THE WISE

V I R G I N
W O R L D S

meet the future

Virgin Worlds is a new imprint. Its aim is to showcase the best in British SF and fantasy, and in particular to discover new talent. Here is the list of previously published titles. See page 472 for press reviews.

MIRRORMAN
By Trevor Hoyle

Frank Kersh is a convicted killer on death row. When the Messengers offer him eternal life, he's not going to turn them down. All he has to do is commit one more crime for them: one final murder.

Cawdor and his family live in present-day New York. He's also a British settler bound for the New World several centuries ago. In all his incarnations, he stands between the Messengers and their plans to inherit the world.

Kersh sets about rubbing Cawdor out – again and again and again.

ISBN 0 7535 0385 9

MNEMOSYNE'S KISS
By Peter J Evans

In the near future, the world isn't an ecological disaster area. Quite the reverse. But human beings still have the capacity to make the worst nightmares come true. Addicts such as Rayanne Gatita consume new drugs to erase the memories of life on the streets; an entrepreneur such as Cassandra Lannigan can still end up with half her brain shot away when a deal goes wrong.

Lannigan wakes up in hospital, unable to remember more than a whisper of her past. But someone's out to assassinate her – again – and her only ally is the street-girl Rayanne.

ISBN 0 7535 0380 8

HAVENSTAR
By Glenda Noramly

The Eight Stabilities are islands of order surrounded by disfiguring, corrupting, lethal chaos. The chaos is encroaching.

Keris Kaylen, daughter of a master mapmaker, is prevented by stifling tradition from pursuing her father's trade. When her father is murdered she sets out across the Unstable and is forced into dubious company, including that of Davron Storre, whose secret is his pact with Carasma the Unmaker, lord of chaos – a secret that, as Keris searches for the maps that will save the world, will one day exact a terrible price.

ISBN 0 7535 0390 5

THE WISE
Andrew Cartmel

VIRGIN
WORLDS

First published in 1999 by
Virgin Worlds
an imprint of
Virgin Publishing Ltd
Thames Wharf Studios
Rainville Road
London W6 9HT

ISBN 0 7535 0373 5

Typeset by Galleon Typesetting, Ipswich
Printed and bound in Great Britain by
Mackays of Chatham PLC

**For
Di Cartmel
(1916–1997)**

CONTENTS

PART ONE

THE ABBEY

ONE

Juliette Race had always considered herself to be good at her job, until the suicide.

Of course, a lot of psychiatrists lose patients to suicide. When you are working with schizophrenics, for instance, it is a recognised and inevitable hazard. But Barlby wasn't schizophrenic.

He was a fat thirteen-year-old boy who had somehow become lost in himself, shutting off the world and pouring out poisonous beams of what Juliette saw as essentially self-hatred.

She took him on for a lot of reasons. It was true that, in some ways, he reminded Juliette of her sister. But she also felt considerable sympathy for the boy's parents, pleasant, ordinary people who were beside themselves, unable to understand how this grotesque behavioural cuckoo had popped up in their loving domestic nest.

Their son was obviously their entire life and they wanted him back to normal, whatever that might be.

When Juliette first met him, the boy, a compulsive eater, was hiding in his bedroom, where he had been holed up for days. The bedroom was musty and airless, curtains drawn tight.

Barlby was in bed hunched under a quilt, surrounded by glittering clumps of foil and the discarded wrappers from chocolate bars. And mounds of books. Juliette paid close attention to the books. The boy had been a prize scholar before he went off the rails.

She sat in the bedroom with him. Sometimes, with some patients, Juliette simply listened, letting them talk and saying nothing herself.

But this time she took a different approach. She tended to follow her hunches and on this occasion she had a strong one. Looking at the books piled around Barlby's room, all science texts, she decided to use the boy's own belief in logic and reason, his God.

She would reason with him.

She talked to him about his eating obsession, his problems with other children at school. His problems controlling his frustration and rage, which could blow up like a storm from nowhere.

With each visit she seemed to make a little more progress – he came a little further out of his shell.

Finally, one victorious day, he left his bedroom and came downstairs, rejoining the life of his family. His parents were overjoyed. Juliette began to wean the boy off her therapy – she didn't want to nurture a dependency in her patient.

No more bedroom visits. Now Barlby came to her. Their last few sessions took place in her office, where they enjoyed what Juliette thought was a genuinely moving rapport, culminating in a final climactic heart-to-heart talk.

'So you see, it is the *satisfaction* you are after rather than the act itself,' reasoned Juliette.

Barlby nodded thoughtfully, receptively. 'You mean the same satisfaction I get from eating I can get from doing something else?'

'Yes. In all sorts of other ways. Go outside and play. Take up a sport. Get out in the fresh air.' Juliette found herself out on a limb, extolling the virtues of exercise and nature hikes which she would never waste time on herself.

Barlby repeated the words 'Sport? Fresh air?' as though they were alien concepts. But she saw his shoulders sag with acceptance. He couldn't argue with the inexorable parsing of her logic.

Juliette quickly added, 'Who knows? You might enjoy it once you get started.'

Barlby left her office that day in a state of complete acceptance. But along with this acceptance came a flash of

4

pure hatred when he looked at her for the last time.

This look unsettled Juliette but, unfortunately, not enough. She was not sufficiently disturbed to ring Barlby's parents and voice her concern. So they had no reason to be particularly vigilant that night.

Sometime during the night Barlby did it. His mother had been using prescription tranquillisers. He gobbled the lot. His mother, ironically, had stopped taking the pills in celebration of the boy's recovery. Consequently she didn't notice that any were missing.

They were accustomed to Barlby coming down to breakfast late in the morning, or not at all. So by the time they looked in on him he was completely beyond reach.

Juliette took it hard. Her professional confidence plummeted. She thought bitterly that she had been right: Barlby had indeed found a new source of satisfaction. In this act all his tightly knotted passive aggressive hatred had come welling out in one final flow like a draining wound.

Unfortunately, the draining of the wound had killed the patient.

Juliette's colleagues were all tediously supportive and sympathetic. Tediously but quite genuinely; some of them had two or three suicides or more under their belts.

Juliette was amazed at the hostility she felt towards the late Barlby. His suicide seemed a spiteful blow against his parents, and against her.

She had been moving in the direction of specialising in children – perhaps not surprisingly, in light of her sister's condition. It had seemed like a fascinating area and it had given Juliette's life a great sense of purpose.

Well, now she had to abandon all that. The heart had quite gone out of her. She cast about for something else to do. She had sufficient insight to know that she badly needed a distraction, a new project to throw herself into.

The next week she was offered the job at the Abbey.

TWO

It was a high white building, an elegant, old-fashioned wedding cake piled against the sky.

Tregemmon stared at it from the window of Danny Bailey's kitchen. 'Did you ever tell me what that place is called?' he said.

Danny Bailey didn't reply. He stared at the bottle of vodka in front of him. It was a rather expensive Russian vodka and he had wasted no time locating and purchasing it after his little chat with Miranda.

Tregemmon came over and picked the bottle up and swirled it around, examining its much diminished contents.

He glanced at Danny. 'Dutch courage?'

'No.'

'Or should I say Russian courage?' He put the vodka down. 'Nothing to be ashamed of.'

Danny took the bottle back and held it protectively, like a baby. He was beginning to feel a certain drunken truculence towards his visitor.

'Well, we'd better get started,' said Tregemmon cheerily. 'Sling your hook.'

This was the moment Danny had been waiting for. 'I'm not coming.'

Tregemmon had taken a jangling ring of car keys from the pocket of his long leather raincoat. Now all his joviality vanished. He turned and looked at Danny with an air of deliberate quiet menace.

There was a complete physical contrast between the two men. Danny Bailey was white and plump, Tregemmon was a tall, thin black man, his lean, pockmarked face framed by a dangling fringe of dreadlocks.

'What did you say?'

'I'm not coming,' repeated Danny Bailey slowly. 'You have to find someone else. I'm taking an early bath.'

Tregemmon's face clouded with anger. He sat down at the table. 'Early bath?' he said. He shook his head. 'I didn't expect you to bottle out on me, you fat fucking chump.'

'I'm sorry.'

'You're sorry? That isn't good enough. Look.' Tregemmon reached into his coat and took something out. He held it casually, so that Danny could see it.

It was a strange, stubby, silver handgun. Danny Bailey knew little enough about weapons, but it looked efficient and dangerous.

Without pausing to think, he lifted his glass, which was still half full of warm vodka, and threw it into Tregemmon's eyes.

While Tregemmon was reacting to that, Danny simply took the gun away from him.

Tregemmon stood in the middle of the kitchen, spluttering and wiping his face. Russian grain spirits dripped from his chin.

'Christ,' he said, his voice more aggrieved than angry. 'Why did you do that?'

'Well . . .' said Danny Bailey, suddenly feeling wrong-footed and foolish. He looked at the gun in his hand. 'You were pointing this at me.'

'Jesus Christ.' Tregemmon wiped his eyes. 'I wasn't pointing it *at* you. I was trying to impress you with the gravity of the situation.'

'Gravity, eh?' said Danny Bailey, experiencing an odd combination of amusement and guilt as he watched his friend busy himself at the sink, leaning under the tap, washing the vodka out of his eyes.

When he looked up from the sink, dreadlocks dripping, Tregemmon was smiling. 'Well, it seems you haven't lost your nerve, anyway.' He opened the cupboard under the sink, picking fastidiously through the tea towels until he found a clean one. He dried his face, then threw the towel at Danny.

7

'What's brought this on, then?'

Danny felt his face getting warm. 'Miranda,' he said.

Tregemmon stared at him in astonishment. 'What?'

'Miranda. We split up.' Danny tried without success to keep a humiliating whine out of his voice.

Tregemmon stared at him for a moment and then roared with laughter. He took the gun back from Danny.

'What is that thing, anyway?' said Danny, anxious to change the subject.

'A Ruger SP101 in a point-three-two magnum configuration with a three-and-one-sixteenth-inch barrel.' Tregemmon's eyes gleamed with amusement. 'The chrome model.' He put the gun away under his coat. 'Look, why don't you come along tonight anyway? It'll be a little light relief. Take your mind off this romantic nonsense.'

'No.'

'Remember, we're talking serious gear here,' said Tregemmon coaxingly. 'You've never had gear like this before.'

Danny shook his head, smiling despite himself. 'No, thank you.'

'And I'll pay you for your help. I pay well.'

'I know you do,' said Danny Bailey, shaking his head. 'But money doesn't mean anything to me at the moment.'

'I'll remind you of that next time you're whining because you're skint.' Danny shrugged. 'Poor bastard,' Tregemmon chuckled. He slapped Danny on the shoulder. And then, as though the contemplation of his friend's broken heart had cheered him up to some critical level, he decisively turned and left.

The tall gate at the back of Danny's garden lurched shakily open, catching on the long trailing vine of green passion flower which Danny could never be bothered to trim.

Tregemmon was halfway out of the gate when all at once he paused, staring up at something.

'What is it?' said Danny.

'That place.' Once again Tregemmon was looking at the

building beyond the trees at the back of Danny's estate. It was a tall building with a grey rectangular roof and high-rising white chimneys. 'I never noticed it before tonight.'

'It's called the Abbey.'

Tregemmon continued staring at it.

'They've got bars on the windows,' he observed.

'On some of them.'

Tregemmon frowned. 'Well, what is it? Some sort of private prison?'

'Private clinic,' said Danny. 'Stars come there to dry out.' Danny was making this up. He had no clear idea what went on at the Abbey. He just wanted to keep Tregemmon here another moment.

He couldn't believe what he was seeing on his friend's face. He couldn't be sure. And now Tregemmon was moving off, striding away into the shadows. He wasn't sure, but just for a moment it might have been fear.

Danny closed the gate and stepped back into his garden. He lingered there for a moment, enjoying the cool evening air. Then, out of the corner of his eye, he noticed a splash of red on the ground.

At first he thought it was a poppy, springing up brightly among the weeds. Then he saw that it was a crumpled piece of paper, folded and angular.

A paper aeroplane. A red paper aeroplane.

Presumably some child had wafted it over his garden wall.

Danny heard Tregemmon's car start up and pull away in the distance. He unfolded the paper aeroplane, noticing idly that there was writing on it.

In large clear letters it read, HERE COMES MR LEIBER.

Danny crumpled it in his hand as he walked back towards the house. He had forgotten it by the time he got inside. He turned out the lights in the kitchen. Through the window the Abbey was just a pale shape against the sky.

9

THREE

Juliette Race nursed her elderly Fiat along the busy road in the South London sun.

Now and then she glanced up into her rear-view mirror and saw her own worried face, coppery dark eyes and twin wings of black hair hanging forward to frame pale cheeks.

She was frantic. She was running late. Where the hell was it? Finally Juliette saw the road and turned.

A man was standing in the open gateway waiting for her. He was a tall man, Indian or perhaps Arab-looking, in a red coat. He stood aside smiling as she sailed through the gate and into the gravel car park.

He came over as she stopped. Juliette opened the window. 'Dr Race?' he said.

'Yes.'

'Hello, my name is Prem. I am the sort of supernumerary and caretaker here at the Abbey.'

'I'm sorry if I'm a bit late.'

Prem directed her to the main entrance. She hurried.

Through the glass doors of the Abbey, in a pleasant whitewashed space, a receptionist was installed behind an antique slab of desk.

She was a plump, unsmiling, middle-aged woman in an unpleasantly shiny nylon suit. She had remarkably synthetic-looking red hair which might have been spun from the same nylon.

'I'm supposed to see Dr Cavanaugh,' Juliette told her breathlessly. 'I'm starting work here today and I'm a little late.' Little late was a big lie.

'Four letters,' said the receptionist. According to a sign on her desk she was called Pamela Croden.

'I beg your pardon?'

'Four letters.'

Juliette suddenly realised that the woman was completely absorbed in a newspaper crossword puzzle. She was holding it concealed out of sight below the desk. In one hand she held a pen, which hovered over the puzzle like a raptorial bird.

'Four letters?' said Juliette.

'The clue is orthopantomogram. What under God's heaven is that? Four letters beginning with an X if you can believe it. Four letters beginning with an –'

'X-ray. Could you please show me the way to Dr Cavanaugh's office –'

'X-ray? That's it. Yes of course.' She looked up at Juliette, focusing on her properly for the first time, as though Juliette had earned her attention. 'Dr Cavanaugh's office. First corridor on your left. Last office on your right.'

Then her brows knotted abruptly with rage. 'But X-ray has a hyphen,' she fumed. 'That should be five letters.'

Juliette hurried down the corridor. She immediately liked the feel of the Abbey. It was a handsome old building, extensively modernised through the judicious use of glass, dark wood and whitewash on the stone walls. Juliette found the effect pleasant and spacious. The tiled corridor was full of light. The graceful parabolic ceilings reminded her of the Colegio Teresiano.

Dr Cavanaugh's office had a pebbled glass door with the words C CAVANAUGH MEDICAL DIRECTOR painted on it in discreet gold script.

Juliette knocked tentatively and was surprised when the door was opened by the man himself. There was no anteroom and apparently no secretary. 'Good afternoon,' said Dr Cavanaugh. 'Please come in.'

He was a chunky, amiable man, muscular and square-built. His hair was pale blond, cropped very short, and he wore some kind of heavy-framed Armani spectacles that caught the light as he looked at Juliette. His smile didn't quite disguise the careful assessment he was making of her.

They shook hands. 'Grab a seat.' He ushered her into the office.

The furniture in the room was all angular and modern – chrome and black leather. The walls of the office were covered with medical diplomas and tennis trophies.

They both sat down in armchairs in front of the desk, as if the office actually belonged to a third party who might join them at any moment.

'I'm sorry if I'm a little late, Dr Cavanaugh.'

'Chad, call me Chad. It's short for Chadwick – but promise not to tell anyone.' He smiled again, an automatic smile that didn't alter his efficient appraising eyes.

Meanwhile, Juliette was making her own appraisal of the man who was going to be her boss.

On his desk were two framed portraits, of Chad himself, in full tennis regalia: action shots with sweat flying from his hair as he slashed at the ball.

'We're delighted, delighted to have you here,' said Cavanaugh absently. He was busy flipping through some papers in a manila folder in his lap. Juliette suspected this was a file about herself. She managed to get a look at the cover and saw that it had the letters MF on it.

What did that stand for? Was it perhaps someone's initials?

Chad glanced up at her. 'I'm glad to say you come to us highly recommended, Dr Race.'

'Juliette, please. Not short for anything I'm afraid.'

Cavanaugh gave a burbling, insincere laugh. He snapped shut the folder, set it aside, then glanced at her and said, 'In particular, we're impressed by the reference given you by Five.'

Five? Had he said Five? Suddenly Juliette's heart was beating quickly. She hadn't expected this. Five? She had assumed this would be an ordinary job.

But maybe she hadn't heard Cavanaugh properly. He had hurried on to other matters. He was now saying, 'I hope you don't mind if we get right down to business. I'm running a little behind.'

'Yes, I'm sorry I'm late. My car –'

Cavanaugh cut her off bluntly and rudely. 'I want you to take a look at a patient.'

Juliette stared at the man. How could he be so rude? She controlled her temper. She had to. This man was going to be her boss.

'I wonder if you'd mind having a preliminary chat with him this afternoon.'

'Of course not. Just let me see his notes –'

'No notes,' said Cavanaugh, cutting her off again. Juliette felt another spark of irritation.

'You must have some reports on him.'

'Oh, plenty,' said Cavanaugh. 'But I'd prefer it if you approached him without any preconceptions. Cold, so to speak.' He flashed her that smile again, the gleaming athlete's smile. 'I'd consider your raw impressions very valuable.' The smile didn't alter his cold blue eyes.

Juliette stood her ground. 'That's very complimentary but I don't feel I can do a proper job unless I have adequate background on the patient.'

Cavanaugh considered this. 'He isn't on any medication,' he added grudgingly.

'I'm afraid I need a little more than that,' said Juliette firmly.

This time Cavanaugh's smile was a mirthless baring of teeth. 'Is this the sort of competitive obsession with standards you wrote about so well in your paper?'

Juliette felt herself flush. 'Which paper?' she said. It was a piece of bravado. The only one that anybody ever read was of course the one about Emily.

Cavanaugh ignored the question. 'It was a fascinating piece of work. I thought you showed considerable insight into the odd kind of sibling rivalry you must feel for your sister.'

'Are you analysing me, Dr Cavanaugh? Because if so I'm very flattered but –'

'Don't be so defensive, Juliette. I merely read your paper about your sister and wanted to congratulate you on it.' He leant forward across the desk. The smile was almost convincing this time. 'And I also wanted to say that it can't be easy living with someone who is ... blessed in that fashion.'

'Or cursed, Dr Cavanaugh.'

'Or cursed. Call me Chad.'

'Chad, can we forget about my sister and talk about my patient?'

'All right. His name is Christopher Matthew.'

FOUR

Christopher Matthew was making paper aeroplanes when she found him.

He was standing in the corridor outside the library, staring out of a narrow window reminiscent of the arrow slit in a medieval castle. The sunshine and the afternoon breeze came in through the window, the sunshine falling in long slices through the steel bars to slant diagonally across the whitewashed corridor. Christopher Matthew squinted carefully in the bright light as he aimed the aeroplane.

He let it go with a snap of his wrist. The aeroplane went sailing out of the window. He smiled with satisfaction, then turned to look at her. 'Greetings.'

'Hello.' Juliette smiled at him, her best professional smile. Her patient was a large man with the look of a rumpled academic. His hair was long and floppy – hippie length. It was also a startlingly pure shade of white.

He was wearing a baggy, grey, silk sweater, blue corduroy trousers and tennis shoes.

He nodded at the window. 'Look at it go.' She stood beside him for a moment watching the bright-red flash of the aeroplane as it sailed over the trees and the wall, towards the small houses of the estate behind the Abbey.

'Excellent throw,' said Juliette. She was grateful for the aeroplane. It was as good a way as any of starting to talk to her patient.

After chatting for a few minutes, meaningless small talk as she sounded him out, Juliette found herself beginning to take a reluctant liking to the man.

And, although it was very early to form an impression, to her Christopher Matthew seemed lucid, intelligent and

15

untroubled. In other words, sane.

She began to feel a little puzzled at the fact that she had been asked to evaluate him. Nonetheless, she persisted, anxious to do a thorough job for Chad.

'Is it your first day here?' said Christopher Matthew suddenly.

'Yes.'

'Seen the library yet?'

'No.'

'Let me show you around.' He was holding the door open for her. Juliette walked into the library. It was a spacious, sunny room with old-fashioned, highly polished, wooden tables and tall shelves lined with books.

'Did Chad unleash you on me?' said Christopher Matthew casually.

'Who? Oh, Dr Cavanaugh.'

'That's right.' Christopher grinned. ' "Call me Chad." Did he come bounding up to greet you with a tennis racket clenched in one meaty paw?'

Juliette suppressed a flicker of amusement. 'Something like that.'

Standing by the library window were a pair of tall, gaunt, red leather armchairs that looked as if they belonged in an Edwardian men's club. Christopher wandered over and sank gratefully down in one, sighing. Juliette watched him. He wasn't handsome, but there was something about him. Charisma.

He glanced at her around the high-winged back of the chair. 'Chad's all right,' he said. 'He's actually pretty sharp. But he roars around in a Porsche Carrera.'

'And that counts against him?'

'It would be all right for a Beverly Hills plastic surgeon who does tit jobs,' said Christopher. 'But one expects a little more gravitas from a man who is supposed to heal troubled souls.'

Juliette perched on the arm of a chair opposite him. Troubled souls, she thought. She looked out of the window, where she could see the car park and, beyond that, the front gate of the Abbey.

16

'I saw you arrive,' said Christopher. 'Had a bit of trouble with the car, eh?'

She looked at him. 'What makes you say that?'

'Well, you are driving a thirty-year-old Fiat.'

'It's not thirty years old,' said Juliette defensively. Ridiculously, her pride had been pricked.

'Are you joking? There are wanted posters out on that car. The Beast of Turin. Approach with caution.'

'You seem very interested in cars. Chad's Porsche, my Fiat.'

But Christopher didn't seem to hear her. 'Have you read any RD Laing?'

'Quite a bit.' It was almost as if she was having an ordinary social conversation. She felt very relaxed with the man.

'How about *Wisdom, Madness and Folly*?'

'His autobiography.'

'Exactly. You know, for me the most interesting part is where Laing goes into a Glasgow theatre and sees a mind-reader at work.'

'A mind-reader?'

'This man is up on stage telling people what's in their wallets and so on. And Laing buys it totally. He believes he witnessed something extraordinary that day.'

'Well Laing was always something of a mystic,' said Juliette.

'Plus all those acid trips didn't help, right?' Christopher Matthew grinned. 'But let us suppose that he was reporting accurately on this occasion.'

'Why suppose that?' said Juliette. 'We didn't witness the event. We can't corroborate it. It's far too tenuous an anecdote to justify accepting . . .'

'Accepting that someone can read minds.'

'Yes.'

'Ah, but your main stumbling block is that, as a scientist, you can't posit a causal mechanism.'

'Posit a causal mechanism?'

Christopher grinned at her. 'I occasionally like to use a ten-dollar word.'

'And what is this mechanism?'

'Imagine a group of humans, sitting together in the darkness of a Glasgow theatre. Sitting in the dark, waiting for the show to begin. Although they don't know it, they are all communicating with each other. Communicating in subtle ways. Seventy per cent of all communication is nonverbal anyway, correct? We're exchanging subliminal signals all the time. Sharing some kind of group communication. So, anyway, the mind-reader gets to work. He asks for a volunteer from the audience. At the back of the theatre, RD Laing or someone takes out his wallet and looks inside it. On the stage a hundred yards away the mind-reader tells him that he's got five pounds and a shoe-repair ticket in it. Or something. And he's right. How could the mind-reader possibly know?'

Juliette leant forward. 'He knows because the man with the wallet knows,' she suggested.

Christopher grinned with approval. 'That's right. And somehow the knowledge is passed through the audience, up towards the stage, like a ball bouncing on a trampoline.'

'The ball is the information,' said Juliette. 'And the trampoline is the . . . web of subliminal communication shared by the people in the theatre.'

'Exactly! Somehow the mind-reader has tapped into this subconscious communication system.'

Christopher leant back in his chair. He looked at her and smiled.

Juliette shrugged. 'So why don't we all communicate in this way? All the time?'

'That's just my point. We do.' Christopher moved his hands in the air, trying to explain. 'Without realising it, we are all responding to subliminal signals from people all the time.'

'But we can't all guess the contents of somebody's wallet from the other side of a theatre. What makes you think your mind-reader can?'

Christopher looked smug. 'Well, he's a special individual. You might say he's learnt to work the system.'

'A special individual?'

'That's right.'

'And do you see yourself as this kind of special individual?' she said softly.

Christopher looked at her in mild surprise. 'Yes,' he said. 'Yes, I suppose I do.'

Juliette smiled at him. She felt a sudden rush of professional excitement, a sense of things beginning. At last she had a clue to her patient's problem.

This talk about special individuals and mind-reading. They were the first signs she'd detected of delusional thinking.

'Delusional thinking?' said Christopher cheerfully. He was sitting in the armchair in a patch of sunlight, grinning up at her. 'Hey, which one of us is driving the thirty-year-old Fiat?'

Juliette managed to successfully smother her impulse to laugh. Which was just as well because she knew it would have turned into one of her full-blown snorting laughs, which made her sound about as ladylike as a pig rooting after truffles.

An hour later Juliette had finished at the Abbey and was driving north in the slanting autumn sunlight. The Fiat behaved itself immaculately all the way home. What had Christopher Matthew called it? 'The Beast of Turin.'

Juliette found herself thinking about her patient as she drove. She felt a definite mounting excitement. The sense that something was beginning.

She tried to tell herself that it was purely professional excitement, but she found herself thinking about Christopher Matthew's eyes and the way he smiled.

Just then an odd thought occurred to her.

Juliette was driving along the Westway, cruising on the elevated road high above London, when it struck her. Christopher had made a joke about delusional thinking, a rather rude joke about her car. It had been in response to Juliette's own observation about *his* delusional thinking.

Juliette gripped the steering wheel tight. Sunlight slashed through the windscreen, heating the interior of the car like a

19

solarium. But a cold trickle of sweat had suddenly fringed her ribs.

She hadn't said it aloud.

She hadn't said anything about delusional thinking. She was certain of it. There was no way she would say such a thing in front of a patient.

She hadn't said anything aloud. She'd merely thought it. How could he know what she was thinking?

FIVE

After Tregemmon left, Danny Bailey began to brood. He didn't want to, but he just couldn't stop thinking about Miranda.

Miranda Lang.

Danny had first met her on a rainy autumn Wednesday when her art gallery was invaded for an advertising shoot. Danny was driving a van and rigging lights for the company.

The gallery itself was a cosy little space tucked away in an alley off Lots Road. Its discreet lighting, dove-grey carpets and ludicrous collection of giant earthenware vases seemed to meet with the art director's approval. He did the minimum of dressing and got on with the shoot.

Miranda was being paid some ungodly sum for the use of the place, and she was getting it by the hour.

Danny Bailey could no longer remember what the shoot had been about. Fat-free nondairy spread? High-absorbency tampons? Shampoo and conditioner in one bottle?

What he remembered was Miranda.

She was a lithe compact blonde. A patrician beauty with a full sullen mouth and greyish blue eyes that were so pale they looked almost blind.

It had been raining when Danny Bailey first saw her, endless veils of colourless rain sweeping down over Chelsea Harbour and the long slow river. The colour of that downpour reminded him of Miranda's eyes and after that he always privately thought of her as the Girl with Eyes like Rain.

On the last day of the shoot he surprised himself by asking her out, and she surprised him by accepting.

* * *

On their first date Miranda turned up a fairly standard twenty minutes late. By then Danny was hungry. He decided to abandon his original plan, which required their listening to something tortuous and modern by a rather severe string quartet, followed by an expensive meal in one of the fashionable riverside restaurants.

Instead, he hailed a taxi to carry them across Waterloo Bridge. They cut through the Strand and soon arrived at a battle-scarred little café just off Denmark Street, full of gleaming stainless-steel tables. Frequented by off-duty taxi drivers, it was the sort of place where Danny Bailey, left to his own devices, enjoyed eating.

Miranda frowned at the handwritten menu and demanded to know what on earth a BCMLT was.

'Sort of a BLT that had a radiation accident,' replied Danny. His mouth was watering so much he could hardly talk.

They both ordered one, and soon the huge sandwiches arrived, perched on chipped china plates: triple-decker confections of white bread toasted golden brown and slathered with mayonnaise. Fat pink rashers of fragrant bacon dangled from the side. Between the layers of bacon and toast were stacked cheese, lettuce, mushrooms and tomato.

'These are almost impossible to fit into an ordinary human mouth,' said Danny, tucking in.

Miranda merely nodded. She was herself busy eating. With her first bite some of the filling squirted out on to her fingers. She licked them and carried on.

She did this in such a daintily ladylike fashion that a grinning Cypriot waiter hurried to provide her with a knife and fork. By that time, though, she had virtually polished the sandwich off.

They caught a taxi back to his place. Miranda stayed with him until dawn and then caught another taxi back home to shower and then stagger like a zombie to her job at the gallery.

Three weeks later Danny Bailey found himself making

love to her in a car parked outside her parents' house in Enfield while her mother laboured over the spattering Sunday roast in the kitchen and her father reclined corpulently in pale-blue television light, watching motor racing.

Neither the father nor the mother seemed to notice the two vague shapes in Danny's car, faintly moving in the autumnal drabness.

The car was dangerously close to the house and to Danny there seemed a terrible likelihood that one or both of Miranda's parents might glance out at any moment and take note of the fervid carnal activity in its cramped confines.

This notion, however, served only to sharpen Miranda's appreciation of the event. And in the end that got Danny going, too.

It was altogether an exciting affair. And it intensified, not just physically but emotionally, until Danny was walking on air. Things just seemed to be getting better and better!

That was when she gave him the elbow.

Danny tried not to think about Miranda. Each night he sulked over a bottle of vodka and attempted to obliterate her from his mind. Or, failing that, obliterate his mind.

He slept heavily and, as far as he knew, dreamlessly. But one night he was suddenly awakened. Emerging through the bleary layers of vodka intoxication he found himself surfacing to consciousness through jangled fragments of a dream about Miranda.

A dream of shocking erotic intensity.

He sat up, blinking his gummy eyes in the predawn darkness. It took him a moment for his confused mind to reassemble his consciousness. His heart was jolting violently. What had snapped him awake with such suddenness?

He soon found out, because it happened again. A violent pounding at the front door.

It was Miranda. Somehow Danny knew it.

Miranda, come in the middle of the night for a reconciliation. Come to apologise to him, to beg him to take her back. To initiate a hot tearful reunion in the tangled sheets of his bed.

Danny pulled on a robe and hurried downstairs, flapping lights on as he blundered to the front door, and flung it open.

Tregemmon was standing there. In one hand he was carrying a battered metal briefcase. The other arm was held high, leaning on the doorframe. The arm was wrapped in a long white bandage. Blood was seeping through the bandage in a jagged red stain.

Tregemmon brushed past Danny and walked into the house. He looked tired, his pockmarked face tense and nervous.

'What happened to your arm?'

'Cut,' said Tregemmon. 'It's clean and it's not deep.'

'I can see that it's a fucking cut,' said Danny Bailey. He was scared and being scared made him angry. He slammed the door shut and followed Tregemmon into the house. 'I meant what the fuck kind of a bandage is that?'

Tregemmon had wandered into the kitchen. Now he turned and looked blankly at Danny, and then at his own arm. The crude bandage on it consisted of a series of Häagen-Dazs napkins secured with silver gaffer tape. Tregemmon looked at it and grinned.

'I had to use what I found in the glove compartment. It's all right. They were clean.' Tregemmon picked at the loose edge of one of the napkins. 'You know, this stuff has nothing to do with Denmark. It comes from New Jersey.'

'Tregemmon, *what is going on*?' Danny's voice trembled with anger. He glanced out of the window. Was Tregemmon in trouble? Was someone after him?

Tregemmon sighed and set the metal briefcase on the kitchen table. 'You were smart not to come along.'

'What?'

'Along on that job. I took someone else and it got a bit nasty on us and he got himself arrested.'

'Could you be a little more vague?'

Tregemmon sagged into a chair. 'I don't want to tell you about it,' he said. 'Not yet.'

He nodded at the metal briefcase, gleaming on the table.

Danny noticed that it was dented in one corner. The dent was about the size of a large grapefruit.

'I'd like to leave this here for a few days.' Tregemmon stared across the dim kitchen at Danny Bailey. 'I know I'm asking you a favour. I'll make it worth your while.'

Danny shrugged impatiently. 'Are you offering to *pay* me, Tregemmon? Fuck that. Just tell me what's going on.'

Tregemmon rose and went to the kitchen window. He peered out. A helicopter was sweeping through the night sky, red and green lights gleaming on its insect body. Tregemmon watched it for a moment. 'They won't think of looking here,' he said.

Then his shoulders suddenly quivered violently, like a dog shaking off water.

'Are you all right?' said Danny.

Tregemmon waved him away. 'Ever heard that expression? Someone walking on your grave?'

'It's loss of blood. That's all you're feeling. They call it shock.'

'Something like that, all right.' Tregemmon was still trembling. He looked up at Danny, his eyes pale in his dark face. 'You know,' he said, 'I've been through some disturbing shit in my time. Nowadays I get a definite feeling when things are not quite right.'

Danny laughed. 'Tregemmon, your arm is slashed, your friend is in prison, someone is after you; I'd say it's fairly obvious that things are not right.'

Tregemmon shook his head. 'No, that's normal. I mean I get the feeling something *strange* is going on.'

He glanced at Danny. He had an odd, haunted expression on his pockmarked face. 'And believe me. I know about strange. I've been there.'

Danny Bailey watched his friend carefully. Tregemmon was acting very weird. Was he on drugs? Or maybe the more realistic question was, which drugs was he on?

Tregemmon had risen restlessly from his chair again and now he was standing at the kitchen window. The moon came out from behind a cloud and cold light flowed down on him.

He stood there in the moonlight peering suspiciously up at the looming shape of the Abbey. The building was a vague white mass, rearing over Danny's house. Its north face was high and pale against the night sky.

For a moment Danny had the ridiculous feeling that Tregemmon might start sniffing, like a bloodhound picking up a suspicious scent.

Instead, he just turned away from the window and nodded at the dented metal briefcase on the table. 'I don't suppose it will do me any good to ask you not to look inside that.'

'Of course it won't.'

Tregemmon went to the door. He turned back and smiled. 'If I'm not back by dawn Thursday, help yourself. Open it.'

He went out the door and Danny followed him into the small back yard. Tregemmon took one last look at the Abbey and then he left. The gate clattered shut behind him.

The night became silent and still. Danny Bailey went back inside and stood by the sink, staring out of the window.

Behind him on the table, gleaming in the moonlight, stood the metal briefcase.

SIX

Juliette parked, set the handbrake and nervously checked her watch. She was grievously late for her appointment.

She stepped out of her car on to the winding gravel drive. Grey storm clouds were drifting over the Abbey, swallowing the sun. Two young uniformed nurses were climbing into an orange Mini nearby. They glanced up at Juliette with frank curiosity as she hurried past them, heading towards reception.

Juliette ignored them. She was thinking there would be no time for a proper briefing with Chad.

She would have to blunder straight into her crucial second session with Christopher Matthew.

She was so late. Juliette suppressed a shiver. She couldn't help it; there was something horrifying about the truly irrational.

Juliette was late because she had somehow managed to misplace her palmtop computer. The computer was a small grey rectangle of plastic, but Juliette thought of it as the receptacle into which she poured her secrets.

She kept all her patients' notes on it. Confidential, uncensored details of everything they discussed in their sessions. It was hardly surprising she began to panic when she couldn't find it. Her patients trusted her. What if it fell into the wrong hands? It would be ripe material for blackmail.

She searched her office in an increasingly panic-stricken fashion. The maddening thing was, she knew exactly where the palmtop had been just a few hours earlier.

She'd used it first thing that morning, just after arriving

at her office in Vauxhall Cross. And since then she hadn't left the office and no one else had come in. So where could it have gone?

This small grey piece of plastic eluded her for an entire hour and she searched with a mounting feeling of hysteria. But the worst part came when she actually *found* it.

Because it turned out that the computer was right there on her desk, in plain sight.

The very first place she had looked. How could she have missed it all this time? She scooped it up with a sweaty hand and slammed it into her briefcase.

That was why she was now hurrying into the Abbey, running a spectacular two hours late.

The rain was pouring down in fat drops as she marched through the front door and into the cool stone reception area. Pamela Croden was frowning over the *Independent* crossword puzzle and merely nodded at Juliette as she hurried past and fled into the ladies' to repair the damage the rain had done to her hair.

As she peered into the mirror she found herself startled by the intensity of the anticipation she felt. Just the thought of seeing Christopher Matthew triggered a deep visceral fluttering in her.

Juliette shook her head, as if trying to shake ridiculous notions out of it. Christopher was a patient. She was his doctor. Ethics obviously forbade any involvement. And then there was the small matter of his sanity.

She found him in the games hall, a large room opposite the library with cream walls and green carpeting. It contained a ping-pong table, a pool table and some kind of computer-games console.

There was a long, low, suede sofa the colour of toffee which occupied the centre of the room. At both ends of it were stationed tall, floor-standing, brass lamps with green felt shades.

The lamps were on, giving the room a cosy buttery glow as the rain fell steadily and drearily outside, sucking all the light and colour out of the day.

Christopher Matthew was ensconced at one end of the sofa. He got up when she came in and waited for her to sit before settling again.

'Good to see you,' he said, smiling and wiping his long white hair back from his creased, smiling face. Those remarkable eyes were shining. He was clearly very pleased to see her.

'I'm sorry I'm late,' said Juliette.

'No need to apologise. Anyway, I'm the one who should apologise.' Christopher's smile faded and his expression became suddenly serious. 'I have to apologise for what I'm about to tell you.'

Juliette Race felt an odd sinking sensation. 'I see,' she said, choosing her words carefully. 'And what exactly do you have to tell me?'

Christopher stirred restlessly on the sofa, also searching for words. 'I want to say some things without prejudice. I only ask you to hear me out before you pass judgement.'

'Of course,' said Juliette. She heard the rain dripping and splashing on leaves outside the window. She felt her heartbeat lurch and accelerate. 'You can tell me anything you like, Christopher.'

'But let me tell you the whole thing. Let me explain it all to you. And try not to panic.'

Juliette felt a small pulse of anger. 'Of course I'm not going to panic,' she said. She turned slightly on the sofa, crossing her legs, getting comfortable.

'OK.' Christopher eased around to face her. 'I'm not a specialist in eyes –'

'In what?'

'*Eyes*. I'm no specialist, but I understand all human beings have got blind spots. I mean literal, physical blind spots. Something to do with where the optic nerve enters the eye.'

'I'm not a specialist either.' Juliette frowned, remembering her anatomy classes. 'But the optic nerve enters the eyeball just to one side of the fovea. It is the one place in the retina where photoreceptors are entirely absent.'

'My God, I love it when you talk shop.' Christopher

shook his head ruefully. 'So, anyway, there are these blind spots and we don't notice them in the course of our everyday life because we've learnt to compensate for them, correct?'

'I suppose so. Of course. Correct.'

'Compensate for them both physically and mentally. But, nonetheless, they *do* exist and, if something happens to fall under your blind spot, you can't see it.'

'Obviously,' said Juliette. 'By definition.' She wondered what he was getting at.

'OK, good. Now let's leave the question of the blind spots aside for a moment.' He shifted on the sofa, hitching a little closer to her. 'Let's go off on a tangent.'

For some reason Juliette felt an impulse to move away, exactly the same distance Christopher had moved towards her.

Outside, silent lightning flickered through the window like a giant flashbulb igniting. Christopher said, 'Would you agree that sometimes we don't consciously know what we are doing, even while we're doing it?'

'Naturally,' said Juliette. She tried not to sound scornful. 'I'd say that's a given of modern psychiatry.' Lightning flickered at the window again. This time it was followed by a long, slow roll of thunder.

'Let's invent a story,' said Christopher. 'Say for instance a girl is about to get married. It's the morning of her wedding. She's rushing around getting ready and she falls down the stairs, breaks her ankle. Ouch. So the wedding is postponed. Everybody is very understanding. But in the end, a few months down the line, she breaks off the engagement altogether. Deep down inside she knew it wasn't going to work. But she couldn't face actually cancelling the wedding . . .'

'So she fell down the stairs and broke her ankle, thereby stopping the wedding without having to confront her feelings.'

'Exactly.' Christopher was watching her, his eyes gleaming in each flash of lightning. 'She didn't exactly fall down the stairs deliberately, but something inside her *made* her do it.' He smiled. 'Now, Freud would buy that, wouldn't he?'

'Certainly. All you're talking about here is the sub-conscious mind. A fairly well-established concept,' said Juliette dryly.

'But not a proven fact.'

'No, but –'

'But it's important to keep an open mind about these things, correct? All right, well this is where the blind spot comes back into the argument. Let's talk about perception and subconscious manipulation of the blind spot.'

'Manipulation?' Juliette suddenly felt uneasy again.

'Certainly. We can subconsciously make use of the blind spot to edit what we perceive.'

'Edit in what way?'

'By making an object vanish. The object falls under our blind spot. It vanishes. Don't get me wrong: I'm not saying we're consciously aware of this. But, like the bride falling down the staircase, we're making it happen.'

'What you're saying is –'

'What I'm saying is that you subconsciously select what you see. Or what you don't see.'

Juliette felt herself start to sweat. She forced herself to speak. 'There's just one problem with that.'

Christopher looked at her with alert interest. 'And that is?'

'We have two eyes. They synchronise so that whatever falls into the blind spot of one is picked up by the other.' Juliette felt her confidence coming back as she spoke, dredging her memories of her first-year medicine. 'The eyes compensate for each other.'

Christopher waved a dismissive hand. 'But they don't synchronise properly all the time. Ask anybody who suffers from a lazy eye. We have the power to move them independently. You see the implications, don't you?'

'No.'

'Well, this enables us to subconsciously make an object vanish, and then magically reappear.'

Juliette forced herself to take a deep breath and remain

31

calm. Christopher had of course just described what had happened to her that morning, when she lost her palmtop computer.

Lightning flashed through the window, a huge white sheet that dimmed the electric lights to insignificance. At the same time, the thunder came like someone slamming a door in the sky. The sound was so immense that Juliette jumped in her seat.

Christopher, however, wasn't at all startled. He just sat watching her calmly. All at once Juliette found his calmness irritating. Intolerable. She decided to terminate the interview.

'I'm afraid I have to go now.' She rose from the sofa. Christopher watched her. Lightning flickered across him like white paint thrown across his face.

His dark eyes were sad as he watched her go. 'Doctor,' he said. 'You really ought to read up on the Sapir-Whorf hypothesis.'

Juliette listened to her own heels clattering along the hallway. She was furious. She didn't understand exactly what her patient was doing, but she knew he was fucking with her mind.

Manipulating her. Trying to frighten her.

She felt stickily ashamed to think that, only a few hours ago, she had been wrestling with the notion that she might have a crush on this man.

Her professional feelings had become caught up with her sexual feelings. She wanted to help him. To heal him. But Christopher Matthew didn't need help. He was as sane as anyone. Cool and calculating. Completely manipulative. It had felt like he was playing handball with her brain.

She thought of his mocking smile and that ugly, lank, white hair. How could she have ever imagined she was attracted to him?

She composed herself as she approached the frosted-glass door of Chad Cavanaugh's office.

'Come in. Good to see you, Juliette.' Chad was seated

behind his desk, the first time Juliette had seen the medical director in this position. She felt she had finally caught a glimpse of the beast in its natural habitat.

Chad was clutching a pen in one slablike hand, staring up at her. Despite all his efforts at democratic chumminess, he radiated bullnecked authority. And, thought Juliette, a total disregard of any opinions other than his own. But he smiled pleasantly enough as Juliette came in and sat down in front of him. There was a folder lying open on his desk, which he moved quickly to cover with papers. Before he managed to do so, Juliette noticed the name at the top of one page: Matthew Franklin.

She said, 'I'm sorry we missed our meeting –'

'Forget it,' said Chad. He consulted the chunky sports chronometer on his wrist. 'I'm glad you dropped by. I have a dinner commitment. But before I go I'd like to fill you in a bit on our patient.'

'Fine,' said Juliette, although at the moment she couldn't have been less interested in their patient.

Because he was the worst kind of man. Arrogant. And so manipulative. Like some kind of creepy Svengali.

But Juliette Race didn't say that. Instead she said, 'Yes, I'd find that very interesting,'

And then she sat back and listened.

33

SEVEN

She swung open the heavy oak doors of the library and saw Christopher inside, sitting curled up in one of the big leather armchairs, reading by the light from a small, bright, art-nouveau lamp. Behind him rain pecked at the dark window.

Lightning flashed as Juliette walked across the room. It seemed to take a long time. Long enough for her to realise that he was sitting exactly where he'd sat during their first interview.

Christopher casually set his book aside as she approached. Juliette saw that it was a large illustrated volume about Aboriginal art. He reached up and switched off the lamp. 'If it isn't the angry psychiatrist.' A smile spread across his face.

Juliette came further into the library. 'I'm sorry I reacted badly earlier.'

Christopher shrugged. 'What made you change your mind and come back?'

'Dr Cavanaugh and I had a chat.'

'Chatting with Chad. I see.'

'And he told me a little about your past.'

Christopher fell silent. He was looking at her, and there was no mistaking the anger smouldering in his eyes. 'He had no right to do that.'

'Christopher –'

Christopher Matthew set his book aside. 'I am not a fucking microbe on a slide,' he announced. 'You people don't have the right to hold my life up for inspection.'

'I know,' said Juliette quickly. 'Don't be angry. I'm sorry. I just want to help.'

'I'm going to wring Chad's fucking neck. He had no right

to tell you.' He got up and went to the library window.

Juliette waited a moment. Then she went over and joined him. The storm seemed to have cleared. Red and yellow leaves lay soaked and flattened on the tarmac of the wet car park below. By the walls of the Abbey the dark tangled limbs of the trees were just visible against the deepening blue of the autumn sky. Night was settling fast.

'What did he tell you?' said Christopher, his voice tight with anger.

'That you were an anthropologist. You wrote a couple of books. You're highly regarded in your field . . .'

Juliette had resolved to say nothing more, to let her patient dictate the pace of their encounter, but suddenly she blurted it out. 'It must have been terrible, losing them both like that.'

Christopher didn't reply. Juliette repressed the urge to put her hand on his shoulder.

'How exactly did it happen, Christopher?'

For a long moment he remained silent and she didn't think he was going to reply. But then he said, 'Motorbike. It was at a pedestrian crossing. The motorcycle was over-taking. Went shooting past the cars, didn't see them until it was too late. Hit both of them. Both dead.'

Juliette winced, imagining the brutal sledgehammer impact. They were silent for a moment. The last of the light had faded from the sky. Juliette stood beside Christopher and stared out into the cold London night.

'How old was the little girl?'

'Five.'

It must have been incredibly painful to lose them both, thought Juliette. Wife and child.

'Yes,' muttered Christopher quietly.

Juliette glanced around at him, but he seemed to be speaking absent-mindedly to himself.

Then he turned from the window and looked at her. 'What else did he tell you?'

'How you walked out of your house when you heard about the accident. And never went back. He told me how you lived rough.'

'He's got the chronology screwed a little.'

'And then he told me about the office where you worked.'

Christopher looked at her, suddenly on his guard. 'The Brain Trust?'

'Yes. How you got the job there. How you were sleeping in the park.'

'Yes, that's right.' Christopher relaxed and smiled reminiscently. 'I was staying in the park, sleeping rough. I'd sit there during the day, too. It was a nice park. It smelt good, all the growing green things. It cheered me up. After a while I started saying good morning to people walking through. The regulars. They became familiar faces. A lot of people came through that park on their way to work. There was this big building opposite. It was a company that called itself the Brain Trust. Kind of a think-tank. You know. Brainstorming solutions for big corporations. And I gradually came to know the people who worked there. I suppose from their point of view I was just the crazy homeless guy who lived in the park. But from my point of view, they were a nice bunch of people. I suppose they took pity on me. They gave me a job carrying boxes into the building. Soon I was supervising deliveries. Then they made me doorman and after they got to know me a little better they gave me a proper job. I had to wear a suit and tie again. And live in a house. It made an interesting change from sleeping under the open sky.'

'Was it interesting work?'

'Yes. Rather too interesting.' His voice was strangely bitter. 'There was another man who joined and worked with me. He had some particularly fascinating theories about the human mind. Did Chad tell you about him? His name was Mr Leiber.'

'No he didn't.' Juliette sensed that he was on the verge of an important disclosure. 'What were these theories?'

Christopher didn't seem to hear the question. 'You know, even after everything that happened, I can't help feeling grateful to the Brain Trust. They gave me a place among other people again, made me feel accepted again.'

He laughed, but it was a false, humourless sound. 'You might say they made me whole again.'

'What do you mean?'

Christopher shrugged evasively. 'They gave me money. A roof over my head. I was on top of the world.'

So what happened? thought Juliette. But she didn't pursue it. Instead she said, 'Why did you mention the Sapir-Whorf hypothesis?'

'Are you familiar with the term?'

'It's anthropology, isn't it?'

'Yes. Linguistic anthropology. Edward Sapir and Benjamin Whorf. Do you know what it means?'

Juliette frowned, trying to recall her university reading. 'It's to do with cultural relativity and the role language plays.'

'In our construction of reality,' said Christopher. ' "Language-mediated interpersonal agreement". So for instance, a culture which doesn't have a word for war might not be able to entertain the concept of war. A nice thought, but sadly unlikely. The important thing about the Sapir-Whorf hypothesis, though, is that it introduces you to the notion that reality is not fixed. It is something we create around us as a group endeavour.'

'And why is it important that I should appreciate that?'

'Because I want to prepare you,' he said, suddenly serious. Juliette stared up at him.

She felt as if her hands might start rising of their own volition, like balloons. Reaching up to touch his face.

'Prepare your mind for the notion that sorcery can exist,' said Christopher.

'Sorcery?' The word had an ugly irrational sound.

'It's just a term. A way of describing something. Let me put it like this. If you were a young aboriginal woman – and I'm sure you'd look good in the costume –'

Juliette smiled. 'Or lack of it.'

'Or lack of it. If you were a young aboriginal woman you could experience sorcery at first hand. You might see extraordinary things. You might witness the *karadji* – the shaman – point the killing bone at someone and cause

37

their sudden death simply by willing it.'

Christopher watched her as he spoke. His voice was soft and low.

'You might witness such a thing,' he said. 'And it might frighten you. But it would not shock you out of your mind. Because you live in a society which accepts that magic is real.'

He moved away from her and sank into one of the armchairs by the window. 'But you are not an aboriginal woman. You're a modern Western woman, and you don't have any cultural buffers to protect you.'

'Protect me from what?'

EIGHT

Danny Bailey was sitting in his kitchen, looking at the metal briefcase.

He had left it on the kitchen table exactly where Tregemmon had set it down. All he had done was clean a few dark stains off it, trying to kid himself that they didn't look like blood. He also tried to avoid speculating about what was inside the briefcase.

But in fact the question was a welcome distraction: it stopped him thinking about Miranda.

Perhaps he should have handled it differently with her. Perhaps there was something he should have said or done, that would have made it all all right.

Miranda said goodbye to him for the last time at the same spot where they had met for their first date. By the river.

They were standing by the second-hand bookstalls that spanned the embankment under an awning. Miranda said they reminded her of Paris, then she gave him a sisterly peck on the cheek and turned and walked away, heels clicking as she headed up the steps towards Hungerford Bridge and then back across the river.

The Girl with Eyes like Rain, walking out of his life, and there was not one damned thing he could do about it.

He sat in the darkness of his kitchen, remembering that final bitter parting. It was so late it was almost morning. Outside, the city streets were quiet and empty. He had been sitting like this all night, brooding about what might have been. Waiting for the birds in his garden to start singing at dawn.

Dawn on Thursday.

The kitchen was gradually growing brighter. The first light began to creep across the sky and then a slow grey luminescence invaded the house. In this cold half-light Danny sat looking at the briefcase.

He remembered Tregemmon, his bloody bandage of ice-cream napkins. 'If I'm not back by dawn on Thursday . . .'

Danny Bailey got up from the table. Through the window he could see the Abbey standing high and white over the rear wall of the estate.

The sky was pale pink now and growing brighter. Dim shapes of tree branches were appearing against the pearly clouds.

He turned to the briefcase, flipped the catches and opened it.

In his efforts to extinguish his memories of Miranda, Danny had first tried vodka.

When the vodka didn't work, he'd driven north in pulsing rain through sluggish grey traffic and paid a visit to a pub in Kilburn. There he scored an eighth of an ounce of grass from a chunky amiable Irish girl. The girl had told him frankly that the grass wasn't much good.

'There's a shortage about.'

'There's always a bloody shortage about.'

'No, seriously now.' She pronounced *now* as *nigh*. 'It's to do with the red spider mite.'

'What's that, some kind of crop parasite?'

'Yes! Except it's being spread deliberately by the police. The Drugs Squad are breeding them and dropping them by helicopter.'

'Like cloud seeding.'

'Yes!'

Danny had taken his eighth of grass and driven south towards the river, leaving the Irish girl to her fantasies of biological warfare. His mind flared with paranoia every time he passed a police car but he arrived home without incident and as soon as the door was locked behind him he hungrily unwrapped the grass.

But the Irish girl hadn't exaggerated. Danny smoked

the entire eighth hoping that it would ease him into some kind of painless realm where a broken heart was a matter for easygoing laughter.

Instead it had merely given him a dry mouth and a dull throbbing headache. He had wished at the time for some decent weed, something strong and effective.

And every day since then he'd tried to get hold of some. But there had indeed been a drought on, a drought of such epic proportions that Danny had begun to reconsider the notion of red spider mites being dropped from helicopters.

Now, staring down into Tregemmon's briefcase he gave a low, awed whistle.

The case was tightly packed with bricks, each about the size of a pound of butter. The bricks were wrapped in aluminium foil and each sealed in turn in a transparent plastic bag. This extensive wrapping had done remarkably little to reduce the enormously pungent odour that wafted from the briefcase.

This was, after all, why they called it skunk.

As Danny dug out a brick something shifted in the briefcase. Something heavy. He took out a few more bricks to get at the object. It was angular, heavy and metallic, also wrapped in plastic.

He freed a final brick and suddenly the object tumbled out on to the kitchen table. It was a gun. The Ruger that Tregemmon had been carrying a few days ago.

Danny stared at it. Snub-barrelled and ugly, it lay there on the table, an unlikely, lethal, chromed artefact.

What on Earth was this thing doing in his house?

The sinister appearance of the gun threatened to sour the festive discovery of the skunk weed. Danny decided to put it back in the briefcase and pretend he hadn't seen it.

The block of grass was a dark-brownish green, with dusty orange pods honey-glued into it, sticky with resin. Danny carved a parsimonious slice off the brick with a Swiss Army knife. Then he flaked the compacted weed apart. By the time he was finished, his fingers were sticky with dark resin. It left smudged brown stains on the single cigarette paper.

Lipstick kisses, he thought as he rolled a needle-thin joint. Then he thought of Miranda and felt a stab of pain.

Danny licked the joint, trimmed the end and wandered into his sitting room and turned his stereo on. This proved to be a terrible mistake. From his speakers came wafting the lovely old Ray Noble ballad, 'The Very Thought of You'.

The problem was, it had been *their* song. He remembered Miranda wandering around his house, unselfconsciously nude, slender line of legs and smooth flowing arch of back swaying as she strode gracefully to the stereo.

She would put this song on before turning to smile and join him on the sofa, where a towel was spread ready.

He would never be able hear this song again without thinking of Miranda. He felt a sharp visceral pain as the first lingering, shuffling piano notes began to play.

> *The mere idea of you*
> *The longing here for you*

Where was the bloody remote? He searched madly. He had to turn this shit off. But then the smoke from the joint began bleeding into his lungs and in the end he gave up searching for the remote control and sat back to savour the sensation.

> *I see your face in every flower*
> *Your eyes in stars above*

He sat there, letting the smoke and the music wash over him. It was probably better to face the pain anyway. Get past these memories and forget about her.

He closed his eyes and took another deep puff from the joint. The hot smoke floated to the back of his throat. A faint taste like gunpowder brought back memories of childhood and fireworks nights.

Danny Bailey's lungs expanded, accepting the smoke. It flowed into him. He held it in his lungs as long as he could. Then he exhaled, hoping to feel some kind of esoteric impact.

Nothing.

Not a sausage. Beyond the pain of the Miranda memories, Danny began to feel a faint glimmer of amusement.

Tregemmon had been ripped off. This stuff had all the potency of lawn clippings.

He inspected the smouldering joint with contempt. He put it to his lips again and inhaled mightily, taking in an enormous breath of smoke prefatory to stubbing the thing out.

It filled his lungs. They expanded like balloons. He choked and coughed up an involuntary mouthful of smoke.

The oily smoke dispersed in the air in slow layers. It hung in front of his face like a milky shimmering veil.

Presently Danny began to feel very strange indeed.

Time seemed to expand languorously. He glanced around the room and his eyes were drawn to an odd glow.

The quality of the early-morning light had changed. It angled through the window and fell across the sofa with a sulphurous yellow luminescence like the light just before a storm.

Danny slowly exhaled, the barely visible smoke easing out of his body. He found, somewhat to his surprise, that he still needed to breathe. He inhaled the cool room air, breathing deeply, feeling every subtle muscle and sinew involved in the process.

Something very strange was happening. Danny felt a powerful buzzing in his brain. He sat there, the yellow thunderlight shining on him, like the vast silent detonation of some distant nuclear device.

He looked around the room. He saw the familiar walls and furniture of his sitting room but all at once it was a different place. He'd been thrown into another dimension, to a distant corner of the universe which had been cunningly fashioned to resemble his room, right down to the smallest detail.

What a strange notion. His scalp crawled with the curiousness of it and for a moment Danny felt his sanity wobble like a circus clown cycling across the abyss-spanning tightrope.

Then he got a grip on himself and a deep resonant calm settled over him. The saffron glow hovered around his body. Time seemed to have slowed down in the small room. The moment froze into a hard golden nub like amber.

That was when it happened.

He had an abrupt sensation of falling.

Feel of rain on his face. Then he could smell cool clean air wet with rain. And he could hear something, too.

The buzzing roar of traffic. Cars whipping past on a busy street. A tremor of anxiety, never dispelled since childhood, flickering deep down in you at the prospect of crossing the road in the face of the rushing traffic.

Look left. Look right. Swinging your head but it's hard to see because of the long sheaves of golden hair that sweep across your vision. Thumb the hair back behind your ears in exasperation, stare for a moment, wait for a gap in the traffic.

A taxi driver grins and slows down to let the pretty girl run across the road.

Flash him your second-best smile and your heels clip the tarmac neatly, swiftly. You're through the traffic, across the road, safely at the other side, and you slow down and suddenly for some reason you're standing on the Kings Road in a faint mist of early-morning rain, thinking of Danny Bailey.

On your way to the twenty-four-hour shop. A pint of milk. Some stamps. Minor random errands before you go to the gallery, to start the day with your business partner Della Cooper who is there already, making the coffee and impatiently waiting for the milk.

But Danny Bailey has come flapping into your mind like a bird swooping unexpectedly in through an open window.

What's happening? Traffic roars past on the Kings Road. You feel the rain on your face and it feels very strange. A wizened man with a drooping cigarette clamped in his jaws is taking bundles of flowers out of a

44

van, placing them in pale-green plastic buckets on the pavement. Bright wilted bundles of carnations, lilies, irises.

I see your face in every flower

The old song comes roaring back into your mind. You remember listening to it in Danny's flat. Suddenly you feel very strange.

You almost feel stoned.

You stumble into a lamppost. The Indian man opening his grocery shop looks at you with a momentary flicker of concern, swiftly replaced by contempt. He sees some drugged-out blonde. High or drunk at this early hour of the morning, when the decent people are starting their working day.

You push away from the lamppost. Ignore the man. What is happening? There is something in your head. Like an echo. Your thoughts are coming at you from strange angles.

They don't feel like *your* thoughts at all.

You shake your head. Fear and anger flash inside you like a match to petrol.

Get out of my mind!

Danny Bailey jolted forward, wincing with pain. Then, like a man coming awake, he shook his head to clear it. Had he drifted off? Had he been dreaming?

He was sitting on his sofa, still clutching the roach of his joint. How much time had passed? What the hell had happened?

He wandered into the kitchen, lost in thought. He poured himself a glass of water and sipped it slowly.

Danny didn't believe in ESP. Yet that strange flash had been so vivid, so convincing. Just like being inside Miranda's mind. All the thoughts had the distinctive flavour of her, right down to that final fierce flash of rage.

It had blasted him right out of her head.

Danny could still feel a distant tremor in his skull, the menacing promise of a massive headache somewhere in the background.

He was wandering out in the garden, getting a breath of fresh air, when he saw a splash of bright colour on the ground. At first he thought it was some late blossoming flower. But it was another of those paper aeroplanes.

This one was also fashioned from bright-red paper. Danny picked it up and unfolded it. It had writing on it. He read the slanting words: IT'S NOT JUST THE DRUGS. IT'S THE MUSIC.

NINE

The accident would never have happened if Juliette hadn't been in such a hurry.

She was hurrying because, as usual, she was late for her appointment at the Abbey. Her appointment with Christopher.

As she hurtled through Fulham, aiming south for Hammersmith and the river, she was already composing apologies to her boss in her mind.

Juliette was busy silently rehearsing these explanations and justifications to Chad when the accident happened.

A knot of traffic was waiting at the lights on the narrow road leading towards Hammersmith Bridge. The autumn evening was closing in and drivers beginning to switch on their headlights. The buildings across the river were already vanishing in the further gloom.

Sitting in her Fiat, Juliette watched the traffic lights turn to green and duly accelerated forward on to the handsome old Victorian bridge. The note of her tyres on the road surface changed. She saw the muddy banks of the Thames spreading to her left and right, the smooth spread of water, the ornate iron pillars of the bridge flickering past.

In front of her was a small group of bikers. Four young men in leathers and tattered denim sitting astride powerful motorcycles, buzzing forward through puddles, white tongues of spray sizzling up from their tyres.

Ahead of them was an orange bus with the silhouette of a wheelchair emblazoned on it.

The bikers were halfway across the bridge when the orange bus abruptly braked to a halt in front of them, responding to some unseen traffic situation at the far end of the bridge.

The bikes screeched neatly to a stop behind the bus, their red brake lights winking on. Following them, and taken somewhat by surprise, Juliette braked too.

At least, she tried to.

She mashed the pedal to the floor but found, to her horror, that the Fiat just kept moving. Despite the brakes being fully engaged, the car was sliding along the damp surface of the bridge, straight towards the immobile cluster of bikers.

Juliette clutched the steering wheel. She kept pushing at the brake pedal with all her strength, to no avail. The car kept sliding.

Time seemed to slow down and Juliette found herself watching the accident beginning to take shape. There was nothing she could do as the Fiat slid inexorably forward, aquaplaning on the wet road.

The bikes were parked in a loose diamond formation, one man at the front, two behind him side by side, and the fourth biker at the rear. Juliette clutched the steering wheel and stared during the sickening slow-motion instant it took.

The fourth biker was a thin young man with red hair. Juliette got a good look at him. He seemed to sense that something was wrong and glanced over his shoulder just before the moment of impact.

It wasn't a particularly violent impact but it swung the rear of the motorcycle around and knocked the rider off. The look of surprise on the biker's face and his windmilling limbs were horrifyingly comical.

The Fiat finally came to a halt, having nudged the heavy motorcycle a metre or two diagonally across the road. The redheaded biker was picking himself up, apparently unhurt.

Seeing this, Juliette allowed herself to breathe again.

The other bikers had all parked their machines on the kickstands and were busy dismounting now. The one in the front, evidently the leader, went over to the redheaded biker and reached down, offering to help him to his feet.

The leader was massively fat but powerful-looking. He wore an armless denim vest over his black leather jacket with an inept painting of a jackal on it.

The redhead cursed and slapped the jackal man's proffered hand aside. He climbed to his feet unaided, then walked shakily to the edge of the bridge and stared over the rail at the water, as though recovering his composure.

The big man chuckled, watching him. He turned to look at Juliette and shouted something. She wound down her window so she could hear him.

'Lenny's pissed off,' said the man jovially. The two other bikers made a beeline for Juliette's car as soon as they heard her window opening. One of them was a portly little man with a stubbly grey fringe of beard. He looked about fifty.

The other was a tall, gangly, sharp-faced kid with the beady dark doll's eyes of an amphetamine freak. They glared at Juliette, then turned to look at Lenny, who was now wrestling his motorcycle up off the road with the help of the big man.

All the bikers except Lenny were grinning, apparently amused by the accident. Lenny's bike seemed miraculously undamaged; nonetheless he carefully inspected it.

Juliette leant out of her car window. 'Are you all right?' she called cautiously. Lenny ignored her. Juliette decided she had to get out of her car and face the music. She swung the door open and reluctantly stepped out into the rain. But Lenny ignored her, concentrating on his examination of his bike.

'Let me give you my insurance details,' said Juliette. Her voice sounded shrill and hysterical, even to herself. She felt like some stupid irresponsible woman driver.

'I'm sorry,' she said. 'I had the brakes on full but it just didn't seem to want to stop.' She hated the note of whining that had crept into her voice.

The small, older biker with the bristly grey beard came over to her. 'You should have pumped the brakes,' he said helpfully. 'Next time, don't just freeze on the pedal. Let it up, then put it down again. Pump it. That way you dry off the brake pads.'

The leader came over. He ignored Juliette. 'Don't try and explain anything to the stupid cow, Shorty,' he said. 'She shouldn't be on the road in the first place. She's not fit to drive.'

He returned to his own bike and straddled it, knocking it off the kickstand.

The school bus had moved on now and the bridge was clear. Juliette was acutely aware of the line of cars building up behind her, waiting to go past.

The leader gunned his motorcycle and that seemed to be a signal. The others mounted up and roared away without a backward glance.

But as Juliette approached the intersection before the Abbey, she happened to look in her mirror, and there they were.

All four of them. The bikers. Hanging in close formation on the road behind her.

They must have been waiting in one of the side roads. Waiting for her to go past so they could follow her.

As soon as she glanced in the mirror, the group of bikers split up into two pairs. One pair zoomed ahead of her and drifted over in front of the car. Lenny and the leader, the big man with the jackal emblem.

They slowed down until their motorcycles hovered just a few yards ahead of her car.

Julia's heart began to ripple erratically in her chest. She peered anxiously into the mirror and saw that the other two bikers, Shorty and the speed freak, were right on her tail.

They had boxed her in.

Juliette had no idea what they planned to do next, and no desire to find out.

Her Fiat was just passing a small lane. On an impulse she wrenched the steering wheel violently to the right and sent the car skidding into the road.

The two motorcycles behind nearly collided with her

rear wheel arch as she made the manoeuvre. The two in front sailed blissfully on, unaware of what she had done.

Juliette heard shouting and the squeal of brakes behind her. She stamped hard on the accelerator, leaving the main road behind. The country lane flashed by.

It was a quiet little lane with a ceiling of dense dark branches. Not the route she would normally follow, but Juliette felt a warm flush of triumph. She'd got rid of the bikers.

But the feeling of triumph soon vanished. She found herself glancing into the rear-view mirror, anxious for the first sign of pursuit. She was concentrating so hard on watching the mirror that she almost ran into the railway junction.

She stamped on the brakes, jerking forward in her seat. The Fiat came to a stop, nose lurching downward, just inches from the skeletal metal gate. Juliette cursed.

These metal gates were lowered whenever a train was coming and they stayed down, preventing the car from crossing the rails, until the train was safely past.

Juliette bit her lip. What if the bikers caught up with her before the gates were raised again? She craned her head out of the window to look at the red lights that flashed to warn approaching traffic.

That was when she noticed something very disturbing. The red lights weren't flashing. In fact they appeared to be dead.

What was going on? Juliette looked back at the barrier in front of her and saw that there was some kind of black and yellow hazard-warning tape wrapped all around the metal uprights of the gate. The loose ends of the tape flapped in the wind.

That was when she finally saw the annoyingly small sign at the railside that announced ROAD CLOSED FOR ESSEN-TIAL REPAIRS. Beneath it was the logo of Wandsworth Council.

Juliette wrenched the car door open and jumped out. She looked back. The road was empty behind her. She was in a heavily wooded section of parkland and realised suddenly that it was a very lonely place.

Chestnut trees spread over her and above them she could see the distant white roof of her destination, the Abbey.

There was a flare of light from the roof of the Abbey. The reflection of something bright in the last rays of sunset. It was tantalisingly close. For a moment Juliette considered abandoning her car and continuing on foot.

But she couldn't quite bring herself to relinquish the protective shell of her car.

She turned back to the railway barrier and stared at it. On the other side of the tracks she could see abandoned machinery and a large excavation. No workmen in sight. They must have finished for the day. The road on the other side wound through another heavily wooded patch of parkland.

There was no way forward. She would have to turn back and shunt the car around the narrow lane in a U-turn. Then drive back towards the main road.

Juliette cursed and bit her thumbnail. Her instinct screamed for her not to turn back. She had the strong feeling that the bikers might be following her.

What should she do?

A cold wind weaved through the trees and damp leaves stirred sluggishly at her feet. Juliette glanced back at her car. There was no choice. She had to abandon it.

She felt as if she was leaving her only protection. A warm safe womb of metal. But already there was a sound in the distance, a faint traffic sound. Could it be motorbikes? Could they even now be hurtling towards her along the winding lanes?

She turned to the railway barrier, hesitated for a moment, choosing the best way over, then hitched up her skirt and began to climb. As she scrambled up, a buffeting noise came echoing at her through the dense screen of trees. It was unmistakable now.

The sudden guttural rumble of a motorcycle engine, startlingly close.

TEN

Juliette didn't look back. The sound grew louder, plural. At least two motorcycles. She swung a leg over the barrier.

The Fiat blocked the road behind her. The motorcycle came to a stop behind it. The rider scrambled off. Juliette didn't see which one it was, but she heard him. He was coming for her.

She swung her other leg over the barrier.

Her tights snared on a scrag of wire at the top of the barrier. The other motorcycles had arrived. They were rumbling to a stop behind her Fiat.

Juliette wrestled with her snared tights. She desperately wrenched herself forward, ripping them on the wire, lunging over the barrier.

Lunging free, dropping down on to the cinder railbed.

Free.

A hand grabbed her on the shoulder and clamped with an unrelenting leathery grip. Juliette tried to struggle loose but the man dragged her around to face him.

It was the biker's leader, the big man, reaching over the barrier at shoulder height, the muscles on his tattooed arm bulging. Juliette heard a roaring noise in her ears. The man was shouting something but she couldn't hear him because of the roaring noise. The other bikers were running to the barrier now, coming to help their leader.

The noise behind Juliette was now a long continuous scream, matching the scream of terror in her mind.

Then she finally recognised the sound. She could see it. The hurtling approach of a juddering shape, sweeping nearer in the evening light.

A train.

All four of the bikers had their hands on her, an eight-limbed beast clutching her.

She writhed and struggled against the beast even as it dragged her back over the barrier, back to safety.

The train thundered past, its warning siren screaming.

'You stupid bitch,' panted the leader. 'You nearly got yourself topped.'

The train rattled off into the distance.

'Never mind that – she nearly topped me.' Lenny came over to Juliette and stared into her face.

'Worse than that, she might have damaged your bike,' said the big man who was still holding Juliette. The others all laughed. But it wasn't the sort of laugh that released tension.

It had an ugly note to it and Juliette sensed that these men were not going to stop at verbal abuse. She had to get away from them as quickly as possible.

Lenny was leaning over her. He was so close that she could smell his leathers. His pale-blue eyes were alight with excitement.

'You nearly wrecked my bike and you nearly killed me,' he said. He was uncomfortably close to her. She could smell the acid tang of his sweat now. Juliette tried to move away but the big man, the leader, was still holding on to her.

When she tried to move, he tightened his grip. Juliette's first impulse was to struggle further. Instead, she forced herself to relax. When she spoke she tried to sound casual but firm.

'Nonsense. I knocked you off and I'm terribly sorry. I offered to exchange insurance details and you ignored me. But I didn't come close to killing you. That's a ridiculous exaggeration.'

'How do you know?' demanded Lenny. 'I might've cracked my skull.'

'You were wearing a helmet.'

'Helmet.' The skinny teenager chuckled moronically, gleaning a sexual meaning from the word. There was a sudden silence on the darkening stretch of country lane.

Juliette didn't like the sudden change of mood. 'Let go of me, please,' she said, trying to put a note of authority in her voice.

'All we're saying is that we want an apology,' said the small man with the scraggly grey beard. He hurried over. 'Just an apology.' But his own voice sounded apologetic.

'Shut up, Shorty.'

'That's all we want,' persisted Shorty. He looked worried. 'Just an apology.'

'That's all we *did* want,' corrected the leader. 'But then we got a look at you.' He reached up with a grimy callused hand and stroked Juliette's cheek. She couldn't stop him because the speed-freak kid had hold of her again.

Two pairs of hands on her.

'Let go of me,' said Juliette. She could hear her voice wobble with fear.

'We can't let go of you,' said the leader softly. 'We've seen you now. And it's your own fault. You let us get a good look at you. You got out of your car. You were climbing that fence with your legs apart, provocatively flashing your knickers at us.' He caressed her face again.

Juliette saw that he had a name tattooed on his fingers. 'Suze' in jagged blue letters. She wondered numbly if that was a name, and if it would be a useful detail for the police.

'You got us all worked up,' said the biker. 'The excitement of your near miss with the train and all.' He rubbed his chin nervously with his tattooed fist. 'You might say it stimulated us.'

'Please let me go.'

'We can't. Not now that we've had a good look at you. You're lovely. Isn't she, lads?'

'Come on,' said Shorty. 'That's enough. Let her go, Jackanory. You've scared her. She's good and scared.'

'She's wetting her knickers,' Lenny leered.

'That's only fair,' said the skinny teenager. 'She made you cack yours when she knocked you off your bike.'

'Let her go, lads,' pleaded Shorty.

'Please.' Juliette could feel herself beginning to cry. Tears of rage and humiliation.

'We can't let you go,' said the big man called Jackanory.

'My name is Juliette Race. I'm a doctor. I work just up the road,' Juliette spoke swiftly, matter-of-factly. It was essential that she make these men begin to perceive her as a human being, a person with a life. Not some anonymous object on to which they could project their sexual fantasies and their rage.

Juliette hurried on. 'I come to a private hospital every afternoon where I have a patient.'

The bikers hadn't loosened their grip on her but they were listening to her and they seemed to be looking at her differently from the way they had a moment ago.

Was she getting through to them?

'My name is Dr Juliette Race,' she repeated. 'I'm on my way to work. I'm very late.' She tried to make her face smile.

'You're more than late, Dr Juliette Race,' said Jackanory. 'You're horny. I bet men are always telling you that.'

Juliette hesitated. She wanted to keep talking, keep a dialogue going, but not on this sexual footing.

'You're made for it,' said Jackanory. 'Has anyone ever told you that? I'll bet they're always telling you that. It's your mouth. But not just your mouth. It's everything about you.'

He suddenly put his hands on her breasts and Juliette felt a sick breathless shock, as if she had been punched in the stomach.

She writhed, straining to escape his touch but there was nothing she could do. He kept on touching her, and, when they saw that it was all right, the others began touching her, too.

'Leave her alone,' said Shorty. His voice was shaking. 'Come on, boys. Enough's enough.'

The others ignored him.

Shorty lurched forward. He tried to peel the men off and Lenny swung around and promptly hit him, smashing him to the ground.

As soon as Shorty went down, Juliette knew she was finished. The others started dragging her away from the railway barrier now, back to the grass on the roadside under the dark spreading trees.

Juliette smelt mould and loam, the bitter stinging scent of nettles. She felt as if this was all happening to someone else.

Someone in a dream. She wondered if it would do any good to scream.

Jackanory was crouched over her while the other two bikers held her down. He had his hands hovering between her legs.

His gaze was locked on the torn black fabric of her tights and the whiteness of flesh underneath. 'You poor thing,' he said, his voice a horrid falsetto parody of concern.

'They're ruined. Your lovely stockings are ruined,' he crooned. Now his voice thickened with lust. 'Let me help you take them off.'

The touch of his hand on the bare flesh of her thigh gave Juliette a shock as though someone had reached into her chest, spread her ribcage and squeezed her heart.

She tried to kick him, but the skinny teenager was holding her legs with bruising strength. She couldn't move.

The leader began to jerk her tights off. 'I think Lenny should do the honours first,' he chuckled throatily. 'After all, it was Lenny she rear-ended.'

'Now I think I'll rear-end her,' said Lenny quietly. He began to unbuckle his belt.

Juliette stared up, past the bestial faces, past the spreading branches, up into the darkening sky. It was a Thursday afternoon in October with intermittent rain showers.

This couldn't be happening.

'I'm a doctor,' she heard herself say.

'That's good. You'll know all about anatomy, then.'

'Please let me go.'

The biker leader ignored her. He looked at the others. 'First Lenny, then me, then you, then Shorty,' he said.

'I don't want any part of it,' said Shorty. He stood a small distance away, wiping blood off his beard. Juliette tried to catch his eyes, to plead for help, but he wouldn't look at her. He was too frightened.

'You're going to get a helping whether you want it or not,' said Jackanory. 'Everybody joins the picnic.'

'It's just that Shorty gets leftovers.'

'Sloppy seconds.'

'Sloppy thirds,' said Lenny

'Sloppy fourths,' said the teenager. His voice was squeaky with excitement.

'I'll scream,' said Juliette.

'You've picked a good place for it,' said Lenny amiably. 'Go ahead. Scream your heart out.' He had finished unbuckling his heavy silver belt and now he unzipped his leather trousers.

That was when Juliette realised it was actually going to happen. She stared at the dark branches above her. There was no stopping it. She closed her eyes hopelessly, retreating to some numb corner of her mind where she might survive this intact.

With her eyes closed the universe was reduced to a dark world of primitive sensation. Sound and touch. The man kneeling between her legs was having trouble ripping her underwear off. And he was getting impatient.

Juliette distantly registered his laboured breathing. He obviously had some kind of respiratory trouble – probably a heavy smoker. Then Juliette heard another sound, from the direction of the rail barrier. A sharp metallic rattling. There was a heavy thud and then the rattling again.

One of the bikers called out. Shorty. He gave an abrupt wordless cry of warning and Juliette felt the men release her.

She opened her eyes. Everything was happening at once. Jackanory and the teenager had let go of her and were stumbling towards their motorcycles.

Lenny, who had been kneeling between her legs, was a little slower off the mark. He was still struggling to his feet and, seeing her opportunity, Juliette jerked forward, trying to drive her knee into his face.

But the man deflected the blow with ease, taking it harmlessly on his shoulder. Then he scrambled to his feet and fled to his own motorcycle. The other three bikes were already on their way, roaring off down the quiet country lane.

Juliette turned to see what they were fleeing from.

A policeman was running towards her.

The metallic sounds she had heard were the railway barriers yielding as the policeman had vaulted over them. He was dashing towards the last biker just as Lenny mounted his motorcycle and sped away.

The policeman was a big middle-aged man, wearing a loose-fitting blue bomber jacket. He stood for a minute, watching in frustration as the bikers zoomed away.

Juliette was still stunned by the suddenness of the man's arrival. He had saved her. The bikers had scattered at the first sight of him.

Scattered like crows, she thought.

The policeman's hair was pale. Pale and unusually long, Juliette realised. It was tucked into the back of his collar to conceal it. Long pale hair. White hair, in fact . . .

Then he turned to face her and she saw that it wasn't a policeman at all. It was Christopher Matthew.

He came over to her, his face a mask of anger and concern.

'Are you all right? Did they hurt you?'

'Christopher.'

'The bastards,' he growled, staring after the bikers. 'Did they hurt you?'

'Christopher. What are you doing here?' Juliette felt that, on top of everything else, Christopher's arrival was too much to comprehend. Her mind refused to take it in. All at once she found she was too exhausted to remain standing.

She sank down and sat on the grass at the roadside, her ruined tights pooling baggily around her knees. Christopher sat beside her, took her hand and squeezed it tight.

'I thought you were a policeman,' she said.

'Good,' said Christopher. 'That's what I wanted those bikers to think.'

He seemed to feel that settled the matter. But Juliette persisted: 'Christopher, this is very strange. When I looked at you I was *certain* I saw a policeman.'

'It's the jacket. Official blue. Very intimidating.'

Juliette reached out and fingered the fabric of his bomber jacket. It was made of blue silk, old and torn and oil-stained. 'It wasn't just this. It was the way you moved. It was everything about you.'

'All right.' Christopher squeezed her hand gently and released it. As he climbed to his feet, he brushed off his jeans. 'I admit I was trying to convey that impression.'

'Trying to convey . . .?' Juliette shook her head. She retrieved her handbag from the ground, then finally gathered the strength to stand up. Christopher put a hand around her shoulders and helped her.

He smiled. 'After all, there were four of them and only one of me. I wanted to spook them as much as possible.'

Scattered like crows, thought Juliette. She was beginning to realise that she had witnessed something extraordinary, but she wasn't quite sure what it was.

'I don't understand. How did you know what was happening to me?'

'I saw it.'

Juliette repressed the urge to shiver. She glanced at the Abbey in the distance, a white shape over the darkening treetops. 'That's not possible,' she said. 'You can't see this spot from any of the windows of the Abbey.'

'No.' Christopher smiled. 'But you can see it from the roof.'

'From the roof? What on Earth were you doing on the roof?'

'Launching these.' Christopher unzipped his jacket and took out a fan of bright-red paper aeroplanes.

'You get more accuracy and better lift from the roof.'

'You saw me . . .'

Christopher reached into another pocket and took out a small pair of binoculars.

'I was looking through these. Watching my planes land. That's what I was doing when I spotted you.'

Juliette remembered the flash of light on the roof of the Abbey. 'But you aren't allowed to leave the grounds.'

Christopher smiled again. 'I'm not allowed on the roof either, but I know how to get in and out of the Abbey without being observed.'

Juliette was nodding, looking at the bright-red sheets of paper in his hand. There was writing on them. Just a few words here and there, hidden or distorted by the sharp angular folds of the wings.

Christopher noticed her gaze and put them away, tucking the sheets of paper into his jacket in an unhurried fashion.

'What's that?' she asked.

'What's what?' he said innocently.

'The writing on those paper aeroplanes. You've written something on them.' Juliette had a sudden intuition that this was important. 'Let me have a look.'

'It's nothing,' said Christopher. He was beginning to look embarrassed. 'It's just a little ritual I have. Before I launch the aeroplanes I like to write something on them. I just jot something down without thinking about it. The first thing that comes into my head.'

'Let me read some,' said Juliette. Christopher shook his head, grinning weakly. 'No. It's too embarrassing.'

'Why?'

'Because it seems a little bit crazy. I mean, what a ridiculous thing to do.' His smile grew a little more sincere. 'Though I would argue that it's certainly no crazier than painting a jocular message on the side of an atom bomb before you drop it on a large metropolis full of your fellow man.'

He put the binoculars back in his jacket, zipped it up and turned towards her car, as if this signalled the end of their discussion.

Juliette felt a rising flood of irritation. She knew that Christopher was not going to yield. He was not going to show her what was written on the paper aeroplanes.

She was also certain that she had just been told any number of lies, but she was too exhausted to pursue the matter.

Christopher opened the door of the Fiat for her. 'Do you have the keys?'

Juliette fumbled in her handbag and passed them to him. He started the car, switching on the headlights and carefully reversing until he came to a place in the road that was wide enough to allow them to turn around.

ELEVEN

Juliette forced herself to remember the facts of her situation. The man sitting beside her was supposed to be locked behind bars.

She had, in theory, just been rescued by an escaped lunatic.

She looked through the window of her Fiat and saw that they were approaching the final stretch of road leading to the Abbey. As if he'd read her mind, Christopher suddenly said, 'All this talking is making my throat dry. Let's have a drink before we go back.'

'A drink?'

Juliette's horror must have shown in her face because Christopher laughed. 'I'm not exactly eager to go back behind bars, you know.' He glanced at her. 'I mean, I'll do it, but I'd love to have a drink with you first. Just one drink as a free man. Please permit me that.'

Juliette didn't see how she could refuse. After all, he had just saved her life. And, besides, he was the one who was driving, and there wasn't much she could do to stop him.

She stared forlornly out of the window as the Abbey whipped past.

'I believe there's an interesting little pub not too far from here.' Christopher was peering into the darkness as they barrelled along the road, heading south, away from London. Into the countryside.

Juliette was acutely aware of the fact that she had gone AWOL from a private clinic with one of its star patients.

Somehow, seeing the Abbey disappear in the Fiat's rear-view mirror had brought that fact home with unpleasant force.

As if sensing her mood and wanting to distract her, Christopher said, 'Let me ask you a question as a psychiatrist.'

'As a psychiatrist?' Juliette shrugged. 'All right.'

'Do you think it's true that when we're kids we look to our parents for interpretation?'

'What do you mean by interpretation?'

'To give meaning to our experience, to define it for us?'

'Of course,' said Juliette tersely. She was feeling fretful and bad-tempered. 'Christopher, can we turn around and go back to the Abbey? I'm very late and –'

'Go on, Juliette. Be a good sport. Just one quick drink. All right?'

'I suppose.'

'Good! Now, where was I? Oh yes. As children we look to our parents for interpretation of events. But even as adults we tend to look to others for a similar kind of validation. Do you know what I mean?'

'Yes, I think so . . . I'm not sure.'

'Have you ever heard the term "local-reality commander"?'

'No.'

'That's hardly surprising, because I just made it up.' Christopher chuckled as he slipped the car into third. 'I like to think of reality as a force, just like gravity. And, just as physicists talk about gravity varying from place to place, I think we can talk about a thing called local reality.'

He was going to continue, but Juliette cut him off. 'Hence all your references to the Sapir-Whorf hypothesis. You're suggesting we shape our own reality.'

'Someone shapes it,' said Christopher grimly.

Christopher was peering into the darkness over the steering wheel, apparently searching for a landmark, when they finally slowed down. He said, 'Ah, yes. Here we go.'

Before Juliette knew it, he had set the indicator signal to winking a left turn. A moment later the Fiat was bouncing on to a weed-grown square of stained concrete that served as the unkempt car park of a small dingy pub.

Christopher switched off the engine and climbed out, carefully locking his door before coming around and opening Juliette's. She climbed out of the car. Their feet splashed in puddles as they crossed the pockmarked concrete towards the shadowy block shape of the pub.

Music from a jukebox thumped powerfully within. Juliette picked her way carefully among the puddles. It was very dark. It seemed there had once been a row of lights strung over the pub sign, but the bulbs had all been smashed.

So Juliette was almost through the door of the pub before she noticed the things.

There on the threshold of the pub she froze, staring at them. Christopher, who was ahead of her, leading the way, didn't notice anything until he had the door half open. Music and light poured out, and a flow of warm air heavy with a boozy smell of stale beer and cigarette smoke.

'What is it?' said Christopher.

Juliette didn't reply. The light from the doorway showed that she hadn't been mistaken. The shadowy shapes were now clearly outlined, chrome gleaming.

She looked around the car park and saw, with a chill feeling of astonishment, that they were everywhere. Parked under trees, leaning against the wall of the pub, blocking the shackled entrance to the beer garden.

Motorcycles.

Dozens of motorcycles.

'Christopher . . .' she said, with a dawning feeling of horror.

Christopher stood impatiently in the half-open door of the pub. 'What is it? What's the matter?'

Juliette forced herself to lower her voice so that no one in the pub could hear her. 'It's a bikers' pub.'

'So?'

'So?' Juliette was suddenly furious. How could he be so insensitive as to bring her here, after what had happened – or almost happened – beside the railway tracks?

'Oh, come on, Juliette,' said Christopher. 'No one will hurt us. Most bikers are decent people. You merely had the misfortune to run into a few nutcases.'

Merely? Juliette felt herself boiling with rage. 'A few nutcases who are probably in there swilling pints of fucking beer right now.'

She realised that this was the first time she had sworn in front of Christopher. The first time she'd ever sworn in front of one of her patients.

'Come on,' said Christopher in a wheedling tone. 'You have to rub shoulders with them, otherwise you'll permanently have a hang-up about people like this. It's like getting back on a horse after you've been thrown. I mean, you don't want to develop a complex, do you?'

Juliette felt her rage becoming diluted with exasperation. Christopher seemed to be nominating himself as her psychiatric counsellor, instead of the other way around.

Now he stepped into the pub, holding the door open for her. Juliette considered going back to the car and sulking there, but instead she found herself following him inside.

The pub was warm and smoky and noisy. The clientele seemed to be almost exclusively bikers. Although conversation didn't exactly stop when they walked in, it grew subtly quieter and there was definitely a sense that they were outsiders who were being scrutinised carefully.

Juliette had pulled her ruined tights up in the car but now she was acutely aware that they were beginning to bag around her knees en route to her ankles. What she really needed to do was take them off altogether.

She sank gratefully into the seat Christopher found for her, an old wooden pew by a table squeezed in between a dartboard and a cigarette machine. He left her there while he went to the bar to order drinks.

Juliette took the opportunity to inspect her surroundings. It was a traditional pub with a wood-beam ceiling which had apparently last been decorated sometime in the late 1950s. The ceiling and walls had acquired the distinctive yellowy-brown glaze that only decades of nicotine could impart. There was a gleaming mass of machinery mounted on a slab of mahogany over the bar, with a plaque identifying it as a Harley-Davidson engine.

The people sitting and standing around the bar were wearing worn jeans and leathers, with a lot of bare flesh and tattoos and body piercing in evidence. The customers ranged in age from a pair of tarty young girls in spangly satin boob tubes who were obviously under eighteen, and drinking illegally, to several grizzled old greybeards hovering like hawks over the pool table, who might have been upward of sixty.

The clientele was predominantly male and rowdy but there were quite a few girlfriends, and perhaps even wives, in evidence. Juliette was looking around for the door to the ladies', so she could change out of her tights, when Christopher returned with their drinks – a bottle of mineral water for her and another mineral water and what looked like a triple brandy for himself.

Christopher lifted the brimming brandy glass in a salute to her. 'A taste of freedom,' he said. 'You can do the driving on the way back.'

Juliette inspected the glasses they'd been given and was surprised to see that they were clean. She tipped the slice of lemon out of her glass into the ashtray, then twisted the neck of the bottle, unscrewed it and filled her glass.

Christopher was already sipping some of his water, as a chaser for the brandy. He frowned as he tasted it.

'What is it?' she said, watching him alertly.

'It tastes sweet,' he said. 'Try yours.'

Was it just the power of suggestion? Or maybe fear and dehydration had made her saliva more saline. But Juliette found that the water did indeed taste subtly, delightfully sweet.

She found herself checking the label on the bottle to see if there was added sugar. Of course, there wasn't.

'That's a good sign,' said Christopher.

'What are you talking about?'

'The fact that the water tastes sweet. It means that we're welcome here.'

Juliette peered closely at Christopher to see if he was pulling her leg. He appeared to be completely serious.

'Don't ask me why,' he said. 'But this has happened to me before.' He sipped some more of the water. 'And it's always a good sign.'

'Well, it's never happened to *me* before,' said Juliette. 'It sounds like a load of mystical cobblers.' She had been willing to accept many of the things that Christopher had said in the car, but this really was the limit.

'Besides,' she said, 'how can you say we're welcome here?' She nodded at the crowd around them. The people in the pub were increasingly boisterous, but were still pointedly ignoring them.

'Maybe they're not as unfriendly as they seem,' he said.

'Sweet water means you're welcome in a place? Honestly, Christopher. It sounds like something out of the Old Testament. I can't believe you're serious.'

'Believe what you like,' he said. 'But, if you're ever somewhere and the water tastes unaccountably brackish, then be on your guard.' He glanced at her. 'Brackish means salty,' he added.

'I know what brackish means,' said Juliette bad-temperedly. She wished he wouldn't keep banging on in this bogus-mystical vein. Up until now she'd been quite impressed with Christopher and some of his observations about human behaviour.

And, if the truth was told, she was actually rather enjoying the fact that they were having a drink together.

Enjoying it in a way that no psychiatrist should feel with her patient. Juliette sipped the sweet water again and found herself wondering if Christopher had somehow spooned some sugar into the bottle.

She was interrupted in these speculations by a rather odd incident. They had been lucky to get a seat in the pub. It was now packed, the sweaty crowd swaying to the constant booming of the jukebox.

Then all at once there was a ripple in the crowd. A fat woman emerged from the crush and waddled towards the rear of the pub where Christopher and Juliette were sitting. She was wearing frosted denim and had two grubby, tired-looking children in tow.

There was nowhere left to sit and Juliette was beginning to feel sorry for the woman, and guilty about her own seat, when a pair of bikers arose from a table and offered it to the woman.

That was the first clue Juliette had that something strange was happening. Because as the men stood up they glanced over at Christopher Matthew.

There was something very odd in their glances.

They moved off swiftly and the big woman gratefully set her bag down at the table. But the heavy, obviously foot-weary woman didn't sit down herself.

Instead she gave the seats to her two children, a skinny young boy and girl. The children were now sitting opposite Christopher. Juliette noticed that they cast nervous sidelong glances his way.

Indeed, despite the bustle and the noise of the pub, everyone seemed to be covertly looking at Christopher. Watching him and waiting for something to happen.

Christopher didn't seem aware of this sudden attention. He had downed most of his brandy rather swiftly and was now contentedly engaged in peeling the label off the plastic bottle. He was apparently completely wrapped up in this meaningless task, and he leant forward, bowing his head over the table in concentration.

As soon as he bowed his head, the mother and her children dropped their own heads in what Juliette could only describe as a pious fashion. They were like worshippers in church.

The jukebox was still hammering away and pockets of loud conversation continued, but around the family's table there was silence. Everyone was surreptitiously watching the strange tableau of Christopher and the kids.

At that instant the father appeared with a drink for himself and his wife, and bags of crisps for the children. He took in his silent, hunched family, then gave Christopher a swift suspicious look.

Right, thought Juliette with a flare of fear. Now there's

going to be trouble. But instead of striding towards Christopher to angrily challenge him, as she'd expected, the man just set his drink down. And then, astonishingly, he too bowed his head.

The family remained that way for a moment, worshipfully paused before Christopher as though receiving a blessing from him. All around them people were remaining respectfully silent and trying not to look. The whole event had a tense, oddly ritual quality. A synchronised precision, like a dance sequence.

A moment later the father looked up and hauled his kids to their feet. He dragged them away from the table and his wife followed.

As they went they glanced back at Christopher a final time. Juliette found it impossible to read their expressions. Perhaps fear or awe.

Perhaps even gratitude.

Once the family had disappeared, conversation resumed in their immediate vicinity and a couple quickly slipped in to occupy the chairs at the vacant table. The noise level was soon back to its original raucous volume, or perhaps louder.

And was there a more relaxed quality to the noise? As if tension had been built up in the crowd, and then released?

No one was looking at Christopher now. He still had his head bowed, in a pose that resembled meditation. Then he looked up and smiled at Juliette.

'Let's hit the road,' he said.

Juliette was relieved to escape through the door into the cool night air. She turned to him as they walked towards the car. 'What was that all about?'

Christopher looked at her with swift interest as they strode across the gravel. A cold moon was rising in the October night.

'Did you see it?' he asked.

'I could hardly help noticing it.'

'What exactly did you see?'

'That family brought their kids to sit in front of you and then it was as if . . .'

'Yes?'

'It was as if they received a blessing,' said Juliette reluctantly.

Christopher was nodding excitedly. He unlocked the Fiat and passed her the keys as she climbed behind the wheel. He sat in the passenger seat beside her as she started the engine.

'Yes,' he said. 'That's my interpretation, too. Or at least it's as close as I've ever come to explaining it before.'

'Before? This has happened to you before?'

'A few times.'

'In that pub?'

'In places like it.'

'Well.' Juliette shrugged helplessly as she steered the Fiat out of the pub car park. The whole thing seemed extraordinary. Inexplicable.

Was Christopher telling the truth? Yet she had witnessed the incident with her own eyes. 'What does it mean?'

'I don't know. But, as I was telling you, some of our group behaviour is deep in our genes. And ancient behaviour patterns can still be triggered in certain contexts.'

'What contexts?'

'Tribal.' Christopher frowned, and then he smiled at her with a strange nostalgic sadness. 'I was going to write a book about tribal behaviour. And how it surfaces in modern society.'

Juliette remembered that Christopher had been a highly respected anthropologist. Once again she felt her curiosity tugged by the mystery of this man. 'What happened to the book?'

'Let's just say I did the research, but I never wrote it.' He smiled a bitter smile. 'I did the research all right.'

'What do you mean?'

Christopher ignored the question. 'Lévi-Strauss has described the tribal lifestyle as a kind of hothouse for genetic variation,' he said. 'But it is also a hothouse for behavioural mechanisms. And those bikers back there in that pub are leading something close to a tribal lifestyle in the modern world.'

'What was so tribal about what we just witnessed?'

Christopher leant over and played with some controls on the dashboard, turning up the heat in the little Fiat.

'You must remember that the shaman was an important figure in tribal life.'

'The what? The shaman?'

'Yes.'

'So you're saying what happened was like tribal children being given a blessing by a shaman?'

'Or a priest,' said Christopher. 'Or a sorcerer.'

TWELVE

Back at the Abbey, Juliette finally had a chance to change out of her torn tights. She threw them into the bin in the ladies' and then hurried back to join Christopher in the games room.

As she walked along the dimly lit corridors of the sleeping institution, Juliette felt a sudden shudder of emotion. An emotion she was shocked to recognise as lust, pure and simple.

For weeks now she had been struggling against the realisation that she was falling in love with Christopher Matthew. The realisation was a dangerous one, because it was a transgressive love, violating boundaries Juliette was sworn to honour. Boundaries of doctor–patient ethics.

So far she had managed to keep this feeling under control, but today it had all got seriously out of hand. Christopher had rescued her.

Her saviour, in his ragged old bomber jacket.

And then at the pub he had demonstrated that not only was he sane but was on to something. Some kind of crucial discovery about the deep sources of human behaviour.

In her mind Juliette had already co-authored an award-winning paper with Christopher Matthew. And she was only just holding herself back from naming their children as she hurried towards the games room.

Juliette swung through the doors of the games room and there he was, standing hunched over the pool table, long white hair hanging down over his face, concealing those remarkable eyes. Then he looked up and those eyes were staring right into hers. He smiled the ironic smile she had come to know and her heart clenched.

He came over and stood close to her.

Not close enough. She wanted his mouth on her mouth. His hands on her breasts. Juliette found herself looking at the sofa and wondering if they should wedge a chair under the handle of the door to give them some privacy and then simply climb on to that sofa together.

It was total madness. It flew in the face of everything she had been taught. But it was going to happen.

Juliette felt that her face was flushed, glowing crimson, revealing all her innermost thoughts. She forced herself to be cool, to compose herself. To play the role of psychiatrist.

'Come and sit down over here, Christopher.'

He was smiling at her. Did he know? They sat down on the sofa, at opposite ends, a cautious distance between them. Christopher sat cross-legged. Juliette kicked off her shoes and slid her legs under her. 'Well, Christopher . . .' She tried to sound all official, full of authority, but her mind was miles away. How would she get him to kiss her?

That was the question. How to close that gap between them? Only the width of two cushions, but it seemed like miles.

She forced herself to say something, to behave like a psychiatrist.

'Well, Christopher, at our last appointment you were telling me how you found an office job after the accident, after you became homeless.'

'That's right,' said Christopher. There was a gleam of amusement in his eye. He did know, damn him. He knew that this was all just a game and soon they would cross the dividing space and they would be in each other's arms.

'You were quite happy at that office, weren't you?'

'Sure. It was a nice place.'

'That was the impression I got,' she said. Any moment she was going to abandon this charade and reach across the sofa. If he didn't kiss her, she was going to kiss *him*, by God.

One or two more questions, just for appearances' sake.

'So, why did you leave there?' Her voice sounded

impatient, perfunctory, even to herself. 'You were happy, so why did you leave?'

Christopher shrugged. 'I didn't exactly leave,' he said.

'What do you mean?'

'I mean Dr Cavanaugh came and kidnapped me.'

Juliette was silent for a long moment. 'Did you say *kidnapped* you?'

'Yes, he kidnapped me and brought me here.' He looked at her a little sadly as he said it, as though he was reluctant to tell her the truth, but it was the truth all the same.

Juliette stared at him. It was obvious he wasn't joking. She felt the lust and all the other good feelings inside her begin to congeal into a cold lump.

She forced herself to remain calm. 'And why would he do a thing like that?'

'Because he knows about Mr Leiber.'

'Mr Leiber?'

'Yes,' said Christopher. He scratched his head nervously in a monkey-like gesture. He was speaking very quickly now. Almost babbling.

'And he knows that I know about him.' He leant forward, eyes gleaming intently. Juliette repressed the urge to move away from him. 'Of course I do. But he doesn't know the full truth. He can't quite bring himself to believe it.'

A glittering drop of spittle sprang from Christopher's mouth as he spoke. 'He doesn't know the full scope of my powers. Or Mr Leiber's powers . . . And he doesn't know of the awesome conflict which is to come.'

Juliette couldn't think of anything to say.

'I've wanted to talk to you about Mr Leiber for a long time,' said Christopher, after Juliette had let him ramble uninterrupted for a while. There was a thin film of sweat shining on his forehead. 'It's good that I've told you about him at last.'

'Yes, Christopher, it's good,' said Juliette. She tried to remain calm despite the sickening, sinking feeling inside her.

Christopher Matthew was quite clearly out of his mind.

75

THIRTEEN

Chad glanced up as Juliette wandered wearily into his office.

The medical director was busy dusting his tennis trophies, an absurdly large yellow feather duster clamped in his meaty fist. But Juliette didn't feel any amusement at the incongruous sight.

She wondered if she would ever feel anything again, except numbness.

Whatever his faults, Chad Cavanaugh was a perceptive man. 'What is it, Juliette?' he said. 'What happened?' He set the duster aside as she sank wearily into one of the armchairs in front of his desk.

Chad sat opposite her in the other armchair. He was watching her closely while trying to appear casual. 'Has something happened to upset you?'

'No, not really, no,' she lied. 'It's just that I've had a setback with Christopher Matthew.'

Cavanaugh looked instantly wary. 'I thought you two were getting along famously.' Was there a note of anxiety in his voice?

'Let me try to explain.' Juliette was surprised to find that her own voice was steady and strong. 'This might also account for the fact that I seem a little upset . . .'

'Take your time,' said the medical director, and he said it in such a condescending tone that Juliette astonished herself with a fleeting, savage impulse to grab one of his heavy silver tennis trophies and brain him.

She took a breath, controlling her rage. 'I suppose the problem is that I began to pay attention to his strange theories.'

Of course, in truth the problem was her own feelings, and the way they had betrayed her. But she'd die before she admitted as much.

'Paying attention to your patient is your job,' said Chad in a syrupy, sanctimonious voice. 'To make clinical progress with someone is to share a common ground with him. But that common ground can sometimes be a minefield.'

Juliette was getting the stealing, somnolent impression that she was hearing an oft-repeated lecture.

She interrupted impatiently. 'I admit, he's very plausible. I was almost ready to give him a clean bill of health myself.'

Chad suddenly became very casual. 'Ah. And what happened to alter that opinion?'

Juliette fought to steady her voice. She was on the verge of tears. 'It happened when I began to interview him today. I was feeling very positive about his prognosis. But then I just asked a few questions, routine questions. And . . .'

She looked up at Chad, who was listening carefully.

'It was like walking down a staircase and suddenly there's no more steps. You're stepping into thin air.' Juliette made an effort to pull herself together and went on. 'We were talking normally when he began to display what I can only characterise as florid paranoid delusions.'

Now Chad looked genuinely worried. 'What exactly were you discussing when you made this . . . step into the void?'

'I asked him how he came to leave his job.'

'Ah,' said Chad. Juliette found that she was suddenly unable to read her boss's expression.

'And he told me that you kidnapped him and brought him here,' said Juliette.

Chad sagged forward in his chair, sighing with relief. 'Oh, that.' He immediately brightened up.

Juliette was silent for a moment, watching him, trying to interpret this sudden change of mood. Cavanaugh was actually chuckling now. His blue eyes twinkled at her as he exercised all his bullnecked charm. 'I think you can return to your earlier estimate of our patient.'

He wagged a large finger at her indulgently. 'He may not be quite ready for release, but he's certainly not some kind of deeply paranoid personality.'

'But you didn't hear him. The way he described being brought here. It was classic textbook stuff. Descriptions of persecution –'

Chad held up a big hand to silence her. 'It's not your fault, not your fault at all. I can see how you might have been misled –'

'Misled? He said that he was *kidnapped*.'

The medical director chuckled. 'Kidnapped is putting it a bit strongly.'

'A bit strongly. He said he was brought here at gunpoint.'

'He's somewhat exaggerating the case.'

'Exaggerating? What do you mean exactly?'

'Well, all right, there was an armed escort with him when he arrived at the Abbey.'

'And why wasn't I told about this? Why was I left alone with him, with no instructions and no warning that he was dangerous?'

'He isn't dangerous,' said Chad impatiently. 'The armed guard was there to protect him.'

'Protect him?'

Cavanaugh fell silent. He looked uncomfortable again, as though he'd said more than he'd intended.

It was obvious to Juliette that she was supposed to stop asking questions now. She didn't give a damn. She was furious. She pressed on.

'How on Earth am I supposed to distinguish between delusion and truth on behalf of my patient when you won't even tell me what the truth is?'

All the smiling charm faded from Cavanaugh's face. His blue eyes went cold, the true nature of the man shining clearly through. 'The truth?' he said sardonically.

'I think you owe me that.'

Chad got up from the comfortable armchair and went back and stationed himself behind his desk, symbolically resuming his position of power.

He looked at her as if she were a rather unprepossessing job applicant. His voice was polite and neutral. 'Dr Race, do you remember doing some profiling recently?'

Juliette looked at him in surprise. How could Chad know about that? It had been strictly confidential work.

'I'm not sure I'm at liberty to discuss –'

'Oh, loosen up for God's sake, Doctor.'

'I signed the Official Secrets Act.'

Chad stifled a yawn. 'Who hasn't? You've worked for Five, so have I. In fact they recommended you to me.'

'Five?'

Chad regarded her coolly. 'Don't play dumb. The fashionable nickname for MI5. Britain's oxymoronically named intelligence service . . . *Spies*.'

A thought suddenly occurred to Juliette. 'You mean this place where Christopher worked, the Brain Trust, was something to do with the intelligence community?'

Chad smiled and nodded.

Juliette was silent. Finally she said, 'Do you believe that Christopher Matthew is sane?'

She could see Chad's mind whirring away swiftly as he weighed up the consequences of various replies, and the consequence of not replying swiftly enough.

Then he smiled his most plausibly charming smile. What Juliette had privately come to think of as his politician's smile. 'I'm not about to offer a snap diagnosis on such a complex and problematical issue. But I will tell you this. The things he told you today, the things which you – quite understandably – took to be delusions are in fact nothing of the kind. Essentially he was telling you the truth.'

Juliette considered this little speech, and then she said, 'Even when he was talking about Mr Leiber?'

Chad gave her an unreadable stare and then he said, quite casually and blandly, 'What precisely did he tell you about Mr Leiber?'

'Nothing precisely. Vague ramblings. I thought he was ranting. I got the impression that this Mr Leiber was some kind of personal bogeyman. I didn't think he existed.'

'Oh no,' said Chad in the same bland voice. 'Mr Leiber exists.'

Juliette strode down the corridor, towards the reception area where Pamela Croden sat wrestling with her endless crossword puzzles.

Today she was busy with the *Mirror*.

As she walked towards the front door, Juliette noticed for the first time the small camera angled discreetly in a corner of the ceiling, peering down at her, a light blinking on its side.

Juliette realised that there were similar cameras outside. She had seen them without ever really registering their presence. They had blended into the background.

Like the TV screens behind Pamela Croden's desk. The plump woman was smoking a cigarette and looking at them now, reluctantly forsaking her crossword for a moment while she watched Juliette's departure.

She pressed a button on her desk and released the lock on the doors and Juliette stepped out into the night. The air was cool and smelt of fresh-cut greenery. Prem was still trimming the hedges, working by torchlight as she crossed the car park. He paused when he saw her, and smiled and waved.

As he waved his red coat sagged open, revealing some kind of harness over his white shirt. The harness held a small metal object snugly against his ribs.

Juliette hurried to her car and drove away from the Abbey. All the way home she thought of her final conversation with Chad. She regretted one small act of cowardice. One failure of nerve.

When he'd asked her about Mr Leiber, she'd described him as some kind of personal bogeyman to Christopher. But that wasn't really the truth at all.

She had got the distinct impression that Mr Leiber was more than just a bogeyman.

He was the devil himself.

FOURTEEN

The sun was sinking low in the sky. The last rays shone across the roof of the Abbey and through the window of Danny Bailey's kitchen, silhouetting a figure.

Tregemmon stood there. He had opened the metal briefcase, which sat on the table, and was holding one of the blocks of the weed, the one Danny had been using for his personal smoking.

He was listening patiently.

Danny said, 'It was just like being inside Miranda's head. It was like a psychic connection between us.'

Tregemmon nodded as though he understood. 'Young telepaths in love, huh?' There was perhaps a hint of mockery in his voice.

Danny sighed. 'You seem to have a very open mind, Tregemmon. I mean, how many people would sit through a story like that and even think about believing me?'

'Listen,' said Tregemmon. He nodded at the skunk weed piled in blocks inside the metal briefcase. 'Do you know what they call this stuff?' He picked up a block. 'You've heard of Northern Lights and Chronic and Kali's Mist?' He touched the weed, almost caressing it. 'Well, they call this little lot ESP.'

He set the block down and an odd look came into his eye. 'And anyway, why shouldn't I believe you? I've run across weirder shit.'

'Anyway,' said Danny, 'I wanted to apologise for smoking so much. Caning your inventory. After Miranda blasted me out of her head, I smoked masses because I wanted to re-establish contact with her.'

'And did it work?'

'Not exactly. Nothing was happening. But then I got this.' Danny took out a bright-red sheet of paper. There were sharp creases in it where it had been folded into the shape of an aeroplane.

He smoothed them out with the edge of his fist as he turned the paper over and showed Tregemmon the message written on it: IT'S NOT JUST THE DRUGS. IT'S THE MUSIC.

Tregemmon snapped his fingers. 'Of course,' he said. 'That song that you were listening to when it first happened.'

'It was *our* song,' said Danny simply.

'So you smoked *and* you listened to the song. Did it work?'

Danny nodded. 'Then I discovered that I don't need the skunk weed. In fact, I don't even need the music. I just have to get into the right frame of mind.'

But Tregemmon wasn't listening. His expression had become suddenly grim.

He stared down at the red sheet of paper, frowning at the handwriting. He looked at Danny.

'So where did this thing come from?'

'I don't know.'

Tregemmon turned and stared out of the window. Danny realised he was looking at the Abbey. 'I think I'd better be going,' said Tregemmon.

Tregemmon opened the garden gate and stepped into the street. He swapped the briefcase to his left hand and shook hands with Danny.

As he turned to go, he once again paused to peer bleakly up at the Abbey. 'I tried to come here a couple of times to collect this.' He lifted the briefcase. 'But I had to turn back.'

'Why?'

For a moment it seemed Tregemmon wasn't going to answer. But then he said, 'Because I discovered that you were under observation.'

'Under what?'

By way of reply, Tregemmon pointed to a vehicle that

was parked under a street light just up the road. An orange school bus.

With its wheelchair emblem on the side, the bus was a familiar sight. Danny often saw it when he was going back and forth between home and the local shops.

'You must be joking,' he said.

Tregemmon shook his head with weary disgust. 'Haven't you ever wondered why you've got a school bus parked out here every day when you haven't got a school?'

'But it's for the disabled kids.'

'You ever see any disabled kids in it?'

'No.'

'And you never wondered about it?'

'No.'

'Well, that's what I call sharp-eyed observation,' said Tregemmon disgustedly. He moved close to Danny and his voice dropped to a whisper. 'Trust me,' he said. 'That's no school bus. They've got surveillance gear on board.'

'Right.' Danny decided that Tregemmon was pulling his leg. 'Surveillance gear.'

Tregemmon looked at him bleakly. 'State-of-the-art equipment. The sort of kit that can pick up a conversation in a room by shining a laser on the window. And they've got ordnance, too. Weapons.'

Danny Bailey felt like calling Tregemmon's bluff. His friend was obviously trying to frighten him. 'Well, how are you going to get past them with that?' he said. He indicated the steel briefcase, which, for all his cloak-and-dagger stories, Tregemmon was holding in plain sight.

To Danny's surprise Tregemmon began to laugh. 'Because I got it wrong. They aren't after us, fool. It isn't you that's under observation.'

'Who is it, then?'

'That place,' said Tregemmon.

He pointed at the big white building that rose beyond the wall of the estate. The Abbey.

Suddenly Danny didn't know whether to believe him or not. He said, 'But why are the police watching the Abbey?'

'Oh, I don't think they're the police,' said Tregemmon cheerfully. He slapped Danny on the shoulder and left.

Ten miles north, the last rays of sunset glittered on the slow-moving waters of the Thames and slanted down over Chelsea Harbour. Gloom was gathering among the antique shops and brasseries and pubs and people quickened their stride in the chill autumnal darkness.

Miranda Lang stood looking through the window of her little art gallery and shivered as she watched the last light fade from the day.

Ever since that strange encounter in the Kings Road, she had been in such a state of turmoil. It was as if she'd suddenly begun sharing her mind with someone else.

She had felt him there as emphatically as you feel someone putting a hand on your shoulder. Someone *in* there with her. In her most private of places.

Danny Bailey.

Sharing her mind, in some kind of unimaginable intimacy.

She had remained tensed up for days afterward, waiting for him to do it again. A few times she had experienced a fleeting, uneasy feeling, like a shadow flitting across the back of her mind. It reminded her of the feeling you get on the back of your neck when someone is watching you.

But that was all. Perhaps she had just imagined it.

By now she had almost managed to forget about the whole incident. She locked up the gallery and caught a taxi into town, where she joined some friends for dinner and a quick drink. A quick drink turned into several. The next thing Miranda knew, it was closing time and she was standing in the surging neon wilderness of the West End Friday night.

Her friends loyally flagged down a taxi for her in Piccadilly Circus and gave the driver instructions as Miranda folded up in the back seat in an undignified, giggling heap. The whole problem of Danny Bailey was quite forgotten.

Luckily, she got home before she started throwing up.

And she soon made the unhappy discovery that the throwing up was just the prelude to a spectacular bout of stomach-wrenching nausea, interrupted now and then by shocking spasms of diarrhoea. It had to be food poisoning. But what? That fucking Greek place. The chef probably hadn't washed his hands since the 1960s.

She spent the rest of the night hunched on the toilet, hopping up at horridly regular intervals to throw up into the sink.

This was the position she was in when, suddenly and emphatically, she felt the presence of Danny Bailey in her head.

Up until that moment, Miranda believed things couldn't get worse. What she had taken for granted was her privacy. At least no one was able to see her in the process of this ultimate humiliation, spinning from toilet to sink like a kind of ghastly gastric Catherine wheel.

But now, without warning, that privacy was ruptured and Danny was there.

She was hunched over the loo, miserably preoccupied with the mephitic churning of her bowels, when he arrived.

There he was in her head. And as soon as he realised what was going on he was gone again, vanishing unceremoniously into the void.

It might have been funny if Miranda hadn't been so miserable.

Finally the food poisoning passed off and Miranda lay trembling under her duvet, as weak as a kitten. As she dozed her way into a sweaty oblivion she decided that perhaps it was just a hallucination, a fever dream.

After all, how could Danny Bailey invade her mind?

The next day was Saturday and Miranda slept until noon, occasionally waking and opening bleary eyes to try to discern the face of her alarm clock. When she finally surfaced into full consciousness, the sickness was quite gone and Miranda just lay there feeling happily limp, delighting in the sensation of being well.

This sense of wellbeing was a cosy warmth that slowly altered its nature, moving southward from her stomach and transforming into an erotic yearning as it moved.

Miranda yielded to the ticklish ache in her loins, lifting the covers with one hand and sliding the other slowly between her legs. It felt very nice. A reassertion of life and vitality after the terrible night she had just spent.

She teased herself delicately, then with increasing tempo, letting images flow unbidden into her mind. She saw limbs, movements, flashes of specific sensual activity as she imagined herself opened, held, touched, tasted and deftly penetrated.

Hands touched her, a knee moved between her knees, gently nudging her wide open.

The wiry black hair on a chest hovered over her, flexing with the effort of moving against her. Arms were around her, a hot mouth pressed against her neck as she lost herself in the increasingly fragmented, increasingly urgent race to reach the point where she could just let everything go and be swept away.

That was the point where Miranda slowed everything down and let it linger, holding on to the moment before climax, stretching it out as much as she could endure. The images came spontaneously into her mind, unplanned. Faster than she could create them. With the hypnagogic intensity of a mind on the edge of sleep. On the edge of dreaming.

She saw a fraction of a gleaming liquid eye. A swell of familiar skin. She could smell her lover's sweat.

The heavy curve of Danny's shoulders.

Danny Bailey.

At the point of recognition Miranda was on the edge of orgasm. But the shock of recognition didn't shatter her mood. On the contrary, it intensified everything she felt, driving it up to a higher level.

She felt herself carried up to a new plateau of sensation where she lingered almost painfully. She was quite beyond thought now, transformed into a self-stimulating mechanism, wringing every last drop of sensation from herself.

She came explosively and repeatedly, her mind filled

with a collage of images. Mouth, lips, hands, cock. A face.

Danny.

Then Danny came, too, and everything intensified further. Like a star exploding, spreading and dispersing into space as the thinnest of gases. Miranda felt her awareness thin out and disperse until for a moment her identity was lost. She didn't know who she was, where she was, what she was.

Gradually, awareness returned and Miranda found herself lying in her bed. In her bed, sweaty and drained and disorientated. And alone.

What had happened? She had never felt anything remotely like this. Was she going mad? Had Danny Bailey really been there? Had she just had sex with a phantom?

She searched her mind for any trace of him and, sure enough, in a corner of her consciousness, she detected a warm residue of Danny's personality. But it was a simplified, slumbering presence.

He was still there, but he'd fallen asleep.

Typical, thought Miranda.

She felt Danny's presence attenuate and then begin to slip away as he drifted into unconsciousness. The connection between their minds became vague and then lapsed altogether as he disappeared.

When he went, he went with a final dying flare, like the fleeting orange glow you get from a candle when you blow it out.

He was gone, and for a moment Miranda felt abandoned and terribly alone.

Then rage swept over her.

She kicked the duvet off the bed and scrambled out. Wrenching her nightshirt off, she stomped into the bathroom. She showered under a blazingly hot spray and scrubbed herself raw, trying to eradicate any trace of the violation she had just experienced.

Then she towelled herself and dressed swiftly, applied a

savage slash of lipstick and stalked out of her flat, slamming the door behind her. There was a black cab pulling up just as she emerged from her building. She hailed it and jumped in the back, giving the driver Danny's address.

She was going to put an end to this once and for all.

FIFTEEN

Danny Bailey lay in the cooling water of his bath, feeling stunned. He had just had the most explosive sexual experience of his life, and it had occurred while he was here, alone except for the bobbing idiot presence of a bright-yellow plastic duck.

He had run the bath to relax himself. A relaxed state of mind seemed the best for making contact with Miranda.

He'd found this process growing easier each time he tried. This time he'd settled into the steaming water, leant back with a folded towel behind his head and almost instantly he'd found himself inside Miranda's mind. In the middle of the most erotic experience of his life.

Miranda was masturbating, and it was as if Danny found himself shovelled into a furnace, a furnace where the flames could consume him but somehow didn't hurt.

On the contrary, they were intensely pleasurable. The power of Miranda's libido, at first hand, had been astonishing.

Danny had been feeling bad about eavesdropping on her the previous night when she'd been racked with food poisoning. He was sure she'd spotted him. He'd even wondered if he could somehow convey an apology to her.

But all his good intentions had evaporated as he was swept up in the fierce sexual surge of the moment. He'd gone from contrite suitor to compulsive voyeur in the blink of an eye.

And then from voyeur to avid participant.

When it ended he had simply slipped into sleep, out of

her mind, like a detumescing lover leaving her body.

He didn't know how long he had dozed in the bath afterwards, but the water was distinctly chilly when he awoke. Danny blinked, looking at the rubber duck afloat on the scummy water, leering at him with its idiot good humour. 'What are you grinning at?' he said. And then the doorbell rang.

Danny climbed out of the bath, cursing and dripping. Hastily wrapping a towel around himself, he lumbered to the front door. He opened the door and shivered as the cold air struck him.

But then all thoughts of physical discomfort were scoured from his brain.

Miranda was standing there.

Miranda Lang, irritably wiping a long strand of straw-blonde hair back from her face. That lovely face. Vivid red lipstick, pale grey eyes. So pale they looked almost blind.

The Girl with Eyes like Rain.

She breezed past him, striding in uninvited. Danny closed the door behind her, feeling a surge of joy. This was the moment he'd dreamt of.

Miranda had come back to him.

He hurried after her, leaving wet footprints on the carpet. She was standing in the middle of the sitting room, lighting a cigarette. He'd forgotten how she moved. Her every gesture was elegant, economical. Music enacted in space.

'Miranda –' he said.

'First off,' she said, interrupting him, smoke floating from her mouth, 'let's get one thing straight. I don't know what you're doing or how you're doing it, but it's over.'

'Let me explain.'

'I don't want explanations. I don't give a shit about explanations. All I want is for it to stop. Do you hear me?'

'You don't understand,' said Danny, spreading his hands helplessly. 'This isn't something I planned. I didn't intend for it to happen.'

'You didn't intend it? Christ.' Miranda gave a brief, harsh bark of laughter. 'How do you think *I* feel? I'm walking down the street one day and you come barging into my brain.'

'But –'

'Shut up. I was crossing the road. There was traffic. You could have got me killed.'

'I'm sorry, I didn't mean to –'

'And when I'm on the bog last night, spewing my guts up, you come leering and prying. What are you? Some kind of sick pervert? Why don't you just drill a hole in the wall of the women's toilet?'

'I'm sorry about that. Miranda, I wanted to apologise. That's why I made contact this morning and –'

Danny Bailey fell silent. He felt his face turning bright red. He'd just remembered what had happened that morning.

'Yes, you are some kind of pervert, aren't you?' remarked Miranda. She was speaking in a light, conversational tone which was incredibly hurtful.

'But wasn't it great?' said Danny breathlessly. He didn't intend to say it – it just slipped out.

'Wasn't it what?' said Miranda dangerously.

'Wasn't it the most amazing feeling? You and me together like that? Our minds together and the way we both –'

'You really are insane, aren't you?'

'Miranda, don't you see? I've never felt this way before. Not the way I feel about you. You mean everything to me. Don't you understand what this means? How could we read each other's mind if there wasn't something special between us? We have a unique connection. It must mean something. We can't just throw it away . . .'

Danny's voice was choked with emotion. Unfortunately this was the point where his towel, already sagging damply around his waist, decided to let go and slap to the floor. It landed in a wet heap around his ankles, leaving him exposed and naked and ridiculous.

He immediately spun around, trying to preserve his dignity as he bent over, scrabbling desperately on the floor to retrieve the towel. He realised too late that this manoeuvre merely presented Miranda with an uninterrupted view of his fat hairy arse.

Danny clumsily knotted the towel back around his waist. He hardly dared turn to look at Miranda.

She stood watching him for a long moment in silent disgust and then she said, 'You like spying on all my most intimate moments, do you? You want to read my mind, do you?'

She smiled at him and it wasn't at all a pleasant smile. 'Then read this,' she said.

Miranda closed her eyes and concentrated.

Before Danny had made contact with her, Miranda had never imagined that such a thing was possible. But each telepathic encounter had taught her a little more. Now she used everything she'd learnt.

Somewhere in the restless orange-brown darkness behind her eyelids she reached out for Danny's mind with her own. It was like breathing out cigarette smoke, her mind sending forth expanding tendrils of thought.

Except that the smoke had the supple strength of a root extending through loam. Her consciousness reached out and found Danny's, and wrapped around it. There was a flash of contact and then they were sharing a single consciousness, sharing thoughts in a haphazard, overlapping pattern until the contact became decisive and clear.

Danny could feel her presence. He knew what she was thinking. A direct contact that went beyond touch or words, primal and immediate, with no barriers. Her experience was his, uncensored and direct.

That was when she let him have it.

She imagined fingernails screeching down blackboards, hard foam blocks squeaking and crushing. The brassy clamour of alarm clocks smashed peaceful sleep into a million pieces. Factory whistles shrieked and teeth bit down on to a fragment of bone in a mouthful of soft meat. The teeth crunched to bits.

Dentists' drills bit into inadequately anaesthetised nerves. A bare foot thudded down with meaty weight on to the long point of a steel nail.

Bile, vomit, tears, menstrual cramps and migraine headaches.

By the time she was finished, Danny was writhing on the floor. His towel had slipped off again, but he hadn't noticed.

He didn't notice when she left, either, quietly slipping the front door shut behind her.

Miranda walked away from Danny's little house, along the winding tree-lined drive that cut through his estate. She felt tired and drained and rather hungry. The cool air cleared her head as she walked and she began to think, in a calm methodical fashion, about what had just happened.

It had gone more or less the way she had planned, although it was true she had rather lost her temper towards the end. Lost control. She had gone a little too far, blasted him too hard, but she couldn't help herself.

Her emotions were rubbed raw. She was more than a little frightened by what was happening to her. To them.

And then there was the bald fact of what she still felt for Danny Bailey.

Danny might not realise it – indeed, he'd have to be some kind of genius to realise it, after what had just happened – but Miranda still loved him.

That was the one absolutely certain thing that had emerged from the turmoil of the last twenty-four hours.

Every word Danny had said was true. How could they share this psychic link unless there was something special between them? He was right. It was some kind of uniquely rare bond, a once-in-a-lifetime sense of communion. Not to be discarded lightly.

Not to be discarded at all.

Miranda winced when she remembered the expression on Danny's face after she'd floored him. That had been a mistake.

It wouldn't be surprising if he never tried to make contact with her again. She frowned as she walked along, only half aware of the traffic on the road beside her. She would have to come up with some way of encouraging him.

Some subtle way of getting things rolling between them again. But how to achieve that without being too obvious? She would think of something, as soon as she got back to her flat. Which shouldn't be long, provided she could find a taxi.

Miranda became aware of the rumbling sound of an engine trailing along behind her. It sounded like the throbbing of a diesel and, wondering if perhaps it was the lucky appearance of a black London cab, she turned to look at it.

But the vehicle wasn't a taxi. It was an orange school bus with a wheelchair emblem.

The bus was rolling slowly along parallel with her, and, as she turned to look at it, it braked to a halt. Miranda couldn't see inside the bus because the windows were that odd kind of smoky mirrored glass you saw sometimes in limousines. Obviously a measure to protect its disabled passengers from prying eyes.

But now the folding doors sighed open with a pneumatic hiss, revealing the driver.

He was a young man with a vivid crop of freckles on his thin angular face and a ludicrously synthetic peroxide-blond dye job.

'Excuse me,' said the driver, smiling, 'but I'm totally lost.' He held up a small paperback book, a street map of London. He looked quite pathetic, indeed very much lost. Before she knew it Miranda was climbing up the low steps into the bus.

The bus wasn't large. Behind the driver's compartment was a deep square alcove containing two folded wheelchairs and a stack of aluminium flight cases. The rest of the bus consisted of half a dozen seats on either side, and a wide back seat on which another man was lolling.

A beefy middle-aged man with snow-white hair framing his otherwise bald pink head. He was the only passenger. There was no one else on board.

'Can you help please, miss?' The driver had now spread the book out to show to her. Miranda bent over it.

She heard the doors hiss shut behind her.

'We've been driving around for hours,' said the driver. 'It's ridiculous but I just can't find this street.'

'Here, let me have a look.'

The driver gratefully surrendered the book to her. 'Thanks. I've been going around the twist. It's sort of turned into a nightmare. It's like that film where the bloke goes into the phone booth and finds that the door's locked behind him and he can't get out again, whatever he does . . . What's that film called?'

'*The Phonebooth*,' called his friend from the back of the bus.

'Oh yes. Very imaginative guess,' said the driver sarcastically.

'No, really. It's a short film. A short Spanish film. Made in the seventies.'

'No it wasn't,' said the driver. 'It was called *The Phantom Tollbooth*.'

'No, that was a feature-length American animated cartoon, not a Spanish short film,' said the large man, getting up from his seat and ambling slowly towards the front of the bus. 'It was directed by Chuck Jones.'

'No it wasn't.'

While they bickered, Miranda was frowning at the map book. She flipped it shut and studied the cover, then gave the driver a sardonic look.

Because the book was a street plan of Manchester, not London. No wonder they couldn't find any familiar reference points in it.

'You're in the wrong place, mate,' said Miranda.

The driver was watching her with an odd expression, furtive and excited.

'So are you,' he said.

* * *

A hand closed over her mouth.

Miranda promptly bit the big man's hand. Before he could wrench it free, she managed to take a sizable chunk out of his thumb.

He pulled his hand away. She took a deep breath with the intention of screaming the place down. But another hand clamped on to her mouth. The driver was on top of her while the big man danced around cursing, shaking his bleeding hand in the air.

'She bit me. The cunt bit me.'

'Grab her. Comstock! Quick. Help me.'

Miranda writhed and kicked, but together the two men managed to wrestle her to the back of the bus. They pressed her down on the long back seat. One of them grabbed her arm and rolled up the sleeve. The other one took something out of the breast pocket of his overalls. At first Miranda thought it was a pen. Then she realised with a flash of terror that it was a syringe.

She made a final convulsive effort to fight free of the men's grip. Their heavy sweating weight didn't even budge.

Then she saw the needle hovering over the exposed flesh of her arm. It dipped and entered her vein. Blood blossomed in the glass barrel of the syringe and then she began to feel it take effect.

The men let go of her. She tried to scramble away from them but her body wouldn't move.

'I'm going to have to get a tetanus jab,' said the big man, sucking at the wound on his hand.

'It's your own damned fault.'

'She bit me. I didn't expect that. It wasn't like in *The Collector*,' whined the big man. 'I want a tetanus jab.'

The men's voices were becoming oddly boomy to Miranda.

'You'll have to wait until we get back,' said one of the boomy voices. 'Dr Buckminster can sort it out.'

'Why don't we stop at a chemist's on the way?'

'We'll be late. And Mr Leiber wouldn't like that.' Slowly the booming sound of this voice faded, drowned out by the general roaring that filled Miranda's ears.

Suddenly her body seemed to be melting away, beginning at the extremities.

She lost all sense of feeling at the tips of her fingers. And her toes went too, and then the numbness spread swiftly inward along her limbs. In a swoony instant the only feeling left in her body was just above her eyes.

Miranda gathered herself and, with the last of her strength, used this final tiny nub of awareness to cry out for help.

She cried out to Danny Bailey, knowing that he was out there somewhere, that, even if no one else in the world was aware of her plight, he would hear.

As her consciousness melted away, Miranda stretched every fibre of herself, reaching out into the void with all her strength. Reaching out towards Danny Bailey as the drug slugged her down into oblivion.

Then she felt him.

Out there in the darkness, in the void, she touched him with her mind. Like a strong, solid island in an endless ocean. Firm dry land under her feet after an eternity swimming.

Danny Bailey.

She had done it. Home and dry. Back in contact. From the last remnant of her melting consciousness, Miranda reached out feebly and told Danny about her plight. She sent a simple, vivid message. Two men. An orange bus. A needle, an abduction. Still close, but carrying her away. Come now. Call the police. I'm only just up the road, but hurry . . .

And she felt the message fail.

It bounced off Danny's mind, sliding feebly away. Because there was a barrier in Danny that hadn't been there before.

A barrier she had created when she'd lashed out at him. It had formed, like scar tissue, in his mind. Now her feeble message was like the touch of gossamer on that scar tissue.

He couldn't feel her.

Couldn't hear her.

Miranda realised that Danny couldn't hear her any more. And in that final sad moment she became aware that she was profoundly alone.

And then awareness slipped away altogether.

SIXTEEN

When Emily Race finally found the book she wanted, it was on the top shelf, of course. All the interesting books were always on the top shelf. Visible, alluring, but quite unreachable.

In this case, the book wasn't even visible. Emily knew it was there only because of the class number assigned by the library. She followed the numbers on the spines of the other books as they ran along the shelves and, sure enough, the sequence indicated that the volume must be tucked somewhere up there, out of sight.

She backed away and squinted and caught a glimpse of the book's mint-green dust jacket with the authors' names emblazoned on the spine.

Hopeless. The library shelves were at least a metre and a half high, and the top ones were well beyond her reach.

Life was never simple, Emily thought as she went in search of a chair. She was dragging one back when the librarian spotted her.

Emily saw that it was a new librarian, one who didn't know the ropes.

Here we go again, she thought.

The librarian was at her side now. She put a restraining hand on the chair and Emily ceased, knowing it was pointless to fight against the woman's superior strength.

'Now, where are we taking that?' She was a pretty, chubby girl with her glossy black hair cut short in the manner of the silent-film star Louise Brooks. Emily thought that she was very young, only a teenager. Not a proper librarian, even.

'Let's put this back, shall we?' said the girl. She was

addressing Emily in the loathsome tone of voice that they all used with her at first. Seeing the chair vanish, Emily felt like crying with frustration. Instead, she did what she had learnt to do. She swallowed her emotions and forced herself to stay calm and try to explain.

Preferably in words of one syllable.

'I need the chair,' she said. 'Please can I use it?' They always liked it when you said please. The young librarian hesitated, holding the chair.

'Please,' repeated Emily. It really was impossible to lay it on too thick. 'I'll be very grateful. I'll put it back immediately afterwards.'

The idiot girl was smiling at her now, evidently quite charmed. You could see her thinking how bright and well spoken Emily was. 'Immediately after what?' she said. She set the chair down and hunkered down so that she was at eye level with Emily. A little tête-à-tête. 'What would you like to do with our chair?'

Emily considered and swiftly rejected a violent and anatomically implausible suggestion. It would have been satisfying but more trouble than it was worth.

Instead, she told the truth, trying to be patient and keep it as simple as possible. 'I need to stand on it so I can –'

'Oh you mustn't stand on it,' said the librarian in mock horror. 'You might fall off!' Her teenage eyes were twinkling with merriment. Emily could have killed her.

'I need to stand on it, so I can get a book from the top shelf,' said Emily, speaking quickly and trying to keep the rising tide of sarcasm from her voice. 'I can't get at it otherwise. I'm not tall enough.' There. That should be simple enough for even this moron.

'Oh,' cooed the librarian. 'I can help you with that. Let me help. Show me where the book is.'

Emily shrugged and led her over to the relevant shelf, pointing out the fat green book as they approached. But she could see a look of growing uncertainty on the librarian's face and she got the sinking feeling she always experienced when things were about to get complicated.

'Are you sure that's the book you want?'

100

'Yes.'

'But these are all very grown-up books.'

'Yes, it's called –'

'Very technical grown-up books.'

'It's called *Fundamentals of Timesharing in Operating Systems*,' said Emily patiently. 'It's by Kernighan and Esslin. Here's the class number.' She showed the librarian the details she'd jotted down.

It was clear that the teenage girl didn't know what to think. Finally she said, 'Wouldn't you be happier with a nice book from Kiddies' Corner? There are lots of nice books there for little girls.'

Emily thought that if the librarian said 'nice' one more time she was going to bite the stupid bitch on the ankle. But she forced herself to remain calm and said, 'I want something on time sharing and multitasking in mainframes.' She smiled her most innocent smile. 'Do you think they're likely to have that in the Kiddies' Corner?'

After the librarian finally got the book down for her, Emily decided she might as well make full use of the stupid girl. So she got her to reach down a few more volumes as they made their way back among the rows of tall shelves.

Emily selected a book on Husserl, a couple of Richard Gregory titles she hadn't read, *The Living Brain* by Grey Walter – hopelessly out of date but still exhilarating in the breadth of its speculation – and *Gödel, Escher, Bach* by Douglas Hofstadter, an old favourite. Then, since the books were rather large and heavy, she got the librarian to carry them to the checkout desk for her.

By now the girl was bewildered, but passively obedient. Perhaps she didn't realise she was waiting on Emily hand and foot. 'Is there anything else?' she said.

'Yes,' said Emily. On their way to the desk, she got the girl to stop at Kiddies' Corner to pick up a copy of *The Witches* by Roald Dahl.

'I do occasionally like a little light reading,' explained Emily. The expression of relief on the librarian's face was pathetic to behold.

101

By way of retribution for the chair business, Emily got the girl to carry her books all the way out of the library for her and through the arts centre to the trendy little cafeteria adjoining the museum. As they walked along together Emily reflected that she was beginning to rather enjoy having a slave.

'Is your mummy waiting for you here?' said the librarian, evidently anxious to fit Emily back into some kind of normal domestic context.

'No, but my sister is.' She pointed to the table where Juliette sat, waiting. 'That's her over there.'

'She's very pretty,' said the librarian.

'Yes, isn't she? Quite bright too. She's a psychiatrist. She once wrote a paper on me. Perhaps you'd like to read it.'

The librarian had turned bright red. She obviously didn't know what to say.

'*I've* read it,' continued Emily. 'About what you'd expect from a second-rate mind. Don't misunderstand me. It's not a bad paper but it lacks insight. And what is a psychiatrist without insight? If you really want to know about the phenomenon of child prodigies, you'd be better off reading something by one of the Americans. Feldman's *Beyond Fundamentals in Cognitive Development*, perhaps.' She smiled up at the young librarian. 'You must have heard of it.'

But the girl was too flustered to reply. As soon as they were in the cafeteria, she just set the books down on her sister's table and fled.

'What have you done to that poor girl?' said Juliette, frowning at her over a folded newspaper.

'Nothing she didn't deserve,' said Emily. 'Now can we go home?'

'So who is he?'

'Who is who?' said Juliette. She avoided her mother's gaze. She was blushing and she was hoping her mother wouldn't notice.

But her mother noticed all right, her plump face glowing with approval. She was a fat woman with a red face and long black hair streaked only here and there with grey. In honour of her long tradition of wearing embarrassingly horrid clothes she was currently decked out in a long, flowing, black silk robe figured with bright flowers. The robe served to conceal her considerable bulk. She padded around the kitchen in her big bare feet.

Juliette's mother was unfailingly cheerful despite the fact that Juliette could detect very little in her life to be cheerful about.

'The man, of course.' Her mother beamed at her. 'The new man in your life.'

Juliette bridled. 'Who says there's anyone new in my life?'

'I do. A mother knows these things.'

From the alcove beside the kitchen came a sardonic snorting noise.

Juliette turned to see her little sister sitting there. Floral curtains were stirring gently in the breeze and the sun was shining through the window on Emily's smooth, intent, childish face. Propped in front of her on a table was a fat book which she was carefully reading.

'She heard it when you spoke to him on the phone,' said Emily. 'Apparently it was something in your tone of voice.'

She returned her attention to the book. It was an extremely fat volume, too large for Emily's tiny hands. She had to use the toast rack plus an array of jam jars to prop it up. Juliette recognised the book. It was the Hofstadter. She had read it herself, when she was a medical student, but she'd found the computer-programming bits rather heavy going.

But seven-year-old Emily was turning pages in the book at the rather alarming rate of two or three a minute.

And rudely ignoring her sister.

Juliette turned back to the kitchen and her mother. 'Is that right?' she demanded. 'You think you heard something in my voice and on the basis of this you've extrapolated that I'm in love?'

'Extrapolated. That's a nice word,' called Emily.

Their mother bustled back and forth in the narrow galley-style kitchen, briskly opening and closing cupboards. 'Why don't you just tell us about him, dear?' She opened the refrigerator and peered inside for a moment before emerging with the butter dish in one hand.

Juliette said nothing.

'I think she's being evasive, Mum,' called Emily. 'What do you think?'

'I think it's lovely having your sister home.' Her mother selected a heavy old frying pan, blackened with a thousand meals, and sparked the gas cooker to life. A star of blue flame flared on the hob; her mother set the frying pan over the flame and forked some butter into it. She methodically stirred the butter with a wooden spoon as it began to sizzle and melt.

Emily hopped down from the table next door and painstakingly lifted the large book, hugging it to her chest. She carried it into the narrow kitchen and barged past her mother and her sister. 'Excuse me. I have to go upstairs.'

'Mind where you're going, Emily.'

'If you weren't so clumsy you wouldn't be in my way,' said the little girl. She started up the staircase on the far side of the kitchen, not bothering to glance back.

An hour later, as soon as lunch was ready, Emily rejoined them; she always had an unerring instinct for mealtimes, appearing just as the food was served.

'I think you've excelled yourself this time, Mum,' she said, sniffing the various dishes as her mother brought them through from the kitchen.

'Did I hear you at the door just now, love?'

'It was just some Jehovah's Witnesses,' said Emily. 'I got rid of them by telling them we're a den of atheists with the odd agnostic thrown in.'

When all the food was set out, their mother poured another glass of wine for herself and Juliette and some organic apple juice for Emily, and then finally sat down with a sigh. She sipped her wine and looked at Juliette and said, 'Why don't you tell us all about this mystery man, then?'

'I'll say this for him,' said Emily. 'Some of his ideas are very interesting. Do I detect Gruyère in this sauce, Mum?'

'Why yes, dear,' said her mother, her face lighting up. 'Do you like it?'

'Delicious. Don't go back to using that vile Cheddar you normally employ, will you?' Emily looked at her big sister, who was staring at her.

'What did you mean by that?' demanded Juliette.

'About the cheese?'

'About his ideas! Whose ideas?'

Emily stirred her food around on her plate. 'Christopher Matthew,' she said quietly. 'It's just that some of his ideas about group behaviour and subliminal communication are quite interesting, that's all.'

'The point about the Cheddar,' said their mother, 'is that it's so much cheaper.'

Juliette ignored her. She stared at Emily, her eyes steely. 'And what do you know about Christopher Matthew's ideas?'

'Oh,' said Emily airily. 'Not much. Just what you recorded on your computer.'

'You've been looking at my computer?'

'You shouldn't leave it lying around.'

'Juliette! Don't hit your little sister! You're a grown woman and a psychiatrist.'

'I'm not going to hit her,' snarled Juliette, wadding her napkin and dropping it on to her plate.

'Aren't you going to finish your meal?' said her mother in a pleading voice. Juliette ignored her. She was busy glaring at Emily.

'I can't believe the behaviour of this nasty little sneak thief.'

Emily was standing on her chair, frowning as she leant across the table and clumsily carved herself a thick chunk of bread. 'Thieves take things. I don't think the illicit perusal of data actually constitutes a theft. But I could be wrong. It's an interesting distinction.'

She sat down and began to apply a thick layer of butter

to the bread. 'By the way, what's all this nonsense about his glowing mystic eyes?'

Juliette stared at her little sister. Her face began to redden. 'What?'

Emily turned to her mother. 'That's what she wrote in her diary, about this Christopher bloke.'

'You broke into my diary?' hissed Juliette.

'Since I was already ransacking your computer, I thought I might as well.' Emily had placed a large piece of fried tomato on her buttered bread. 'You really ought to put a password on that machine.' She folded the bread over to form a sandwich. 'That would keep prying eyes out.'

'I wouldn't need a fucking password if I didn't have a sister like you.'

'Don't swear, dear.'

'She's a . . . bogging little sneak!'

'She's one to talk,' said Emily through a mouthful of food. 'Being a spy and all.'

There was silence at the table.

'What do you mean?' said Juliette.

'Don't be tediously obtuse. I know you're working for MI5, Britain's internal-intelligence apparat.'

'That's not true.'

'Of course it is. You spy on the people of this fair isle at the behest of its own duly elected government. Some people would say that you are a menace to a free society.'

'For God's sake, don't dramatise, Emily. I did some routine profiling work at the MOD. For a few hours each week. It was ages ago.'

'That's not what Christopher Matthew says.'

Juliette stared at her sister.

'What do you mean?'

'He says that your new job is also part of a covert operation for MI5.'

'He never said that.'

'Yes he did. He told me as much himself.'

Juliette set her fork down.

'Are you all right, dear?' said her mother worriedly. 'You look very pale.'

'When did you speak to him?' said Juliette.

'Oh, about ten minutes ago,' said Emily casually. She continued to eat, not looking up at her sister. 'If you want to know more, why don't you ask him yourself.' Now Emily did look up.

'He's upstairs. In your bedroom.'

SEVENTEEN

All the way up the long creaking staircase Juliette told herself that it must be some kind of joke. That Emily was lying. But, when she reached her bedroom and opened the door, Christopher was there.

He was sitting on her bed, among the dusty collection of soft toys, reading a copy of *The Prophet* that a boyfriend had insisted on giving her in another lifetime.

Juliette's mother had preserved her bedroom like a shrine ever since she had left for university in London, and there was an almost unwholesome feeling of suspended time about the place. It was a kind of museum of her adolescence. On the walls there were sun-faded posters of the Human League and Gary Numan.

Juliette stared at Christopher, unable for a moment to relate him to these familiar surroundings. He looked up at her and smiled, holding up the copy of *The Prophet*.

'Well, it was either this or *Siddhartha*,' he said, nodding at the meagre contents of her bookshelf.

'What are you doing here?'

'I came to see you.' Christopher set the book aside, sliding it under one of the toys on her bed, a fat badger called Benny who was leaking stuffing from his seams. Juliette registered every tiny detail, as if she was in a state of shock.

'How did you find me?'

'I sneaked into Chad's office. Your mum's address and phone number were there in the on-call register. So I got a train down here and phoned. I spoke to Emily and she told me to come over. She's quite a girl, isn't she?' Christopher shook his head in bemusement. 'I'd read your paper but even that didn't prepare me for meeting her.'

'How did you get out of the Abbey?'

'Oh, come on, Juliette. You know I can sneak out of there any time I like. Nobody even knows I'm gone. And they're not going to notice until bedtime, unless I'm very unlucky.'

At the mention of the word 'bedtime', Juliette felt an unwanted and oddly powerful stirring of desire. She realised that Christopher was sitting on the same bed where she had conjured her adolescent fantasies. The thought made her irrationally angry.

'What do you want from me?' Her voice was strained and hoarse.

'I told you. I had to see you.' Christopher reached out and took her hand. Juliette immediately snatched it away, but she was aware that something had passed between them at the moment of contact, something she couldn't conceal.

Suddenly all the anger leaked out of her, like the stuffing leaking out of Benny the Badger. She slumped down on the bed beside him, feeling numb and exhausted.

For a moment they sat there in silence among the jumbled soft toys. They didn't say anything, or even look at each other, but there was a relaxed, familiar quality to their being together. Like an old married couple, thought Juliette despairingly.

She had managed to conquer her feeling of lust, but it hadn't gone away. It had merely transformed into something else, something more deeply treacherous. A feeling of profound comfort as she sat on the bed beside him. It felt so natural and right.

The bed sagged under her and she found herself sitting with her head against Christopher's shoulder. It felt nice. They sat there together, motionless, watching the sunlight move slowly across the floral wallpaper, across the little wooden bookshelf, which did indeed contain a copy of *Siddhartha* – and *The Little Prince*. The volumes of Tolkien were missing, long ago requisitioned by her mother.

She had no idea how long they sat there. 'I'm going to have to take you back to the Abbey,' said Juliette finally. She realised that Christopher was holding her. She gently freed herself from his grasp. It was surprisingly difficult to let go of him.

'Fine.' Christopher smiled. 'That will give us a chance to talk.'

There was no way they could drive back to London. The Fiat was in for repairs and Juliette had no intention of waiting for it to be ready. It would have meant hanging about for another hour or two in her mother's house, and the thought of that was quite unendurable.

As it was, her mother insisted on pouring Christopher three cups of tea and feeding him an enormous slab of fruitcake, all the while grilling him, with an elephantine attempt at subtlety.

Juliette had rung for a taxi, but it seemed to take forever to come. She went back and rang again, demanding to know what the delay was about, and her mother followed her into the parlour.

'He's ever so nice, dear,' she said, her eyes glowing. 'He really has the most remarkable aura. I wouldn't be surprised if he turned out to have all sorts of extraordinary powers.'

Juliette didn't bother to reply. She simply turned and fled back upstairs to the kitchen, where she found Christopher working his way through the piece of fruitcake while Emily sat opposite him saying, 'But if everyone has a distinctive rhythmic pattern to their brain activity then that implies that some people will be synchronised while others are asynchronous.'

'Exactly,' said Christopher, with a mouth full of cake, nodding.

Juliette left the room, feeling like she wanted to scream.

The taxi finally came and carried them to the station. The Victoria train was waiting on Platform One and they boarded it seconds before it pulled out. A uniformed guard came and sold them tickets. Juliette paid for Christopher, a gesture that he didn't even acknowledge. He was too busy spouting his usual blend of semimystical gibberish.

'I'm sorry if I startled you, turning up like that,' he said. 'But I had to see you and explain to you. There are so many things I have to tell you about, to prepare you for. And there's so little time.'

He babbled away along similar lines all the way back to London. Juliette made the occasional encouraging noise, but hardly listened. Her one thought was to get Christopher back to the clinic safely. He was her patient. Her responsibility.

They changed trains at Clapham Junction, then got another taxi from Richmond for the final leg of the journey back to the Abbey. After Juliette had paid for the taxi, Christopher insisted on her waiting outside for five minutes while he sneaked back into the clinic via his secret route.

The whole thing was a farce, but Juliette didn't have a better idea. She could hardly see herself marching back through the front door with an escaped patient at her side. The very thought made her feel hot and sticky with guilt.

Somehow the fact that Christopher had come to her when he broke out made it look as if she was to blame.

Nonetheless, as soon as she got inside she was determined to find Chad and tell him the truth. They would have to keep a closer eye on Christopher in the future. Find out how he managed to escape from the Abbey at will and block his escape route.

Things couldn't continue this way.

Juliette stood under the gently swaying branches of a horse chestnut tree, staring at the pitted wall of the Abbey and, just up the road, a school bus.

She slowly counted to three hundred as she had agreed to do. She felt terribly self-conscious standing there, but at least no one else seemed to be around.

Except the bus. The bus looked oddly familiar; it was an orange vehicle with mirrored windows.

Then Juliette remembered where she'd seen it before.

111

On Hammersmith Bridge, on the day when the bikers had assaulted her.

The memory caused a stab of anxiety and she decided she'd waited long enough.

She walked in through the open gateway and up the drive. The Abbey seemed surprisingly peaceful. A sense of weekend quiet pervaded the place.

The wind rustled through the grass and shrubs. A flash of scarlet among the apple trees behind the Abbey signified the presence of Prem in his red coat, no doubt busy pruning or raking. Juliette hurried towards the building. There were only three cars parked outside, including Chad's Porsche.

She saw the reflection of her own unhappy face as she pushed through the glass doors into the reception area. A cigarette was smouldering in an ashtray on Pamela Croden's desk, but there was no sign of the receptionist. Perhaps she had run out of crossword puzzles and momentarily abandoned her post to go off in search of a new one.

Juliette was hurrying down the hallway to Chad's office when some atavistic instinct warned her something was wrong.

The building was oddly quiet. The only sound was her own footsteps echoing off the parabolic ceiling of the corridor. She stopped walking and immediately the silence closed in on her.

Now the only thing she could hear was the beating of her heart.

Juliette tried to tell herself that she was behaving irrationally, that there was nothing to be afraid of. But the fear kept welling up inside her. She couldn't force herself to take another step.

At the back of her mind a warning was flashing. Telling her not to go on, to turn around instead.

After fighting it for another moment, she spun on her heel and fled back to the reception area.

That was when she found the bodies.

EIGHTEEN

After she found the receptionist lying on the floor, Juliette fled from the Abbey.

She wasn't thinking clearly, merely acting on the first impulse that came. She found herself running out to the orchard where she'd seen the caretaker, Prem.

Prem always had an air of strength and good-natured competence. If she could find him, everything would be all right. But, when she found Prem, everything just got worse.

Juliette believed she'd seen the caretaker working among the trees behind the Abbey. But in fact all she had glimpsed was the bright colour of his coat stirring in the breeze. Now she saw that the coat was hanging limply from Prem's shoulders, like a rag draped on a scarecrow.

Prem himself was leaning slumped in the crotch of a tree, held upright by the V-shape of two thick trunks. Even from twenty yards away, she was certain he was dead.

Nonetheless, she forced herself to get close to him and check for vital signs. She walked around the tree until Prem's crusted, lifeless eyes were aimed at her. Then she made herself touch him, looking for a pulse.

Nothing.

Tree branches rattled over her head as the wind picked up speed, dislodging dead leaves which drifted lazily down on her. Juliette looked away from Prem and stared up into a blue autumn sky. She saw the distant glinting silver of a jet plane climbing for altitude, carrying off hundreds of people. People who were still living in a sane, safe world.

The plane roared away and abruptly she was all alone in the orchard. The cold sun shone down on her as she turned away from the tree and started back towards the Abbey.

Behind her the wind was growing wild in the trees; it seemed to be calling to her in strange voices, trying to tell her something. Juliette fought off the bizarre notion.

She knew that she had to master this situation or it would overwhelm her. But it was like swimming against a huge and violent sea.

She went back into the Abbey. Back to the body of Pamela Croden.

The receptionist lay on the floor, dyed red hair shockingly bright against the pallor of her skin. The body was behind the desk, concealed from any casual passer-by. But one of her shoes had come off and the glossy patent-leather toe of it was poking out, just visible under the desk. Juliette suspected that it was this shoe she must have seen out of the corner of her eye, registering it subconsciously as she hurried past.

This was the subliminal warning that had brought her back to the reception area and possibly saved her life.

Juliette glanced along the dimly lit corridor. The Abbey was silent and still, apparently deserted. She reached for the telephone on Pamela's desk. As she began to dial 999 she realised that she felt oddly self-conscious about what she was going to say. I have two murders to report. Perhaps more. And I know who's responsible.

Christopher Matthew.

As her mind emerged from a red tangle of panic, it was sickeningly obvious to Juliette that Christopher had killed them all, and then come to get her and bring her back here, to witness it. Like a cat bringing its kill into the house and proudly showing it to its owner.

He was more deeply disturbed than any of them had guessed. He'd killed the staff at the clinic and then travelled down to Brighton to find her. To bring her back here and presumably add her to his total.

Juliette lifted the phone with a shaking hand and pressed it to her ear for several seconds before she realised that she couldn't hear a dial tone. The phone was dead. Juliette cursed herself for leaving her overnight bag in Brighton. Her cellular phone was in it, lying useless on a chair in her mother's poky little sitting room.

She glanced over her shoulder at the long corridor that led into the Abbey. Fluorescent light gleamed on the black and white tiles that were like a cold chessboard on the floor.

On either side of the corridor were doors that led to offices. Perhaps in one of them there was a phone that was working. But Juliette had no intention of finding out.

She hurried back to the door of the Abbey. She was just about to push through and escape when something fell into place in her mind. She felt a deep, cold shock. She realised that she must be wrong about Christopher.

He couldn't be responsible for the killings. She had been with him for the last three hours, and, although Juliette wasn't a forensic expert, she knew that both Prem and Pamela Croden had certainly died more recently than that.

Much more recently. Juliette remembered the cigarette smouldering in Pamela's ashtray. It was only now finally burning itself out, leaving a charred yellow stub of filter.

And, if Christopher hadn't killed them, that meant he was trapped somewhere in the Abbey. With the real killer.

Juliette stood in the half-open door, feeling the cool fresh air of freedom stream in past her. She couldn't leave. She had to go back for him.

Christopher was her patient. She was responsible for him.

That was a lie. She loved him. A distant part of her mind realised this was why she had been so ready to blame him. It had been a strange final attempt to deny her feelings for him.

As she walked down the corridor, Juliette felt lighter than air. She had a strange feeling that might almost have been exultation. Everybody in the Abbey was dead. Soon she might be dead too.

But, whatever happened, she was walking towards her destiny.

The door to Chad's office was unlocked. She swung it open and went in. The telephone was right in front of her. It was sitting on top of a pile of papers on his desk. Juliette shut the door quietly behind her and started towards it.

She was halfway across the room before she realised that she wasn't alone.

There was someone else in the office, behind her. As Juliette turned around she seemed to be moving in slow motion. The office spun around her with the stately grandeur of planetary rotation. Objects streamed past at the periphery of her vision, framed diplomas on the wall, pictures, Chad's gleaming tennis trophies.

There was a man sitting on the floor. Sitting with his back against the wall and his long legs spread out in front of him. A shocking red corona of blood soaked the white carpet around him.

For a moment panic paralysed Juliette's mind, and she thought it was Christopher Matthew. But then awareness fought through and she saw that the man was Chad.

Dr Chad Cavanaugh, wearing his neat black trousers and Prince of Wales check jacket, looking dandified and ready to hurry to some party or social function. But his spectacles hung crookedly askew on his face, and his shirt and tie were stained with a heavy patch of red.

The shock of finding him sitting there was nothing compared with the shock she got when he opened his eyes and looked at her. It lasted only an instant but it was a droll, self-deprecating look. As if to say, Look at this mess.

As his eyes drifted shut again Juliette hurried and knelt beside him, the carpet oozing wet under her knees. She touched him, moving methodically, her medical training taking over. She loosened his tie, removed the broken spectacles from his face and set them carefully on the floor, as if they were something precious.

He watched her steadily for a moment, with the bright, quiet, enquiring gaze of a bird. Then his eyes drifted shut.

116

Juliette began to examine him. The big man looked drained, shrunken. There was considerable blood loss. She could hardly believe that he was still alive. Unlike the others, though, this didn't appear to be the result of gunshots. Perhaps a knife wound. It was high on his chest, displaced slightly to the left. Very bad. The worst possible locus for a penetration injury.

She tried to gently unbutton his bloody shirt and open it, teasing it away from the skin to inspect the wound. But as soon as she touched him his eyes flashed open again and awareness came swimming back into them.

'Knife,' said Chad. His voice sounded shockingly normal, as if he was resuming an ordinary conversation, a workaday conversation in their office. 'Not even a very big knife. Maybe two-inch blade. Went right in.'

His face was filmed with sweat and so pale it was almost grey. But his eyes were steady and alert. Full of intelligent interest. 'Small but very accurate,' he said. He nodded at his bloody shirt front. 'Some other wounds, but that's the main one. Aorta or vena cava, I think.'

Juliette had known patients, on the verge of death, who'd experienced a final burst of vitality. It came flowing down their central nervous system to carry them on one last tiny journey of life. They lost the cachectic look of chronic illness and suddenly became almost radiant. A postman with liver cancer had once told her, shortly before he died, that he was fit as a fiddle, had never felt better in his life.

Now, in the midst of this massive trauma, she saw the same kind of terminal energy flowing in Chad Cavanaugh as his eyes focused on her and he began to speak calmly and consecutively. It was as if he'd been patiently waiting for her to arrive.

'I'm hypovalaemic,' he said. 'Bleeding internally. Could be fairly massive.' He spoke with detached precision. 'Depends on the size of the nick . . . Only a little knife. Oh, I told you that.'

Then, as she watched helplessly, he faded out for a moment. She checked his pulse. It was rapid and thready.

His forearm stirred in her grip, and, as rapidly as he'd gone, he faded back in again.

'Juliette, you've got to get out of here,' he said.

'Chad –'

'Don't waste time. They're still here. They'll find you. Go.'

'I can't. Christopher is inside.'

'Forget it. Forget him. He'll be dead by now. Get out.'

'No. He was with me all afternoon. We've only just come back.'

Chad slowly absorbed this information. 'Thank God,' he said finally. His eyes flickered shut. For a moment Juliette thought he was gone, but his eyes opened again and he stared at her. 'Then you have to find him,' he said.

'Let me try to find a phone.'

'No! Just shut up and listen. You can't call anyone.' Chad's eyes flickered but remained open. 'You don't know what was really going on here. You don't have any idea. It was all a setup. From the beginning.'

'What do you mean?'

'Why do you think I never gave you the background on Christopher? I never intended to. You weren't supposed to be given the full picture.'

Chad's face twisted and at first Juliette thought it was contorting with pain. But then she realised that he was smiling at her. 'But now I've got to tell you. You weren't hired to cure Christopher. You were just supposed to keep him amused. Do you understand? The whole thing was a charade. He wasn't a patient. He was the bait for a trap.'

'Let me try to find a phone.' Juliette shifted position. For a horrible second her knees adhered to the sticky carpet. 'Please.' It seemed obscene, to be pleading with a dying man for the right to save his life.

'No! I told you, there's no one you can call.' Chad's pale face twisted again, and this time it was a grimace of pain. 'No one who'll believe you.' He fell silent, breathing in ragged shallow gasps, then he rallied and looked up at her.

'Try to understand. The Abbey is a real clinic. There were some real patients, but they were just . . . window dressing. Christopher was brought here so we could keep an eye on him. It was a trap . . . Was supposed to be. Everything went wrong. We underestimated . . .'

His eyes dimmed and he squeezed them shut for a moment, like a man who'd been too long without sleep, fighting for consciousness.

When he spoke again, his voice was perceptibly weaker. A fierce hissing. 'Christopher was here as bait. Like staking out a goat to draw a lion. Do you understand?'

'I, I think so. But I don't understand why. I don't even understand who he is.'

'Most of what we told you . . . about Christopher Matthew was true, as far as it went. He turned up out of nowhere, living rough . . . Got a menial job at the . . .'

'The Brain Trust.'

'Yes. His abilities are recognised. He's promoted. Becomes valuable. But . . .' He tried his ghastly smile again. 'We didn't tell you . . . what the Brain Trust was really doing.' He looked at her for confirmation.

Juliette remembered what Christopher had told her. 'Some kind of think-tank.'

'No. It was a government . . . research unit. Under control of the security services. Its job . . . was weapons development. Very special new kind of weapon. Psychological warfare. Studying crowd behaviour. Subliminal communication. Trying to manipulate human behaviour through use of . . . of special individuals.' Chad pronounced the words with great precision. 'Special . . . talent. Special . . . abilities. Turned out Christopher Matthew was the perfect subject.'

Chad gave a little wheezing laugh. 'Quite a coincidence, don't you think?' The laugh turned into an ugly snoring noise and then his breathing subsided, becoming so faint she could hardly hear it.

Juliette bent over him. He was fading fast. It went against her training to do anything to disturb him, but she had to ask the question.

'You said it was a trap?'

Chad spoke slowly, with great effort. 'Yes.'

'You said he was like a goat staked out for a lion.'

'Yes.'

'Who's the lion?'

'Leiber. Franklin Leiber. He was . . .' Chad blinked at her. 'He was another recruit at the research unit. Lion is right. His abilities made Christopher's look . . . look like nothing. Surprised us all. Came out of nowhere. But then, then things began to go wrong. Leiber is too . . . unstable. Too dangerous. Project terminated. Leiber is arrested, for everybody's safety. He escapes. Christopher goes after him. Tries to stop him. No good. Leiber got away. We thought he would come back, though, come looking for Chris.'

He looked up at Juliette, his eyes unhappy. 'Looks like we . . . were right.'

The medical director's voice was slowing, like a mechanism winding down. Now he fell silent, gasping. His eyes drifted shut. Juliette could see that he didn't have long. Sweat was thick on his brow. He turned his face to his shoulder, trying to rub it on the rough fabric of his jacket. He was too weak and clumsy even to do that.

Juliette reached out and gently touched his face, wiping the greasy film of sweat away with her hand. He twitched at her touch, eyes opening to look at her again. Eyes that were oddly clear, the expression pleading.

'Scared,' he said. 'Please hold my hand.'

She took his hand and squeezed it. It was damp, and cold as ice.

'Juliette,' he said, his breathing laboured, voice almost inaudible. 'I want . . .' She leant close to hear him. His breath was a feeble stirring on her face. 'Want you to . . .' But then his eyes flickered fearfully towards the door.

Juliette twisted quickly around. The office door was opening. Someone was coming in.

Juliette wrenched herself away from Chad, getting to her

feet, looking for something to defend herself with. Any-thing. On the desk. A paperweight –

Then she saw who it was. Christopher Matthew.

The swift impact of their bodies knocked the breath out of her. Their arms wrapped fiercely around each other. For a long moment they hugged, the present nightmare disappearing from Juliette's consciousness, squeezed out by the totality of his physical presence.

Then she eased away from his embrace and the fear came lapping in again.

'Chad's badly hurt,' she said. 'We have to get him out of here.'

She turned back to the medical director. Christopher crouched beside her. Chad's eyes were shut and he didn't seem to be breathing.

'Chad?'

His eyelids trembled, failed to open. Then they did open, but his eyes stared out at them without recognition. They drifted shut again.

As they watched, his face became oddly still. There was no explicit change, nothing Juliette could have singled out, but something was suddenly absent.

He was gone.

She got up and went to the desk, reaching for the phone.

'Forget it,' said Christopher. 'They're all dead. Some-body must have disabled them at the switchboard.'

She put the phone down. 'Chad said we mustn't ring for help anyway.'

'He's right,' said Christopher. 'Forget about calling the police. They can't help.'

The corridor outside the office was cold and quiet. At the far end was a watery glow of daylight, coming in through the glass doors of the reception area. Juliette wanted to run towards the daylight, but she made herself walk calmly beside Christopher.

As they moved down the corridor she noticed that one of the doors on the left was open. Had it been open before? She turned to Christopher, intending to say something. But, as soon as she opened her mouth, he clamped his hand over it.

He was dragging her through the open door, kicking it shut behind them. For one dizzying instant Juliette thought that she had been wrong, and that Christopher was the murderer after all.

But then he released her, holding a finger to his lips, urgently gesturing for silence. He turned to the door, which was still open an inch or so, and peered out. Juliette didn't understand what he was doing.

Then she heard the voices. Low voices echoing down the corridor. Men. At least two of them.

Christopher eased the door shut with great caution and the voices gradually faded. He let go of the door and turned to her, and she saw the fear on his face. He put his mouth to her ear and whispered.

'We have to hide.'

Juliette looked around the room. There was a desk in one corner, shoved up against the wall. Two spindly chairs stood on it, stacked one on top of the other. On the other side of the room was a plump, dusty sofa piled with box folders and textbooks. The only other piece of furniture was an old, green, civil-service filing cabinet.

Christopher went to the sofa and eased it away from the wall, grunting with the effort. When she realised what he was doing, Juliette hurried to help.

As soon as there was room Christopher slipped behind the sofa, crouching and measuring the space available. He got up and adjusted the position of the sofa slightly. 'Come on, there's room for both of us.' He clambered behind it. 'No one will see us.'

Juliette hesitated. Just then there was a sharp noise in the corridor. A door slamming. Then another.

'Come on!' Christopher beckoned to her urgently. 'Quick. They're coming this way.'

Juliette slipped into the space behind the sofa. The carpet was thick with dust and she could feel it irritating her eyes and nose. Out in the corridor the slamming of the doors continued, getting closer.

Juliette felt hysteria begin to well up in her. Outside this office were the men responsible for the slaughter, and here she was hiding behind this sofa like a child playing a game. It was pitiful.

It would never work. They would be found and killed. The only sensible thing to do was run while they still had time.

Juliette began to writhe out from behind the sofa. Christopher looked at her for a moment in horror, then grabbed her.

'They'll find us!' she hissed.

'No they won't.' He pulled her back. 'We can fit behind here.'

Maybe he was right. The sofa was just high enough to conceal their heads. If they dragged it back towards them they would be out of sight.

It might just work.

Juliette slipped her shoes off and put them in her lap. Then she folded her legs and flattened herself against the wall the way Christopher had.

'Good,' he whispered. The slamming doors were closer now. 'Help me drag it back.' They put their hands over the top of the sofa and began to pull.

Juliette was astonished by its weight. It refused to budge. Then she remembered the mounds of books and papers piled high on it.

Instead of moving towards them, the sofa rocked violently back and forth, tilting and then thudding back down into the same position as before. Clouds of dust rose around Juliette and she furiously fought off the desire to sneeze.

Again, the sound of a door slamming. This time it sounded dangerously close. 'Try again,' whispered Christopher urgently. Once again they pulled the sofa; once again it rocked back briefly before slamming back down exactly where it had been before. Juliette stared around helplessly.

They were hopelessly exposed.

Christopher was leaning close to her, whispering furiously

in her ear. In her panicked state it took a moment for the meaning of the words to penetrate.

'The legs.'

Christopher groped under the sofa, searching for its stubby wooden legs. Juliette understood now, and tried to help. She reached down. The rough edge of the sofa chafed her wrists. Her fingers slithered over the dusty carpet, blindly searching for the rear legs of the sofa.

Now voices could be heard clearly through the opening door. 'They aren't here.'

'They must be,' said a second voice. 'Keep looking.'

The door was almost fully open. Juliette fumbled under the sofa. Nothing. Nothing. Her hands were scouring through the dust in broad sweeps and finding nothing. The door was fully open now, the vague shape of a man visible in it. He was dressed in a denim jacket.

He was turned away from the room, talking to someone in the corridor. That was the only reason he hadn't seen her yet.

Then her hands closed around the hard knob of wood. She grabbed the sofa leg and pulled it towards her with all her strength. The sofa lurched and moved, grinding silently back across the dusty carpet.

She heard the man in the door say, 'I think I've looked in here already.'

'Shut up and look again.'

Juliette flattened herself against the wall and dragged with both hands. The sofa surged towards her until the fabric of it was pressing hard against her nose. She felt the pressure of ruptured ancient springs straining under the fabric, pressed against her face.

The sofa wouldn't move any closer. This would have to do. She carefully drew her hands out from under it. They were bruised and scraped. Juliette felt no pain. She felt safe and warm and hidden.

She folded her hands over her shoes in her lap and sat there with her back hard against the wall, Christopher beside her, their knees touching.

The man in the denim jacket came into the office, cursing.

She heard his feet scuffing softly across the carpet.

Juliette emptied her mind. She made herself pretend she didn't exist. There was no one behind this sofa. This office was empty. The man was moving around, searching an empty office.

Somewhere inside her a childhood memory stirred, a memory of playing hide and seek. Playing and winning. They would never find her.

Juliette sat absolutely still. The only motion she could feel was a residual trembling in the old wooden frame of the sofa, a vibration set up by the violent motion of dragging it.

'Well, they're not in here,' said the man. She could hear him wandering around, angry about this pointless search, impatient to be gone.

And then two things happened.

Juliette realised where she'd heard those voices before.

And the trembling in the frame of the sofa reached a crescendo and suddenly turned into a horrid slithering sound, as if something was tearing. Juliette couldn't identify it, and then abruptly she knew what it was. The huge pile of books on the sofa had been dislodged. The action of tugging it had further unsettled them and now the whole chaotic mess was beginning to slip off.

A few small pamphlets slid to the floor with a whispery sound. After a pause a few more joined them.

Then there was a steady rustling noise and suddenly large books were tumbling off the sofa, followed by whole sliding piles.

An avalanche of paperwork, pounding on to the floor. More and more, in an unstoppable slide.

And the door, which had almost swung shut, creaked swiftly open again and footsteps hurried into the room. Outside, far down the corridor, a voice called, 'What was that?'

'A load of shit just fell off this sofa,' said the man in the room. His voice was low and amused and intimate. And very close. Juliette could hear him approaching the sofa.

'What?' There was the sound of footsteps in the corridor as his companion came hurrying back.

'In here. The sofa. I think somebody's hiding behind it.' The voice was almost a chuckle now. It sank down into a parody of a childhood game, crooning, 'Come out, come out, wherever you are.'

Juliette recognised the voice. It was one of the bikers who had tried to rape her beside the railway tracks. The skinny teenager. The speed freak.

Time had frozen for her. She sat there, defenceless and helpless, holding her shoes in her lap as someone grabbed the sofa. It shuddered as the man began to wrench it away from the wall.

Then she heard something else, a swift confusion of sounds in the hallway. Footsteps running. A voice crying out.

The door of the office was bashed open. And, a second later, there was a series of strange popping noises. The sofa trembled violently. There was another cry, more popping sounds and then silence.

Christopher started pushing the sofa away from the wall. Juliette was too shocked to stop him. She blinked in the light as her shelter vanished.

Christopher was standing up shakily. He turned to her and helped her to her feet. He virtually had to pick her up. There was no strength left in Juliette's legs. They were trembling violently, as if she had just run a marathon.

As she stood up, she saw what had happened. On the floor of the small office two men were lying motionless. One wore a denim jacket, the other was in leathers. She had been right when she thought she recognised the voices.

The speed-freak kid and the big man, the leader of the bikers. They were sprawled on the carpet in awkward positions, like puppets whose strings had been cut in the middle of a performance.

A ribbon of blood was worming out from under the bodies.

Standing over them was a tall young black man. His hair

was braided in dreadlocks. In one hand he held a pistol and it bobbed up and aimed at them as they rose from behind the sofa.

Then he saw Christopher and his eyes opened wide in surprise. 'Oh shit,' he said. 'Oh shit.'

The gun dropped to his side again.

Juliette saw that Christopher was grinning at the man.

'Hello, Tregemmon,' he said.

NINETEEN

'Oh shit,' said the man called Tregemmon. 'I should have known.'

He stared at them wearily, his gun dangling loosely in his hand.

Christopher climbed slowly out from behind the sofa. He stepped carefully over the bodies on the floor, walking towards him.

For a moment it looked as if Tregemmon was going to run, but he stood his ground.

'Thank you,' said Christopher. He held out his hand but the other man ignored it. 'You saved our lives. Thank you for that.'

The other man didn't respond. 'Shit,' he repeated, talking more to himself than Christopher. 'I should have known.'

He put his gun into the pocket of his coat. He glanced at Christopher. 'I should have known it was you.'

Juliette was only vaguely registering the conversation between the two men. She was examining the bikers.

Both had been shot through the head. They were so brutally plainly dead that she felt very strange as she checked them each in turn, feeling the necks under their ruined faces, looking for a pulse.

'It's good to see you again,' Christopher Matthew was saying.

'I wish I could say the same,' replied Tregemmon. 'I guess this means I'm dead, doesn't it?'

Juliette looked up sharply from the bodies on the floor. 'What do you mean?' Her voice was harsh and ugly. She could hear a ragged edge of hysteria in it. 'These men are dead. And you're still very much alive.'

Tregemmon turned to look at her. There was a cool flash of anger in his eyes. 'What I mean is, I've hung out with the Edge before.' He nodded at Christopher. 'I was damned lucky to survive that time.' He turned and moved towards the door.

'Why does he call you the Edge?' said Juliette.

'Well, it's not because he plays guitar with U2,' said Tregemmon. He left the room.

On the way out of the building they paused in the reception area. Christopher went through the drawers of Pamela's desk. Tregemmon went over to join him. Juliette watched the men.

'You two know each other?'

'We haven't seen each other for years,' said Tregemmon.

'Then how did you know we were here? How did you know we were in danger?'

'I didn't,' said Tregemmon impatiently.

'What do you mean?'

'I came here for another reason. You'll see in a minute.'

He opened the glass doors and stepped outside. Juliette and Christopher followed. It was cool outside. A fresh autumn breeze smelt of leaf mould.

She was surprised to see that it was still daylight. It felt as if it had been a lifetime since she entered the Abbey.

'I don't understand. Are you saying this was a coincidence? That you arrived at the exact moment when you saved our lives, and it was a *coincidence*?'

Tregemmon shrugged. 'If you hang around with the Edge you'll find things like that tend to happen.' He nodded at the Abbey, his dreadlocks shaking. 'Those wankers in there didn't have any idea what they were up against. They should never have tried anything with your boyfriend.'

'He's not my boyfriend,' said Juliette impatiently.

Tregemmon gave Christopher a droll look. 'Well, excuse me,' he said. 'What is the setup then?'

'Juliette's a psychiatrist and I'm her patient.'

Tregemmon chuckled. 'Then she's got her work cut out for her, hasn't she?'

TWENTY

'The first thing I want to say,' said the man, 'is I'm sorry.'

His face was deeply sunburnt and pitted with dirt, except for a clean pale band of skin across his forehead. Juliette assumed this was usually covered by his motorcycle helmet.

The man was the biker called Shorty.

Juliette had recognised him the instant she'd climbed on the bus. It was hardly surprising. After all, as he himself kept pointing out, Shorty was the only one who'd made any attempt to prevent the gang rape beside the railway tracks.

'I'm sorry about everything that happened,' he said. 'It just got out of hand. I didn't mean for any of it to turn out the way it did. And I'm sorry for the bad things that happened to your people.'

He glanced back at the Abbey, which was now receding in the distance, and looked pleadingly at Juliette. She stared bleakly back at him. His gaze wavered and he lowered his eyes.

Whatever he was looking for in Juliette's face – forgiveness, perhaps – he failed to find it.

Shorty sat in the strange smoky light that came through the mirrored windows of the school bus, looking shamefaced and shifty. He was tied up on the back seat, secured with what looked like a length of plastic clothesline.

Juliette had been delighted at this sight. She hadn't realised it, but she'd been holding in a vast hot ocean of anger against the bikers. Now she felt a fierce joy at seeing one of her erstwhile tormentors trussed up and helpless.

'We weren't supposed to hurt you,' said Shorty. 'We

were just supposed to scare you a little.'

'I don't understand.' She spoke so harshly that Shorty flinched.

The bus was rolling along familiar streets now, heading towards Richmond Park. Christopher Matthew was up front by the driver – a young man called Danny Bailey, who looked rather scruffy and unreliable to Juliette.

Outside the bus were joggers and cyclists and families shopping in the sunlight.

Shorty said, 'We were shadowing you every day and you didn't even know it.'

'Let me get this straight,' said Juliette. 'You claim someone paid you to follow me?'

'That was just one of our jobs. We were also keeping an eye on the Abbey where Mr Matthew was staying.' He nodded towards the front of the bus where Christopher stood. 'And we weren't the only ones on the job. There was also Comstock and Brilly. They kept an eye on the estate next door. Where *he* lived.' Shorty indicated Danny Bailey.

Juliette felt a sudden flare of impatience. This was all getting too complicated. 'Why were you watching me?'

'And how much money did they give you?' said Tregemmon suddenly.

Shorty's eyes shuttled nervously back and forth as he decided who to reply to. 'Not money,' he said. 'Drugs. They had this bent GP who said he could get hold of anything we wanted. Dr Buckminster.'

'He sounds like a hospital doctor, not a GP,' said Juliette.

'You're probably right,' said Shorty sycophantically.

'And this is the man you're working for?'

'Oh no. The man I'm working for is called Mr Leiber.'

Juliette jumped at the sudden sound of a loud voice from the front of the bus. 'Is anybody going to tell me where we're going?'

Danny Bailey was shouting at them from the driver's seat. Why did he have to shout like that? The effect of the sudden noise on Juliette's frayed nerves sent her shimmering from near tears to anger.

Danny went on bellowing in the same irritating fashion. 'After all, I'm driving this bloody thing. It would be nice to know where we're headed.' He was staring back at Tregemmon. Danny seemed overwrought and short-tempered.

'Just keep on driving around,' said Tregemmon in a level voice.

Juliette leant close to Tregemmon. 'Who is he?' She tried to keep her irritation from showing.

'Danny? He's a friend. He's the whole reason I got into this.' Tregemmon smiled a thin smile. 'Or, at least, I thought he was.' He glanced at Christopher. 'Now it looks as if the Edge was pulling the strings all along.'

It made Juliette uneasy when Tregemmon said things like this. This casual acceptance of extraordinary powers. It was something she herself was far from ready to concede.

Tregemmon nodded towards Danny. 'He has a sort of special connection with his girlfriend. This morning they had an argument, a knockdown row by all accounts. But after she left Danny began to get a nasty feeling that something had happened to her. And he began to get flashes. Like a mental picture.'

Tregemmon patted the metal frame of the seat he was sitting on. 'Of this bus.'

Juliette shook her head in disbelief. 'And that convinced you?'

Tregemmon shrugged. 'I'd already clocked that the people in this bus were up to something. I had reason to believe that some weird shit was going down.'

He glanced at Christopher standing at the front of the bus. 'I just didn't know how weird.'

'So where does this girlfriend come into the picture?' said Juliette, a little impatiently.

'She doesn't. Not any more. That's the problem.'

Tregemmon nodded at the trussed biker. 'That's what we were asking our friend Shorty here. We found him in this bus, parked outside the Abbey, sweating bullets.'

'The bus belongs to Comstock and Brilly,' said Shorty helpfully. 'We borrowed it from them.'

'Whatever,' said Tregemmon. He looked at Juliette.

'Anyway, as soon as we started asking questions, Shorty spilt his guts about what was happening in the Abbey.'

'And you came in and saved us,' said Christopher. He had drifted back down the bus to join them.

Tregemmon shrugged off this attempt at thanks. He turned away. 'Whatever,' he repeated. He walked to the front of the bus.

Now Juliette and Christopher were alone with their captive. As soon as Christopher sat down beside him, Shorty seemed to sense that things had grown more serious.

'What's happened to Danny's girlfriend?' said Christopher in a no-nonsense way.

'I told your mate,' whined Shorty. 'I honestly don't know. It honestly wasn't nothing to do with me. It was Comstock and Brilly. They lured her on to this bus and took her.'

'Took her where?'

'I don't know.'

'Oh come on,' said Christopher. There was a dark gleam in his eyes that Juliette had never seen there before.

'No, really, sir. They never told me any more than was strictly necessary, I –'

'There must be something.' Christopher's voice was soft and wheedling, but there was something threatening in it, too. 'Some small piece of information. Some little scrap.'

'No,' said Shorty, shaking his head.

'Some little scrap,' insisted Christopher.

'They never . . .' and then Shorty fell silent.

'What is it?' said Christopher. Juliette felt a rush of excitement. It was clear Shorty did know something.

'Well, sir. The last time the doctor was supposed to pay us off, he came up short. The boys were getting angry. So he said what the hell, and got out this pad . . .'

'A prescription,' said Juliette.

'That's right, ma'am. He didn't have all the pills we wanted, but he said he'd write us scrips for the rest. And that's what he did. He gave me a prescription for some downers.'

133

'And you still have it?'

'Right here in my pocket,' said Shorty eagerly.

It was a small pink scrap of paper, folded in half.

Christopher watched her as she fished it out of Shorty's pocket, carefully checking for sharps. The prescription read 'codeine phos 60mg x 100'. The doctor's signature was quite indecipherable, but this didn't matter since his name and the address of his practice were helpfully printed on the top.

'Is it any good?'

'Dr EG Buckminster,' read Juliette.

'Superb. Does it have his address on it? His home address?'

'No, just his practice.'

'Well, what does that mean?' said Christopher. He was beginning to sound exasperated. 'Can we find him or not?'

Juliette shrugged. 'I suppose I could get his home address off the Medical Directory.' She felt an odd reluctance to help.

'Good.' Christopher turned to face Shorty. 'Who were these other men you mentioned? Comstock and Brilly?'

'They're serial killers,' said Shorty in a trembling, credulous voice.

Juliette sighed disgustedly. But Christopher still seemed to be listening with keen open-minded interest. 'And they're staying at Dr Buckminster's house?'

Shorty nodded. 'They're all staying at Dr Buckminster's house.'

Christopher nodded again. 'Excellent.'

Juliette tapped her foot restlessly. She couldn't help herself. 'And I suppose Dr Buckminster's a serial killer, too,' she said sarcastically.

Shorty looked at her as if she was beginning to get the idea. 'That's right,' he said, apparently altogether sincere. 'But Comstock and Brilly have a very different technique from the doctor.'

'Technique.'

'Yeah. They always use their beloved bus. They travel

everywhere with it. Nobody notices nothing. Nobody knows they're doing it.'

'Doing what?'

'Serial killing,' said Shorty, a trifle impatiently. 'They use the bus to pick up their victims. They strap them into wheelchairs and load them on board.'

Juliette sighed audibly. Shorty didn't seem to notice. 'Every now and then they paint it a new colour and move on somewhere else,' he said. 'Fresh territory. Nobody suspects a bus. They've been prowling the roads for years, always one step ahead of the police.'

Christopher was still listening with noncommittal interest. But Juliette couldn't stop herself making a sound of disgust through her nose.

'I don't know how Mr Leiber discovered them,' burbled Shorty. 'As far as serial killers go, they must be in the top rank. At least in England and Western Europe.'

Juliette shook her head in exasperation. 'And they were all working for Mr Leiber? Comstock and Brilly and now this Dr Buckminster?'

'Yes.'

'Why?'

'He promised them a special reward. A prize pair of victims.'

This situation was rapidly becoming frankly unbelievable. Juliette felt a sudden vivid wish to be somewhere else, free of it all.

'And they're all working for Mr Leiber?' said Chris. Juliette gave him a sharp look. But Shorty nodded enthusiastically. 'Yes, that's right.'

'And what were all these people doing, these minions of Mr Leiber?' said Juliette. 'What are they up to?'

'Preparing for the final conflagration is the way Mr Leiber put it,' said Shorty.

'Drugs weren't the only means of payment, I take it,' said Christopher.

'No. That's why his girlfriend is missing.' Shorty nodded at Danny. 'Dr Buckminster was promised something tasty as a reward.'

'Hey!' yelled Danny Bailey from the front of the bus.

At first Juliette thought he'd heard them discussing his girlfriend. But he was agitated about something else. Juliette began to take a sharp interest in events.

Tregemmon raced forward to join Danny. He peered out of the window for a second and then came back. 'We've got company,' he said in a low voice.

'I knew it,' whined Shorty. 'Mr Leiber is going to punish me for failing him.'

Everyone ignored him. Chris and Tregemmon went to the front of the bus. Juliette joined them. At the rear of the bus Shorty continued to make frightened noises.

'Here it comes,' he said.

TWENTY-ONE

The bikers were everywhere. Clustered all around the nose of the vehicle, matching the speed of it.

They reminded Juliette of porpoises swimming alongside a whale.

Within five minutes they had forced the bus to turn. They jolted on to a deserted-looking street in a sprawling urban wilderness occupied by offices and industrial units. The bikers herded them into a cul-de-sac and when the bus finally, inevitably, braked they came to a stop all around.

'Any bright ideas?' said Tregemmon, turning to Christopher. Then, in alarm, 'What the hell are you doing?'

Christopher was opening the door of the bus. 'I'm going outside.'

'Uh, are you sure that's a good idea?'

'Christopher, you're not serious,' said Juliette.

'Those greasers out there don't look like a welcoming committee,' said Tregemmon.

'You might remember that I have a knack with group dynamics,' said Christopher. He seemed to be addressing both of them.

'Shut the door behind me,' he said.

Juliette watched helplessly as he left the bus.

She had once seen a motorcycle rally en route to Brighton. That was the only other time she'd seen so many bikers gathered together.

Mostly dressed in leather and denims, often with aggressively decorated helmets, both men and women were in the group.

The bus doors sagged open and Christopher Matthew stepped out among them.

* * *

He approached them calmly, talking to them as they climbed off their motorcycles and came angrily forward to confront him. Danny had sealed the doors of the bus again, so Juliette couldn't make out what was being said. But at one point the exchange became quite agitated and the cluster of bikers in front of Christopher Matthew began to shout.

But Christopher remained calm, speaking to them slowly and quietly. Juliette watched him with a queasy stirring of fear in the pit of her stomach. She had the feeling that something dreadful was going to happen at any instant.

Tregemmon stood comfortably close behind her, following the unfolding drama with keen interest.

Only at one point did Tregemmon look like he might interfere. The bikers had finished talking to Christopher for a moment and had turned away to converse among themselves. Then they seemed to come to some kind of decision. They turned back to Chris, surging towards him in a mass, engulfing him.

When he saw this, Tregemmon drew his gun from his coat pocket. 'OK, Danny,' he said. Danny reached for the door control.

But then the bikers surrounding Christopher drew back. One of them held Christopher's left hand in the air, the way a referee might hold up the hand of a winning boxer. Chris was smiling, and all around him the bikers were grinning with approval.

There seemed to be something tied around Christopher's wrist, although at this distance Juliette couldn't make out what it was. Some of the men were slapping him on the back in a congratulatory fashion. The scene reminded her of a gathering of primitive warrior chiefs.

Now the crowd of bikers released him and allowed him to walk back towards the bus. They turned to watch him go, and, as they looked at the vehicle, Juliette noticed that the smiles faded from their faces.

'Shit,' said Tregemmon with reluctant admiration. 'Trust the Edge. He walks into a gang of bikers all set to cut his balls off but instead they end up giving him a friendship band. Open the door, Danny.'

As the doors swished open and Christopher climbed on board, Juliette saw that Tregemmon was right. There was a friendship band tied around his left wrist: a thin piece of braid with bright colours woven into it, purple and black and an eerie green.

'Nice one,' Tregemmon was saying. 'Whatever you said to them, it obviously worked.'

'I just told them the truth,' said Christopher. He leant over and had a brief whispered conference with Tregemmon. Juliette couldn't catch any of it. Then he said, 'Start the motor, Danny.'

'You mean we can just go?' yelled Shorty from the back of the bus. He had been following the encounter with bated breath. Now his voice was trembling with relief.

Christopher walked to the back of the bus to face him.

'*We* can,' he said. There was a note of sadness in his voice.

Shorty stared up at him. 'What do you mean?' he quavered.

'You're staying here.'

'Your friends want to see you,' said Tregemmon. 'They're not too pleased about someone else dealing drugs on their turf.'

'No!' screamed Shorty. He began to writhe frantically, trying to fight his way off the bus seat. But the cord that secured him was wound around one of the upright poles and he couldn't move more than a few inches.

Christopher returned to the front of the bus. 'Open the door,' he said quietly.

A group of bikers had gathered outside, patiently waiting. As soon as the door opened they flowed on board, moving quickly down the gangway. Tregemmon and Juliette and Christopher climbed into the seats on either side, out of their way. The bikers converged on Shorty. Juliette saw the gleam of a knife and for a moment her heart stopped.

But the men merely cut the cord that bound Shorty. A moment later they were dragging him along the gangway and back through the door of the bus.

'OK,' called Christopher as soon as they were gone. 'We'd better get moving.'

Danny Bailey shut the door and released the handbrake. The bus shuddered and moved off, following the crescent road that led out of the industrial estate.

As Juliette looked back over her shoulder, the last thing she saw was Shorty disappearing into the mass of bikers. He was shouting something, but she couldn't hear what it was.

She watched the dwindling drama, her heart sinking. Out of the corner of her eye she saw someone ease into the seat beside her.

'What's the matter?' said Christopher, touching her on the shoulder. He could read her moods with dismaying ease.

Juliette kept staring out of the window. 'What are they going to do to him?'

Tregemmon heard her and came over to join them. 'Why are you fussing over Shorty? I thought he was one of the freaks who attacked you by the railway tracks.'

'He was the one who tried to *stop* them. He tried to pull them off me and they hit him.' Juliette remembered the blood on the little man's beard. Poor scared Shorty trying to defend her. 'We shouldn't have handed him over to them.'

'We had no choice,' said Christopher. 'Put it out of your mind. We have more important things to concern us.'

Juliette glared at him. 'Such as?'

Christopher nodded towards the young man driving the bus. 'Danny's girlfriend. Mr Leiber's people are holding her captive. We have to find out where.' He dug in his pocket and took out a scrap of paper.

Juliette recognised it as the prescription Shorty had given them. Christopher looked at it and then up at her.

'And for this we're going to need your help.'

* * *

An hour later Juliette was leafing through a large red volume of the Medical Directory in the library of the Charing Cross Hospital, a white fortress-like building which stretched an extravagant distance along the Fulham Palace Road.

Christopher was standing beside her. The hospital bursar waited patiently outside the door. The library had been closed when they arrived but when Juliette identified herself he had grudgingly allowed them in as a professional courtesy.

'Here it is,' she said. She indicated the entry in the book. Halfway down the right-hand column was the name Buckminster, Ellbert Garrin, followed by a sprawling string of initials which indicated his medical credentials, and an address.

'Sometimes they only give the surgery address,' said Juliette. 'But it looks like you're in luck. That's his home.' The address was in a small village near Rainham in the Medway towns.

Christopher leant over and took the book from her, beaming. 'Excellent. Well done.'

'Would you excuse me for a second?' said Juliette. 'I've got to use the loo.'

'Of course,' said Christopher. He began copying the address from the big book.

Juliette turned away and hurried out of the library, nodding at the bursar. As she left the library she passed the ladies' room on her right. She didn't even slow down. Instead she hurried past and descended the stairs, moving as quickly as she could.

She wanted to be gone before Christopher noticed that anything was wrong.

The sliding glass doors of the hospital were in front of her now. Out in the car park was the orange school bus, blending into the background with its wheelchair emblem. It was over to the left.

Juliette stepped out into the windy autumn evening and turned right.

She kept her head down as she hurried away. The rain

stung her face. She walked towards Hammersmith Broadway and flagged down the first unoccupied taxi that happened along.

She'd had enough. Let Christopher and the others pursue this madness.

She was getting out.

TWENTY-TWO

'Did you know,' Emily announced to her mother, 'that there really isn't any such thing as a gene?'

She scrambled up to sit on the kitchen counter beside her plump bustling mother, who was busy chopping red chilli peppers and occasionally consulting a cookbook spread open on a heavy cast-iron book holder.

'I must remember not to rub my eyes,' said her mother as she picked up the slices of red chilli.

'The exact point where a gene becomes a gene is impossible to fix,' continued Emily. She sat on the counter top, swinging her legs and noisily drumming her heels against the kitchen drawer beneath her. 'Quite impossible.' Cutlery rattled in the drawer, but that didn't bother Emily.

'There are things that are more like genes,' she added. 'And things that are less like genes. But there's no such thing as a gene itself. It's a definition which Lewis Carroll would have appreciated.'

'That's interesting, dear,' said her mother. 'Then a gene is a little like the truth, isn't it? Sometimes we're nearer to the truth, and sometimes we're further away from it. But no one knows the absolute truth.'

Emily grunted noncommittally. She didn't like it when her mother came on all mystical-cum-philosophical like this. She drummed her feet impatiently against the drawer until the cutlery inside sang.

'Will you stop banging your feet?' snarled a harsh voice from the doorway. Emily looked up to see her sister Juliette standing there, glaring at her.

Juliette looked terrible. Under the dark wings of her hair, her face was pale. She stood holding a book with one

143

finger inside it, to mark her place. Emily recognised it as one of their mother's books. Some fat tome about witchcraft and magical practices around the world.

Emily had briefly skimmed through the book herself, before discarding it in disgust. She had no patience with woolly thinking and the section on alchemical lore had made her head ache with the sheer stupidity of the whole enterprise.

Now her big sister turned away and stomped up the stairs, carrying the book.

Emily waited until she was gone and then she said, 'What does she care if I bang my heels or not? She won't hear me when she's upstairs.'

'But it *is* very distracting, dear. Personally I'm glad you've stopped.' Emily's mother stooped and opened the oven door. Slipping on padded mittens, she took out a deep Pyrex dish containing a pie with golden leaves of pastry folded gracefully across the top.

For a moment the warm golden vision of the pie and its wonderful aroma distracted Emily. Then she returned to her thoughts.

'Mum, why is Juliette always having some kind of crisis over some man?'

Emily's mother frowned thoughtfully as she tested the crust on the pie. 'Oh, I think it's a little more than that, dear,' she said. 'A little more than just a man on her mind.'

'What exactly?'

'I don't know.' Emily's mother returned the pie to the oven. 'But it's clearly got Juliette very worried.' She clanged the oven door shut and turned the heat up. 'I'm sure she'll tell us when she's good and ready.'

Just then the doorbell rang. Emily hopped down from her perch on the counter and galloped downstairs towards the front door.

'Don't run, dear.'

'That must be Professor Romilly!' called Emily, peering through the window on the landing.

'He's right on time. That's a good sign.' Her last tutor, Dr Markowitz, had always been at least fifteen minutes late, as if to assert the fact that *he* was in charge, not the upstart child he was teaching.

Perhaps it helped to take away the sting of Emily beating him at chess seven games out of ten.

Emily was glad Markowitz was gone. She scrambled down from the window and, ignoring the warnings from her mother to slow down and be careful, dashed down the stairs to meet her new tutor.

She was enormously excited. Her tutors usually turned out to be second-rate minds, but you never knew. There was always the possibility that one of them might be intellectually challenging. And Emily was determined to give Professor Romilly a fair chance.

After all, her mother was paying good money for him.

Juliette came hurrying down the stairs, clutching her book. She peered into the kitchen. 'Who was that?' she demanded.

Her mother was twisting the dial on a small, turquoise, ceramic cookery timer in the shape of an egg. She finished adjusting it and set it beside the stove, where it ticked busily. 'At the door do you mean, dear?' she said.

'Listen, Mum. If it was Christopher Matthew or any of his cronies, tell him I don't want to see him. Tell him I haven't called the police yet, but I might. Tell him I want him out of my life. I just want to be left alone. I want nothing more to do with him.'

'That's all right then, love,' she said. 'Because it wasn't Christopher at the door. It was Emily's new tutor.' She wiped the flour off her hands, observing how her daughter's face fell with disappointment.

She reached out and touched Juliette on the cheek. 'Are you sure you don't want to talk about it, love?' Her fingers still carried a trace of flour and she inadvertently left a streak of it across her daughter's smooth, lovely cheek. The sight of Juliette's beauty still pinched her heart, giving her an oddly mixed feeling of pride and pain.

Pain because she knew she couldn't protect her daughter from the vagaries of the world. She felt the same way about

Emily when she thought about her growing up. She wished she could protect both her daughters for ever.

'Please tell me what's bothering you, Juliette,' she said. Juliette was standing there in the doorway, pale and unhappy, looking as if all the cares of the world were on her shoulders.

'I can't.'

'Something bad happened when you went to London with Christopher, didn't it?'

Juliette sighed and set the heavy book down on the kitchen table. Her mother looked at the illustration on the cover: a witches' Sabbath by moonlight. 'You wouldn't believe me, Mum,' she said finally. She stared at the book cover for a moment and then looked at her mother. There were smooth indigo half-circles of exhaustion under her eyes.

'Maybe I would believe you, dear.'

Juliette gave a mirthless chuckle. 'Yes, you might at that. And maybe that would be even worse.'

'What do you mean?'

Juliette idly studied the book on witchcraft. 'I'm a scientist, Mum,' she said. Her voice was fierce and anger gleamed in her eyes. 'I believe in rationality and the world of empirical analysis. I am clinging to all that by my fingernails. I am trying not to let craziness engulf me. The last thing I need is for someone to weigh in on the side of the craziness.'

'And that's how you see me, is it?' She could not prevent her voice betraying the hurt she felt.

Juliette sighed and was evidently trying to frame a reply when she was interrupted by the doorbell ringing again.

'If it's Christopher Matthew I'll tell him you're not here.' She turned away from Juliette and marched out of the kitchen.

'Wait a minute,' said Juliette. She hurried out after her mother, who was already halfway down the stairs, moving surprisingly quickly for such a large woman. Juliette paused at the landing window and cursed. There in the street below, parked behind her Fiat – now repaired – was the orange bus that Christopher and his friends had commandeered.

Christopher was here. Juliette's heart flip-flopped in her chest. She heard her mother downstairs, opening the front door, and then she couldn't resist any longer. It was all she could do to stop herself running as she hurried down to join her.

She got to the door just as her mother was cautiously opening it on the chain.

'Oh, Mum, for God's sake,' she said. She reached forward and dragged the chain off the door, flinging it open wide. There standing on the steps were Tregemmon and Christopher, both looking a little hesitant and sheepish.

'I thought you'd be here,' said Christopher.

'We were worried when you just disappeared like that,' added Tregemmon. 'You should have left a note or something.'

Juliette opened her mouth to reply, only then realising she had no idea what to say. She was still coping with her reaction to seeing Christopher again.

She'd told herself dozens of times that she never wanted to lay eyes on him again. But now that he was standing on her doorstep, in the flesh, she felt her resistance melting away.

'Why don't you both come in for a cup of coffee?' said Juliette's mother, beaming anxiously, talking to fill the awkward silence. She stood back, allowing the men to troop in. As they did so, she shot Juliette a shy, pleased look. Somehow that look irritated Juliette and the irritation gave her a solid footing for her hostility.

Anger sprang up in her as she hurried after Christopher.

'Why did you come here?'

'I told you, I was worried about you.'

'Just show your friends into the parlour, Juliette. I'll make the coffee.' Juliette frowned at her mother as she hurried up the stairs towards the kitchen.

She reluctantly led the men into the downstairs parlour. 'That's not the real reason,' she said, glaring at Christopher.

'It's not the entire reason,' he conceded. 'I also came because we need your help.'

'Help for what?'

'We've got to get Danny's girlfriend back,' said Tregemmon. 'God knows what those freaks might do to her.'

'I found the address for you,' said Juliette harshly. 'What more do you want?'

For a moment it looked as if Christopher might lose his temper. 'Juliette, this girl's life is in danger.'

Juliette shook her head, refusing to listen. 'I've had enough. I'm a doctor. I can't just keep following you into places full of dead bodies.'

'This isn't going to be like that,' said Tregemmon laconically.

'Oh no?'

'No. Because they're not dead yet. That's the whole problem.' Tregemmon gave her a thin rueful smile. She turned away from him to look at Christopher.

He spoke softly. 'Please, Juliette, I need you.' He reached out to touch her, but she dodged away. 'Please,' he repeated. 'Danny's girlfriend is being held prisoner by some of the worst people on the planet.'

'I'm sorry, Christopher,' she said, speaking flatly and with great finality. 'But it's not my fight.'

From the hallway outside there was a strange cry and all of them spun to face the door. Tregemmon reached for his gun, not relaxing again until he saw Juliette's mother come hurrying in.

She stared at them. Her plump face was strained, her eyes tight with anxiety.

'Emily's gone,' she said.

TWENTY-THREE

The headlights on the school bus cut through the motorway darkness. A heavy rain was still falling, battering at the vehicle, but the steady scything of the windscreen wipers kept the glass clear. Juliette peered out at the dark rain-slashed road ahead, willing the bus to go faster. She jumped when Danny Bailey spoke.

He was sitting beside her, peering out over the steering wheel. 'Maybe they didn't take your little sister,' he said.

Juliette resisted the temptation to bite his head off. After all, his girlfriend was in the same boat as her little sister.

'Maybe it's got nothing to do with them,' persisted Danny.

Juliette shook her head. 'It's them all right.'

'But maybe this bloke, this tutor, just took her out somewhere.'

'No. We rang the real tutor up and he was still at home. He told us someone phoned him and cancelled this evening's lesson. A man, he said.'

Juliette peered out into the fan of their headlights that shone along the motorway. The dark road kept rushing towards them, vanishing under the bus. For a moment her vision swam with tears.

'Someone else came for her,' she said.

She felt a hand on her shoulder. It was Christopher. 'Come and sit down.'

Juliette shook her head. She felt she should stand here beside Danny, urging the bus forward into the night. It seemed like a necessary penance.

She couldn't forget how she had stood in the parlour, steadfastly refusing to help rescue Danny's girlfriend.

Now they were racing to rescue not only her, but Emily as well.

Juliette felt as if her little sister's kidnapping was some kind of punishment for her refusal to help.

As if sensing her distress, Chris put a gentle hand on her face. 'Come on, love. You're distracting the driver.' He tried to make a joke of it, tapping the small warning sign that advised her to avoid doing just that.

Juliette reluctantly allowed him to lead her to the back of the bus. They had to make their way past Tregemmon, who was crouched in the aisle, opening the large metal flight cases they had found on board.

He was working by torchlight, holding a small halogen-bulbed Mag-Lite in his mouth, shining the beam down at the glittering contents of the cases. As they brushed past him, he took the torch out of his mouth and said, 'This is quite a find. A veritable treasure trove.'

'What have you got?'

'Surveillance equipment. I knew about that. But also a lot more weapons than I expected. Other assorted combat gear. And enough ammunition to fight a small war.'

He grinned up at them, his teeth shining in the darkness. 'Which may be exactly what we're about to do.'

Juliette slumped into a seat and took out her palmtop computer and a cellular phone. 'There must be something else I can do to help.' She switched on the phone, then after a moment switched it off again. She looked at Christopher.

He was shaking his head. 'You've rung everyone you know who might be able to tell you anything about Dr Buckminster, haven't you?'

'I suppose so,' said Juliette reluctantly. 'I've been racking my brains but I can't think of anyone else.'

'That's probably just as well. We don't want to alert him that someone's asking questions. As far as he knows, no one is aware of his involvement. Let's keep it that way.'

Tregemmon joined them and nodded in agreement. 'That's our main advantage. Surprise.'

He smiled again. 'These fuckers don't know we're

coming.' He took an oddly shaped gun and fitted it back into the flight case, then snapped the case shut.

'Are you sure your mother's going to be all right?' said Christopher.

Juliette nodded. 'She seems to have given up the idea of phoning the police.'

'Wouldn't do any good,' said Tregemmon tersely.

'Well, I was astonished that Chris managed to talk her out of it.' She looked over at Christopher Matthew. 'She seems to have a lot of respect for your opinion.'

He shrugged. 'Tregemmon's right. It wouldn't do any good.'

The dark miles slipped by under the bus. They seemed to be driving for ever through the rain and getting nowhere. The waiting was torture for Juliette. Finally she switched on her palmtop and forced herself to review the notes she'd made.

The medical world was a small close-knit community and it hadn't proved difficult to track down a friend of a friend who knew a GP called Ellbert Garrin Buckminster.

In the hour since they had left her mother's house, Juliette had been busy on the phone, gleaning all the information she could, and making notes.

Now she'd managed to piece together a short biography of the man. Christopher had said any information could be useful.

But of course there was always the chance that Emily hadn't been taken to Dr Buckminster's house. Buckminster might have no idea where she was. Juliette tried not to think of that possibility. Buckminster was their only lead.

She peered at her neatly typed notes on the slender, glowing screen. 'Let me just review what we've found out so far,' she said.

'Dr Buckminster,' said Tregemmon, interrupting her. 'Mid-fifties,' he recited. 'Respected general practitioner. Former hospital doctor. Author of a highly regarded work on the ethics of euthanasia. Comes from a distinguished medical family. His grandfather was an aviation nut,

"Bucky" Buckminster. Flew against von Richtofen in the Great War, et cetera. Father drove racing cars as well as keeping up the flying tradition and also practising medicine. Busy bunny, eh? Both father and mother died tragically when Ellbert was a kid. Drowning accident. Family was filthy rich. Ellbert inherited it all and invested it all and now *he's* filthy rich. He doesn't need to practise medicine but he likes it. He's very dedicated. Doesn't seem to spend any of his considerable wealth. Still lives in large family mansion where he grew up. Did I miss anything out?'

'No,' said Juliette in a small voice.

Tregemmon shoved the flight cases aside and came and sat between her and Christopher.

He smiled at her. 'Look, I know you want to help,' he said patiently. 'I know you're going spare worrying about your sister. But just try and chill. We may need you fresh and sharp when the show begins.'

Juliette nodded but didn't say anything. She turned away and peered out of the rain-smeared window, so the men wouldn't see the tears on her face.

As she gazed out into the darkness a huge flash of lightning exploded on the horizon, followed by a lingering rumble of thunder. A gust of wind rattled the window of the bus. Juliette shuddered. The world seemed to be at war with itself.

She felt Christopher take her hand. 'We'll be there soon,' he said.

Just then Danny leant out from the driver's seat and called. 'Tregemmon. You'd better come up here.'

Tregemmon strode up the swaying length of the bus and stood beside him. 'What is it?'

Danny was frowning, a band of light across his eyes from the rear-view mirror. 'Those lights,' he said. 'The same car's been there ever since we left.

'Somebody's following us.'

The thunderstorm was fully developed by the time they reached the tiny village of Westenham, just south of

Rainham. Thunder and lightning rolled across the sky, illuminating the neat geometry of hop fields and apple orchards, and then later the bare tangled branches of heavily forested land nestling along hillsides.

Shrieking winds buffeted the bus but Danny Bailey kept it moving smoothly and steadily along the winding road.

'Are they still following us?' said Juliette.

Danny nodded. 'It's definitely the same car. Following at about the same distance. They're trying to stay out of sight but they're not very good at it, especially on these country roads.'

'Are you still OK to drive?' said Tregemmon. 'I could spell you. You must be knackered.'

'No. I'm all right.' Danny waved his hand impatiently. 'I'd rather be busy. Otherwise I'd just be gnawing myself to pieces worrying about Miranda.'

Amen to that, thought Juliette.

'Also, I've discovered a weird thing,' said Danny. 'You know the term "highway hypnosis"?'

'It's sort of a trance state,' said Christopher. He was sitting with Juliette and Tregemmon. They were all clustered at the front of the bus now as they were nearing their destination. 'People drop into it when they're driving on long journeys, especially through unvarying landscapes.'

'Well, I've been feeling something like that,' said Danny.

'Maybe I should take the wheel after all,' said Tregemmon hastily.

'No, I'm fine. I'm perfectly alert,' said Danny. 'But I've found that it's the ideal state of mind for trying to make contact with Miranda.'

'You mean you're picking up her thoughts?' said Juliette. She was still torn between fascination with Danny Bailey's story of telepathy and finding the whole thing ridiculous.

'Not really thoughts,' said Danny. 'Just images. Just one image in fact.'

'So, what do you see?' said Christopher.

'A tree up on a hill. It looks like it's been struck by lightning.'

'I wouldn't be surprised if there's a few more of those before the night's over,' said Tregemmon, looking out into the storm-torn landscape.

'I hate to interrupt the telepathy symposium,' said Juliette, 'but shouldn't we do something about the people following us?'

'Don't get impatient,' said Tregemmon. He got up and stood crouched beside Danny, staring into the rear-view mirror. 'Leave this shit to me,' he murmured.

Then he turned back to them and smiled. 'I'm thinking we'll prepare a little surprise for them. I was just waiting until we were off the main road.'

He winked at Juliette. 'Wouldn't want any law-abiding citizens getting caught in the crossfire.'

In the end Tregemmon settled for a simple expedient. He got Danny Bailey to extend his lead on the car following them. Then, when they were far enough ahead, Danny stopped the bus and parked it in a sprawling diagonal across the road, blocking both lanes.

Tregemmon watched the manoeuvre with approval and slapped him on the shoulder. 'You've chosen a pretty good spot. Nice and quiet.' He peered out at the rainswept road. 'But you better keep an eye on the road in the other direction. Some cars might turn up. And they'll be somewhat surprised to find a dirty big coach blocking the road.'

'What do I do if one comes?' said Danny.

'You'll think of something.' Tregemmon slapped him on the shoulder again and moved down the dark length of the bus to where Christopher and Juliette were sitting.

He crouched beside Juliette. 'I've taken some cushions off the seats and put them on the floor. You just stay down there, out of sight and out of the firing line. Don't even look up until I come back and say it's all clear. I've left a gun with Danny in case things get rough.'

He turned to Christopher. 'I didn't bother finding one for you. If memory serves, you prefer other methods.' He smiled a strange smile and then he was gone, out of the bus into the rain and darkness.

154

Juliette saw him vanish among the trees on the side of the road, and then she felt Christopher's hand on her shoulder, urging her down on to the floor.

She lay there breathing the vinyl smell of the old cushion, feeling its smooth pressure against her face. Sweat gathered on her cheek and she could feel her heart beating in the darkened bus, so loud that it seemed the others must hear it.

Christopher was a comforting presence, sitting beside her. She couldn't see him, but she could feel him there.

The motor sound grew nearer and then Juliette saw the bleary headlight beam sweeping above her, creating tall angular shadows of the seats that marched down the bus.

There was the moaning sound of brakes, then the smearing splatter of tyres trying to bite on to wet road. The headlights shuddered and came to a stop, shining in through the bus windscreen at an angle. The motor of the car was still running.

Juliette tried to rise up and see what was happening outside. Christopher's hand pressed her firmly back down. She felt like a frightened child who was being made to stay out of grown-up affairs.

Like a frightened child . . .

Suddenly her mind was filled with thoughts of her little sister. These were the people who had taken her.

Juliette heard the car engine go off. When it died, the headlights went off too, dropping the interior of the bus back into sudden darkness. Juliette found herself blind. She couldn't see to distinguish the bus from the road and the countryside outside.

Then, after a hesitant pause, there was the sound of the car door opening followed by the sound of a seatbelt snapping open.

Then silence.

The silence was the worst thing. It seemed to go on for ever. Then there came a sharp rapping on the door of the bus, so loud and so peremptory that Juliette nearly convulsed with shock. Before she could react, Danny was scrambling into the driver's seat and activating the door control.

The doors hinged open and someone was instantly striding on to the bus. Juliette saw the shape of head and shoulders in the darkness, the distinctive sway of dreadlocks, and knew it was Tregemmon.

'OK, Danny,' he said. 'Get this bus straightened out on the road before someone crashes into it.'

Tregemmon had a disgusted expression on his face. He leant over Danny and flipped a switch and the interior lights of the bus flickered on. Juliette looked up, blinking.

'You can get off the floor now,' said Tregemmon.

'What is it?' said Juliette. 'What happened?' Then she fell silent as she saw the face of the woman who was peering timidly in through the open door of the bus.

It was a plump, red, middle-aged face, moistened by the rain draining off the rim of the ridiculous, brightly coloured Tibetan wool hat she was wearing.

The woman stared sheepishly at Juliette.

'I'm sorry,' she said. 'I couldn't just stay at home and wait, dear.'

TWENTY-FOUR

They made Juliette's mother follow in the car and a quarter of an hour later they arrived at Dr Buckminster's house.

The house was situated in substantial grounds in a small valley, a cup of land surrounded by four hills. It soon became evident that their bus was parked on the fourth and tallest hill, situated to the northwest, screened by trees.

Juliette braved the rain to clamber through the muddy woods with Christopher and Tregemmon and peer through binoculars at the house.

These were some sort of image-intensification binoculars which Tregemmon had found on the bus. They made things visible in ghostly shades of green and he proudly adjusted them for Juliette, focusing until she could make out the house below.

As she peered through the binoculars Tregemmon leant over and whispered to her. 'Don't you just love technology?'

Juliette hardly heard him. She was staring at Dr Buckminster's house, imagining Emily being held prisoner there.

'Weird-looking place, isn't it?' said Christopher.

'Now don't start with that mind-fuck stuff,' said Tregemmon amiably, borrowing the binoculars again to survey the house below. 'The Edge tends to establish a weird sort of reality around him,' he said in an aside to Juliette.

Juliette too was staring at the house in the valley. Even without the binoculars she could see the big ghostly shape of it beyond the trees.

'Did you ever tell the lady about your local-reality-commander theory?' said Tregemmon, passing the binoculars on to Christopher Matthew.

'I might have mentioned it in passing.'

'I'll bet.'

'Can I have the binoculars again?' said Juliette.

She was keyed up and tense, wondering if her little sister was in the strange house in the rain-soaked valley below. A flash of lightning lit up the valley and the house became clearly visible: a sweeping block of white stone in a broad spread of lawns facing south. It was a thick semicircle, a broad enclosing arch with a flat roof. At one end of the roof was some kind of large radio aerial.

The house was three floors high, the top floor all glass; a solid bank of floor-to-ceiling windows on every side. The top floor was dark but there was a random pattern of lights in the other windows; someone was obviously at home.

On the right of the house were the remains of a large tennis court, now cracked and pockmarked with holes. Puddles glinted in these, reflecting the lightning.

Weeds were clustered in the cracks in the tennis court. The torn nets hung in sad tired loops. Beyond the court the lawn was interrupted by large squares of ground which had apparently once contained a magnificent spread of flower beds. These were now as neglected as the tennis court, weed-grown and running wild.

Directly behind the fat white curve of the house was a swimming pool, in an even sadder state of repair than the gardens or tennis court. Its dark water was thick with leaves. Its diving board had been reduced to a chewed-off stump.

'Not exactly a proud house owner with a tidiness compulsion,' said Tregemmon.

'What's that?' asked Juliette. 'A Roman road?' Further to the left, where the trees thinned out, an arrow-straight ribbon of tarmac ran up towards a tall structure which looked like a barn. The tarmac ran straight up to the dark open mouth of its doorway.

'No, not a road,' said Tregemmon. 'It's a runway. That building there is the hangar.'

'Hangar?'

'Yeah. See the drums of aviation fuel? If you remember, Granddaddy Buckminster was a flying enthusiast.'

'Doesn't look like anybody's done any flying in recent years, though,' said Christopher.

'Or swimming or tennis or gardening,' said Tregemmon.

'The house itself is in good repair, though,' said Chris. 'And that top floor made of glass is bad news.'

'Why?'

Tregemmon answered. 'Just one or two observers up there can keep a three-hundred-and-sixty-degree sweep surveillance. No blind spots. Makes approaching the house a ticklish business.' He took the binoculars back from Juliette and inspected them proudly.

'They're beauties, aren't they? That bus is full of groovy hardware.' Then he turned away and led Juliette and Christopher back through the dripping trees.

They came to the edge of the woods and crossed a loop of the road. A flash of lightning suddenly slammed the woods around them into stark contrasts of black and white. As the thunder followed, Juliette's eyes gradually recovered from the glare and she saw the lights of the school bus ahead.

There were lights on inside the vehicle but also an odd shifting glare underneath it.

As they got closer, Juliette saw why. Danny Bailey was crawling around in the mud, shining a torch under the bus. She remembered that he had heard a disturbing rattling sound when they pulled off the road and guessed that he was inspecting for damage.

On board the bus, Juliette could see the silhouette of her mother moving around busily. 'Getting our supper ready,' said Tregemmon happily as they picked their way through the mud and small saplings.

Juliette's mother had brought along a hamper of food in the Fiat when she had followed them – the evening meal she had been preparing when Emily had disappeared.

Now they clambered, cold and dripping, into the warm dry bus, and found her laying the food out on clean tea towels draped across the seats. There was a chicken pie,

159

rice salad, a bowl of vegetarian chilli, two green salads, bread, cheese, fruit, and some bottles of mineral water.

When Tregemmon saw the food he smiled from ear to ear and said, 'Hey, Mrs Race, you can come along any time.'

Juliette's mother beamed and started to cut wedges of pie and serve them on paper plates. The doors of the bus opened again, letting a gust of cold air in as a soaked and mud-smeared Danny Bailey climbed aboard.

'I found something under the bus,' he said. 'Some kind of plastic or fibreglass pod.'

'It's probably for smuggling,' said Tregemmon.

'I tried to open it or take it off, but I couldn't get at it. I need better light and better tools and someone has to give me a hand.' There was an irritable note in Danny's voice. He wiped the back of a dirty hand across his damp, pale face, leaving a black smear. He looked exhausted.

'Don't sweat it,' said Tregemmon. 'We can investigate that later. Now get yourself dry and try to get some sleep.'

'Sleep?' said Danny in a scandalised tone.

'Yes. We can't do anything until this storm lets up. You might as well get as much rest as you can. We don't know what we're up against.'

'Sleep?' repeated Danny, in exactly the same disgusted voice. 'I don't want to *sleep*. Not until I *eat*.'

He flopped down in the seat nearest to the food and scooped up a paper plate laden with chilli and salad. Juliette's mother handed him a plastic fork and he moved back to the door of the bus, shovelling food into his mouth as he went.

'Hey, where are you going?' said Tregemmon.

'I'm not leaving those tools outside to rust.' Danny climbed back out into the howling night.

'Bloody perfectionist,' said Tregemmon. 'Now let's see about this chicken pie, Mrs Race.'

Juliette's mother served him. She was trying to smile but it was obviously an effort. Juliette could see that she was struggling to hold back tears. Christopher Matthew had noticed, too. He set his plate aside and touched her on the arm.

160

'What's the matter?'

Juliette's mother swallowed and spoke in a trembling voice. 'Is it true that these people . . . those men that you told me about – Comstock and Brilly – is it true that they are . . . killers?'

Tregemmon forked a slice of pie into his mouth and chewed it thoughtfully. 'Listen, Mrs Race. Very soon we're going to make a move. And, once we do, those freaks down there in that house aren't going to be a danger to anyone. Not ever again.'

He looked over at Christopher Matthew, sitting beside Juliette. 'Just ask the Edge. Isn't that right?'

'Comstock and Brilly aren't our main concern,' said Christopher.

Juliette glared at him. She could hardly believe her ears. 'How can you say that? These people have taken Emily!'

'Forget Comstock and Brilly. Forget Dr Buckminster. However dangerous they are, they're nothing compared with Mr Leiber.'

Juliette noticed that Tregemmon wasn't listening. He had stopped eating and was staring tensely out of the window, into the dark tangle of trees across the road.

'What is it?'

'Danny's gone,' he said. 'He was out there gathering up the tools but there's no sign of him.' He stared out of the window. His voice was taut with anxiety. 'He's vanished.'

When he set off to search for Danny, Tregemmon insisted that the others join him, including Juliette's mother. 'I don't want anyone else disappearing,' he said.

Tregemmon had a gun in one hand and a torch in the other. He used the light sparingly, guiding himself by the occasional flash of lightning.

Juliette flinched with each bolt of lightning and each subsequent rolling rumble of the thunder. Her heart had sunk inside her. Everything was hopeless. Emily was lost and so was Danny's girlfriend, and now Danny himself.

All of them gone for ever.

But, after ten minutes searching through the dripping

woods, they found Danny.

He was quite unharmed. He was sitting on a tree stump on the ridge of a steep slope. His plate of food was on the ground beside him. The paper plate had become soaked in the rain and begun to disintegrate. The food on it was untouched, except by the steady flow of rainwater that had begun to wash it away.

The rain was falling steadily on Danny, too, but he sat on the stump apparently unaware of it. Tregemmon came sliding down the steep muddy bank to alight beside him.

'What the hell are you playing at?'

Danny turned to stare at Tregemmon and the others. His broad pale face and dark eyes looked oddly blank in a flash of lightning.

Juliette took Christopher's hand and together they skidded down the bank to join the two men. Juliette's mother remained standing on the crest of the hill, apprehensively clutching some branches in case she tripped and fell.

'Don't wander off and leave us like that,' Tregemmon was saying, raising his voice to make himself heard above the storm. 'We thought they'd got you.'

'Oh no, they haven't got me,' said Danny slowly. 'But they've got Miranda.'

He got up and pointed at the stump he'd been sitting on. 'Here it is,' he said.

For a moment Juliette didn't understand what he was talking about, and then she saw the long dark body of the felled tree beside the jagged stump. The dark charred smears on trunk and stump confirmed her guess.

'It's the lightning-struck tree,' she said. 'The one you saw in your mind. The one Miranda saw.'

Danny nodded dumbly, rainwater dripping off his broad face. He turned to stare at the big white house, visible beyond the trees in the valley below. Small squares of light glowed in the windows.

'Miranda's down there,' he said. 'They've got her down there in a room where she can see this tree.'

TWENTY-FIVE

The first thing Miranda Lang saw was the dim green lines of the hillside. All she remembered was that she had been drugged and now she was fighting that drug, fighting her confused way back to consciousness.

She couldn't move. The drug seemed to have paralysed her. She sat staring out of the window, looking at a wooded hillside in the late-afternoon sunlight. One of the trees on the hillside was a jagged, charred stump with a long seared trunk lying at an angle beside it.

She slowly concluded that the tree had been struck by lightning.

Then Miranda noticed something else. On either side of her, at the periphery of her vision, she was aware of curved red shapes. The puzzle of their identity irritated her and preoccupied her mind. Eventually she concluded that she was sitting in an old-fashioned, high-backed, red-velvet armchair, and that the curved shapes were its sides.

She gazed through the window and, when the daylight began to fade, resigned herself to having nothing to look at.

But then a small man in a cardigan bobbed into her field of vision. The man had a neat little spade-shaped beard the colour of ivory and he was smoking a cigar and cradling a large glass of brandy.

He appeared in front of her, leaning in from her left, and said, 'Interesting drug, isn't it? Somewhat similar to curare in some of its effects. Not quite such a catastrophic muscle relaxant, though.'

Then he wandered out of her vision again, his carpet-muffled footsteps receding slowly into silence.

* * *

He didn't come back for a long time and Miranda began to believe he had been some kind of hallucination. As night settled over the hills outside, the window glass slowly turned into a mirror and Miranda could see a reflection of herself and the room behind her.

She was in some kind of sitting room, furnished in dark wood and pastel fabrics. The walls were white.

When night came, the storm came with it. Lightning swept across the white walls, and with each blast of light and sound her heart leapt. Fear lanced through her.

Thank God Danny Bailey was there – the sense of him steady and comforting in some distant corner of her mind, just a ghost of his presence, but enough. That presence stopped her going mad.

Then the little bearded man came back. This time he had a girl with him. She was an odd-looking girl with her hair dyed a flat, dead shade of black and cropped close to her skull. She wore red eyeshadow which gave her a slightly unearthly appearance. She had on a black leather jacket.

'My name is Dr Buckminster,' said the man. He nodded towards the punky-looking girl. 'This is Nuala Crosswell. She's a journalist.'

'I work for a webzine called *Profile*,' chirped the girl. She had a soft, raspy, rather pleasant voice with a faint twang of a Welsh accent. 'You may not be familiar with *Profile*,' she added. 'It's only distributed electronically, over the Internet.'

'It's a dubious little subculture,' sniffed the doctor.

Nuala shot him a glance. 'It is rather a specialist publication,' she conceded.

'Specialist? Bunch of bloody anoraks,' murmured Dr Buckminster. 'Anyway, what she's getting at is that she wants to ask you a few questions.'

He withdrew from Miranda's field of vision, leaving the punky girl to take out a small tape machine with a microphone attached to it. 'Just let me get a cassette sorted,' she said, 'and then we can start in. I only need a few details about you. Some background colour, really, as part of a larger article I'm working on.'

The girl slid a tape into the machine and clicked it shut. She pressed a button and smiled triumphantly as a green light came on. 'You see, I came here to interview Dr Buckminster.'

'That's right. And she's not the only one.' The little man lurched back into Miranda's field of vision. Once again he had a glass of brandy in his hand. The amber liquid slopped around unsteadily in the big balloon of the glass and Miranda realised that he was slightly drunk. He leant close to Miranda and suddenly she could smell the ripe aroma of the brandy on his breath. 'There are two more journalists on their way – a man and a woman. They know an important subject when they see one. And they're bringing a *video* camera.'

'And I suppose you're going to let them film you?' said Nuala sardonically.

'Behind a curtain or something,' said Dr Buckminster. 'We'll work something out. Preserve the mystery. The point is that they want to interview *me*.' He jabbed himself in the chest and glowered owlishly at Nuala.

The girl gave Miranda a weary look. 'Please, Doctor,' she said. 'The tape is rolling.'

'I thought you had a telepathic link with this girl,' said Juliette impatiently.

'She has a name,' said Danny Bailey. He glared bad-temperedly at her and then returned to the task of trying to dry himself off. He was sitting on the back seat of the bus, rubbing at his soaked clothes with some ridiculously small tea towels which Juliette's mother had taken from her picnic hamper.

'Her name is Miranda,' he said.

Juliette took a deep breath. 'I'm sorry,' she conceded. 'But this waiting is getting to me. And my sister has a name too. It's Emily. And she's being held prisoner down there with Miranda. And it seems insane that you can't use this . . . gift to help us.' Juliette didn't add that she didn't really believe in this gift.

Danny shrugged unhappily. 'It's not like talking to each

other. It's not as though I can just send a message or receive one. It's more like seeing through her eyes. And vice versa.'

'Shared experience,' said Juliette.

'That's right.' Danny set the soaked towels aside and began to glumly shovel some cold chilli into his mouth from the plate that Juliette's mother handed to him.

'Well, if you can see through her eyes, what have you seen?' said Juliette. 'Have you seen my little sister?'

'Don't badger him, dear,' said her mother. 'Let the poor man eat.'

Danny Bailey was shaking his head. 'Miranda can't see much of anything. She's still drugged to the eyeballs. She can't even move her head.'

'So perhaps Emily is there,' said Juliette eagerly. 'Right there in the same room, but your girlfriend just can't see her.'

Christopher came back down the bus to join them. 'Juliette, your mother's right. You shouldn't pester Danny.'

'Pester him? Emily is down there with those people and –'

Danny Bailey interrupted. 'No, it's all right,' he said. His jaw bulged as he chewed his food. 'Maybe she's right. Maybe her sister is there. But all I know is what I've told you.'

'Let me see if I'm clear on this,' said Juliette. 'This girl is some kind of murder groupie.'

'That's right.'

'And she writes for a fanzine aimed at other serial-killer enthusiasts. And there's also a camera crew on the way.'

'That's right.'

Juliette shook her head. 'I'm sorry. But it all seems so far-fetched. I mean, magazines and videos dedicated to killers. Legions of fans avidly tracking them down. The notion that these people are celebrities, that they will deign to be interviewed, and that their fans will conspire to keep their identities secret. It smacks of paranoia. Elaborate conspiracies. An entire corrupt subculture, for heaven's sake.'

Juliette looked at Christopher. Now it was her turn to plead with him. 'I just find it very hard to believe that I live in a world where such a thing is possible.'

'You didn't,' said Christopher.

'I beg your pardon.'

'But that's the world you're living in now. Conspiracies of serial killers and their fan clubs. Maybe it wasn't possible before, but it's happening now all right. And Mr Leiber made it possible.'

He took Juliette's hand and squeezed it. Out of the corner of her eye, Juliette noted with irritation that her mother was smiling and pretending not to notice. In her mind she had probably already married Juliette off.

'We're dealing with the reality he's created.'

'I suppose he's another local-reality commander,' said Juliette dryly.

'Not just another one,' said Christopher. 'I can't stress this too much. He is extremely dangerous. You have to expect reality to grow increasingly strange as we enter his zone of influence.'

He squeezed her hand again. 'It's going to get worse before it gets better.'

The doors of the bus folded open, admitting a gust of cold wind and rain as Tregemmon climbed aboard. 'OK,' he said. 'I'm set. I've picked a spot where I can watch all the approaches to Buckminster's house. I'll take the car down there in a minute. So long as Mrs Race doesn't mind me borrowing it.' He smiled at Juliette's mother.

'Of course not, Tregemmon.'

'Then I'll be able to spot the camera crew coming. And stop them.'

'And that's where I come in,' said Juliette's mother proudly.

They all stared at her.

'What do you mean?' demanded Juliette.

'Well, our best bet is to capture the camera crew and tie them up and then send two of us along to the house pretending to be *them*. That's what you said, isn't it, Tregemmon?'

Tregemmon nodded.

'And according to Danny,' continued Juliette's mother, 'the camera crew consists of a man and a woman. So it will have to be me who takes the place of the woman.'

'I can't believe I'm hearing this.'

'Well, it can't be you, dear,' said her mother gently and reasonably. 'These people were keeping the Abbey under surveillance. They'll know very well what you look like. But none of them have ever seen me.'

A delighted smile slowly spread across Tregemmon's face. 'That's what I like. A lady with guts who can cook, too. Ever considered remarrying, Mrs R?'

Juliette cut in. She could feel herself starting to lose control. 'Stop it. You're not going anywhere, Mum.'

'Emily needs me, dear,' said her mother simply.

TWENTY-SIX

Dr Buckminster smiled at Miranda with quiet satisfaction. 'You see,' he said, 'I feel it's important that you understand what's going to happen to you. I mean, that you understand the reasons behind it.'

He gestured towards Nuala with his brandy glass, the liquid slopping around inside it. 'What this young lady has failed to explain is, well . . . me.'

'What do you mean I failed to explain?' said Nuala petulantly. 'I told her what you are.'

'What, but not the *why*,' said Dr Buckminster, sipping his brandy. He rolled the balloon-shaped glass between the palms of his hands, warming the liquor. 'You see, Miranda, I am a unique creature.'

He smiled at her, his neat little beard twitching, his bright eyes watching her steadily, imploring her to understand. 'There is no time for false modesty now. And, besides, my uniqueness reflects on you. I may be special, but you are very special, too.'

'Get to the interesting bit,' said Nuala from somewhere behind Miranda's chair. 'Tell her how you got started.'

Dr Buckminster frowned at the girl for a moment, and then he cleared his throat. 'My earliest excursions were as a young trainee doctor working long hard hours on the wards of the great London teaching hospitals, following in the footsteps of my father and grandfather. Although they, of course, were purely preoccupied with *saving* lives.' Buckminster took a sip of his brandy and sighed.

'I must confess that my early experiments were unambitious. Furtive, hurried little consummations in the terminal wards. An oxygen embolism here, an undetectable insulin injection there. Sometimes something as

169

simple as a pillow held over the mouth until the struggling stopped under the bed sheets.'

He glanced up at Miranda and suddenly he didn't seem at all drunk. 'I watched their eyes and, on more occasions than you might imagine, I saw gratitude shining there.'

Miranda found herself swallowing back a sudden column of acid bile that was rising in her throat.

Buckminster continued speaking, casually sipping his brandy, his eyes focused on the distant horizons of his past.

'My pursuits led me into areas of philosophical speculation about the doctor–patient relationship and the ethical arguments for euthanasia. This led to a paper which was rather well received and, over the years, numerous appearances at conferences here and in the Netherlands and Scandinavia, where I spent many a lively hour arguing the issue with my medical colleagues.'

He smiled nostalgically. 'None of them of course were aware that I was uniquely well qualified to take part in this debate. I had relieved the suffering of so many.'

He poured himself another nip of brandy and returned the bottle to the floor. 'But you will be different, my dear.' He smiled at Miranda, saliva gleaming on his neat small teeth. 'You will be leaving life in your prime.'

There was the sound of a door opening and a man's voice from the back of the room.

'He wants to see you,' said the voice.

Buckminster blinked and drew back from Miranda. There was a pause and then he said, 'Well, I'm rather busy just at the moment.'

'Suit yourself. I'm just passing the message along. But if I were you I wouldn't keep the man waiting.'

There was the sound of the door closing and then Nuala said in a hushed voice, 'Don't you think you ought to go?'

Buckminster's face coloured. 'Whose house is this?' he demanded. 'I will not be peremptorily summoned or generally ordered about under my own roof. Your friend is a guest under my roof. As indeed are you, my dear –'

'Dr Buckminster?' said a voice from the doorway.

Miranda couldn't turn around to see who it was, but she could hear that it wasn't the same man as before.

Buckminster had fallen silent. Those two words seemed to have taken the wind out of his sails completely. Miranda saw all the drunken antagonism drain from the small man. He glanced to the door and obediently hopped to his feet.

'Yes, Mr Leiber,' he said. 'Right away.'

As he neared the door Dr Buckminster made a deliberate effort not to hurry. He reminded himself that this was *his* drawing room, in the house that he had inherited from *his* beloved parents so many years ago.

The hallway was long and dimly lit and elegant, with royal-blue carpeting and walls, hung here and there with McKnight Kauffer tapestries. Normally Buckminster felt rested and confident in this place – centred. But now he looked at the man waiting for him, and felt nothing but fear.

The man was sitting some distance down the hallway on a lovely old Biedermeyer sofa. There was a discreet sconce light on the wall above his head but he was sitting at such an angle that his face was in shadow.

Then the man turned to look at him, and his face became visible in the sconce lighting. He was as unremarkable and undistinguished as the Biedermeyer was elegant and beautiful: a big burly nondescript man with thinning hair and a swelling waistline.

An office man of some sort, an undistinguished middle manager from some anonymous company. There was dandruff on the shoulders of his cheap suit. You might pass a dozen like him during the rush hour on any day in any big city. You might stand beside him on a train for ten minutes and not one detail of his appearance would register on you. He'd be gone from your mind as soon as you looked away . . .

If it wasn't for his eyes.

Now he turned his face slowly towards Buckminster. There was a dreamy, somewhat vague expression in those eyes but it was clearing rapidly, as if he was returning

171

from the contemplation of a profoundly distant inner landscape.

Dr Buckminster braced himself as the full weight of Mr Leiber's attention was suddenly brought to bear on him.

It was like being buried in a landslide. 'I wanted to speak to you,' said Mr Leiber.

'Yes, sir.' Buckminster couldn't stop himself. The word just slipped out. The man commanded instant respect. Fear, even.

Buckminster asked himself once again why this unlikely man should have such power. It was as if the dark gods had taken the mundane fat husk of a random mediocre commuter, hollowed him out, then poured some terrible primal essence into that empty shell.

Buckminster somehow managed to muster his courage. 'Look here, Mr Leiber. You really ought to show a little respect. This is my house. I refuse to be ordered about under my own roof. You bring these other people to stay and conduct their own pursuits, using my home as a base, motorcycle riffraff and Comstock and Brilly with their school bus and God knows what.'

For a moment Mr Leiber didn't respond. He just sat there, head cocked to one side, patiently waiting to see if Dr Buckminster had anything else to say. Then he spoke.

'Doctor, I don't think you quite understand the nature of our relationship. Perhaps this is because you are basically a deeply unimaginative man. Yet you have no trouble believing that you live in a world where serial killers have adulation and a cult following bestowed upon them.'

'But we do. At least I do.'

'I know that's terribly old hat.'

'Serial killers?' said Dr Buckminster. 'Old hat?' He noticed with embarrassment that a gleaming spray of spittle had accompanied these words. He hastily wiped his mouth with the back of his hand. 'What are you on about?'

'I don't expect you to understand, Doctor. But I have to surf the currents of public consciousness. I weave the reality of those around me. When I stumbled on Nuala and her pals I began to create a most remarkable reality based on their beliefs.' He smiled that empty smile. 'You see, Nuala moves in a world where the likes of you and Comstock and Brilly are possible, indeed real.'

'I'm afraid I don't know what you're on about.'

Mr Leiber sighed. 'I wish Christopher was here. He would understand. Mind you, if he was here I'd have to deal with him.' Mr Leiber's voice was almost wistful.

He stood up. 'But don't feel badly, Dr Buckminster. You may not understand, but neither does the fragrant Nuala or those colourful bikers. But they *believe*, and that is enough. They laid the foundations for the local reality I created. The reality we now inhabit.'

Mr Leiber smiled. 'And so Comstock and Brilly need never question whether they've actually been cruising the country for years in their school bus, preying on their victims. Or whether they only existed as a potential, them and their beloved bus just spectres floating in the cold fog of possibility. Taking shape out of the soup of chaos only thanks to *me*.'

Buckminster felt a ridiculously well-defined chill travel down his spine. He decided that he must have misheard Mr Leiber. 'I'm sorry. I didn't quite get that last bit.'

'Of course you did.' Mr Leiber rose from the sofa and started down the hallway. Buckminster found himself scurrying along beside the man, like a servile and faithful dog.

Leiber started down the long elegant staircase with its beechwood steps and swooping chrome handrail. Buckminster followed. He let his hand glide along the gleaming handrail now, automatically inspecting it for dust. He had allowed the grounds of his house to fall into squalid devastation, but the house itself he looked after with almost religious devotion. Tomorrow it would be time for the handrail's weekly application of polish.

'And, by the way, I want you to deal with that young woman in the drawing room,' said Mr Leiber over his shoulder. 'What's her name? Miranda.'

Dr Buckminster couldn't believe what he was hearing. 'But I can't. I have to wait for the camera crew to arrive. I promised I'd do that one on video.'

'I'm afraid there isn't time. Do it now.'

'But I simply *must* wait for the camera crew. These people are coming miles especially to record the event.'

'I'm afraid there's just no time. Events are moving much too quickly now.' Mr Leiber smiled blandly.

Dr Buckminster hurried after him. At the foot of the stairs they turned left, away from the big sitting room with its cubist white-leather furniture and walked towards the back of the house, to the kitchen.

For a moment Dr Buckminster was surprised to see that the door to the kitchen had been closed, but then he noticed Mr Leiber taking out a key and he remembered their other guest.

She looked up as the door swung open.

'Hello, Emily,' said Mr Leiber.

TWENTY-SEVEN

The small girl nodded sombrely, but didn't reply. She was sitting on several cushions on a chair in front of the big wooden oval of the kitchen table. In front of her was a litre carton of ice cream which she was dipping into with a large silver spoon, in what Dr Buckminster felt was a distinctly uninterested fashion.

'Don't you like the ice cream?' he said coaxingly.

Dr Buckminster didn't pretend to understand children. He had a number as patients, of course, but he had never really developed a convincing bedside manner with them. He found them rather baffling small creatures and was glad that he had never made paediatrics his field of speciality.

'What do you expect?' Emily was saying sulkily. 'I've eaten a whole carton already and, despite the widely held belief that children have an insatiable sweet tooth, I personally find that I soon reach a limit.'

She pushed the carton of ice cream aside. 'Perhaps because I'm aware of the amount of sugar and fat in this stuff and I'm not particularly eager to lay the foundations for diabetes and heart disease later in life.'

There was a note of arrogance and superiority in the little girl's sulky voice which Dr Buckminster found distinctly irritating. He bit back the urge to tell her that the diseases of later life were the last thing she need worry about.

This effort at control made him feel nervous and bad-tempered. He had the sudden overpowering urge to quaff another fragrant glass of brandy. The decanter was upstairs in the drawing room where he had left it, of course, but there should be a bottle or two in the pantry.

He turned away from the table and started towards the pantry door.

Just then the little girl piped up sharply behind him. 'You see, Dr Buckminster,' she said, 'I've read all the latest research on cholesterol and blood sugar. But I quite understand that, as a busy GP in an embattled health service, you don't have time to keep abreast of the literature.'

Her voice was so snotty and insulting that Buckminster was stung into replying. He quite forgot his intention of opening the pantry door.

He spun around, his mouth half open, about to speak, when Mr Leiber held up a hand and gestured for him to remain silent.

'You really are quite a fascinating creature, aren't you?' he murmured. He sat down opposite the little girl. 'An old soul in a young body.'

'That's rather a mystical way of putting it. I prefer a more down-to-earth and scientific interpretation.'

'Such as?'

'Well, Mikhalyi Csikszentmihalyi at the University of Chicago, for instance –'

'For instance,' Mr Leiber chuckled indulgently.

'Csikszentmihalyi insists that a child prodigy is purely a cultural invention,' continued Emily, frowning at the interruption.

'Fascinating.'

'Yes it is. Can I go home now?'

Mr Leiber patted her on the head. It was an oddly clumsy gesture, as though he was imitating behaviour that he'd heard about, but never actually witnessed.

'Soon. But first you have to go on a wonderful adventure. Is that all right, Emily?'

'Not really,' sniffed the little girl. 'But what choice do I have?'

Dr Buckminster and Mr Leiber left Emily at the table and walked to the back of the kitchen, where a glass and metal door led out to the conservatory. This door, too, was locked, but Mr Leiber produced the correct key from his pocket without hesitation.

It gave Dr Buckminster an odd feeling to see the keys of his house being handled with such ease and familiarity by this man.

It was quite a nasty feeling, really. As if he had surrendered control of his house to Leiber.

More than his house, in fact.

Mr Leiber locked the door behind them and they entered the old tiled space of the conservatory. Spindly metal chairs stood gauntly among plants in large ceramic pots, all of them dead or dying from neglect.

The room still smelt of the long day's trapped sunlight. It reminded Buckminster of happy hours spent there with his parents. His father pouring the morning coffee and his mother tending the thriving army of plants which Buckminster had tried so pathetically to emulate.

To the left of the conservatory was a door in a brick wall, which led to a small adjoining room. This had been the workshop so beloved of his father. Mr Leiber pushed the door open and Buckminster followed him in.

Among other enthusiasms, Buckminster's father had been a dedicated radio ham and this workshop had been the focal point of his hobby. Thick clumps of wire ran along its whitewashed walls, passing through a neatly drilled hole to the tall antenna that was clamped on the side of the house, rising up towards the lip of the roof and towering several metres over it.

The room was crammed with metal shelving units and work benches covered with pieces of equipment. Capacitors, resistors, vacuum tubes, spools of rusting wire. But pride of place was reserved for the large, old-fashioned radio which sat in the middle of a square table by the window.

At least, it had previously sat in the middle of the table. It was now shoved to the back, displaced by the gleamingly new and far smaller pieces of equipment that were being examined by the red-bearded young biker.

'Hello, Lenny,' said Mr Leiber.

The young man was perched on a stool, sitting on his leather jacket. He turned to look at them with his pale-blue eyes.

'Hi.' The red-bearded lad twitched a smile. 'Sorry about moving your dad's radio, Doctor. But it's safe and sound. It's just that your old equipment isn't much cop. Not for the sort of job I need to do.'

Dr Buckminster nodded. He had to admit that Lenny had a talent for technical matters. His natural skill and respect for mechanical things were evident in the way he looked after his motorcycle, now parked carefully out of the rain behind the old hangar.

'Are we ready then, Lenny?' said Mr Leiber.

'Ready to rock,' the young man asserted.

'With regard to what exactly?' said Dr Buckminster.

But, before Lenny could reply, there was a rapping at the window of the workshop. They all glanced up and saw two men standing there in the garden, sheltering under the eaves of the house from the storm. For a moment all Dr Buckminster could see were dark shapes, but then lightning flashed and he recognised Comstock and Brilly.

Lenny frowned with distaste. 'I meant to tell you, Mr Leiber. Those two have been watching me all afternoon, hanging about like bad smells. I think they suspect something.'

'We'd better put them in the picture then. Tell them to come in out of the rain and join us.'

Dr Buckminster frowned. Put them in the picture about what?

Lenny turned to the window and tapped on it with a spanner. 'All right, you plonkers,' he yelled. 'Come on in.' Buckminster watched the men leave the window and lope around to the door of the conservatory. He turned to Mr Leiber. 'What is going on exactly?'

'Just tidying up a few loose ends.'

Comstock and Brilly came hurrying through from the conservatory, shaking rain off their hair and leaving wet footprints behind them.

Brilly came first. He was fanatically combing his dyed blond hair, trying to lash every drop of rain out of it. He was younger than Comstock by several years but nonetheless seemed to be the dominant one in the partnership.

Comstock followed and stood awkwardly in the small room staring at the radio. Both men wore orange overalls with the words SCHOOL BUS printed on the back.

'It reminds me of that film,' he muttered to his friend. 'The one set in the Arctic research station where they're being killed off.'

'*A Cold Night's Death*,' said Brilly instantly. 'Directed by Jerrold Freedman. Wait a minute. Was it black and white or colour?'

'Black and white.'

'Then I stand corrected. It was *The Thing from Another World*. Directed by Howard Hawks.'

'No, it wasn't. It was directed by Christian Nyby,' said Comstock.

'No it wasn't,' said Brilly. 'There was a remake but it was by John Carpenter.'

'Not the remake, the *original*, numbnuts.'

'Gentlemen, please,' said Mr Leiber. 'We have more important issues to resolve.'

'Then why were we stuck out there?'

'That's right. We were stuck outside in the rain. Now we're soaked.'

'It's your own fault,' said Lenny. 'Nobody asked you to spy on me through the window.'

'We needed to keep an eye on you. We know you're up to something,' said Brilly.

'We knew it as soon as you fixed that thing on the bottom of our bus,' added Comstock, giving Lenny a poisonous look. 'Great huge thing it was.'

'That "thing" as you call it, mate, was a specially adapted fibreglass case. The kind designed to keep your fishing rods dry when you drop them overboard. Only it doesn't have fishing rods in it.' Lenny smiled at them, his teeth looking feral in his wiry red beard.

'What does it have in it?'

'Radio-control unit, detonator and charge.'

For a moment Comstock and Brilly were silent with shock. Then, with comical precision, they turned and stared at each other, then back to Lenny again.

'You bugger,' said Brilly. 'You rotten little swine.'

'The radio-control unit and detonator is bigger than it should be,' said Lenny equably. 'That's because it's quite a complex device. Just one signal won't set the charge off. It takes two separate and different signals at a precisely timed interval to trigger the charge. You see, the airwaves are clogged with so much shit these days, there was no guarantee that some fucking passing minicab wouldn't detonate it.'

'You mean we've been riding around on a bomb that could go off at any moment?'

'No, thicko. Listen. That's what I'm telling you. That's why I designed it so that it takes two separate signals, at two different wavelengths, to set it off. The odds against getting both those signals within the correct time span are bloody microscopic.'

Brilly didn't appear to hear any of this. 'We were riding on a bomb and you didn't tell us?'

Lenny grinned and said nothing. The bomb was just a small shaped charge but he'd fitted it under the petrol tank, so when it detonated the whole bus would indeed go up in one fast beautiful blast. If something had gone wrong while Comstock and Brilly had been aboard, they would certainly have been fried in tiny pieces.

In truth, he wouldn't have minded if that happened. Lenny didn't like these two.

While Brilly was growing outraged at this latest revelation, Comstock was still working on an earlier concept. 'We're going to lose the bus,' he said. 'I knew we should never have loaned it to those biker wankers.'

'Who are you calling wankers?' said Lenny in a dangerous voice.

'Gentlemen. No bickering please. We had need of that vehicle. But now its usefulness is at an end.'

'That bus was part of our lives,' said Brilly. 'Mr Comstock's right. It deserves to be put in a museum, not blown up.'

'Well, I'm afraid that it's a foregone conclusion that your bus has now fallen into the possession of the enemy,' said Mr Leiber. 'It has been hours since Shorty should have returned. I believe that he and his companions have come to grief at the hands of Christopher and Tregemmon and company.'

'And our school bus along with it.'

'Never mind, gentlemen. Cheer yourselves up by thinking of the triumph that lies ahead of you at the Halloween.' He nodded towards the glass door of the kitchen. Through it Emily could be seen, listlessly stirring her ice cream with a spoon.

'New fortunes under new skies, eh?' said Mr Leiber. 'That's worth the loss of your beloved bus, isn't it?'

'I suppose so,' muttered Brilly.

'Good. Now I want the two of you to prepare for immediate departure. As for you, Dr Buckminster –' Mr Leiber put a hand on his shoulder and guided him towards the kitchen '– I want you to go upstairs and get that paralysed girl.'

'I can't just do it indoors,' said Buckminster petulantly. 'I need to take her out to the swimming pool.'

'Do what you must, but do it now.'

The doctor left, muttering sulkily. 'And the weather's stinking, too.'

When he was gone, Mr Leiber turned to the young biker sitting by the radio. 'As for you, Lenny,' he said, 'I want you to send that signal and blast the school bus into oblivion.'

'Now?'

'Now.'

TWENTY-EIGHT

At the front of the bus, Christopher was deep in conversation with Danny Bailey. They were examining the wristband the bikers had given to Christopher.

It was a hippie sort of thing. You gave one to a friend and they were supposed to wear it until the band of cloth wore out and fell off. Juliette was familiar with the concept – she'd seen a lot of her mother's tediously New Age friends wearing the things.

The one on Christopher's wrist was just a tightly twisted black braid with a fine tracery of bright-green and purple thread. But Juliette noticed that the bikers had tied it on his left wrist instead of the right, which she had understood to be customary.

'Friendship band' seemed an odd name for it, considering that the bikers who had given it to Christopher had probably turned on Shorty a few moments later and brutally beaten him to death.

Juliette forced her mind away from these grim thoughts. She had an important matter to discuss with her mother. She walked down the length of the bus and sat down beside her on the back seat.

'Mum.'

'Yes, dear.'

'Do you know what you're doing?'

'Why are you whispering, dear?'

Juliette suppressed her annoyance. It was true that she was speaking in a whisper. She glanced up to make sure that the others weren't listening.

Then she turned back to her mother. 'Mum, you didn't really mean it when you said you'd pretend to be one of the camera crew.'

'Of course I did, dear.'

'But you don't understand what it entails.'

'Yes I do, dear.' Her mother screwed her brightly coloured woolly hat more tightly down on her head, as if this helped her to concentrate. 'It entails me waiting here until Tregemmon comes back. Right now he's stationed down on the road where he's going to intercept the camera crew.'

'Intercept? Mum, you're not on *Mission: Impossible*.'

'He'll intercept them and bring them back here,' said her mother firmly. 'The camera team consists of two people, a man and a woman, according to our intelligence.'

'Intelligence?' hissed Juliette. 'You mean according to what Danny Bailey claims to have picked up from his girlfriend by telepathy.' She glanced quickly at the front of the bus. 'I'd say that was the opposite of intelligence.'

Her mother tugged at the long earflaps of her woolly hat.

Juliette realised with a shock that her mother was tight-lipped with anger.

'Don't you dare be so negative and sceptical.'

'But Mum – telepathy!'

Her mother ignored her and resumed repeating her itinerary. 'The camera crew will consist of a man and a woman. And I'll put on the woman's clothes, assuming they fit.' Juliette's mother surveyed her bulky body with a certain amount of distress. Then she squared her plump chin and continued firmly. 'But, even if I don't fit the clothes, I'll go up to the house with Danny Bailey and we'll pretend to be the camera crew and get inside.'

'And then what?'

'I don't know what,' snapped her mother. 'But we will do something. We have to.' Then, with a great effort she managed to regain a measure of her normal serenity. 'So you see, I know exactly what it entails, dear.'

'But it's the way you perceive the situation that really worries me, Mum.'

'The way I perceive it?'

'That's right. Tell me exactly what's going on here,

Mum. What is this all about? This situation we find ourselves in?'

Her mother pursed her lips thoughtfully. 'Well, it's about a white wizard.' She glanced up the bus at Christopher and a certain dreamy tone came into her voice. 'And the white wizard is fighting the evil forces of the dark wizard and his sinister lieutenants.'

Juliette was silent for a moment. Then she said, 'You see, Mum. That's delusional thinking based on your semi-mystical, so-called New Age beliefs and obsessions.'

Her mother turned and stared at her, real anger in her eyes. Juliette was shocked by the force of that anger. 'How dare you denigrate my beliefs when it is your own lack of belief that got us all into this?'

'W-what do you mean?'

'Instead of staying with Christopher and Tregemmon and helping them, you came fleeing down to hide at our house.'

'But Mum, I had to. I –'

'And that's how we got dragged into this. And that's why they took Emily.' Lightning flashed outside and Juliette saw her mother's broad face, normally so placid, contorted with rage and hatred. 'You led them to us. Those people got Emily and it's your fault.'

Juliette sat staring at her mother for a moment. She was shocked to the core, but there was no faulting her mother's logic. It was true.

She got up from the seat and wandered numbly to the front of the bus. She didn't want anyone to see how upset she was. Juliette turned to the picnic hamper her mother had brought and blindly fumbled out the first thing that came to hand. A small plastic bottle of mineral water.

She wasn't thirsty but she twisted the lid, breaking the seal, keeping her head down so that Christopher and Danny wouldn't notice her tears.

But it was no good. Christopher was immediately at her side. 'What is it?'

Juliette shook her head. 'Nothing.' She turned away and began to drink from the bottle. She had swallowed half a mouthful of the water before she realised that there was something badly wrong with it.

Juliette almost choked. The water was thick and salty and foul-tasting. She hastily set the bottle aside. To her chagrin she found that tears were welling up in her eyes and had begun to flow down her cheeks in a steady stream.

She turned and leant against one of the handrails in the gangway of the bus. The foul taste of the water lingered in her mouth.

She was vaguely aware of the bulk of her mother beside her. A tentative hand tugged at her sleeve.

'I'm sorry, dear.'

'Oh, Mum,' sobbed Juliette.

'No, dear. It's all my fault.' Her mother's arms were around her.

'You were right. It's all my fault that they took Emily.'

'No, no, dear. It was wrong of me to blame you. I'm so sorry. I was just cross.'

She could smell the wet wool of the ridiculous hat as her mother's face pressed against her shoulder.

'No. It was my fault.'

'Stop that. It wasn't. Tregemmon said they must have been watching us for weeks. Watching our house. They'd been planning to take Emily away.'

As her mother's words began to penetrate, Juliette felt herself relaxing. It was true. She hugged her mother in a gentle rocking motion, as if she was a child being lulled to sleep. The smell of her mother's woolly hat began to grow unpleasant, though. It was Tibetan, allegedly, and it smelt like a mountain goat when it got wet.

But Juliette didn't care. Her mother was right. It wasn't her fault after all.

She was so overcome with relief that she quite forgot about the water and absent-mindedly took another swig from the bottle.

The water hardly touched her lips before she spat it back in the bottle. It tasted even worse this time. Vile and brackish.

Brackish. What had somebody told her about water when it tasted like that? Something Christopher had said, that night when they were in the biker pub . . .

But so much had happened to her since then. Juliette was exhausted. She could hardly think straight. She was trying to force herself to concentrate when a dazzling glare of white light swept across her face. The headlights of a car.

At the front of the bus Christopher called, 'It's Tregemmon. He's back.'

Juliette and her mother hurried to the front of the bus as Danny opened the doors. The sound of the storm was blown into the bus on a wave of cold damp wind.

Tregemmon had parked the Fiat and was climbing out. Christopher jumped down from the bus to meet him, and Juliette followed. Tregemmon stood there in front of them, rain dripping off him. Juliette could see his smile in the darkness. She could just make out two dark figures in the back of the car behind him.

'Come on,' he said. 'I've got something to show you. You're going to love this.'

They followed him to the car. Tregemmon opened the back door and lifted his torch, shining a beam into the darkness.

A chubby unhealthy-looking young man wearing an anorak was sitting there, blinking at them. Beside him was an equally chubby girl, also in an anorak. The young man blinked uncertainly in the white beam of light. Thunder rumbled overhead and he flinched.

'Tell these people who you are,' said Tregemmon.

'My name is Dominic Wheatabix,' said the young man. 'That's not my real name of course. It's my pen name.'

'Pen name?' barked Tregemmon.

'Yes, sir,' the boy continued with a quaver in his voice. 'I'm, I'm a journalist.'

'Now, Dominic, tell these nice folks who you work for.'

'I, I work for a limited-edition videozine called *Breakfast Serial*.'

'Serial, get it? Tell them the award bit.'

'In the underground press multimedia awards I've been voted journalist of the year working on a specialist subject.'

The chubby girl leant forward into the light. 'I'm afraid I'm just the cameraperson.' She held up a Sony videocam to show them. Juliette noticed that the red recording light was gleaming on the camera.

She was about to say something but Tregemmon had already spotted it. 'Turn that damned thing off,' he said. He spoke in a quiet voice but the girl instantly obeyed, and set the camera down on the floor of the car. As the girl leant forward, something glinted on her wrists. Juliette saw that the boy was also wearing them. Handcuffs.

'OK, OK,' said Tregemmon. 'Now just sit tight unless you want me to blow some random pieces off your bodies.'

The two kids nodded, obviously terrified. Tregemmon switched off the torch and slammed the car door shut. He turned to Juliette and Christopher.

'They're even wearing anoraks,' he snorted. 'Sick, huh?'

Juliette absent-mindedly took a sip from her bottle and discovered that the water tasted all right now. She watched the handcuffs glint on the wrists of their prisoners.

'Did you get those handcuffs from the bus?' said Juliette. She was still a little disturbed by the sight of them.

'Too right,' said Tregemmon proudly. 'It's a treasure trove. Night-vision binoculars, listening devices, laser-sighting mechanisms. I just love all that.' He grinned. 'Not to mention the guns.' He turned away. 'I'm going to take the car back down the road. Just for five minutes to make sure that nobody else is following those wackos.'

He turned and got into the Fiat as Juliette followed Christopher back to the bus. He climbed on board.

'OK, Danny,' he said, 'it looks as though you might be in luck. The chap in the camera crew looks about your size. You too, Mrs R. When Tregemmon gets back you can put on their clothes and we can get the ball rolling.'

Juliette stood in the doorway of the bus. She took a sip of water from her bottle and almost gagged. Her stomach convulsed at the horrid taste of it.

'Christopher –'

He turned and looked at her sharply, sensing something in her tone of voice.

'What is it?'

'This water. When we got off the bus it tasted OK, but when we're on the bus it tastes horrible. I was thinking about what you said to me –'

But Christopher wasn't listening to her. 'Everybody off the bus. Now.'

Danny and Juliette's mother were staring at him. Danny leant over to grab a roll of tools.

'Leave it,' yelled Christopher. 'Leave everything. Get off. Now!'

He turned and pushed Juliette back out through the door of the bus. She stumbled to the ground and almost lost her balance, but then Christopher was beside her. He helped her.

'Run,' he shouted. His voice was lost in an echoing rumble of thunder. Juliette's feet splashed through puddles. Behind her she was vaguely aware of her mother blundering along beside Danny Bailey. They ran off the road and into the dark cluster of trees.

Juliette couldn't see where she was going, but Christopher dragged her along. Branches lashed her face. Tears of pain mingled with rainwater on her cheeks.

She couldn't see her mother or Danny now. She was just aware of anonymous dark shapes blundering through the woods.

And then, behind her, came a sound louder than any blast of thunder. A powerful warm wind buffeted at her back with the force of an ocean wave and Juliette was nudged off her feet.

She slammed forward on to the wet forest floor and lay there, panting. Fragments of branches and leaves swirled through the air above her, flapping and clicking madly. Her ears rang with the great booming sound.

At first she thought lightning must have struck the ground behind them, but then she looked back and saw the torn hulk of the school bus, burning like a guttering candle.

'It's a shame we lost all that good food you brought, Mrs R,' said Tregemmon.

'That's not all we lost with the bus,' said Christopher.

Tregemmon shrugged. 'Tell me about it.' He spread the fingers of his hand and began to count. 'Half a dozen side arms, three rifles, binoculars, ammunition, smoke grenades, and God knows what else.' He sighed wearily and set his coffee down on the floor of the van. 'So right now our entire arsenal consists of this.' He reached into his coat and drew out his chromed revolver. 'We don't even have any spare ammunition.'

'The bomb must have been in that pod underneath the bus,' said Danny Bailey. 'I knew I should have taken a look at it.'

'I'm glad you didn't,' said Christopher. 'If you'd touched it it might have gone off.'

'Never mind, dear,' added Juliette's mother. They were all crowded together in the cramped confines of Dominic Wheatabix's van.

It was a rusty, white Ford Escort van. Juliette and her mother were in the front seat, Danny and Tregemmon and Christopher in the back. Juliette's mother was busy pouring a cup of coffee from a silver thermos flask. She passed the cup to Danny.

'At least those camera nuts brought some coffee with them,' said Danny, accepting the cup gratefully.

'And this van,' said Christopher. 'I'd hate to see all of us trying to fit into the Beast of Turin.' He glanced out of the back window at the Fiat parked on the roadside. The chubby boy and the girl with the video camera were sitting disconsolately in the back seat.

'So what are we going to do?' said Juliette. Her nerves were ragged and she made no attempt to conceal the ugly note in her voice.

'Do?'

'Yes, now that you've lost all your bloody infrared binoculars and buggering sniper scopes.'

'We'll go ahead as planned,' said Tregemmon calmly.

'But you've seen your entire arsenal blown to Kingdom Come.'

Tregemmon shrugged laconically. 'Never mind. I'm happier with my Ruger anyway.' He checked the gun carefully and slipped it back into his coat.

Juliette shook her head. 'I don't believe it. You're just going to blunder in there and take these people on with one gun and six rounds of ammunition?'

'Five,' said Tregemmon. 'I never keep one under the hammer.' He grinned. 'It's safer that way.'

'But this is suicide,' said Juliette.

'You're wrong,' said Christopher. 'But that's because you don't know my friend here.' He picked up Tregemmon's coffee cup and returned it to him. Then he looked at Juliette, his face in shadow, expression vague. 'You see, the name "Tregemmon" is Yardie patois. It's a corruption of "Trigger Man".'

Christopher moved forward and his face shifted into the light. He smiled at her. 'He got that name for a good reason.'

Juliette felt like she was fighting a rising tide of insanity. 'Why don't we just call the police?'

Tregemmon shook his head. 'And take a chance that your sister will be dead before they get here? I'm sorry to be blunt but this is the only way to play it.'

'But they'll be expecting us. They must have heard the bus blow up.'

'I don't think so,' said Tregemmon. 'We were a fair distance from the house and, what with the storm, I imagine they'll just think it was thunder. Anyway, if they think we've blown up they're more likely to drop their guard.'

'What if you're wrong?'

'Please, dear,' said her mother. 'Stop making negative vibrations.'

190

There was a sudden sharp gasp. Juliette turned to see Danny Bailey staring at them. His face was white with shock.

'We have to go now,' he said. 'It's Miranda. Something's happening to her.'

TWENTY-NINE

'It's a shame about the rain,' said Dr Buckminster. His voice was wistful, full of longing and nostalgia. He stared up at the moon. 'Apart from the rain, it was on a night very like this that my parents died.'

He turned to the swimming pool. 'They died in that.'

The pool glittered in the moonlight, the big white house reflected in it. Heavy rain was dappling the surface of the pool and falling steadily on the garden all around. Miranda could see why Dr Buckminster had elected to wear his ridiculous yellow oilskin. It would keep him nice and dry.

Miranda herself had no such problem. Before carrying her outside, Buckminster had removed all her clothes. There hadn't been anything sexual in the way he did it, and in a way that made it worse.

Miranda felt no discomfort. The chill of the rain was lost in the cold numbness that the drug conferred on her body.

Buckminster got busy, fumbling excitedly in his bag, a big, old-fashioned, leather, doctor's bag. He held an umbrella over it to keep its contents dry.

Miranda turned away and looked at the swimming pool. All that was left of the diving board was a jagged stump, as if a giant mouth had bitten the board in half.

Clumps of rotting leaves lay thickly on the surface of the pool. Miranda watched the rainwater dimpling them.

She liked the gentle persistent touch of the rain, on the swimming pool and on her own body.

She found herself being lulled by it.

Dr Buckminster began to speak. 'That pill was a euphoriant, to make things more pleasant for you. And this . . .' said Buckminster, holding up a disposable plastic syringe, 'this little potion inhibits the parts of the brain which control respiration and heartbeat.'

Miranda tried not to pay any attention. The sky above was a steady flow of dark clouds. Miranda concentrated on watching the sky. It was the last thing she'd ever see.

The clouds broke open and she glimpsed a white chunk of moon shining down on her. There was a halo around the moon, glowing in the damp night sky.

Miranda felt an oddly peaceful sensation as if her life had reached a natural completion and everything added up and made sense. As though she'd lived a long and full life.

Instead of being murdered in her prime by a madman in a rainsoaked garden.

Dr Buckminster came and stood directly above Miranda, blocking out the moon, occupying the sky with his head and shoulders enveloped in his ridiculous yellow coat. Rainwater splashed and danced on its slick surface.

'I really am terribly sorry about this. It's all become something of a rush job. Not at all the way I envisaged it.'

He looked around the garden, rain dripping from the rim of his hat. 'I had this all planned. I wanted it to take place on a fine clear evening. I wanted to dig out my father's old outdoor loudspeakers and fit them on poles, so we could enjoy a little music to go with the occasion. Nothing dramatic or upsetting of course. Mantovani or Stanley Black. The sort of music my parents would play at their parties.'

Dr Buckminster smiled fondly as his mind filled with memories. He blinked his eyes as if they were correspondingly filling with moisture.

'I'm so sorry, old girl,' he said, patting Miranda on the shoulder. 'I had such grand plans for you. I was even going to mow the lawn and do a little work on the garden. Perhaps even skim the pool, although I've found it hard to put much effort into caring for that thing.'

He turned his head sharply and looked at the swimming pool, raindrops spilling from his coat. 'I suppose in a way I blame the pool, although of course it's silly to blame an inanimate object.'

Then he turned and looked at Miranda again. 'But it is, after all, the place where my parents died.'

He squatted down on the lawn beside her. Water dripped off the looming shape of him on to Miranda's naked torso. He was so close that he blotted out the entire sky and suddenly Miranda felt a cold, queasy stirring of fear. Now she was cut off from the sky, and the sky had been her only comfort.

She had begun to think perhaps she would go up into the sky when she died. It was a nice thought.

But maybe it wouldn't happen if Dr Buckminster was blocking the way.

'My parents enjoyed their parties,' said Dr Buckminster. 'They were *bons viveurs*. They enjoyed good food and drink and music. And, occasionally, what we would nowadays call recreational drugs. Being a doctor, of course, my father had access to all manner of things.'

Dr Buckminster frowned. 'To this day I don't know exactly what it was they took. There was a post-mortem of course but the details were hushed up. You know what the medical community is like. Or you can imagine. Especially in the early 1950s. It must have been a very shocking thing. But in any case I imagine it was some kind of powerful barbiturate or opiate.

'Obviously it was only many years later that I pieced all this together. When it actually happened I was only an infant. I was in my cot, by the side of the pool. They were very insistent that I remain in the cot until they deemed me old enough to swim. They felt it was safer that way.'

He looked up at the sky, wiping the rainwater from his face. 'As I said, it was a fine night. It was one of the rare occasions when my parents didn't have any friends around. And it was this, in combination with a few other factors, that ultimately proved fatal.

'It was just the two of them. And me of course. They had come outside to have a swim before dinner, as was their ritual. And they had several gin martinis by the poolside, as was also their ritual. And then they took this drug, whatever it was. My father was a doctor and no fool.

So perhaps someone lied to him about the composition of the drug, or perhaps it was some freak dosage accident. But for whatever reason the drug, in combination with the alcohol, proved massively too powerful. They had hardly climbed into the pool for their pre-dinner swim when the overdose took hold. I watched helplessly, trapped behind the bars of my cot, just a poor little chap, as they thrashed and weakened and eventually drowned, sinking helplessly in a few feet of water.'

Dr Buckminster's voice was steady and reflective. 'My father held my mother out of the water for as long as he could. He was a strong man. But then finally even he weakened. The last thing I saw was the water closing over her face.'

Dr Buckminster reached down and wiped the rain off Miranda's face. His touch was gentle. When he spoke again, his voice was steady and businesslike. 'The drug obviously seriously disrupted motor control and fatally weakened their muscles. Obviously it wasn't a pleasant thing for a young child to watch. But I've come to terms with it.'

He loomed over Miranda, smiling, his face as big as the moon. 'You see, I concluded that it wasn't so bad for them. They were lucky really. What a pleasant way to go. Just imagine, your consciousness floating off as you sink in the water. It must have been like floating into a dream. So gentle and so peaceful . . .

'A gentle restful easement into a tranquil oblivion,' said Dr Buckminster, his voice heavy with treacly sentiment. 'I invented that little phrase myself and I have to say I'm quite proud of it. I always say it to one of my friends just before I help them on their way.'

He smiled down at Miranda. 'You're one of my friends now, you know.'

He squared his shoulders against the wind and the rain. In his yellow oilskin he looked for all the world like a plucky little yachtsman rounding the Horn on a gallant solo voyage, braving the elements.

He lifted the syringe. Miranda tried to watch the sky, the

peaceful slow parade of clouds, but her eyes kept straying to the approaching syringe in Dr Buckminster's hand.

There was a clap of thunder and Miranda wondered for a moment if the storm was beginning again. Then she realised that it couldn't be thunder. It was much too small a sound, and too close at hand.

And something odd was happening to Dr Buckminster. He was walking around in a funny little half-circle, like a man who has dropped something in the grass and is searching for it. He wandered unsteadily over to Miranda and sat down beside her.

He sat down hard and all at once. Miranda saw that he was holding a hand against his chest.

He looked at her with a bemused expression.

'I've been shot,' he said. He tried to open his raincoat but his hands slipped away from the button. He sighed and slumped forward, rolling over on his back so that he was lying beside Miranda.

They were like two children lying on the lawn, staring up at the night sky.

Dr Buckminster was still talking, but his voice had sunk to a whisper.

'It's all right,' he was saying. 'Death will be pleasant. Comforting. A peaceful letting go.' He spoke the words to himself swiftly, desperately, as though they were some kind of prayer which would protect him.

'A gentle restful easement into a tranquil oblivion . . .'

In the distance Miranda could hear running footsteps approaching.

'Peaceful and pleasant,' whispered Dr Buckminster. 'Nothing . . . to be . . . afraid of . . .' Then he fell silent and Miranda thought he was gone.

But a moment later he hissed sharply, 'No. Not what I expected at all! Oh no. Oh, dear God, no.'

Then his voice sank to a whisper, until it was hardly audible. Lying so close, Miranda could still hear him. She wished she could move away, but of course she couldn't. So she lay there in the rain listening to the dying man as he whispered of the horrors that engulfed him.

THIRTY

The footsteps were getting nearer. Miranda concentrated on them until the tall black man came striding out of the rain.

He was holding a silver gun in one hand and he looked around carefully before he turned to her. Rain splashed from his dreadlocks as he swept his head first to the left, then to the right.

When he was satisfied there was no one else nearby, he hurried over and briefly examined Dr Buckminster. A grim smile appeared on his face.

'Not a bad shot for a handgun at that distance,' he said. The doctor was obviously dead. The man was tugging off his raincoat now, rolling the small body over until it spilled out of the coat and on to the lawn.

Dr Buckminster's neatly dressed little form was exposed to the mud and the rain. The man callously turned away. He turned to Miranda and spread the raincoat across her.

Then he sat down beside her and whispered, 'It's all right, honey. You're safe now. I'm Tregemmon.'

He smiled at her. 'I'm a friend of Danny Bailey's. Danny filled me in. I know they've got you doped.'

He lay down in the grass beside her, the gun in his hand, staring into the night. 'But don't worry – it'll wear off soon. We'll just stay here a while and make sure there aren't any surprises.'

He put his arm across Miranda and adjusted the raincoat. Suddenly the smile vanished from his face.

Then Miranda heard it too. A strange high howling noise, growing louder and rising steeply in pitch.

Tregemmon stood up.

'Oh no,' he said. 'Oh shit, no.'

* * *

Juliette wished they'd all just shut up. She was sealed in a tiny car with a trio of chattering idiots. Parked under a tall silver tree which seemed to be funnelling rainwater on to them instead of sheltering them from it.

The rain dripped onto the roof. Juliette's mother kept babbling. Asking questions. And the worst part was that sometimes they'd answer.

'Is your name really Dominic Wheatabix?' said Juliette's mother.

The boy in the back seat remained quiet this time. He seemed to have sunk into a sulky silence.

The girl beside Wheatabix leant forward. 'Dominic doesn't mean to be rude. It's just he's concerned that he's going to miss the big gathering at the Halloween.'

'Quiet!' hissed the chubby young man.

'Don't be worried,' replied the girl soothingly. 'These nice people won't take us to the police. Not if we behave ourselves and cooperate, like the Trigger Man told us. If we do that you'll still be able to get to Las –'

'For God's sake, shut it.'

There was silence for a while and Juliette began to relax, but then the girl started talking again. 'I want to do an interview with that Trigger Man,' she said dreamily. 'That would be a world exclusive.'

Then the boy – or perhaps it was the girl – broke wind noisily.

That was it. Juliette snorted with disgust and cracked open the door of the Fiat. Rain blew in.

'It's cold in here! Would you kindly shut that.' The boy's voice rang from the back seat, heavy with sarcastic politeness.

'Would you kindly shut your mouth,' snapped Juliette.

'Juliette! Don't be so rude. Just because these people are our . . . well, our prisoners, there's no need to be rude to them.' Her mother turned and smiled at the two pale chubby faces that watched them from the back seat.

Juliette sighed with disgust and got out of the Fiat, slamming the door behind her. She turned and stalked off into the rainy night. She heard the car door slamming again as her mother quickly followed her.

'Why don't you stay here, dear?' she said, drawing close, her voice horribly reasonable and patient. 'That was what Tregemmon said and Tregemmon does seem to know what he's doing.'

'Look, Mum, I am not going to sit cooped up in that tiny car. That boy called Wheatabix has a serious body-odour problem.'

'It's not his fault. He's probably just frightened, dear.'

'We're going to have to have the car fumigated when this is over.'

They both fell silent, sharing the same thought. When this is over. Of course, if anything happened to Emily, it would never be over. This night would replay for ever in their minds.

They would wonder if they should have acted differently. If they should have gone into the house instead of sitting here, waiting impotently under these dripping trees.

'Juliette, what are you doing?'

'I'm going to the house.'

'What? You mustn't!'

'Just to take a closer look.'

'But Christopher said –'

'I know.'

'And Tregemmon said –'

'I know. Mum, I just want to take a look.'

'You mustn't go anywhere near that house.'

The note of near hysterical fear in her mother's voice only strengthened Juliette's resolve. She gave her mother a peck on the cheek and turned to go.

'I'll be back. Just stay in the car and keep an eye on Mork and Mindy. I'll see you.'

Juliette turned away, crossing the road and setting off into the thickest part of the woods.

Behind her, her mother called out. 'Juliette, don't go near that house! It might be protected by witchcraft.'

The thunder had stopped. But the steady rainfall continued, causing an eerie, hollow dripping sound in the dark woods all around her, like the percussion in a strange, modern piece of music.

The noise began to get on Juliette's nerves. She began to imagine she could hear every individual drop of rainwater crashing through the leaves to spatter on the forest floor.

Soon it began to feel like one of those Chinese tortures you read about. Where the relentless dripping of water causes the victim to break.

Juliette forced her mind on to other thoughts. The woods were really quite beautiful in the moonlight. If only she could stop imagining things standing in the shadows, watching her.

Other than the dripping of the rain, the only sound was her feet slithering through the damp leaves on the forest floor. Juliette began to imagine she could hear other sounds, mixed in with the footsteps and the rain. Sounds that had a sinister similarity to human voices . . .

Stop it, she told herself.

But it was hardly surprising if she was imagining things. She had been under tremendous emotional strain for the last few days. Seen people die. People she knew.

Naturally, the cumulative impact had finally caught up with her.

And exhaustion hit her all at once. It was like being slowly smashed down by a foam-rubber steamroller.

The dripping woods became unreal around her. Juliette realised that she had lost all sense of direction. She was hopelessly lost in these wet dark woods.

She had to go on blundering in the only direction that was certain. Moving inexorably downhill, towards the big white house in the valley.

By the time she got through the woods Juliette was in a state of complete nervous exhaustion, walking like a zombie. She paused at the edge of the lawn and studied the white curve of the house in the distance. It was hard to remember why she had come here, but Juliette knew that the house was the source of danger. She remembered that much.

She moved cautiously across the wide lawn towards one

of the outbuildings at the left of the house. It was a large structure which looked like a barn, its dark mouth gaping open. She was halfway there, wading through the dense, wet grass, when she felt the unexpected sensation of tarmac underfoot.

Juliette stepped out of the long grass and stood on the tarmac. The moon came out from behind a bank of cloud for a moment and she saw that she was standing on what looked like a strip of road running towards the barn.

Suddenly Juliette felt terribly exposed. She stepped back into the long grass, feeling a horrid certainty that someone had just seen her.

What a ridiculous thought. But it was hard to think. Her exhausted mind seemed fogged in; thoughts were forbidden to land and circled out in the ether.

Then abruptly the sensation of being watched intensified. For some reason Juliette remembered what her mother had said about the house being protected by witchcraft.

A gunshot rang out in the night.

It seemed to come from somewhere near the house. It was a flat, undramatic sound, but Juliette was certain it was a gunshot.

It seemed to have come from over by the swimming pool. The sound caused Juliette to freeze. A cold spasm of adrenaline blossomed in her body.

Someone was shooting at her. She threw herself to the ground. She lay there panting, her blood pumping in her head with swift massive surges.

The sensation of being watched had not left her. Juliette felt the hairs prickle on the back of her neck. She held her breath, trying to listen. Was someone coming towards her? No. All she could hear was the rain.

She was intensely vulnerable crouching here in the long grass. She began to crawl forward. As she did so, Juliette heard a sound that pierced her. A tortured rising shriek, inhumanly loud.

All the fears of the day rose up in her mind. The bomb on the bus and the foul-tasting water. Her mother babbling about dark wizards and witchcraft.

The shrieking grew louder.

She scrambled frantically through the grass, the noise washing over her. She tried to flee from it, to flee the big white house. She would be safe if she could only get back to the woods. Please, God, let me get back to the woods.

The noise was getting louder now, as if some great beast had been unleashed into the night and set to hunt her down.

Panic saturated Juliette's mind. She became a simplified organism, an animal intent on escape. Pushing through the tall grass, she burst on to a hard flat surface and with a jolt of terror she realised she was back on the tarmac.

She thought she was fleeing the house, but in her confusion she had turned full circle and come back to it.

The howling was impossibly loud now and something came rushing at Juliette out of the night, a sweeping predatory shape. It was huge and its eyes glowed like something from hell.

Fear closed down Juliette's brain as she curled up into a ball and lay there like a rabbit on the motorway.

The monster thundered towards her, screaming in a torrent of noise that tore at her ears. Juliette covered them and gabbled a prayer as the thing loomed over her and then swept past, clawing its way into the night sky.

The earth trembled with its passing. She saw streaks of blue brightness, like flames. She lay there huddled on the tarmac in the rain. Juliette wasn't certain how long she lay there, as the trembling slowly subsided, both in the air above her and in her terrified mind.

Then she felt familiar hands on her face and looked up to see her mother looking down at her, her plump face taut with concern, her Tibetan hat askew on her head.

'Are you all right, dear?'

'You were right, Mum,' said Juliette. She was surprised at how calm her voice sounded.

'Right about what, dear?'

'This house being protected by magic.'

'Magic?'

'Yes! And I believe you now. Because I saw it. I saw it

with my own eyes. It was some kind of . . . I don't know . . . Some kind of dragon or demon or something.'

Her mother looked at her sourly. 'It was an aeroplane, dear.'

'An aeroplane?'

'Yes. You were lying in the middle of a runway. It was an aeroplane taking off. My hat's a sopping ruin,' she added. She took it off and wrung the water out of it, spattering emphatic drops on the tarmac. She sighed. 'Really, dear. You're right in the middle of a runway. Didn't you realise? The plane was coming straight at you . . .'

Abruptly her voice began to tremble. She looked at Juliette, her lips trembling too. 'Juliette, love. You could have got yourself hurt.'

Juliette sat up on the runway as her mother hugged her. Now that the fear was ebbing from her mind, she felt ridiculous. Her mother was snuffling on her shoulder, her smelly, goaty, Tibetan hat squarely in Juliette's face.

'I know I was supposed to stay in the car,' said her mother, her voice shaking. 'But I had to follow you, dear. Who knows what might have happened to you?'

Juliette accepted the embrace woodenly. She could see the barnlike building over her mother's shoulder, and now she remembered with embarrassment that Christopher had told her it was a hangar.

There were rapid footsteps on the tarmac and they both looked up. A man was running towards them from the direction of the hangar.

Juliette couldn't see his face but then a flicker of dreadlocks in the moonlight revealed that it was Tregemmon. 'It was an aeroplane,' called Juliette's mother helpfully.

'I heard,' said Tregemmon. 'Some kind of small jet. A Lear or something.' He crouched beside the women and shook his head. 'This is not good. It's not good at all.'

'Does this mean they've escaped?' said Juliette.

'It looks like it. Flown the coop.' He stared at the big white house and then he smiled. 'But I've got Danny's girlfriend. She's by the swimming pool safe and sound. Apart from her, I guess we're the only ones here.'

He was helping Juliette to her feet when they heard the gunshots from the house.

The shots came from the far side of the house. Tregemmon made Juliette and her mother stay with the drugged girl by the swimming pool. After a few minutes, which passed in absolute silence, Juliette decided to follow him.

Leaving her mother hissing for her to come back, she hurried around the long, curving, white wall.

She found Danny Bailey and Tregemmon standing by the front door of the house. The door was a solid rectangle of oak with jutting metal handles. Just inside it was another door. She stared at it.

The inner door was made of panels of glass and wrought iron alternating to form an elegant pattern. But the glass panels had been blasted out of it and the narrower bands of iron looked like twisted ribbons. They had been misshapen by some kind of blast.

'What happened?' Tregemmon turned to look at her.

'They set a trap for us,' he said. He opened the inner door and Juliette felt a quick flare of shock when she saw a shotgun pointing at her.

But there was no one holding the shotgun. It had been wired to the backs of two metal-framed chairs. The chairs had been wedged against the walls of the hallway so that the gun was firmly fixed in position, pointing at chest level at anyone stepping through the front door.

This ghoulish mechanism was apparently activated by a loose strand of wire looping from the trigger guard of the shotgun to the handle of the inner door.

Then a disturbing thought occurred to Juliette. 'Who set the gun off?'

'Our mate Christopher,' said Tregemmon in an uninflected voice. 'Tell her, Danny.'

'It was like he stepped through the door,' said Danny. 'But suddenly he was jerked back, just as the shotgun went off. So it missed him.'

Tregemmon grinned mirthlessly. 'That's the Edge. He hasn't lost his knack.'

'What happened was that friendship band on his wrist, you know the one the bikers gave him? Well, it got snagged. It snagged on the handle of the outer door just as he stepped through. And it kind of jerked him back, just in time.'

'It still wasn't a very pleasant experience,' said a voice. Juliette looked up and felt a pleasant warm rush as Christopher stepped into the hall. He walked up and inspected the chairs where the shotgun was fastened.

'Not as unpleasant as it would have been if you hadn't pulled that trick,' said Tregemmon.

'It wasn't a trick,' said Christopher bitterly. 'It just happened.'

'Whatever. All I know is that if I met a bunch of bikers they'd smash my car up and take my wallet. You – they give a friendship band to you and it saves your life.'

Juliette couldn't tell if Tregemmon was being coolly sardonic or if there was a genuine note of admiration in his voice. 'The Edge has a knack,' he said.

'If I've got a knack why are we in the shit like this?' said Christopher savagely.

'Not entirely in the shit,' said Tregemmon. Just then Juliette's mother came around the corner. For some extraordinary reason she had snapped into her rare bossy mode. Juliette felt her cheeks flare with embarrassment as she marched over to them and said, 'That poor girl will catch pneumonia lying on the wet grass. Someone has to help me carry her inside.'

'Miranda!' said Danny Bailey. His eyes gleamed with excitement in his plump face and he turned and ran off with surprising speed, back around the house towards the swimming pool.

As soon as he was gone, Juliette's mother lost all hint of bossiness and burst into tears. 'What's happened to Emily? What's happened to my little girl?'

Christopher's voice was tight with anger. 'I'm afraid we're too late,' he said bluntly. 'They're gone.'

'How can you be so sure?'

They had followed Christopher into the kitchen. 'You'd

better sit down, Mrs Race,' he said. 'This might be a bit upsetting.'

Juliette's mother seated herself obediently at the big oval of the kitchen table. Juliette watched, feeling an almost unbearable apprehension as Christopher set an object down on the table. It was a circular piece of white cardboard with writing on it.

Large, childish handwriting.

'What is it?' said Tregemmon.

'It's the lid of an ice-cream carton. Emily has written a note on the inside of it. A note to us. She hid it, wedged under the door of the pantry.'

'Clever kid,' said Tregemmon quietly. 'She must have worked out that we'd open every door in the place looking for her. We open that one and it sticks and, bingo, we find the note. Clever kid.' Then he added, 'Brave, too.'

Juliette's mother began to sob as she read the note. Juliette hurried over to the table and read it over her shoulder:

Dear Mum,

Please don't follow me any more. I know you are following because Mr Leiber is getting stronger. He operates on belief. Your belief is making him stronger. Please stay away.

Christopher will understand. (Christopher – I have a general idea on how the mechanism behind this might operate. Self-hypnosis/internal metaphor. No time to go into detail now. Hope to talk to you about it soon, though.)

I don't know where they're taking me, but from the way they talk it's in another country.

Emily

Her mother slumped forward on the kitchen table, her shoulders pulsing as she wept. Juliette sat beside her and tried to comfort her. There were tears gathering in her own eyes, though. She forced herself to stay calm, to talk. 'Tregemmon, where do you think they might have gone?'

'Well, it was some kind of small jet and the range on

those things is extravagant. I hate to say it, but she could be just about anywhere in the world by tomorrow.'

Juliette's mother began to sob more loudly, a heaving bundle in Juliette's arms.

'Well, we'll just have to find her, then,' said Christopher quietly.

PART TWO

HALLOWEEN HOTEL

THIRTY-ONE

The awful thing was, for longer than she cared to remember, Juliette had resented her little sister and longed to be rid of her.

Now that it had happened, she felt an almost irrational burden of guilt.

'What's the matter?' said Chris. As usual, he had immediately sensed that something was wrong. It could be an irritating habit, but at the moment it was very comforting indeed.

'Just thinking about Emily,' she said, leaning towards him. They were in the row of seats on the left of the plane, Chris sitting by the aisle, Juliette beside the window. That had been a waste – she had hardly glanced out since they took off eight hours ago.

Chris had taken her hand. 'We *will* find her,' he said. 'We will get there in time. In the meanwhile just try not to think about her. I know that's easier said than done, but –'

'Mind if I join you?' said Tregemmon.

He had wandered down from the front of the plane, where he was seated with Danny Bailey and Miranda in one of the middle rows.

'Sorry to barge in,' he said, 'but I couldn't stand it another minute.'

'Why?' said Juliette. 'What's the matter?'

'Danny and Miranda.' Tregemmon's face creased with amusement. 'They're such a couple of love bunnies that they've virtually cleared that half of the plane. Everybody's upgraded to club class.'

Juliette felt a small smile twitch her lips. She peered

along the length of the jumbo to the seats where Danny and Miranda sat, entwined in each other's arms. 'It's natural enough, considering they've been reunited after such a traumatic experience.'

'It's natural enough,' said Tregemmon. 'But when he started calling her the Girl with Eyes like Rain I thought I'd better get out before I started to puke.'

Juliette smiled again. She began to feel a little better. She turned to Christopher. He seemed to be fast asleep, his rapid eye movements visible on his closed lids.

Looking at him, she felt a flow of love and a strange certainty. If anyone could get Emily back, it was this man.

Tregemmon left them and Juliette sank back into her seat. She closed her eyes and let the endless white-noise roar of the engines lull her into something resembling sleep as the big jet began its descent over the desert.

Three thousand feet below, Sharleen Gilmore was waking up to face another working day.

It was a full two hours before her shift was due to start, but Sharleen couldn't sleep. She got up and paced by the windows of her duplex. She studied the heavy mist of condensation on the glass.

She couldn't sleep for worrying about the little English girl.

Behind her in bed she heard Gord stirring. He propped himself up on one elbow and resumed their conversation of the night before in a sleepy voice. 'I told you not to get a job at that place.'

He had correctly read her posture, the worry in her. She felt a little spark of anger towards him.

He got up and put the coffee on. 'I told you it would give you the creeps working there. Get you imagining things.'

'I'm not imagining anything. This girl is in some kind of trouble. It was like she was trying to tell me something.'

'The kid's only problem is the hotel where she's staying,' murmured Gord, sipping his coffee.

* * *

212

The sky was a cool mysterious blue as they set off through the early-morning traffic on Route 95. It brightened rapidly as the sun rose, lifting like a big red balloon from the desert beyond the looming city.

The traffic steadily thickened as they turned off on to Rancho and picked up Highway 15. At Junction 39 they turned left and headed towards the Strip.

Sharleen stared sleepily out of the car window at the familiar glowing neon. It looked diluted and somehow sordid in the strengthening daylight.

Driving south, they passed the Sands and the Treasure Island and the Aladdin. Then they were there.

The Halloween Hotel was a massive structure. The entire building was surrounded by a huge orange façade made of some kind of industrial polymer. From a distance it looked like a giant basketball. But when you got closer you realised it was a giant pumpkin.

A jack-o'-lantern, with a huge curving grin carved in it, serrated with jagged fangs, surmounted by two rather crazy-looking diamond-shaped eyes.

The eyes and grin were brightly lit within, as if by some giant internal candle.

At the top of the building, the jack-o'-lantern wore a kind of crown or tiara around the circumference of its fat forehead, elaborately ornamented, featuring an astonishing variety of dancing chrome fiends and skeletons and gargoyles designed by Robert Williams.

Sharleen knew that the chrome tiara was there to conceal mundane things like satellite dishes and air-conditioning ducts, which might otherwise have spoilt the look of the jack-o'-lantern.

But somehow it always reminded her of the crown of thorns that Jesus wore in paintings of the Crucifixion.

Sharleen changed into her costume as quickly as she could. Then, bracing herself, stepped out into the milling activity of the hotel.

She made her way through the casino towards the restaurant. The hotel was designed so that to go just about

213

anywhere involved a journey through the casino.

Humphrey, the stickman at the craps table, nodded at her as she hurried past. He didn't look too happy. Perhaps because he was surrounded by a cluster of conventioneers, and this week's convention was a real woeful bunch of weirdos. They were here to celebrate the joys of something called ICSH.

Once out of the brightly lit activity of the casino, Sharleen expected to feel a little more relaxed. The Halloween had been designed so that its corridors were only dimly lit, with glowing jack-o'-lanterns set in recesses in the wall at intervals, and luminous skeletons flanking the elevators.

She usually found this pleasant. It was a safe kind of darkness, cosy but at the same time with a little excitement to it. A kind of kids-playing-hide-and-go-seek darkness.

But lately Sharleen didn't feel that velvety excitement. Just lately she had begun to find it all a little creepy.

It was all because of that English girl, although in fact the little girl had merely crystallised a feeling that had been growing in her ever since the convention had arrived.

Sharleen shivered a little in the air conditioning. Her costume was some designer's absurd notion, a confection of black leather and silk and fake fur. Sort of a combination of a witch and a scantily clad cavegirl, with a plunging neckline and black stockings.

The darkness diminished as Sharleen approached the dining area. The restaurant was a long curved room which occupied about a quarter of the giant pumpkin circumference of the hotel, set between the foyer and the kitchens. The light was better in here, with daylight coming in through the windows where the diners could watch the weary pageant of Vegas street life.

There were no windows in the casino, of course, because the gamblers weren't to be reminded of the passage of time.

Sharleen bustled to her waitress station, adjusting her costume, wondering all the while if she would see the little girl again today.

Judy Proudhorn was already at the waitress station,

wiping menus and checking that the busboys had rolled up the correct complement of cutlery in each big orange napkin ready for today's onslaught of customers.

As Sharleen approached the station she saw Judy dodge back to avoid a couple of conventioneers who were heading for the cheap self-service breakfast bar.

They were lean, gnarled men. Pale and furtive, they looked as if they'd just broken cover in a darkened forest.

'Ugh,' said Judy as Sharleen joined her. She made a retching gesture, hooking a finger into her open mouth. 'A couple more creeps from ICSH.'

No one who worked in the hotel seemed to know quite what ICSH stood for, but they were all agreed that the conventioneers were creeps.

'What do you think they're up to?' said Sharleen. She began to check the order books at the waitress station, selecting one that was still fat enough to write on easily, and then set about trying to find a pen that worked.

'My guess is S and M,' said Judy. 'Some kind of kinky sex convention. I saw some of the apparatus the porters were bringing in. It was outrageous, handcuffs and chains and stuff. Sicko.'

'Not as bad as that porno convention we had last February,' said Sharleen. 'Took weeks to get rid of the stains in the carpets. Yuk.' She stopped talking then, because on the other side of the restaurant she saw a couple sit down.

A young man and a little girl.

Sharleen stared at them and then said, 'Is that one of your tables?' There must have been a note of something in her voice, because Judy Proudhorn looked at her curiously. 'Yeah, why?'

'Mind if we trade? I want to look after them.'

'Be my guest. Care to tell me what's going on?' Then she saw the look of urgency in Sharleen's eye. 'OK. Fill me in later.'

Sharleen wondered if she was just imagining things. That was what Gord would say.

She forced herself to smile and speak in a normal tone of voice. She set the jug of orange juice down on the table. 'Good morning. I hope you're enjoying your stay at the Halloween. My name is Sharleen. You folks can either help yourselves at the breakfast bar or order à la carte. That means off the menu.'

'I know what it means,' said the little girl in a surly voice. 'I even know what à la mode means.'

'I'll have bacon and eggs and hash fries,' said the biker, breaking in. 'You don't do black pudding, do you?'

'I'm sorry, sir, no.'

'Never mind. And one helping of pancakes.'

'Blueberry,' added the little girl in a low, expressionless voice.

'Blueberry,' said the biker.

Sharleen wrote the order down, although she could hardly force herself to pay attention. She was desperately trying to think of some stratagem for getting the little girl on her own for a moment so she could ask if she was all right.

'And a pot of coffee,' added the biker.

'Thank you, sir. And anything else for you, miss?' Sharleen smiled at the little girl. She was aware that her smile was glassy and frozen. But it didn't matter because just then the little girl spilt her orange juice, sending a small wave of it across the table.

The biker cursed and shoved his chair back just as the juice reached him, splattering into his lap. 'Fuck,' he said.

'Here, let me,' said Sharleen, reaching into her pouch for one of the emergency mop-up cloths.

'No worries,' said the biker bad-temperedly. 'I've got it.' He began to wipe himself off with one of the paper napkins from the table. Sharleen turned her attention to mopping up the table. It took her only a few seconds and then she reached for her pad and pen.

But the pen was gone.

Sharleen was about to say something but she noticed the little girl looking at her in the strangest way. She didn't know what the little girl was trying to communicate but it was obviously very important.

Then Sharleen saw the pen.

It was on the floor under the table. She bent down to pick it up. She sensed the biker watching her ass as she crawled under the table. That's fine, she thought. Keep your attention on my ass.

Just don't notice what I've found down here.

There on the floor beside her pen was a piece of paper. A note.

Sharleen didn't dare read it. She stuffed it into her pouch and looked up furtively. Had the biker noticed anything? No. He was now preoccupied with wiping the orange juice off his leathers.

Sharleen's heart was pounding. She was sure her face was bright red. She stood up shakily. The little girl was staring down at the table and didn't look at her again.

Sharleen turned away and walked back towards the waitress station. She forced herself to act casual. But what she really wanted to do was rip open her pouch and read the note immediately.

When she got back to the waitress station, Judy Proud-horn was standing there, staring at her with enquiring eyes. Sharleen avoided those eyes. She sent the breakfast order through to the kitchen, then excused herself and hurried to the staff toilets.

She locked herself in a cubicle and took the note out of her pouch. It was folded in half. She unfolded it and read what was written there:

'Help. 572.'

Thirty-two

The numbers on the door were written in the big scary gothic style favoured by the Halloween. The numbers were hard to read in the dimly lit corridors of the hotel and were a perpetual nuisance to the staff.

Sharleen steeled herself, shifted the tray into her left hand and reached up and knocked on the door of room 572.

When the door opened, the first thing she noticed about the room was the eerie orange light that bathed it. It was just ordinary daylight of course, but tinted by the pumpkin-coloured glass of the hotel window.

It was an unsettling colour. Sharleen had once read that you got light just like it before a hurricane. Or was it an earthquake?

The man who'd opened the door stood with his back to the light, peering at Sharleen. Middle-aged, pot-bellied and balding, he was absolutely ordinary. Medium height and build, at first glance he looked like a small-time businessman in a cheap sour suit.

But then you looked again and it was almost as though the businessman was just a shell for something else.

He stepped back and gestured for Sharleen to enter the lounge. She stepped into the cool air-conditioned atmosphere of the big carpeted space. There was a television set on one side and the curved façade of a well-stocked bar on the other. It was the standard layout for a lounge in any one of the Halloween's luxury suites.

These suites were often comped to gamblers with big winnings, to keep them in the hotel and near the casino so that the house had a chance to get its money back.

But these people weren't gamblers.

218

The man stood watching Sharleen quietly. He reminded her of a hollow tree stump she'd once seen on a warm summer night during her Georgia childhood. The stump had fireflies inside it and through the knot holes in the old wood you occasionally caught an eerie glow, a flicker of the strange life stirring within.

Sharleen caught a similar flicker in this man's eyes as he studied her.

'I've brought the club sandwich you ordered, sir.'

'No one here ordered any sandwiches.'

Sharleen began to sweat. She tried to keep her voice calm. 'I'm sure they did, sir. Here's the order.' She showed him the room-service slip.

'Well, the order must be mistaken.' The man was staring at her now with those strange eyes, and the flicker had changed into a steady hard glow and he seemed to be staring right into her. Reaching inside her and seeing everything, every secret.

'I ordered the sandwich.' They both turned to see a girl saunter into the lounge from one of the adjoining bedrooms. She was a teenager, or perhaps in her early twenties, quite pretty but kind of grubby-looking. She wore a leather jacket and sunglasses and her hair was short and spiky. She was gnawing at the black-lacquered fingernails of one hand while she stared hungrily at the tray Sharleen was carrying.

The man relaxed. 'You should tell me these things, Nuala,' he said. 'I'm not a mind-reader you know.' He chuckled.

Sharleen went over to a low marble coffee table and set the tray down, silently thanking God that she'd taken the trouble to arrange a legitimate pretext for her visit.

She had promised Mendez the chef a date if he let her take the next room service order up to 572, and had waited half the day for an opportunity.

'I suppose I had better get this young lady a tip,' said the man. He disappeared through a door to the left. Sharleen felt an immediate sense of relief.

The girl called Nuala had swooped hungrily on the tray

of food. She was sitting on the couch, picking French fries off the platter and eating them with her fingers. She ignored Sharleen.

This was her chance. The little girl must be in here. She had to try to find her.

Sharleen knew the general layout of these suites. They were shaped like curved rectangles, following the contours of the hotel's giant pumpkin façade. Each contained three bedrooms. Sharleen took a deep breath and moved towards one of the bedrooms on the left, just as the door popped open. The man who stepped out was the biker.

His eyes instantly narrowed with suspicion. 'What are you doing here?'

'I orbered a samfwich,' said the girl from the couch, with her mouth full.

The biker stared hard at Sharleen. 'Don't I know you from somewhere?'

'Leave her alone, Lenny,' said the girl on the couch.

Lenny ignored her. 'Didn't you serve us this morning?'

'That's right, sir. Sorry about the orange juice.'

The biker brushed aside her attempt to be friendly. 'What are you doing in here?'

'I told you, Lenny, for God's sake. She brought me a club sandwich and chips. Here, have a chip.'

Lenny ignored the girl and stared at Sharleen coldly. 'I thought the bellhops brought the room-service orders.'

'They do normally, sir. But the hotel is so busy with the convention and everything that we're all helping out.' Sharleen's voice trembled. Her little speech sounded unconvincing even in her own ears.

Lenny's look of suspicion deepened. He opened his mouth, about to ask another question, when the door of the bedroom behind him opened. Sharleen's heart leapt as she saw the little girl step out.

She was carrying a stack of dirty plates and she gave Sharleen the unhappy look that had become so familiar. 'Get back in your bedroom,' said the biker.

'Now, Lenny,' said a voice heavy with authority. Sharleen turned to see that the strange man had come back from the master bedroom. He had a wallet in his hand.

'But she's supposed to stay in the bedroom, Mr Leiber.'

'Don't be so harsh, my boy. There's no need to keep Emily, er . . . "grounded" is I believe the expression. Of course, she *has* been a bad girl. But I certainly think we can let her out of her bedroom.'

The man called Mr Leiber opened the wallet and removed a thick wad of foreign-looking currency. He handed her twenty dollars. A generous tip but not an outstanding one. Over the years high rollers and stupid-drunk winners had given Sharleen vastly larger sums, before the casino had inexorably sucked their money back in again.

Sharleen didn't even like touching this man's money but she accepted the tip, folding the bills and putting them in her pouch. Her mind was working frantically. How could she get a moment alone with the little girl?

She had turned away from Sharleen now and was stacking the dirty plates on the bar. 'What are you doing there, Emily?' said Mr Leiber, his voice booming with false joviality.

'Just getting rid of Nuala's plates,' replied the little girl sulkily. 'It seems she can't eat anything except club sandwiches and chips, with a small gherkin impaled on a toothpick on the side. Her adventurous fascination with world cuisine is admirable but I don't want these things stinking out the room.'

Nuala shot the little girl a venomous look.

'All right, that's quite enough, Emily,' said Mr Leiber. 'If you don't behave yourself you're going back to your room. And as for world cuisine, this is Las Vegas, you know.'

These words were a meaningless echo in Sharleen's ears. All her attention was focused on the greasy plates stacked atop the marble bar. There was a white square of paper jutting out from under the bottom plate.

A note.

Sharleen hurried to the bar to grab the plates. She felt as if everyone in the room was watching her. Sweat prickled along her spine.

She bent over and picked up the plates with great care, sensing Mr Leiber behind her. She had the unaccountable, powerful impression that she'd blundered into a den of dangerous animals.

She could feel the man's eyes on her as she scooped the plates up, trying to look casual. Those weird eyes of his.

Don't let him see the note.

The note.

Where had it gone? It had been there a moment ago. It had been right under the stack of plates. Sharleen was certain she had seen it there.

Now it had vanished.

Her heart jerked. Things didn't just vanish. She could feel hot sweat forming on her body. What was going on?

Then she realised exactly what was going on. She could feel something under the stack of plates. A piece of paper. The note. She had picked it up. It was stuck to the bottom of the plates.

Everyone was staring at her now. Don't panic, she told herself. She held the plates carefully as she turned away from the bar. Her heart was slamming in her chest. She had the note.

No she didn't. The mayonnaise or whatever had stuck it to the plate had let go. The note was dropping.

There was nothing she could do to stop it.

The note was dropping away from the bottom of the plate. Floating out into the air. Into the eerie orange light of the room.

Into the full view of everyone.

And then the little girl sneezed. It was the loudest sneeze that Sharleen had ever heard. It sounded like a gunshot and everybody turned around to look at her.

And while they were looking, the note fell through the air. It fluttered across the dark marble of the bar. To Sharleen it almost seemed like a living thing. Wings of paper anxiously beating in a struggle to escape.

The note dropped out of sight behind the bar.

Sharleen couldn't believe her luck. It seemed that no one had seen it. They were all still looking at Emily. The little girl's sneeze was still echoing in the room.

'Oh, poor thing,' said Nuala, with horrible phoney-sounding sympathy. 'She must be catching a cold.'

Sharleen peered surreptitiously over the edge of the bar. The note was well out of sight, in a shadowy area of shelves where dusty, chrome ice buckets stood. No one would see it down there.

If there was one thing Sharleen had learnt in her years in Vegas, it was the cardinal rule of gambling. Quit while you're ahead.

She hadn't gotten the note, but she hadn't gotten caught, either. Her mission had been a partial success. She had learnt that the little girl was called Emily. And it was clear that these creepy people were holding her against her will.

Now she just had to get the hell out of here and get some help. Gord would know what to do.

She turned away from the bar, holding the stack of greasy plates. But, damn it, Mr Leiber had sensed that something was wrong.

'Can I help you, miss?' he said with horrible politeness. 'Have you lost something?'

He was walking over to the bar. Sharleen knew from her brief glimpse behind the bar that the note was well out of sight. No ordinary human being was likely to spot it. But she already sensed that this was no ordinary human being.

The big cold room seemed to have become completely silent. Leiber's face was in shadow and Sharleen couldn't see his eyes, and that was all the more frightening.

The silence seemed to be deepening in a strange way. Sharleen heard a roaring in her ears.

Then the silence was broken by the scratching of a key in a lock. The door of the suite opened and three men came bustling in.

Two of them were dressed in orange overalls. As they turned to face the Leiber guy, she saw that the overalls had the words SCHOOL BUS stencilled in big black letters on the back. Both of them looked very excited.

The third man was younger than the others, and much less athletic-looking. He had a pale sweaty face and was wearing some kind of green army-surplus jacket with a hood on it. He followed the school-bus men into the room, looking kind of nervous.

Sharleen thanked God for the interruption.

'You'll never guess who we bumped into downstairs,' said the big school-bus man excitedly. He slapped the pale-faced guy on the back. 'Tell them who you are.'

'My name is Dominic Wheatabix,' said the pale-faced guy.

Mr Leiber held up his hand for silence. 'Gentlemen. Excuse me for interrupting you, but you might not have noticed that we have company.'

The men all stopped and turned to stare at Sharleen. The pale nervous one suddenly looked even more nervous.

'I'm sorry, Mr Leiber,' said the school-bus man.

Sharleen decided to get out while the going was good. She took the plates and walked across the living room, the haunted orange light shining in on her.

She could feel the little girl's eyes on her back. Watching as Sharleen left her there, in room 572.

THIRTY-THREE

As soon as the waitress left, Emily felt very alone. It was a sensation like stepping suddenly into cold, deep water.

Something must have shown on her face, because Comstock, the big school-bus man, suddenly winked at her and said, 'Hey, cheer up, little 'un.'

His small rodent-faced friend Brilly sneered and said, 'Oh, leave her alone. She doesn't like us. She thinks we're sickos.'

He glared at Emily. 'You ought to know one thing. You're actually very lucky you fell in with us.'

'That's right,' said Comstock. 'You could have been kidnapped by really unsavoury characters who would do terrible things to a little girl.'

'Perverts,' added Brilly.

'That's right. We're not like that. We're normal.'

'Normal mass murderers,' said Emily bleakly.

Mr Leiber interrupted. 'Comstock. Brilly. Should we be having this discussion in front of a perfect stranger?' He turned to the plump young man in the anorak. 'Who exactly are you?'

'Er, as I was saying, my name is Dominic Wheatabix.'

'My God, what a name.'

'I'm a journalist. I work for a limited-edition videozine called *Breakfast Serial*. I've been voted journalist of the year writing on a specialist subject in the underground media awards.'

'Delighted to meet you,' said Mr Leiber cordially. 'Check him over, Lenny.'

The biker hurried into his bedroom and came back with a small black box not much bigger than a remote control.

Emily could see that there was some kind of LED readout on it.

Lenny walked over to the young man in the anorak, who was staring up at him with an expression of fear on his face. Lenny swept the box over the chubby young man as if he was anointing him with some kind of invisible spray. He studied the LED, frowning, then looked at Mr Leiber. 'He's clean,' he said reluctantly. 'No recording devices.'

The chubby young man stared at them, his face pale. 'I wouldn't try and sneak anything in here. I made it very clear to Mr Comstock and Mr Brilly that I wouldn't record anything they said without their express consent.' He cleared his throat. 'I wouldn't do anything to jeopardise my journalistic privileges.'

'It's more than your privileges that would be jeopardised, mate,' said Lenny sourly.

'I've been looking forward all year to the big gathering at the Halloween,' continued the young man.

'Haven't we all?' said Comstock, making an obvious effort to smooth things over. He went into one of the bathrooms and came out holding a sheet of paper covered with typewritten words, folded to form a crude leaflet. Through the open door Emily could see stacks of such leaflets piled beside the sink.

'We're giving a talk on abduction techniques this evening. You might like to attend.'

'I'd be delighted to.'

'We're going to present it at the Evening Gala just before we do our big stage number.'

Dominic Wheatabix nodded eagerly. 'The rumour around the hotel is that you're going to . . .' and then his voice sank so low that Emily couldn't hear what he was saying. But he kept glancing over at her, as if she was the subject of the discussion.

Comstock concluded the whispered conversation by announcing loudly, 'And it will be the most memorable event of the convention.'

'But aren't you facing some stiff competition?'

'Competition from stiffs, you mean,' said Comstock, and

he and Brilly chuckled, perhaps a trifle nervously.

'But seriously,' said Dominic Wheatabix. He took out a notepad and a pen. 'I understand that the Talbot twins have something pretty special planned.'

'Retards,' said Comstock venomously.

'On the contrary, the twins have a very high reputation in their chosen field.'

Emily was trying to pay close attention to this conversation, to glean some kind of clue to her own fate. But she was distracted by Mr Leiber. A strange expression had come over his face, a kind of watchful wrath, as if he knew something was wrong, but he wasn't quite certain what it was. He wandered restlessly around the suite.

Now his wanderings had carried him to the bar. Emily's heart began to triphammer in her chest. She tried not to stare as Mr Leiber bent over the bar and peered behind it.

'Why, look at this,' he said.

Emily squirmed internally as he bent over to pick something up. A folded piece of white paper. He had found the note.

Mr Leiber came out from behind the bar. Everyone was watching him. He took a pair of reading glasses out of his pocket and put them on. Then he turned his attention to the note. After a second he lowered it and glanced at Emily.

'What a bad girl,' he said, shaking his head.

'What does it say?' demanded Nuala.

Mr Leiber began to read from the note. ' "Dear Sharleen, Is that really your name? It makes you sound like some kind of hillbilly maiden. Anyway, thank you for helping me. But the first thing I must tell you is you are risking your life. In fact, and there is no gentle way of breaking this to you, but ICSH stands for the International Conference for Serial Homicide. That's right. Your hotel is playing host to a convention of ruthless cold-blooded serial killers." '

The men in the room all chuckled but they immediately fell silent when Mr Leiber looked up sharply from the note. 'Sharleen . . .?' he said.

'That was that waitress,' said Comstock, obviously

bewildered. 'The one who was just here.'

'Yes. Lenny, go after her, quickly.'

Lenny got up, muttering. 'I knew something was wrong the instant I saw the bitch.' He left the room, slamming the door behind him.

Mr Leiber glanced at Emily. She stood there helpless as he returned to reading the note. ' "Please act quickly. This evening I'll be dressed up in some infantile child-beauty pageant costume and then there will be some business with shotguns. Something very inventive, I'm sure" . . .' Leiber paused for a moment and chuckled. 'You'll love this bit, Brilly.' He returned to the note, smiling. ' "These people are severely disturbed and obsessional. Their obsession takes the form of ever-increasing elaboration. Please pass that insight on to my sister Juliette, if you ever see her. Tell her I am trying to 'think positive' in the jargon. I have read about hostage psychology and I know that maintaining a positive outlook is essential. PS – If you run into Christopher Matthew, please tell him that I think I've worked out –" '

Mr Leiber fell silent. The smile faded from his face.

'Worked out what?' said Nuala.

' ". . . worked out the source of Mr Leiber's power. Perceptual flicker effect, cf. computer time sharing." '

Brilly wrinkled his nose as if he'd smelt something disgusting. 'Flicker effect? Computer time sharing? What's that supposed to mean?'

Mr Leiber crumpled the note in his fist. He didn't look at Emily and she was grateful for that. 'It means our young guest has been observing far too much. I'm afraid the time has come for a parting of the ways, my friends. Nuala and I are going to take our rental car and venture forth into the Mojave Desert.'

'Wicked,' said Nuala, hopping to her feet in her first display of energy for several days. 'I'll go and get packed.'

Brilly looked pale and worried. 'But you can't leave. You'll miss the big show tonight.'

'I'm afraid I am. Nuala and I must depart.'

'But you'll miss the show,' he said wheedlingly.

'Mr Leiber may be leaving but I will be here,' said the young man called Dominic Wheatabix. No one paid any attention to him. He shrugged. 'Do you mind if I use the bathroom?'

'No, of course not,' replied Brilly distractedly. 'Grab one of our programmes while you're in there.'

The young man who called himself Dominic Wheatabix nodded and got up from the couch. As he rose, he tugged his anorak closer around him as if he, too, found it uncomfortably cold in the air-conditioned room.

He glanced briefly at Emily as she was hustled off to her bedroom. Did she see a gleam of sympathy in his eyes? Then he was gone, into the gleaming white and chrome enclosure of the bathroom.

As he shut the bathroom door behind him, he heard Brilly saying, with a hurt note in his voice, 'But you must stay for the party. And what about the awards banquet?'

Then the door was shut and he was alone and, for the first time in what seemed like hours, he could breathe easily again.

He leant on the sink and stared at his reflection in the mirror. What am I doing here? he thought.

You're brave, said a voice in his head. You're brave and you're trying to help that little girl.

It was Miranda's voice.

Danny Bailey savoured the sensation for a moment. He could feel her pride in him – and her fear for him. And, underneath all that, a strong steady tow of love.

How could she love a face like this? thought Danny, staring at his plump features in the mirror. Then he turned on the taps, letting hot water flow until steam had grown thick on the mirror. He extended one stubby finger and wrote on the steamy glass. Three large sprawling numbers:
'572'.

He filled his vision with the room number. Then he filled Miranda's vision with it. When he was sure she'd seen it, he turned off the taps and wiped the mirror clean with his sleeve.

THIRTY-FOUR

Comstock and Brilly and Mr Leiber were huddled together when he came out. They were standing near the bar, where they'd found Emily's note. They all looked up as Danny emerged from the bathroom.

He felt a powerful buzz of paranoia, realising uncomfortably that he'd forgotten to grab some programmes, as Brilly had suggested.

It didn't matter. Nothing mattered. He was safe now. He'd sent the room number to Miranda. Tregemmon would be here soon. Danny might not know how to handle these people, but Tregemmon –

All at once Danny Bailey felt that he'd made a terrible mistake. Mr Leiber glanced around sharply at him. He turned away from the bar and began walking across the room towards Danny, staring at him in the strangest way.

He paused a few feet away and smiled. When he spoke his voice was mild and pleasant. 'Have you ever heard of someone called Dr Buckminster?'

'Yes, of course,' said Danny quickly. Mr Leiber peered at him.

'Have you really? Well, then, perhaps you can answer this question. There was a camera crew which was scheduled to interview him just before we left England. I don't suppose you'd know anything about that camera crew?'

Mr Leiber spoke so softly that Danny could scarcely hear him over the pounding of his own heart. 'Now, what did you say your name was?'

Danny fought to keep his voice steady. 'Dominic Wheatabix.'

'You see,' mused Mr Leiber, 'I'm certain that someone

with that name was supposed to come and interview the good doctor.'

Danny's mind raced. 'Yes,' he said, improvising desperately. 'That's right. But we were delayed. We had a flat tyre.'

Mr Leiber nodded thoughtfully. 'That certainly would be one plausible explanation for the camera crew's failure to turn up.'

He glanced away from Danny and watched Comstock and Brilly, who were still standing by the bar reading the note. 'There is, however, another explanation,' he said quietly.

Danny began to lose control. His words came out as a rattling stammer. 'W-what do you mean?'

'I mean that, if someone was clever enough, they might have got the information about the big convention at the Halloween from Dominic Wheatabix and put two and two together and followed us here.'

He turned back to stare at Danny and Danny could hardly look into the dark inferno of those eyes.

'Which would mean that the camera crew ran into some acquaintances of mine. Some very old acquaintances. Including a man called Tregemmon.' He spoke the name with great force, peering at Danny keenly. 'Rather a strange name, isn't it? And if Tregemmon is here then so is someone called Christopher Matthew.'

Suddenly there was a flicker of uncertainty on Leiber's face. 'And if Christopher is here then we really must be going. Swiftly.' He turned to the open bedroom door and bellowed 'Nuala!'

'I'm packing.'

'Hurry, my dear.' Mr Leiber smiled indulgently and then turned to Danny Bailey.

Just then the telephone rang, sounding brutally loud in the quiet room.

Mr Leiber went to the coffee table, moving in a leisurely fashion, and picked up the phone. He listened, expressionless, and then said, 'I suppose you'd better come back up, then.'

He hung up and turned to the others.

'Bad news,' he said. 'That was Lenny downstairs. He's unable to find that interfering waitress.'

'But she doesn't know anything, does she?' said Comstock.

'After all, she never got the note,' said Brilly.

'Possibly.' Mr Leiber turned back to Danny Bailey. 'In any case, I'd hate for you to think that we'd forgotten you,' he said. 'Comstock? Brilly?'

'Yes, sir?'

'I think we'd best get rid of this young man.'

'Get rid of him?'

'As soon as possible.'

'But he's supposed to be making a programme about us.'

'I suspect he's misled you grievously in that respect.'

The next moment Danny found himself slammed down on to the carpet, trying to work out what had happened. For a moment he thought he'd received an electric shock. One powerful enough to knock him off his feet.

Then he looked up and saw Comstock towering over him.

It took Danny a moment to realise that Comstock had hit him. The big, dull-looking man had crossed the room with frightening speed and knocked him down.

Danny struggled to catch his breath. The blow had smashed the air out of his lungs. He was just managing one retching inhalation when Comstock bent over and pulled him to his feet. Danny tried to resist but he was bonelessly weak. The big man propelled him towards the bathroom without difficulty.

As he shoved Danny through the door, Comstock turned and called over his shoulder. 'I'm taking him into the bathroom. We'll do it in there.'

'Yeah, yeah, right,' called Brilly impatiently.

Comstock shoved him into the bathroom. Danny turned to fight back. He hit the big man. Comstock just shrugged off the blow. He pushed Danny to the floor.

Danny crashed down, bright chrome and gleaming

surfaces whirling around him. He barely missed smashing his head against the heavy white bowl of the toilet. He tried to get up, but Comstock put a foot down on his belly.

Danny struggled feebly as Brilly stepped into the bathroom and closed the door.

'I think we should give him a goodbye kiss,' said Comstock, sounding a little breathless with the effort of holding Danny down.

'Yeah, whatever,' said Brilly bad-temperedly. 'Let's just get on with it.'

'Have you got the kisser with you?' said Comstock.

Brilly brightened slightly. 'It just so happens that I have.' He took something out of his pocket. It was flowing and translucent. The bathroom light gleamed on it. Brilly stretched it between his hands so that Danny could get a good look at it.

A plastic bag.

They grabbed his head.

THIRTY-FIVE

'Room 572?' said Juliette.

'Are you sure?' said Tregemmon.

Miranda nodded. 'Absolutely. I saw Danny write it in the frost on a window.'

'Frost on a window?' said Tregemmon. He leant against a slot machine, shaking his head. 'I know it gets cold in these air-conditioned gin palaces but that's absurd.'

Miranda shrugged nervously.

Juliette moved back to make way for a group of elderly people in leisure suits who were hellbent on getting to the roulette wheel. Christopher had to move as well. The people were very brusque, rude almost, in their hurrying to get to the gambling. They were like a famished group of refugees hurrying to a sumptuous supper – or like cattle stampeding towards the edge of a cliff.

Juliette was fascinated by the behaviour of the gamblers. Fascinated and not a little horrified. Ever since landing in Las Vegas she had felt that she had been exposed to human obsession in its most primal form; the eagerness of the new arrivals to dash themselves on the rocks of the house percentage was truly awesome.

The gambling madness began at the airport, itself a haven for games of chance, and escalated steadily as Juliette's party had approached the Strip.

Now they were standing in a little telephone alcove adjacent to the casino at the Halloween Hotel. Even in here there were slot machines interspersed between the telephone cubicles.

Tregemmon didn't budge for the surge of impatient octogenarian gamblers and earned himself some hostile frowns.

'It looked like frost on a window,' said Miranda suddenly, 'but perhaps it was steam on a mirror.'

'She only gets general visual impressions,' explained Christopher. 'They have to be filtered through her own brain, her own mind and memories.'

'But you're sure about that room number?' said Tregemmon laconically.

'Absolutely. Five seven two.'

Tregemmon nodded; then he grinned at Christopher. 'Looks like you get to stay here with the girls. Try not to get into trouble.' He smiled again, then he was gone, striding across the casino and off into one of the dark side corridors, the swaying motion of his raincoat on his narrow shoulders echoing the sway of his dreads.

'He thinks that he's starring in a western,' said Christopher admiringly. He turned and smiled at Juliette. 'Mind you, if he thinks that way, maybe he is.'

Juliette snorted impatiently. She'd have no truck with this New Age theologising. Sometimes it seemed that Christopher had simply taken up where her mother had left off, spouting mystical nonsense.

For a moment she felt a flicker of curiosity about how her mother was, back at home in England.

In some ways *she* had the hardest job, just sitting and waiting.

Waiting to hear about Emily.

Juliette couldn't bear to think of Emily, so she steered her thoughts to other subjects. She turned around, surveying the activity in the casino behind her.

'What sort of mentality could fall for the lure of gambling?' she said. She glared at the bustle around the gaming tables. The whole ethos of gambling irritated her. The ridiculous human waste involved.

'In many ways it's a worse addiction than any drug,' said Christopher.

'But the whole thing is so transparently a swindle. What is the appeal?'

'Well, here's your chance to find out.' Christopher handed her a paper cup, brimming with silver coins. He

235

gave a second paper cup to Miranda. 'Silver dollars,' he said. 'To use in the slots.'

'I don't want to use them in the slots,' said Juliette tersely. Any such behaviour seemed to trivialise Emily's plight.

'Well, we really ought to try to blend in.'

Juliette was about to dig in her heels when Miranda reached out and touched her on the arm and said, 'Come on. Let's go and have a little flutter.'

She turned and walked away across the casino. Juliette followed her, trying not to think about what might be happening in room 572.

THIRTY-SIX

'I don't suppose you'd believe me if I told you I had nothing to do with that note,' said Emily.

Nuala shook her head. 'You're supposed to be a child prodigy,' she said. 'You'll have to do better than that.'

Emily changed the subject. 'You aren't really going to leave me here, are you?'

'Leave you here?'

'To become the latest victim of those oafs Comstock and Brilly.'

Nuala shrugged. 'I go where Mr Leiber goes. I do what he tells me to do.' She began stuffing more clothes into her suitcase in a haphazard fashion.

The little girl sighed and wandered over and sat on the edge of the bed beside her.

'If you're going to make loud sighing noises you can go back outside in the lounge and stay with the school-bus boys.'

'No, thank you,' said Emily quickly.

'All right, then. If you're going to stay in here you might as well make yourself useful. Help me pack.'

'All right.' Emily frowned at the piles of belongings still waiting to be packed. Clothes, CDs, books and magazines were heaped at random around the room. 'Are you really taking all of this stuff?'

'It all fitted well enough when I came here from England,' said Nuala, a note of puzzlement creeping into her voice. She really was not terribly bright.

Even in her current state of fear, Emily felt a healthy contempt for the girl. She knew she could run rings around Nuala, whenever she wanted to.

'Well, obviously you've acquired rather a lot of things

237

since you've arrived here,' she explained patiently.

'Those are my convention souvenirs,' said Nuala as she continued packing her suitcase, cramming objects in unmethodically. 'I can't leave them behind.'

'It's either that or get another suitcase.'

Nuala paused, her eyes lighting up. 'Wait a minute. Didn't you bring a suitcase with you from England?'

'Of course not.' Emily rolled her eyes in disgust. 'I was kidnapped. Kidnapping doesn't generally involve a free set of matched luggage for the victim.'

'That's right, no point in giving you any,' said Nuala nastily. 'Since you won't be needing it.'

She examined the swelling pile of clothes in her bag and prodded it in an attempt to impose order.

'Face reality,' said Emily. 'You're going to have to leave some of this clobber behind.' She grabbed a stack of magazines called *Murder Can Be Fun*, which were protruding from the suitcase.

'Not those!' shrieked Nuala, snatching the magazines back.

They spilt on the floor and she cursed, bending over to pick them up. While she was occupied doing this, Emily moved cautiously to the suitcase and plucked something out from among the mass of clothes.

A small, red floppy disk.

She stepped away from the suitcase and hid the floppy disk under her jumper. At that exact moment Mr Leiber came into the room.

He had a curious look on his face, almost as if he had scented something in the current of refrigerated air circulating around the suite.

Emily could feel the floppy disk hidden under her sweater. It felt uncomfortably large and conspicuous.

But Mr Leiber turned to Nuala. The girl was trying to jab more magazines into the unyielding mass of clothes in her suitcase.

'Come along, my dear, time is of the essence.'

'I can't fit my stuff into this bag,' squealed Nuala. 'It's not possible.'

'Then we shall borrow a bag from Brilly or Comstock. But we must be going.'

He stepped out of the room as silently as he had entered, leaving the door open. Nuala went on cursing and wrestling with her suitcase.

Emily ignored her. She was listening instead to a strange noise coming through the open door. A floundering, thumping noise emanating from somewhere in the suite.

Thump thump thump.

Emily didn't know what the noise was or what it signified, but for some reason she found it frightening.

It was a rhythmic sound. But it seemed to be getting weaker, like a mechanism winding down, and somehow that made it worse.

Thump thump thump.

Danny kicked at the bathroom door. He knew that soon he would be too weak to even do that. The kicking wasn't likely to do any good, but he had to try something.

He had to try to stop what was happening to him.

Bright colours flashed behind Danny's eyes. Fireworks exploded in his brain as his lungs flared helplessly, trying to suck in air that wasn't there. Just in front of Danny, an inch from his nose, a whole universe of cool sweet air existed.

But not for him.

His own breath, lethally rich in carbon dioxide, flapped wetly against the plastic bag. A horrid gasping noise filled his ears, inescapable inside the sealed world of the bag.

Danny kept kicking feebly at the door. Perhaps someone would hear him.

Comstock and Brilly had tied him carefully, in such a way that he could see the mirror. That had been Brilly's idea: 'Let him watch himself. Just like that film, what was it?'

'*Eyes Without a Face*, directed by Georges Franju.'

'No it wasn't. It was *Peeping Tom*, directed by Michael Powell.'

'It doesn't matter which movie it was. We can argue about it later. But let him *watch his own death*.'

'Absolutely.'

They secured Danny to the towel rail with tightly knotted towels, soaked in water to turn them into unyielding knots.

Then they left him there with the plastic bag sealed over his face. All he could do was kick at the bathroom door, each kick more feeble than the last. Kick and stare into the mirror, just as Brilly had wanted.

The face in the mirror was an eerie writhing shape. Bug-eyed and blue.

Whose face was it? Danny struggled to remember.

Blue.

Miranda stared at the slot machine in front of her. The spinning symbols behind the narrow window slowed down, steadied, and locked into place. Three cartoon skulls in a row. The other symbols on this machine were jagged black silhouettes of cats and witches and the plump orange sphere of a grinning pumpkin. But no other combination was worth quite as much as the three skulls.

Three blue skulls.

There was something about that shade of blue. Miranda stared at it. Why was it so strange?

She had a crawly sensation of *déjà vu*. An image tried to surface in her mind. Then she was momentarily distracted by the winnings spilling into the silver tray in front of her. Jackpot.

Juliette stared over her shoulder as silver dollars seemed to spill endlessly into the tray of the slot machine. But all Miranda could see was the skulls. Something about the peculiar blue . . .

Then she saw it again, in a flash like memory. A hideous blue shape. A contorted face, tongue lolling between cyanotic lips. The face the same eerie blue as the skulls on the slot machine.

The features of the face were so distorted it took her a moment to recognise them.

Danny.

Miranda turned and ran for the elevators. She didn't hear Juliette calling out behind her.

THIRTY-SEVEN

'Emily, come out here, will you?'

His voice was polite and friendly but Emily felt a cold thrill of fear.

She stepped out of the bedroom with trepidation, peering up at the grown-ups gathered around her.

Someone had fetched sheets from one of the bedrooms. The big white sheets were spread over the carpet at one end of the lounge. The end where Emily was standing.

Opposite her, Brilly was fumbling with a small domestic video camera while Comstock emerged from his bedroom with a long rectangular cardboard box of the kind used by florists to protect expensive blooms.

There was no sign of the pale young man in the anorak who had been here a few minutes earlier. And Emily noticed that the thumping sounds were no longer coming from the bathroom. Somehow there was something horrible about this new silence.

Nuala and Mr Leiber were walking towards the door of the room, Nuala clumsily dragging her suitcases.

'Don't forget to burn the sheets afterwards,' said Mr Leiber over his shoulder.

'We won't,' said Comstock, beginning to open the long cardboard box.

'And don't forget to leave the hotel the instant you're finished.'

'Do we have to?' said Brilly. There was the hint of a whine in his voice. He opened the video camera and took out the cassette. 'I want to see the big show tonight.'

'There isn't going to be any big show tonight. I've made a few phone calls and I've advised your brethren to flee.'

'But why?' said Brilly. He slammed the cassette back

into the camera petulantly. Emily thought for a moment that he was going to stamp his feet.

'Because,' said Mr Leiber patiently, 'I feel it is no longer safe here. The forces of what we laughingly call law and order will soon be swarming over the place. Personally I shall be long gone, with Nuala in tow, and I don't really care one way or the other whether everyone else at the convention is arrested or killed. As no doubt they shall be if they don't heed my warnings. As *you* shall be, Comstock and Brilly, if you don't heed my warnings.'

'All right, no need to be nasty,' said Comstock in a shocked voice. He had paused in his unpacking of the box, which was now open to reveal something that definitely wasn't a bunch of flowers. Emily could see that it was a long object covered in white wrapping paper.

Mr Leiber regarded him coolly with his expressionless eyes. 'The only reason I even deign to warn you is because I feel it would be a shame to waste the intricate forces, the gorgeously complex patterns of chance that have brought you all here to this hotel today. I take a certain almost paternal pride in having brought forth such a rich flowering of talent. I would like to linger here, like a man savouring an afternoon in his garden. But unfortunately we must go.'

He turned to Emily and bowed, an awkward wooden gesture. 'So it is goodbye to little Emily. Say goodbye, Nuala. We'll not be seeing her again.'

Nuala ignored him. 'If we're going to go, let's go.'

'All right,' said Mr Leiber equably, as he held the door open for her. She sighed and dragged her suitcases out into the hall. Mr Leiber gave Emily a stiff little wave and then went, too.

The door closed behind them and Emily was all alone with Comstock and Brilly.

Comstock was removing the wrapping paper from the long object. Now Emily could see that it was some kind of big gun with a polished walnut stock. A shotgun, the kind they called a pump-action.

As Comstock freed the gun of the last clinging bits of

wrapping paper, his friend Brilly moved around Emily, studying her at various angles through the viewfinder of the video camera.

'We never did a child prodigy before,' he remarked.

'What happened to Miranda?'

Juliette shook her head in exasperation. 'She just turned and ran off.'

'With no explanation?' said Chris.

'None at all.'

Chris was annoyed. 'You should have stopped her.'

Juliette shrugged helplessly. 'I couldn't go after her and just leave this.' They both looked at the glittering heap of coins in the maw of the slot machine. 'She'd just won the jackpot,' said Juliette. Christopher looked at her sardonically. 'There's a thousand dollars here,' she added feebly.

She was beginning to feel guilty about not simply abandoning the money and chasing after Miranda. She looked away from Chris and his sardonic eyes, staring around the casino.

The gaudy activity angered her. 'I hate this place. It's nothing but greed and stupidity and random numbers.'

'Maybe not as random as you think,' he said. 'If we could just look at it from the right angle we would probably see that the flow of winning and losing in here forms a beautiful pattern, complex but quite regular. Like a Mandelbrot.'

'Nonsense,' said Juliette. She was trying not to think about her little sister, somewhere upstairs in the hotel, above this arena of pathological greed and gimcrack glamour.

What was happening to Emily? She tried not to think about it and her nerves were being eaten raw by the effort.

Often so sensitive to her moods, Chris didn't seem to notice.

'It's all mathematics,' he said. 'The shifting statistical patterns that dictate who wins and who loses. You're just looking at it from the wrong angle.'

'You want to know what I'm looking at?' said Juliette. 'Those women over there.' She nodded at the group of old women by the slot machines in the next aisle. 'Look at the gloves they're wearing.'

The old women were all indeed wearing thick gardening gloves on one hand, as if it was a kind of uniform or badge of affiliation.

'You know why they're wearing gloves?'

Christopher grinned wickedly. 'So they won't get blisters from endlessly working the handles of the slot machines.'

'That's right. Otherwise they might have to momentarily desist from their folly while they had their wounded hand treated.' Juliette found herself wagging her head to make the point; her anxiety had found an outlet in rage. 'Gambling. What sort of idiot would fall prey to it?'

'Look,' said Chris. He put a hand on her shoulder. 'Don't worry about anything. Just stay here. I'll see if I can find Miranda.'

He moved off into the casino crowd and left her at the slot machine, standing guard over the pile of silver. The jackpot.

A thousand dollars.

Looking at the money made her feel anxious. Her mood veered from rage back to fear. She was alone. Where was Chris? What was happening upstairs?

The activity of the casino continued around her, heedless of her or her problems. Juliette turned away from it and, to escape, put a silver dollar into one of the slot machines.

THIRTY-EIGHT

Comstock began feeding shells into his shotgun.

Emily watched him while Brilly dodged around her, still trying to find the perfect angle with his camcorder.

'You're like something out of *Medium Cool*,' said Comstock impatiently.

'You mean *Blow Up*,' corrected Brilly.

'I mean *Medium Cool*,' insisted the big man. He finished loading the shotgun and walked ponderously towards Emily. 'You know, I can't believe Mr Leiber left us like that.'

'He hasn't merely left us,' said Brilly, settling on an angle and aiming the camcorder at Emily. 'He's effectively cancelled the entire convention.'

'I suppose he has.' Comstock came and settled on his big haunches, kneeling on the floor near Emily. The wrinkled expanse of a white bed sheet covered the carpet all around them.

'I say he's overreacting,' said Brilly.

Comstock nodded at Emily. 'So, should we save her for this evening?'

Brilly lifted his face from the camera, frowning. 'No . . . I don't think so. Let's get on with it. Let me just get this video sorted. How do you operate this thing?'

'I don't know. You're the film buff.'

'Me? Look who's talking.' Brilly pressed another button on the camera and nodded his head as the device came to life. 'We should have done this years ago.'

'We would have been more famous than Dr Buckminster.'

'Right.' Brilly spoke into the built-in microphone. 'Private video archive number seventeen, shotgun-splatter-effect experiment.' His voice was trembling a little with excitement.

Emily took a deep breath, and then began to speak. 'How dare you do this to a little girl!' she said. 'You are weak, craven, worthless men seduced by the meretricious glitter of a media-worshipping culture. Can't you even examine your own motives to the point of seeing how ridiculous you are?'

Comstock looked shocked but Brilly merely grinned. 'This is brilliant. Let's see if we can get it all on tape.'

'I wish Mr Leiber was here to see it,' said Comstock forlornly. At that moment there was a knock at the door.

Comstock and Brilly looked at each other. 'That's him! He's come back,' said Brilly happily. He set the camera down and trotted towards the door.

'Wait a minute, be careful,' said Comstock. He was hanging back from the door, the shotgun in his big hands. He didn't take his eyes off Emily. 'Ask who it is.'

'Ask who it is?' Brilly shook his head in weary disgust. 'Who else could it be?'

'Ask!'

Brilly sighed in disgust. 'Who's there?' he called. He put his ear to the door and listened as a muffled voice came through the wood. 'It's Lenny,' he said. He popped the door open.

The biker loomed in the doorway. 'I couldn't find that bitch of a waitress anywhere,' he said.

'It doesn't matter,' said Comstock. 'Emily isn't going to be passing her any more notes.' He nodded at the little girl, who stood on the wide white sheet, rooted with fear.

But Emily wasn't looking at Comstock. Her eyes were still on Lenny. The biker was behaving oddly. He was still standing in the doorway but he had turned around as if he'd heard something. His body was just beginning to tense up in response to what he saw when suddenly there was a thudding sound and he came tumbling into the room.

246

The sound came again and now Brilly was also reeling back into the room as if someone had punched him in the chest. He looked at Emily with a gaze of blank astonishment and then toppled to the floor.

After that, events began to move so quickly that Emily couldn't really absorb them in any coherent fashion. It was only later, when she had a chance to think, that she was able to piece them together into a proper sequence.

As Brilly fell to join Lenny on the carpet a shape came hurtling through the door. It was a man holding a gun. Apparently he had shot the others.

The man was black, with long dreadlocks which splashed out dramatically from his head as he threw himself into the room. He was wearing a raincoat which flapped out on either side of him like wings.

As he came hurtling into the room, Comstock responded with astonishing speed. He flung himself behind an armchair and crouched there, concealed and protected. He started to lift his shotgun as the black man came rolling across the carpet.

By now Emily was beginning to respond to the situation in the only way that made sense. She attempted to turn and run. But the black man reached one long arm out and encircled her waist, scooping her up. Then he threw himself forward again. The place where Emily had been standing a moment ago was suddenly swarming with a lethal cloud of buckshot.

Emily and the man landed in a heap behind one of the long couches. There was a moment's silence and the man took advantage of it to whisper in Emily's ear. 'I'm here to help you. My name is Tregemmon. Christopher Matthew sent me.'

He said something else but it was lost in the blast of the shotgun as Comstock fired again. A great chunk of the couch vanished, chewed away by the blast. A cloud of foam particles began to settle on Emily and she could smell a bitter, acrid scent, like scorched plastic. Then a second shot tore another hole in the couch, just above their heads.

'Hold on tight,' said Tregemmon. He scooped her up again and tucked her underneath his arm as if she were a rugby ball. Then he threw himself out from behind the couch, rolling across the carpet. Emily rolled with him.

They were in plain view now and Comstock began to fire wildly, pumping the shotgun each time to get another shell.

They were exposed for only an instant and in his haste Comstock missed them each time he fired. Then they were safely behind the bar.

Emily heard Comstock fire the shotgun again, twice. The first blast wiped out a row of bottles sitting on the bar above their heads and Emily found herself showered by broken glass and some kind of trickling sticky liqueur.

The next shot was more carefully aimed and it was followed by a hollow, booming, metallic sound like some-body kicking the side of a dustbin.

She looked up to see that the plywood wall of the bar beside her head had bellied inward with the force of the shotgun pellets. But they hadn't penetrated. She was safe.

Emily was astonished to discover that she felt quite secure, crouching here behind the bar. It was something to do with her companion.

Tregemmon's hand was on her back, a reassuring weight. Then it disappeared. She felt him move and turned to see what he was doing. He was writhing on the floor and for a moment Emily was terribly afraid that he'd been hit, but she realised that he was merely struggling to remove his raincoat.

Tregemmon put a finger to his lips, signalling for silence, as he shrugged the coat off.

Comstock had stopped firing, perhaps having realised that it was futile to try to blast them through the bar. Emily knew, however, that this was only a momentary respite. He'd soon work out that he merely had to move and then he would be able to shoot around the open end of the bar and kill them both.

They couldn't stay in such a vulnerable position. Yet if they tried to leave the shelter of the bar they would be exposed and Comstock could pick them off easily.

The bar, which had appeared to be a safe haven, now began to resemble a trap.

Emily's mind began to move swiftly, weighing alternatives, looking for a solution. How could they get out of this predicament?

It was hard to think. After the shotgun blasts, the silence in the room rang in her ears. She turned to look at Tregemmon again.

He smiled and winked and made a counting gesture, chopping his hand down with first three fingers, then two, then one.

On one he moved, and he moved so quickly that he was just a blur to Emily. He flung his bundled coat out of one end of the bar.

As the coat began to unfurl in midair, he moved to the other end of the bar and stood up. Instantly, Emily understood what was happening.

Comstock saw the coat and thought it was Tregemmon. He stood up and fired at it. But, as soon as he stood up, he exposed himself and Tregemmon was waiting for him at the other end of the bar.

Emily heard three pistol shots in swift succession and then there was silence in the room again. The air conditioning whispered around the suite. Tregemmon, reloading his gun, stepped out from behind the bar. Emily lay where she was, feeling the sticky aromatic liqueur from the broken bottle spreading across her skin and down to the carpet all around her. Then Tregemmon came back, his shoes making soft noises.

He said, 'You can come out now, honey.'

In the bathroom Danny Bailey heard the gunshots.

Or, to be more accurate, a tiny portion of Danny Bailey's mind registered them and began to respond, crawling sluggishly back to consciousness.

He had long ago stopped kicking the bathroom door

and abandoned any attempt to contact Miranda telepathically. He'd resigned himself to dying.

But now the gunshots penetrated his consciousness as though echoing through wet cotton wool. Abruptly, hope was reborn, flaring in his brain. Tregemmon was here.

He was saved. Tregemmon would come in and pull the bag off his head and then Danny could breathe again.

All he had to do was make sure that Tregemmon knew he was in here. That was simple enough. Make some noise.

Kick the door. Danny knew he could kick the door.

He knew his legs could reach. He'd done it enough times earlier.

Danny commanded his legs to kick, to lash out until the door shook in its frame. But nothing happened. His legs didn't even stir.

As he tried to kick, all he felt was a diffuse, warm itching sensation in his legs. His muscles were like dead meat. He tried again. This time he didn't even feel the itching sensation.

Hopelessness rushed in on him, blotting out his awareness of his surroundings. He felt himself lapse back into the dim grey mist and all hope faded.

They didn't know he was in here.

He was going to die in here, with Tregemmon only a few feet away.

'You're officially rescued, honey,' said Tregemmon.

'Thank you,' said Emily, like a polite little girl. She and Tregemmon were staring at each other in the sudden silence of the air-conditioned suite. Emily could smell a lingering, burnt odour in the air. She assumed it was cordite, or perhaps gunpowder.

She began to walk over towards the armchair that Comstock had been hiding behind. 'Don't,' said Tregemmon. 'You shouldn't look. You'll have bad dreams.' He had already put the sheet over the other bodies.

'I'd have worse dreams if I wasn't sure they were dead,' said Emily. So he let her lift the sheet and look at

Lenny and Brilly and then go behind the chair to see Comstock.

She was surprised to discover that she didn't feel any residual hatred or anger towards the men. They just looked so sad and helpless lying there. If anything, she felt sorry for them. And, oddly, a little embarrassed on their behalf.

Tregemmon guided her away from the dead bodies. 'My name is Tregemmon,' he said.

'I know, you told me.'

'We ought to get out of here. Your sister's downstairs waiting for you. Is there anything you need or shall we just cut out?'

Emily hesitated.

'Well, actually there is a rather battered, ugly teddy bear I've become quite attached to.' She led Tregemmon into her bedroom and they gathered up Mr Rafferty, as she had dubbed the teddy bear that Nuala, of all people, had given to her just before they left England.

Emily wondered what vestigial impulse of decency had prompted the girl.

While they were in the bedroom, though, they heard a sound coming from the lounge. The banging of a door and then urgent footsteps. Someone had come into the suite.

Emily turned and stared at Tregemmon wide-eyed. 'Did you leave the door open?' she said.

Tregemmon didn't reply. He just cursed and moved cautiously towards the door of the bedroom. Emily saw that the gun was suddenly in his hand again.

Tregemmon peered through the bedroom door, and then he glided out into the lounge. Emily followed him and, surprisingly, he made no effort to stop her. She saw that Tregemmon had lowered his gun again.

He was watching a pretty blonde girl barging around the suite wrenching doors open. Emily had never seen the girl before, but Tregemmon seemed to know her.

'Miranda,' he said. 'What the hell are you doing?'

The girl didn't reply. She kept frantically pulling

doors open, peering inside and slamming them shut again. Then she came to the bathroom door, and when she opened this one she didn't slam it shut. Instead she darted inside.

From a great distance, a distance as far as the other side of the universe, Danny heard the sound of the bathroom door opening.

Then a rasping, tearing sound. After a moment, his crushed senses managed to identify this: the sound of tape being peeled reluctantly off a surface. A numb tingling of nerve endings told him that the tape had been stuck to his neck.

None of this meant anything to Danny yet.

Then he felt the plastic bag being pulled off his head, and the hot poisoned cloud around his face vanished in an instant.

Odd that something so lethal could be dispersed so quickly. Cool sweet air rushed in, flowing across the clammy surface of his cheeks. Danny could feel it against his nostrils, caressing his mouth.

Then he smelt Miranda's perfume, and felt the tickling touch of her hair against his face. And the next thing he knew the familiar soft contours of her mouth were pressing wetly against his. She forced his mouth open and breathed into it.

Sweet air flowed into Danny.

His eyes fluttered open, and in the mirror he saw Miranda there, her red lips pressed against his pale-blue ones.

As the air hit his scorched exhausted lungs they seemed to reawaken, remembering their function. His chest expanded and he sucked in a wet, ratcheting breath.

Miranda drew her mouth away from his to let him breathe. Danny gasped and choked, losing the rhythm for a moment. Then he began to breathe again, more slowly and calmly. As he sucked the air in, Miranda's cool lips were kissing his clammy forehead.

As soon as his breathing slowed to something like

normal, her mouth drifted back down his face and found his mouth again.

She kissed him hungrily. Danny tasted her, and it was the taste of life.

He heard a sound and he opened his eyes. There in the doorway of the bathroom he saw Emily and Tregemmon, staring at them.

'They're snogging!' said the little girl. 'That's *disgusting*.'

THIRTY-NINE

A ghost, a witch on a broom, a grinning jack-o'-lantern.

The figures spun into Juliette's view on the slot machine.

She was peripherally aware of the activity in the casino all around her. But her attention was focused here. She was caught up in the glazed fever-sweat, compounded of guilt and excitement, that had possessed her ever since she had begun dipping into Miranda's winnings.

A thousand dollars.

It had seemed like so much. It didn't matter if she took just a little, did it?

And, if Miranda could win a jackpot, so could Juliette. It was proof. It was only a matter of time. And then of course she would pay her friend back.

She had intended to hold on to the money for Miranda. To keep it safe for her. But once she had begun dipping into it she was lost.

Juliette kept feeding the coins into the slot machine. Several times she came tantalisingly close to the big jackpot. So close, in fact, that she knew a substantial win must be just around the corner.

Thus she gambled away first fifty, then a hundred, and then eventually eight hundred of Miranda's dollars. She kept feeding the slot machines, sweat flowing like warm oil from her armpits down her ribcage as she pulled and pulled and pulled on the levers until her hands began to ache and she wished she had one of those practical gloves like the ones the old women wore.

Finally it crossed her mind that there was something strange about her behaviour. Indeed, if she had been writing a paper about it, she might have described it as obsessional.

254

'It's fascinating, isn't it?'

Juliette jumped at the sound of the voice and turned around, expecting to see Christopher. It was just the sort of thing he'd say, at just such a moment. And in a hot flash of guilt she was already framing excuses to explain about borrowing Miranda's money.

But it wasn't Chris.

A couple were standing watching her. The girl was young and grubby-looking, dragging two overstuffed suitcases. The man, the one who had spoken, was middle-aged, quite tall, otherwise nondescript. Until you noticed his eyes. There was something so strange about his eyes, simultaneously vacant and intense, that it almost prevented Juliette from returning to the serious business of feeding the slot machine.

'Come on,' whined the grubby girl to the man. 'What are you looking at?'

'Just one small piece of my handiwork,' said the man. He seemed to be talking about Juliette, but she politely ignored him. Las Vegas was full of strange people. She wanted to concentrate on the machine in front of her, the tug of the lever and the spin of the symbols. She just wanted the man to go away and leave her to it.

As if reading her mind he turned to the girl and said, 'Come along, Nuala, let's find a taxi.' The girl heaved her suitcases off the floor and wobbled in the direction of the lobby. The man followed.

Juliette was relieved that they were gone. In her hand she held the final silver dollar. It was astonishing, but there you were. She had used up all of Miranda's winnings, along with every penny of her own.

But it didn't matter. She clutched the coin. This was the one. She knew that this was the one that would win. Win back everything and more. She would repay Miranda with interest.

Juliette put the coin in and tugged the lever. The figures spun in the machine, slowed and settled down into a pattern. Two cats, a witch and a ghost.

Nothing.

She had lost it all. Juliette felt a twinge of fear as normal consciousness came creeping back. She began to feel the crashing comedown of the compulsive gambler at the end of a binge.

And with it came the realisation that the man who'd spoken to her could only have been Mr Leiber.

And she'd let him go.

'But we can't just leave my goodhearted hillbilly waitress in the lurch,' protested Emily. 'Is her name really Sharleen?'

'I have no idea,' said Tregemmon. He was walking down the hotel corridor beside her, moving slowly and cautiously, Emily's little hand entwined in his long fingers.

'She was going to come back and help me,' said Emily. 'I'm certain she was.'

Normally Emily didn't like anyone holding her hand, but she was willing to make an exception with Tregemmon. They had reached the lifts now. Tregemmon pressed the button to summon one. 'Who's this waitress again?' he said.

'I slipped her a note in the cafeteria. Have you visited the cafeteria, by the way? Terrific value for money but their tea is terrible.'

Tregemmon chuckled, a pleasant rasping sound. 'No, I haven't been to the cafeteria, honey. What was this note you passed her?'

'It was a somewhat cryptic plea for help. She didn't seem to have any trouble understanding it, though. I suppose in fact most of our communication was via eye contact. Remarkable what can be conveyed by that subtle medium, don't you think?'

'Mmm.'

'But hardly surprising when you consider its million-year-old role in preverbal communication. I really must discuss the subject with Christopher Matthew.'

'It sounds like it's right up his street.'

'Anyway, I passed this note to Sharleen and, plucky Ozark wench that she is, she's no doubt making a brave attempt to rescue me even now. And I would hate for her to turn up at room 572 and find me gone.'

256

Tregemmon chuckled. 'She'd probably find Danny and Miranda taking a bubble bath together.'

'Yes, I'm sorry about my outburst but that really was the most florid display of physical affection. I could hardly let it go unremarked.'

'I shouldn't worry about it, honey,' said Tregemmon cheerfully. But then his face clouded over, frown lines appearing on his forehead. 'She saved his life. If it hadn't been for her, Danny would be dead . . .' He winced. 'And it would be my fault. I'd forgotten all about him.'

'You did have a few other things on your mind. Like mortal combat with three mass murderers and saving my life.'

'That's no excuse,' said Tregemmon bleakly.

Emily wanted those frown lines to vanish, so she changed the subject. 'We aren't just going to leave Danny and Miranda there, are we? It may not be safe.'

'They'll meet us in the lobby as soon as Danny gets his strength back.'

'Judging by his earlier display, it seems to be coming back rather quickly.'

'It was Mr Leiber and I let him get away.' Juliette felt that she was on the verge of breaking down. She looked at Chris through a shimmer of tears.

He shook his head. 'There was very little you could have done to stop him. Don't blame yourself.'

Irrationally, Juliette felt angry with him. Why did he have to be so forgiving? And why did he finally turn up now, when it was too late? 'Where were you?' she demanded.

Then she remembered: he had gone off in search of Miranda. And remembering Miranda triggered a surge of guilt. 'I lost it all,' she said.

'Lost what?'

'Miranda's money. Her jackpot. All of it.' The words burst out of her. She was desperate to confess.

'I'm sure that's the last thing she gives a damn about. She ran off and left it, didn't she?'

'Yes. Did you find her?'

'No. But we can't afford to worry about that now. If Mr Leiber's jumped ship we don't have much time. When Tregemmon comes back with your little sister . . .'

'When,' murmured Juliette. At that moment she loved Christopher for not saying 'if'.

'When he does that, all hell could break loose. Tregemmon and Emily might come fleeing through here with any number of unpleasant people in pursuit.' Juliette nodded. It made her feel cold just to think about it. 'So we'll need to create some kind of diversion to cover our getaway.'

'What do you have in mind? A smoke bomb or something?'

Christopher grinned. 'I'm sure I can come up with something more interesting than that.'

FORTY

Tregemmon kept on prodding the elevator button, but nothing happened. 'What's wrong with the damned thing?' he murmured.

'Oh, I shouldn't think you'll have much luck with that,' said a voice from the shadows.

Emily's heart leapt with surprise and she turned to see a man walking towards them out of the darkness of the corridor.

He was a roly-poly little man wearing a Panama hat and a white suit. The pink stripes on his shirt matched the pink of his small face, which seemed to melt into a fat roll of double chins above his immaculate winged collar. On his hands he wore white gloves.

Emily couldn't help noticing that these white-gloved hands were trembling. He was carrying a small tapestry valise.

Tregemmon moved forward so that he was standing between the man and Emily, shielding her. 'What's the problem with the lifts?' he said.

'Haven't you heard the bad news? It seems that our convention has come to a premature conclusion.' The man's chins wobbled with dismay. 'That is why the elevators are permanently chock-a-block. All of our fellow conventioneers are rushing to check out before it is too late.'

'Too late?'

'Yes, there is a rumour that some busybody has blown our cover. Summoned the authorities. Possibly the rumour is quite without foundation, but the damage has been done. Everyone is leaving and who knows when we will see such a prestigious gathering again.'

The man was close enough now for Emily to see that he

wore wire-rimmed sunglasses; she wondered how on earth he could see in the dark hotel corridors with those on. He seemed to manage easily enough, though.

He reached into the pocket of his jacket and Emily immediately sensed Tregemmon tense up, but the man merely drew out a large handkerchief and wiped his sweating pink forehead with it. 'Ah well, better safe than sorry, I suppose,' he said.

He hefted his valise. 'I am departing for more salubrious climes myself. But before I go, allow me to introduce myself.'

He swept the Panama hat off his head and reached inside it. Emily thought he was going to take out a business card but instead he drew out a small, wicked-looking scalpel.

Tregemmon's pistol was instantly in his hand and the man backed away shaking his head. 'No, no, don't misunderstand me.' He smiled. He had a tiny rosebud mouth and when he smiled his lips gleamed wetly. 'I was merely identifying myself.'

He slipped the scalpel back into his Panama and set the hat back on his head. 'I go by the name of the Incision Master. Obviously inspired by the chosen tool of my trade.' He made a funny little formal bow. 'I'm no Professor Lazarus,' he said modestly. 'But I've done my small bit for the cause.'

'Stay back,' said Tregemmon. The pistol was unwavering in his hand.

The man sighed. 'I really am terribly sorry. You've got me entirely wrong. I would never try to poach your catch.' He nodded at Emily. 'She's all yours. Professional courtesy, you know.'

Tregemmon took Emily by the hand and began to back away from the man. 'Come on,' he murmured to her. 'We'll take the stairs.' He kept his gun aimed at the man but the man just remained standing where he was. When they reached the fire door opposite the elevators he called out, 'Enjoy!'

Then he smiled and waved at them with his trembling

white-gloved hand as the door sighed shut on its pneumatic hinge.

'What do you mean?'

'I mean maybe I can make use of that pattern of random
chance which is flowing around this casino.'

'How do you propose to do that?'

Christopher cupped a hand to his ear. 'Listen, Juliette,'
he said.

Juliette listened but all she could hear was the noise
of the slot machines. A random, clattering, mechanical
aggregate composed of the obsessive tugging of levers by
the addicted personalities all around her. Flawed, weak
personalities.

Indeed, this was the noise of human weakness. Interrupted occasionally – very occasionally – by the jingle of
coins into a payout tray.

'Doesn't it sound like music to you?' said Christopher.

'No. It sounds like formless noise.'

'Oh, come on, Juliette. Surely even a sceptic like you
can pick up patterns, rhythms.' He paused and let the
casino noise wash over them. 'Perhaps not quite music yet,
but quivering on the edge of becoming music.'

Juliette listened. Christopher was watching her with
those dark remarkable eyes, like a teacher waiting for his
prize pupil to come up with the right answer.

Under the weight of that expectation Juliette began to
imagine that she did indeed hear a tantalising pattern in
the chaotic noise. It reminded her of a metallic, percussive
piece of modern music she had once heard by Ligeti.

Then she shook her head to free herself of this ridiculous
notion. Christopher was making her imagine things. It was
just the power of suggestion.

'Maybe all it needs is a good conductor,' he said.

'A conductor as in electricity?'

'No, a conductor as in music.'

Juliette stared at him in weary disgust. 'Music?'

Christopher smiled and winked. 'This casino is like a symphony orchestra, so perhaps I'll entice it to play a symphony.'

261

He swept his long white hair back with a flourish and walked off, smiling that infuriating smile.

The Halloween Hotel abandoned its dim mood lighting in the areas where the big money changed hands. As you approached the casino the lights grew stronger, and so did the sound.

Sharleen followed Gord as he hurried into the gambling zone. She was overwhelmed by the familiar racket of the slots.

Except that it was no longer familiar. Normally the sound of the slot machines was a kind of perpetual thrashing whirr, composed of the noise made by hundreds of levers being constantly pulled. It was almost like the sound of crickets on the summer nights of her Georgia childhood. A thick musical rubbing noise, interspersed with the silvery plash of the random payout.

But now something was wrong. Sharleen could tell right away. She had worked at the Halloween long enough to become attuned to the complex random sound of the casino.

Now the noise of the big room had lost its randomness. The lever-pulling sounds no longer came in a chaotic cloud. Instead they had become oddly synchronous, creating patches of coordinated sound here and there.

These rhythmic bursts of lever-pulling were punctuated by musical climaxes of coins gushing from the slot machines in payouts.

The other sounds of the casino had also changed, right down to the tick tick ticking of the wheel of fortune as it slowed down at the end of its spin. Even the background murmur of conversation from the gamblers. All these sounds had changed. Now they were woven together in an eerie synchronisation.

The voices of the people in the casino rose and fell in excitement. The ebb and flow of that excitement was synchronised with the activity of the slot machines. It was as if everyone in the casino was somehow synchronised, too. Their movements and mood.

The entire pattern of noise and activity seemed to be knitting together. Turning into one big slab of sound with a meaning. Sharleen sensed that events in the casino were hastening towards a strange climax.

She hurried through the casino beside Gord, trying to ignore the strange feeling. But she couldn't help noticing that the timpani splash of payouts from the slot machines was becoming more and more frequent. She knew they shouldn't be paying out so often. They were rigged to guarantee a house profit. But the house sure wasn't making a profit now. She had never heard the casino sound like this.

She wasn't the only one who had noticed. People were hurrying in excitedly from all over the hotel and the floor bosses were looking distinctly uneasy.

But Gord just bulled his way forward through the ever-thickening crowds, one big arm over Sharleen's shoulder, guiding her along. He didn't seem to realise that any-thing weird was happening. Perhaps because he wasn't as attuned to its normal rhythms as Sharleen was.

But even Gord paused for a second as they passed the telephone alcove where a tall guy was standing.

The tall guy was middle-aged and had long white hair and glowing dark eyes. He had a dreamy expression on his face as he leant against the wall, his body swaying and his hands making small involuntary fluttering gestures.

Normally Sharleen would have thought that the guy was out of his skull on some drug, bopping to some stoned internal music.

But every move he made was in perfect time to the sound around him in the casino. As if the sound were music in a disco and he were dancing to it.

No, thought Sharleen, more as if the music was being played by an orchestra and he were conducting it. His every move seemed to anticipate the flow of sound, to lead and guide it. He dreamily snapped one hand down and three nearby slot machines gushed forth huge payouts in perfect coordination, like a trio of struck cymbals.

People streamed past him and into the casino, and

somehow he seemed to be the source of that, too – the ebb and flow of the crowd.

Gord kept bulling through the crowd, carrying Sharleen along with him, and in a moment the guy was out of sight. Gord cursed as they fought the growing tide of humanity sweeping towards the betting table.

When they got to the elevators they found they were hopelessly jammed. In addition to the gamblers swarming in in a feeding frenzy, there were crowds of conventioneers fighting to get out. All the creepy people from that ICSH convention seemed to be clustered around the front desk, checking out.

'There's got to be another way,' said Gord, staring into the seething crowd. Sharleen could see the bulldog determination in him. Sweat gleamed on his bald spot and Sharleen had an urge to kiss it.

Gord wanted to get upstairs and help that little girl.

'We'll take the stairs,' she said.

Tregemmon closed the fire door and peered down the stairwell. It was only dimly lit, with orange pumpkin signs. 'Stick close by me,' he said.

Emily didn't need any urging. Indeed, she reached up and took his hand. She felt safe with Tregemmon. 'What an extraordinary individual that was,' she said.

'Yes. The Incision Master.' Tregemmon snorted in disgust.

'They really do choose the most ridiculous names for themselves,' agreed Emily. 'It would be pathetic if they weren't so . . .'

'Dangerous,' said Tregemmon. They were descending past the fourth floor, their feet striking rhythmically on the concrete steps, when without warning Tregemmon let go of Emily's hand and whirled around.

His raincoat flapped wildly as he raised his right arm, pointing his gun back up the way they had come.

It took a moment for Emily to make out what he had seen in the darkened stairwell. There above them, the fourth-floor exit door was drifting shut and two figures stood on the landing, pale faces gazing down.

Emily felt an irrational chill; it was as if she was seeing double. The two faces were identical. They were gaunt freckled young women, with jutting cheekbones and sharply angled eyes like those of a cat.

'Who's a naughty boy, then?' said one of the women.

'You know extracurricular activities are forbidden,' said the other one. She wagged a finger disapprovingly, then pointed at Emily. 'You know we're only supposed to use the designated areas at the designated times.' Neither of them seemed the least bit alarmed to have Tregemmon's gun pointing at them.

'You're not supposed to do an unauthorised job in the stairwell,' giggled one of the twins.

'So for Christ's sake don't let any of the convention marshals catch you,' said her sister with a smirk. 'They caught Redball and the Blowtorch doing things they shouldn't oughta. And you know what those sons of bitches went and did to them?'

There was a pause and then Tregemmon said, 'No, no I don't.'

'They sent them back to Kansas,' shrilled the other woman. 'And refused to even refund their room deposit. What bastards!'

'Next year, I swear we'll go to the Miami convention instead, Dianthus.'

'I think you're right, Cessie.'

'OK, ladies,' said Tregemmon. 'It was nice talking to you, but we've got to be going.'

'Oh, we're no ladies,' giggled the woman called Dianthus. 'We're the Talbot twins. Now tell us, who are you? And who's the charming little friend you seem so eager to keep to yourself?'

'Sorry. We've got to be going.' Tregemmon began to lead Emily down the stairs again. He had lowered his gun but Emily noticed that he didn't put it away.

The woman called Cessie nudged her sister in the ribs. 'I know who he is!' she said. Her eyes bulged with excitement. 'He's the Trigger Man.'

Emily felt Tregemmon freeze beside her. He turned and stared back up at the Talbot twins. 'What did you say?'

'You're the Trigger Man.'

'How did you know that?' Tregemmon's voice was tense.

'Oh, we've heard all about you. You're one of us.'

'No I'm not,' said Tregemmon loudly. His voice reverberated in the stairwell.

The Talbot twins just giggled and then they turned away and disappeared back through the door. Tregemmon stared after them. 'I'm not one of you, you sick bitches,' he muttered.

Emily squeezed his hand. 'Of course you're not, Tregemmon.'

Sharleen was surprised at how out of shape she'd gotten. That was waitressing for you. You stayed on your feet all day but you never had any real exercise.

She found that she was winded by the time she reached the second flight of stairs and they had to pause and rest. Gord was good about it, but she could see that he was impatient. He wanted to get up to the fifth floor and rescue the little girl. It had become his mission now.

At first Gord had been hard to convince. But he'd heard the genuine fear in Sharleen's voice, and then when he arrived at the hotel he witnessed the strange cavalcade of the ICSH conventioneers. And somehow, along the way, Gord had become a believer.

Sharleen suddenly thought of something. She turned to Gord. 'Did you bring a gun?'

Gord made a disgusted face. 'Of course I did. I borrowed one off one of the bouncers at the club.' Gord was security manager for a lap-dancing establishment nearby. It was a job where things could occasionally get tricky.

Sharleen immediately felt better upon hearing this. Gord was a crack shot from his days in the army and there wasn't much he couldn't handle. She felt almost safe, following his bald spot up the staircase in the darkness. Then all at once he stiffened, staring upward.

'What is it?'

He gestured for her to be quiet. Sharleen strained to listen. Then she heard it. Voices.

Echoing down the stairwell.

'Come along, Tregemmon. The Talbot twins were just trying to annoy you.'

'Well, it worked,' said Tregemmon darkly. He shrugged and then resumed his descent, taking the stairs slowly so that Emily could keep up. They passed the third-floor exit without incident and Emily was starting to relax again when they rounded a corner.

And found themselves face to face with two people coming up the stairs. A man and a woman. The man had a gun.

'That's her!' said Sharleen. The words burst out of her mouth involuntarily.

But Gord had guessed as much. His nerves were already well and truly frayed and when he saw the black guy with the dreadlocks, dragging the scared little girl down the stairs, he acted without thinking.

He lifted his gun and got ready to shoot. But he didn't have a chance.

The black guy moved and suddenly there was a gun in his own hand. It flared three times and an instant later came the echoing report of the gunshots.

By that time Gord had already felt the impact, three hard blows on his chest. He was hit and he was going down.

Sharleen and the little girl and the black guy were all standing above him, looking down at him. The last thing he heard was Sharleen's scream.

Tregemmon was shaking with what looked like rage. But even on their short acquaintance Emily could see that it was something else entirely.

Shock and regret.

'Look, missus,' he said, his voice fast and high-pitched

with anxiety. 'He was coming at me with a gun. I didn't know who he was.'

The waitress didn't pay any attention to his words. She was kneeling beside the man on the steps, cradling his balding head on her lap. Emily wondered how things could have gone so horribly wrong.

'Come on,' said Tregemmon gently. He moved to Sharleen and tried to talk to her, but she turned away from him, wrapping the dead man's head in her arms. Her face was contorted with silent grief.

'Please,' said Tregemmon. 'Come with us. It's not safe here.' He touched Sharleen and the instant he touched her she began to scream.

Her screams rose and filled the stairwell like a flock of terrified birds. 'Leave me alone,' she shrieked. 'Don't touch me!'

Tregemmon and Emily tried to coax her but she was like a wounded animal. When Tregemmon made another attempt to detach her from the dead man she began screaming again.

In the end, the force of her grief drove them away. Tregemmon took Emily's hand and they resumed their descent, leaving Sharleen with her boyfriend.

The worst part was that they had to step over the dead man to get down the stairs.

Emily could hear Sharleen's sobs all the way down to the bottom.

Sharleen hardly noticed when Emily and the black man left. She was numb with loss. Gord was dead and nothing else mattered. Her entire universe had shrunk to these concrete steps where she sat holding his body.

She didn't know how long she sat there, sobbing, but gradually she became aware that she was not alone.

At first she thought Emily and the black guy had come back and she wished they would just leave her alone. But then she looked up and saw that it was someone else. A funny-looking little fat man in a white suit and a Panama hat. He wore sunglasses and white gloves.

He was watching Sharleen, shaking his head with sadness. His double chins shivered like jelly as he shook his head. 'You poor thing,' he said in a soft little voice. 'Such grief. Such pain.'

He took off his Panama hat, as if out of respect. Then he reached into the hat. Through her tears, Sharleen could dimly see that something gleamed in his hand.

He moved towards her. 'I'll make it all better,' he said.

And, in a way, he did.

FORTY-ONE

'I killed him,' said Tregemmon.

Juliette listened, nodding. As a psychiatrist, she wanted desperately to help this man. Her friend.

She could hardly bear to see the grief etched on his face.

'I killed him. The waitress was coming to rescue Emily and she brought her boyfriend with her. And I shot him dead.'

'There was no way you could have known,' said Emily. The little girl was holding Juliette's hand, staring anxiously up into Tregemmon's face.

'She's right,' added Christopher. He was standing on the other side of Juliette. 'It's not your fault.'

They were all clustered on the pavement beside a construction site, a pit in the ground with a grid of steel bars rising out of it into the Las Vegas night.

Through the gaunt skeleton of the structure Juliette could see the restless neon signs of the Strip flashing on and off. Sirens still howled as police vehicles swept south to the Halloween Hotel.

Now that nightfall had come, the construction site had seemed a good place to stop and talk. At least, better than driving around arguing in the rental car, which is what they had been doing ever since they left the casino. Arguing while the police cars whipped past.

The concept of a casino where people could win – and win every time – seemed to have caused a major civil disturbance in Las Vegas.

Juliette still wasn't entirely sure what she had witnessed, or exactly what role Christopher had played in it. She had watched the extraordinary spectacle and her main reaction had been chagrin: five minutes after she had lost every penny to the slot machines they had begun paying out promiscuously, gushing riches for any fool capable of pulling a lever.

Thinking about the slot machines reminded her that she'd lost all of Miranda's money. Juliette shot a guilty look at the girl.

But her missing jackpot was the last thing on Miranda's mind.

She stood intertwined with Danny, who was gnawing on a hot dog they'd bought on the way. It was a foot long and swathed in bright-red ketchup with golden onion rings spilling from the bun. Miranda had her arms wrapped around Danny as he chomped hungrily through it.

Almost being killed seemed to have given him quite an appetite. For her part, Miranda was clinging to him as if she would never let go, like a gawky teenage girl with the boy she worshipped.

Danny occasionally released his ketchup-smeared mouth from its duty of hot dog consumption long enough to kiss her. As a result Miranda had ketchup smeared all over her face, giving her an ungodly vampiric appearance. But the girl didn't seem to care in the least. They were completely wrapped up in each other, oblivious to the argument that was going on.

'You're full of shit,' said Tregemmon. He glared fiercely at Christopher, who just seemed to shrug off his friend's anger. He was maddeningly calm.

'Try to take it easy,' he said. 'I understand that you're upset.'

'You don't understand anything. The waitress's boyfriend is dead because of me. And by now the waitress is probably dead, too.'

The neon of the adjacent casinos glowed on Tregemmon's sweating face. With her clinical experience, Juliette could read the emotional pain there and she longed to do something about it, take him away somewhere quiet, and let him talk for a few hours.

But there was no place to take him and no time to take him there.

'Tregemmon, you've got to think of it as a war,' said Christopher. 'There are bound to be unintended casualties.'

'Go fuck your unintended casualties,' said Tregemmon. 'I killed an innocent man.'

'Look, we're all exhausted. Let's get off the street. Find somewhere to stay. We all need to get some sleep and talk about this tomorrow. Things will look different in the morning.'

'Nothing will look different in the morning. The Talbot twins were right. I'm a murderer, just like them.' Tregemmon stared at him bleakly.

It seemed the moment for Juliette to step in, but before she could say anything Tregemmon turned away and strode off into the neon-slashed night.

Christopher called after him but Tregemmon just ignored him and kept walking.

Emily stared sadly after the disappearing figure. 'Tregemmon,' she called. 'We'll miss you.'

But Tregemmon was a dwindling figure in the distance now, and it was impossible to say whether he'd heard her.

Christopher sighed and turned to the others. 'Well, that complicates matters. I was counting on his help. I don't know how we're going to manage without him.'

Juliette stared at Christopher. 'Manage? What do you mean?'

'We have work to do.'

'What are you talking about?'

'Juliette, take a look at the situation. Mr Leiber is still on the loose.'

'So? We have Emily safe and sound. I'm going to ring Mum and then I'll take her back to England and forget about all this.'

'Forget about it? My God, Juliette. Do you have any idea of how dangerous Mr Leiber is? We have to find him before he gets another project under way.'

'I agree,' said Emily. The little girl stared up at her, her face serious. 'Juliette, you simply don't understand the nature of the problem. All right, that's not surprising

272

because it's beyond your normal experience. But, believe me, Mr Leiber must be stopped at all costs.'

'Why?'

Emily was furious. 'You simply won't take anything on trust from your little sister, will you? Well, let's see if this gets the message into your thick brain. Think of reality as a painting. For you or me the pigment of reality is fixed and dry. But to Mr Leiber it is still fresh and wet and he can alter it at will.'

Juliette turned to see that Christopher was nodding as if he agreed with this astonishing diatribe. Juliette couldn't endure it. She felt as if she had spent half her life listening to the self-assured cadences of her sister's munchkin voice. Arrogant, absolutely certain of the authority of whatever it was saying. And it just went on and on: 'In fact Mr Leiber has the ability to alter the nature of the image, that is of reality itself – I trust you're following the metaphor, Juliette. I've made it as simple as I possibly can so that you can understand.'

Juliette cut off this egotistical flow. 'All right. You're saying that he can alter reality.'

'Yes, and don't take that smirking tone. I realise that you're a psychiatrist. But you're not used to thinking in the terms that Christopher and I might understand. You need to read some McKenna. Start with *Fiddler's Green*. And bone up your quantum physics.'

Juliette turned to Miranda. She had begun to think of Miranda as an ally and a friend and now she looked to her for support.

But Miranda was too wrapped up in Danny to listen. She had saved her boyfriend's life and nothing else seemed to matter to her. Since the moment that Danny had started breathing again, the couple had hardly had a thought for anything except each other. They seemed quite oblivious to the presence of the others as they caressed and kissed each other.

Juliette turned away from them in embarrassment. Emily was still talking. 'As I said, to us reality is like a painting in a museum. Fixed, untouchable. But Mr Leiber can hop past the museum's security, lay hands on the canvas itself and alter it. He can change it from a friendly photorealist canvas to a Hieronymus Bosch nightmare.'

'Look,' said Juliette. She was struggling to retain her temper. It was deeply maddening to be lectured to from a standpoint of superior intellect by your seven-year-old sister. And, despite having recently been in tears of relief because she was alive and safe, Juliette now wanted to grab her sister and throttle her with her bare hands.

'All right,' she snarled. 'But we've broken up his convention at the Halloween Hotel. Isn't that enough?'

'What about the conventioneers, though?' said Christopher. 'Apart from the ones that Tregemmon put paid to, they're all still alive and at large. Free to murder at will.'

'I'm sorry but that's really not my problem. We live in a world where murdering psychopaths exist. We can't alter that fact.'

'On the contrary, that's exactly what someone like Mr Leiber can do,' said Emily smugly.

'Well, there's nothing we can do. I've had enough. I'm going home and so are you.'

'Actually, I see your point,' said Emily, looking up at her. She was suddenly dangerously polite. 'It would be different if we could actually *do* something about this plague of serial killers which is even now spilling into the Las Vegas night like a swarm of hornets chased from its nest.'

'Yes, exactly.'

'Well, there *is* something we can do.' Emily drew something out from under her sweater. It was the red computer disk, which had nestled there safely ever since she had stolen it from Nuala's suitcase.

'What's that?' said Juliette.

The little girl waved the disk proudly. 'I wasn't entirely idle while I was being held hostage,' she said. 'This is something Nuala wangled from the convention organisers. It's their mailing list. It features names and addresses for all of the attendees.' Emily smiled. 'Credit-card numbers, too.'

'Brilliant!' said Christopher, his face lighting up. 'We can use this to track the bastards down.' He scooped Emily up and hugged her as she continued to waggle the disk triumphantly.

Juliette watched them sourly. 'I see,' she said. 'You're suggesting that we get a road map of the USA and hunt down several hundred active serial killers?'

'No, actually I thought we'd leave it to the police.' Christopher took the disk from Emily as he set her down. 'Deliver this to them and let them get on with it.'

'And how will we do that?'

Christopher tapped the floppy disk thoughtfully on the palm of his hand. 'Drop it in the post,' he said.

But then Danny Bailey spoke for the first time. 'No,' he said. 'No. I'll take it.'

'That's not necessary, Danny.'

Danny ate the last fragment of his hot dog and wiped his hands on a paper napkin. He seemed to be emerging from his dreamy erotic reverie with Miranda and there was a new seriousness in his eyes.

'Well, I think it is necessary. It seems to me that I haven't contributed much to this operation so far, apart from getting tied up in a bathroom and damned nearly suffocated. I'll take the disk to the police.'

'Forget it. We'll post it.'

Danny detached himself from Miranda. His jaw had taken on a stubborn set. Juliette could see that his pride was at stake in this matter.

'No, I'll drop it off in person,' he said, and he took the disk from Christopher.

Finding a police station in Las Vegas didn't prove as easy as Danny had expected.

The local constabulary, or the Metro as they liked to call themselves, had a rather complex divisional structure, with Las Vegas split into a number of sections called area commands.

Each area command had a substation. As far as Danny could tell, he was in the Downtown area. There seemed to be three substations located here, only one of which was called Downtown. But that was irrelevant because Danny couldn't seem to locate any of them as he drove around in his rented car.

After an hour of searching through busy, neon-washed streets, the city began to take on the topology of a nightmare. He wondered if he would still be searching when dawn came up over the desert.

It was almost as if someone was trying to stop him finding the police station. Someone who didn't want him handing in the computer disk.

He shook this thought out of his head. This was no time to get imaginative. It would be too easy to spook himself with thoughts like that. Think positive. Everything was going to be fine. He'd find a police station, drop the disk in, and rendezvous with the others at the motel as planned.

And then he'd be back with Miranda.

He'd been away from her for only an hour, but already it felt like days. Danny felt a momentary pang of regret. She'd wanted to come with him, but he'd insisted she stay behind. And it had been the right decision. He felt more secure knowing that she was safe with the others. Who knew? There might be some unforeseen complication. The police might try to detain him when he delivered the floppy disk.

As he drove, Danny gave careful thought to how he'd hand over the floppy. He felt quite buoyant and cheerful. After all, he wasn't really alone.

He knew that Miranda was there, in his head, only a thought away. His girl, riding shotgun in his skull.

This knowledge comforted him as he searched the streets for the elusive police substation. Finally, with the help of a telephone book and a tourist street map, he began to make sense of the city. It seemed he had wandered wildly off course, right out of Downtown. The Downtown area command was now tediously far south of him, as was the Southeast substation.

But the Northeast substation was nearby, on Mojave

Road, just below Washington Boulevard. Danny was confident that he could find it. He traced his finger across the map. The streets of Las Vegas had bizarre, exotic names which, under less stressful circumstances, he might have found charming.

He had just come off Bonanza for instance, and then on to Tonapah, a place name that reminded him of his favourite song by Little Feat. And now he was on . . .

Danny looked up from the map. No. That couldn't be right. He threw the map down and started the car again, racing down the street, squinting ahead, looking for a sign. He had to check the name.

When he finally found a sign, he had to stop the car and stare at it, trying to control the sudden surge of irrational fear that raced through him.

The street was called Comstock.

Comstock. This was where all his confused driving had led him, as if by some inexorable twist of fate. Danny forced himself to calm down.

At least the cross street wasn't called Brilly, he told himself. With that grisly piece of humour he managed a tense grin. A moment later he started the car again and drove east. Soon he was only a few blocks from the police station.

He parked the car and got out, looking for a public telephone. A quick call established that the captain of the Northeast area command was a policeman called Randy Oaks.

Danny addressed an envelope to Captain Oaks and slipped the floppy disk into it along with a note. Then he locked the rental car and began the short walk to the substation.

He was two blocks away when he became aware that someone was walking behind him, keeping pace with him.

FORTY-TWO

Someone had been following him for some time.

Danny took a quick step to the left and darted into the doorway of a darkened bank, empty and closed for the night. Now he was in a better position to defend himself from attack. He spun around to face the man who had been following.

And he almost burst out laughing.

The man was virtually a caricature of a middle-aged tourist. He wore a ludicrous, ill-fitting Hawaiian shirt, khaki shorts and sandals. The exposed white legs jutting from the shorts had a writhing pattern of varicose veins around the calves. The legs were almost sticklike in their contrast to the man's big bulging torso.

Above the collar of the lurid Hawaiian shirt, the man's balding head was bare. He wore a large pair of cheap plastic sunglasses with heavy black frames and seemed to peer out timidly from behind them.

The slope of the shoulders, the potbelly, the scrofulous ring of thinning greasy hair, all were familiar to Danny. There was no question about it.

It was Mr Leiber.

But he looked so ludicrous that, instead of feeling afraid, Danny experienced an exhilarating leap of defiance. This was the man who had terrified him earlier. But that was when Danny had been helpless, locked in a room with Leiber and three brutal killers.

This was quite a different proposition. On his own, here on the open street, in this ridiculous get-up, Mr Leiber didn't seem remotely so formidable.

And then there was the fact that the cheap sunglasses concealed those remarkable eyes. Normally Danny didn't think he could have looked into Mr Leiber's eyes, but now he stepped back out on to the pavement and faced the man squarely and defiantly.

All he saw was his own reflection in the cheap sunglasses. Danny saw a fierce involuntary scowl forming on his own face, like the snarl of an animal.

And Mr Leiber was backing hastily away from this scowl. As though Danny was frightening *him* this time. That gave Danny a savage stab of satisfaction. Triumph rose like a fire in his belly, warming him. The man who had humiliated him, who had tried to take his life, was cowering before him.

Mr Leiber wiped his mouth and cleared his throat and spoke. His normally colourless voice seemed nervous and uncertain.

'I don't suppose it would do any good to ask you for ... ah ... that object which the young lady borrowed from us.'

'The young lady? You mean the seven-year-old girl you were planning to murder.'

Mr Leiber licked his lips, nervously glancing around them. There was no one else on the pavement nearby, although a swift stream of cars sped past in the street. 'Ah, lower your voice if you don't mind,' said Mr Leiber. 'We are after all rather close to –'

'The metropolitan police substation,' said Danny with satisfaction.

'Yes, look, can't we talk about this somewhere quiet?'

'Talk about what? We have nothing to talk about.'

'Please let me explain. You are in, er, possession of something which belongs to us, belongs to Nuala, and I'm sure we can come to some kind of understanding about it ...'

Mr Leiber rubbed his face nervously. 'Money is no object,' he added.

Danny was getting ready to simply tell Leiber to fuck off. Maybe kick him on to his lardy arse and leave him crying there like a fat baby while Danny strolled to the police station in a leisurely fashion and handed in the floppy disk.

But then a thought popped into Danny's head, and he

279

had to suppress the smile that threatened to spread across his face. A lazy smile of satisfaction and triumph. Because it occurred to Danny that he might be able to deliver Mr Leiber along with the floppy disk.

Hand them both over to Captain Randy Oaks in one neatly wrapped package.

Mr Leiber peered at him timidly. 'Can't we talk about it? Just for a minute?'

Danny rubbed his chin, his mind racing with possibilities. The first thing to do was get Leiber some place where he could be easily trapped.

Maybe humiliatingly locked up in a men's room while Danny made a quick phone call to the police. After all, Mr Leiber's cronies had tried to murder Danny in a bathroom. To use a public toilet as his temporary prison cell would be poetic justice.

Danny came swiftly to a decision. There was a quiet-looking coffee shop half a block away. That would be as good a place as any.

The coffee shop was almost deserted. A tired-looking waitress was pouring refills for a lovey-dovey teenage couple in the far corner, and that was it.

The place had an empty, glaring, late-night feel like something out of a Hopper painting. Danny experienced a moment of intense elation. The coffee shop looked mysterious and beautiful to him, full of significance.

It was to be the scene of his triumph over Mr Leiber.

Mr Leiber entered the coffee shop, blinking and peering anxiously from behind his sunglasses. When he spotted Danny he hurried over to join him, wiping sweat off his forehead. He flopped heavily into the chair opposite, his rolls of middle-aged fat jiggling. 'They drive like maniacs in this city,' he said apologetically. 'I thought I'd never get across that road.'

Danny felt a weird tugging sensation in his mind. It startled him. It was persistent and primal, like a child tugging at your sleeve to get your attention. For a moment he didn't understand what was happening.

Then he realised it was Miranda.

Despite his instructions, she was trying to get in touch with him. Danny felt a little irritated. He wanted Mr Leiber to be put safely in police custody. Then he could relax and enjoy his victory. He would be a hero and it would be a great joy to sense Miranda's presence.

Right now, however, she was just a distraction from the immensely important task of nailing the old bastard. An irritating distraction. Mixed in with his irritation, Danny felt a wave of love.

He couldn't help responding to Miranda and, as she sensed this reaction in him, she built on it, immediately strengthening the link.

In a split second she was there in his head. A warm presence sharing his sensations, looking out through his eyes.

And he felt her instant jangling alarm at Mr Leiber's presence, sitting there across the table from him.

Mr Leiber watched him, staring through the dark lenses of his cheap, smeared sunglasses. 'Is something wrong?' he said.

'Shut up,' said Danny bluntly. He squeezed his eyes shut and concentrated. Then he began the process of forcibly elbowing Miranda out of his mind.

Finally, he opened his eyes and looked at Mr Leiber. There was now a cup of steaming coffee on the table in front of him. Danny looked at the coffee, then at Mr Leiber.

'Sorry, I didn't mean to tell you to shut up,' he said.

'Oh no, please don't apologise.' Mr Leiber simpered sycophantically. He indicated the cups of coffee. 'I hope you don't mind. I took the liberty of ordering for us while you were, ah . . . otherwise preoccupied. You obviously had something important on your mind.'

Mr Leiber added milk to his coffee. 'The mind is a fascinating thing, isn't it?' He tore open a pink sachet of low-calorie sweetener and poured the contents into the cup. 'And you know, in a way, that's what I brought you here to talk about.'

Brought me here? Danny thought it had been the other way around.

But suddenly he wasn't so certain. And with this uncertainty Miranda was suddenly back in his head. She was agitated. She didn't understand why he was letting himself get so close to their deadly enemy.

Mr Leiber was talking and he couldn't hear what he was saying. Danny decided he had to get rid of her. He concentrated again.

The process was much quicker this time because he had hit on an image that he knew would keep her out. He took it from an old film called *The Village of the Damned*. Danny just imagined a brick wall spreading high and solid, right across the back of his mind, sealing off the dark space above the spinal cord, where he imagined Miranda's signals arriving.

He imagined the brick wall in some detail, right down to the thick layer of mortar between the bricks. The trick worked. He smiled with relief. He'd got rid of her.

Mr Leiber was watching him closely, with a quizzical expression. No wonder he was puzzled, thought Danny. Obviously it was impossible for him to imagine what had been going on.

'Some kind of problem with telepathic conflict, is it?' said Mr Leiber.

Danny gaped at him. Mr Leiber sipped his coffee and smiled at Danny. 'Don't look so surprised. I realised right away. It was obvious that a telepathic link was involved. And I imagine it was the girl called Miranda.'

He smiled again. 'I could see that she had the aura of the telepath, just as I can see it in you. One often passes people in the street and sees that they have the gift to some degree, even though they are completely unaware of it. It reveals itself as a fascinating shimmer in their aura, particularly around the site of the so-called "third eye".'

Danny felt a little flicker of returning courage. 'I don't believe in any of that shit,' he said defiantly. 'I don't believe in auras.' It was good to hear the sound of his own voice.

Mr Leiber waved a hand dismissively. 'Obviously I'm not talking about some kind of literal aura, like a Beatles *Yellow Submarine* rainbow. The term is merely shorthand, since you wouldn't understand a more complete description.'

He sighed. 'Our friend Christopher would have no trouble understanding, but you are a considerably less formidable opponent, young man.'

He glanced down at his cup. 'Yes, the two of you are very different.' He stirred and sipped his coffee. 'For instance, Christopher Matthew would be capable of sitting across this table from me, having this conversation, and leaving alive.'

Mr Leiber smiled and put down his coffee cup.

Danny discovered that a layer of sweat was covering his entire body like a warm film of oil. He was experiencing a primal spasm of pure fear. With no conscious command from his mind, his body jerked upright. He wanted to run, to get away. He began to pull himself away from the table, his legs trembling like rubber.

'Sit down,' said Mr Leiber. He didn't say it loudly but there was such authority in his voice that Danny couldn't disobey. The idea of contradicting that voice was unthinkable.

Danny sat down.

'Now, what were we talking about?' said Mr Leiber. He peered thoughtfully into his coffee cup. 'Oh yes. Telepathy. Which leads us to the whole question of the human mind and its potential. As I said, the human mind is a fascinating thing. And the evolution of the mind is an equally astonishing subject to contemplate, Danny. It's rather like staring up at the stars in the night sky and wondering what forces have brought this protean, complex beauty before us. Indeed what is at the root of human consciousness? Well, for one thing, a sophisticated grasp of signs and symbols, the abstractions that hold such a great power for human beings. Indeed a life-and-death power.

'Think of an elderly Jew walking his dog in the old Warsaw ghetto. Just before the Nazis close in. Man and dog pause and stare up at a swastika daubed on a wall. All the dog sees is a shape of paint. The man is terrified. He knows what it symbolises, what it portends. But there was a time when it would have meant as little to a man as it did to his dog. Think of the momentous moment when all that *changed*. Millions of years ago something happened to us, the human race, and the modern mind appeared, beautifully shaped for us by evolution. That was the true turning point in history, Danny. We celebrate the day man learnt to create fire. But with a fire you can merely forge blades of iron. The discovery of fire was nothing compared to the discovery of the symbol. And thanks to the symbol the human imagination has a power that transcends any fire. It has become a superheated blaze in which we can forge weapons more deadly than any blade of iron. Yes, the keen, new cutting edges of the mind, Danny: the symbol and our ability to apprehend it.'

Mr Leiber paused and sipped his coffee. Danny wanted to get up and flee, but a terrible fatalistic lethargy had settled over his limbs. He knew now how the rabbit must feel, frozen in the oncoming headlights.

Mr Leiber set his coffee cup aside. 'Sorry to break off like that.' He stared at Danny from behind the dark lenses of his sunglasses and smiled. 'I needed a drink – my mouth was getting dry. Now where was I? Ah yes. When the power of the symbol was fresh. When the sight of a simple wooden image could kill a man. A small wooden doll with a crude spike driven through its heart literally had the power to kill, through suggestion and the sheer terror concomitant to it. The *idea* of death still had something of the potency of death itself. Our ancient ancestors were in some ways psychologically unsophisticated. Our modern culture exposes us to abstract information all the time. We have developed an immunity to it. If we hadn't, the human race might have died out. Nowadays the symbol has become a debased commonplace, robbed of its once great power.'

A bus shot past outside the coffee shop and Mr Leiber gestured at the bright advertisement emblazoned on the side. 'The power of the image. We have developed a measure of immunity to it. And yet . . .'

Mr Leiber smiled. The sweat coating Danny's body began to cool and form a chill sheen.

'And yet we must not forget that it is the power to conjure an *inner* image that is all-important. The signal outside the head creates a corresponding thought *inside* it. That is what the sight of a voodoo doll did in the "primitive" mind. "But where does one find a primitive mind these days?" I hear you cry. True, man's primal innocence is lost. Those precious tiny enclaves where the voodoo doll once worked to dramatic effect have now been exposed to our devalued coinage of symbols. They are becoming just like us. MTV videos are being pumped in by satellite to contaminate the Kalahari.

'So the question is, the challenge is, how does one trigger a lethal image in someone who is immune to the power of the symbol? A member of our zestfully over-stimulated media culture? Someone like you, Danny.'

Mr Leiber shrugged. 'The answer is simple. The voodoo doll might have lost its power to reach the death trigger in your mind. But the trigger is still there. It simply requires more sophisticated techniques to reach it.'

Mr Leiber smiled. 'How could I possibly know the thought that would kill you? I don't. Of course I don't. But I don't need to, Danny. Because *you* know it. After all, it's your thought.'

Mr Leiber smiled. 'It is waiting deep inside you. It is waiting deep inside everyone.'

And then he did something terrible. He removed his sunglasses.

His eyes were worse than Danny had remembered. They stared right into his soul. There was immeasurable power in them and he was quite helpless before it. He felt a queasy flicker of self-contempt when he remembered how he'd planned to trap this man.

He'd believed he was in control. But Mr Leiber had

been in control, from the moment they met.

Mr Leiber smiled again. 'I don't suppose you've ever heard of Count Tolstoy's white-bear club, Danny? Well, it is quite an amusing conceit. You see, to become a member of this club all you have to do is sit in a corner for ten minutes and *not* think of a white bear. Of course, no one ever gets to join the club because it is impossible to resist the urge to think of a white bear.'

He put his sunglasses on and rose briskly from the table, smiling down at Danny. 'Just as it will be impossible for you to sit here and not think the thought that will kill you.'

He clapped Danny chummily on the shoulder. 'Why don't you keep that computer disk, my young friend? I have the feeling that you won't be bothering the police with it.'

Mr Leiber spilt some coins on to the table. 'Do allow me to pay. It has been very much my pleasure.'

He walked away. After a moment he came back to the table. 'Oh, and one more thing. Since you're telepathic, your girlfriend Miranda will of course be infected by the very same process I have set in motion in your head. It will spread to her. Once she knows about the lethal thought she will find her own version of it, and she too will die.'

Mr Leiber turned and walked out of the café. Danny heard the door close. He remained sitting at the table, unable to move. Strange thoughts were rushing through his head, like fish circling in dark water.

He could feel these thoughts wanting to come to the surface. He forced them back down. He tried to keep his mind blank. What if one of these thoughts was the very one that could kill him?

Danny tried to sit quietly at the table and not think about anything. He felt as if he was balancing a cannon ball on his head. If he wasn't careful, any moment it might wobble off and come crashing down.

The waitress came and went.

Danny tried not to think of anything. Maybe Mr Leiber was wrong. Maybe he could get through this alive.

But then he found himself thinking of a white bear. A huge polar bear. Danny remembered that polar bears were dangerous animals. They often attacked and killed human beings.

He tried to make his mind a blank again. It didn't work. He could feel all sorts of thoughts stirring in the background, trying to break through.

And with horror he realised that it wasn't his own thoughts. It was Miranda, trying to make contact with him.

Danny had no doubt that Mr Leiber had been telling the truth. Those extraordinary eyes allowed no doubt. He had already been killed by words, by a quiet conversation in a coffee shop. His own pride had led him here, condemning him to death.

But his own death was one thing. The idea of Miranda being dragged down with him was quite another. And if she managed to achieve telepathic contact with him there would be no way of preventing it.

She would pick up the death thought and be infected by it. And then she too would die.

Danny Bailey had been frozen, but now he found himself galvanised into action. He pushed away from the table and rose on trembling legs. Moving unsteadily towards the door, he could see the Las Vegas traffic outside in the night, sweeping briskly past in an endless stream.

At the back of his mind he could feel Miranda struggling furiously to get in.

He began to run.

Miranda knew he was hiding something from her and she was panic-stricken. She was trying to get through the brick wall he'd imagined.

Brick by brick she was battering her way in.

As Danny approached the coffee-shop door he closed his eyes and concentrated. He burst through the door with his eyes shut and stood there on the pavement panting, inhaling the hot night air perfumed with exhaust fumes.

Danny tried to concentrate. He squeezed his eyes shut. He had to repair the wall that Miranda was smashing through.

He urgently jammed the bricks back in place, but it was no good. Soon she would find a way through.

He had to act immediately. What could he do? A few feet away, cars sped by, their headlights dim in the neon night.

Suddenly he knew what he must do.

Danny crossed the pavement and stood at the kerb, waiting patiently. By now the screaming in his mind had stopped but he still sensed Miranda there, scratching at the wall, like a faithful dog that didn't understand why it had been shut out.

He had to protect her. There was no other choice. His own life was already lost, but he could still save her.

Danny waited for the right moment, waited for a mass of vehicles moving so fast they could never stop in time. Then he braced himself and stepped out into the street.

Really, it was no worse than when you go swimming, that first moment when you have to step into cold deep water.

He heard the shrieking of brakes, the shrilling of a horn.

His last thought was of Miranda.

FORTY-THREE

McCarran International Airport in Las Vegas was much like any other airport in the world, except for the slot machines.

Juliette hated the slot machines. And they were everywhere. Even in the ladies' toilet.

She stared at herself in the mirror and wondered if this was the face of a deeply flawed human being. She finished drying her face and threw the paper towel away. Her reflection marched briskly across the bright faces of the slot machines as she left the washroom. The door swung shut and suddenly she was back in the echoing space of the airport.

She hurried towards the departure lounge, checking her watch.

It had been easy enough to find the next flight to London and take note of the gate number. Gate 17.

Juliette soon found a likely spot, by a drinking fountain opposite the departure lounge. There she waited until she saw him.

'Tregemmon!'

Tregemmon spun around at the sound of her voice. For an instant he looked pleased to see her, then a guarded expression settled over his face.

'Come to see me off?' he said coolly.

'As a matter of fact, I have.'

'So you won't try and talk me out of it.'

'Of course not.'

'I've made up my mind. I'm leaving.'

'Of course.'

A look of pain crossed Tregemmon's face. 'Juliette, for God's sake, I shot the wrong man.'

'You also shot a lot of the right men. And if you hadn't done that the rest of us would be dead.'

'Sweet of you to say so, but I'm still not coming back to help you.'

'I'm not asking you to, Tregemmon. I just didn't want you to go away taking any burden of guilt with you.'

Tregemmon set his bag down. He checked his flight time on the monitor and then looked at her. The look of distrust was gradually softening and leaving his eyes.

'I know you feel bad about what happened,' said Juliette. 'But you did save us. Thank you. That's why I came here. To say that. And wish you all the best.'

'Straight up?' said Tregemmon wonderingly.

'Straight up. Please don't be haunted by what happened here. Don't spend your life blaming yourself.'

'An innocent man died. I shot him.'

'And you saved my little sister's life. And I'll always be grateful for that.'

'Well, maybe not always,' said Tregemmon drolly. 'I've heard the way you girls argue.'

Juliette blushed. It was true. She and Emily had resumed their usual bickering with dismaying swiftness after their initial tearful reunion. It was embarrassing to think how swiftly all the old sisterly antagonisms had arisen again. She felt her cheeks flaming shamefully at the mere thought of it.

And as she blushed Tregemmon began to smile again. It was good to see him smile, and Juliette shared the relief that spread across his face.

But she was still quite startled when he reached out his long arms and hugged her. She didn't resist the hug, though. After a moment she was returning it warmly.

'That feels good,' Tregemmon suddenly said, and they both laughed. Juliette clung to him gratefully. She knew that life was too short not to show some emotion. Far too short.

After all, look at what happened to Danny.

The thought made her tense up and Tregemmon felt her stiffen in his arms. He instantly released her, perhaps misinterpreting her reaction.

And Juliette couldn't explain. She had promised herself that she wouldn't tell Tregemmon about what had happened. If she did, it would amount to an attempt to make him stay.

So she just smiled weakly as he picked up his suitcases again and glanced up at the screen showing the flight times.

'Thank you for not doing the emotional-blackmail thing,' he said.

'I understand that you have to go, Tregemmon. Good luck.'

'Thanks. The same to you.'

He turned and walked towards the departure gate. As he did so, a figure stepped out of the shadows, from behind a bank of telephones.

'Oh shit,' sighed Tregemmon in disgust. 'What are you doing here?'

Christopher Matthew grinned at him. 'I've come to do the emotional-blackmail thing.'

Tregemmon glanced back at Juliette bitterly.

'Don't blame her, Tregemmon. She didn't know that I followed her.'

'You're sinking to low tactics.'

'I have to. I'm afraid things are getting a little weird right now.'

'Things always get weird around you,' said Tregemmon wearily.

'Tregemmon, I've come here because I need your help against Leiber.'

'Don't do this, man. Christ, I knew it. I shouldn't even have stopped to talk to the shrink.'

'Tregemmon, *she's* not asking you. But *I* am asking you. Leiber is still out there somewhere and I don't stand a chance against him without your help.'

Tregemmon had been staring at the departure screen; now he looked angrily at Christopher. 'Look, you think I'm leaving because I shot the wrong guy in the stairwell.'

'Well, isn't that true?'

'No,' snarled Tregemmon. 'That's not why I'm leaving.'

Juliette could see him make a conscious effort to regain his temper. 'Or it's only part of it.'

Now the anger faded completely from Tregemmon's face. 'The truth is, I'm scared.'

He looked at Christopher Matthew, standing in the shadows, looking ghostly with his long white hair.

'Ever since this thing started I've had the feeling I wouldn't get through this alive.' He looked at Juliette, as if pleading with her to understand. He nodded at Christopher. 'If I hang around with you I'm going to end up dead.'

'Then go, Tregemmon,' said Juliette. But he wasn't listening to her. He was looking at Christopher again. 'Don't try and ask me to stay.'

'I have to,' said Christopher. 'I'm about to go into battle and you're my strong right arm.'

There was the flicker of a smile on Tregemmon's face. 'Like one of King Arthur's knights.'

'If you want to think of it that way.'

Tregemmon's expression became grim again. 'I seem to remember *they* all ended up dead.' He picked up his suitcase.

'Did Juliette tell you about Miranda?'

Tregemmon paused. 'What about her?'

'Didn't you wonder why she isn't here to say goodbye to you?'

Juliette said, 'Don't do this. It isn't fair.'

But Tregemmon wasn't listening. He was shaking his head, a fond smile spreading across his face. 'I assumed she didn't come because she was too busy in bed with Danny. His near-death experience seems to have had an effect on those two like Spanish Fly. Lucky old Danny . . . I wouldn't mind being saved that way. A beautiful blonde giving me the kiss of life.'

Tregemmon was chuckling. Then he looked at Juliette and saw the expression on her face. He turned to Christopher. 'What happened?'

'We don't know exactly, but Danny insisted on going to the police.'

'That was stupid.'

Christopher explained about the computer disk and Tregemmon nodded. 'I can understand that. So what happened to him?'

'Mr Leiber intercepted him.'

'Oh no.'

'All we know is that they went into a coffee shop together and Mr Leiber spoke to him for about five minutes. Then Danny walked out of the coffee shop and deliberately threw himself in front of a taxi.'

'He killed himself?'

'Apparently.'

'The bastard put some kind of mindfuck on him.'

'Yes. That's what we surmise.'

'Perhaps some form of autosuggestion or hypnosis,' added Juliette, reluctantly allowing herself to be dragged into the conversation.

Tregemmon was staring at Christopher with a hard gaze. 'You're telling me this because you think it will make me stay?'

'No, I'm telling you because I know he was your friend.'

Tregemmon's shoulders sagged. He stood silently for a long moment. Finally he reached into his pocket and drew something out. Juliette saw that it was an airline ticket.

He folded it in two and began to tear it up.

'You win,' he said bitterly.

FORTY-FOUR

'Where are we heading?'

'Emily overheard Mr Leiber talking to his girlfriend.'

'She's a sneaky little so-and-so, isn't she?' said Tregemmon.

Emily chuckled from the back of the vehicle.

'And she heard Nuala tell Mr Leiber that she wanted to explore the desert,' said Christopher Matthew. 'And he said that was all right because he had business in New Mexico anyway.'

'And that's all you have?' said Juliette, tugging bad-temperedly at her seat belt as she leant forward to make herself heard. 'That's pretty tenuous, isn't it?'

Christopher shrugged. 'As it happens, I have some friends in this part of the world. They might be able to help us.'

'It still sounds very tenuous to me,' persisted Juliette. 'I feel ridiculous.'

'If you really want to feel ridiculous,' said Tregemmon, 'you should try driving this thing.' He patted the dashboard of the vehicle they had rented, a large, silver, bullet-shaped 'minivan' – as the rental agent had described it. He had also referred to it as a 'people carrier'.

It was a roomy, comfortable vehicle, although it stank with the ghosts of old cigarette smoke. There were three rows of seats and a sliding side door, allowing easy access.

Tregemmon waited for a truck to pass him, then signalled and changed lanes. 'Try driving this piece of . . . excrement.'

Emily leant forward. 'Are you avoiding the use of a more biting obscenity in deference to my tender years?'

'Quiet in the back there.'

* * *

They drove out of Las Vegas, on to 515 towards Route 15. The road hummed endlessly under their wheels as Tregemmon drove through the long night, manoeuvring the vehicle with concentration and skill. When his seemingly limitless energy finally waned, Christopher took over at the wheel. When exhaustion finally claimed him, too, they stopped and checked in at a motel.

That was the pattern for the time that followed and, for Miranda, the motels began to blur. There was nothing to distinguish one day from another.

Until the nightmares began.

Miranda never remembered the content of these troubling dreams. But it was embarrassingly obvious that she was suffering, because one day Emily came up and offered her battered teddy bear, Mr Rafferty, to her.

'He'll help you sleep,' said the little girl. Obviously Miranda had been crying out in her dreams. She accepted the bear, rather touched by the gesture. And it did actually seem to help, this cuddly soft toy in her bed.

'Now you're just borrowing him,' said Emily. 'Is that quite understood?'

But then one night at a motel just outside Flagstaff, Arizona, Mr Rafferty failed in his duty and Miranda once again had a nightmare, and one that she would have cause to remember.

She had a room to herself at the motel, on the opposite side of the motor court to the others. As soon as she'd closed the door she had dropped her clothes on the floor and crawled gratefully between the cool clean sheets of her bed.

Slumped forward with her face pressed into the sterile, synthetic smell of the motel pillow, Miranda had been too tired even for grief. But as she drifted off she began to think, inevitably, of Danny.

She slipped into dreams, thinking of the brick wall he had built in his mind. The one he had built to keep her out.

As the motel air conditioner hummed and buzzed, Miranda dreamt sad dreams of that brick wall. Rolling restlessly around on the motel bed she could see every detail of the pitted red bricks and the thick grey mortar that locked them into place.

There was a thin clinging coating of lichen on the brick, as if the wall had been standing a long time.

Danny was behind this wall now.

When she touched it, the bricks were cold and hard and solid. Miranda wondered if this was what death felt like. This cold solid finality. She caressed the gritty surface of the wall, fingers tracing the massive stability of the bricks.

Then something astonishing happened. The bricks moved, pulsing outward under her hand. She was sure of it. Miranda pressed her hands to the wall again and felt it quiver once more.

She stared at it. Dust drifted down on her. Particles of bricks and crumbs of mortar were spilling off the wall. Then she saw a brick dislodge itself and drop out, plummeting past her face.

Suddenly there was a gap in the wall.

Miranda's heart surged with joy. Danny wasn't sealed away from her after all. He had begun to break down the barrier that had come between them. Miranda felt tears of joy course down her face. Their love was so strong it had overcome death.

The gap in the wall was widening. Dust showered from it and bricks were falling in a steady rain. They were virtually flying as she smashed through the wall.

In fact, Miranda realised, it wasn't so much as if she was smashing through the wall. It was more as if something was smashing through it towards *her*. But the realisation was masked by her excitement at the thought of seeing Danny.

The gap in the wall was big enough to see through now. Beyond the wall was darkness. And in the darkness stood a man.

But it wasn't Danny. It was a nondescript middle-aged man, overweight and pasty-faced and balding.

It was Mr Leiber.

He stood there, smiling at her from the other side of the

wall. And his smile was disturbingly meaningless, the rictus of a corpse. 'Good evening, my dear,' he said. 'I am so delighted to see you. After young Danny flung himself under that speeding automobile and there was that very loud and very final crunching sound, I feared our paths would never cross again. You know you really were very lucky to have found such a brave and gallant lover. One who was willing to die for you.'

Mr Leiber stepped casually through the hole in the wall and Miranda stepped back in fear.

'And, since I have managed to make contact with you, perhaps you'd be kind enough to pass a message on to Christopher Matthew.'

But Miranda had turned away from Mr Leiber and was fleeing in terror. Behind her, standing in the ruins of the wall, he called after her. 'All right, then. It's a very simple message. Just tell him, "This is for you." Have you got that? "This is for you." '

Miranda snapped awake. What a dreadful nightmare. It had left her feeling unclean. In her grief she had been longing to make contact with Danny, but instead she had made entirely the wrong kind of contact.

It was like reaching out in the dark and putting your hand in something filthy.

Her heart was beating so hard that her whole body trembled. Get a grip, Miranda told herself. She was just beginning to calm down when a thought wormed its way into her head. Perhaps it hadn't been a nightmare at all.

Perhaps it had been real.

What if the message was real? What if Mr Leiber shared the gift of telepathy? That's what Danny had believed.

It was frightening to imagine someone like that possessing the power, but it was possible. After all, Miranda was in no position to deny the reality of ESP.

Perhaps he really had been inside her head. The dream had certainly seemed real. What was it that he had said to her? A message she was supposed to give Christopher Matthew:

'This is for you.'

What could that mean? Miranda wrestled with the question, her mind still blurry with sleep and residual fear. She felt very strange. Her heart was slamming with panic.

It hadn't calmed down at all. Instead it seemed to be beating so hard now that it was causing the bed to shake.

Not just the bed, but the whole room. And there was a sound outside like a freight train rattling past. A freight train big enough to rock the whole building.

That was impossible. They were miles from any railway. But the room was shaking. The shock of this realisation brought Miranda fully awake. She was alone in a motel room in the middle of the desert and suddenly the world had gone mad.

The ground, which Miranda was accustomed to thinking of as permanently solid, had suddenly changed into a trembling, shifting mass.

The furniture was dancing around the room in the moonlight. A heavy-framed painting of horses tilted and then crashed from the wall.

Miranda lay in bed clinging to the sheets like a little kid and praying for the nightmare to end. But the nightmare didn't end, and all at once the bed itself began to move, leaving the wall and joining in the dance of the furniture around the room. It moved with a grating sound like some kind of vehicle starting up.

It felt horridly as if the bed had come to life. Miranda was lying on top of a big beast that had decided to carry her off.

She tore the sheets away and jumped off the shuddering mattress, landing barefoot on the cold floor. Sickeningly, the floor was no more stable than the bed. It trembled violently under her feet. Miranda tried to get her balance and then suddenly she saw the big wooden shape of the bed dancing towards her, juddering across the floor.

She jumped out of its path and it crashed into the wall. Clouds of dust floated in the moonlight.

By now, Miranda was running for the door.

She was stark naked but she didn't even think about

pausing to grab any clothes. The door frame was squeaking around the door as the wall flexed around it and for one awful moment the door jammed. Then suddenly the frame let go like a big mouth opening and the door sprang free. Miranda ran out of the motel into the concrete car park.

A whiskery old man from the next unit was already standing out there, hopping around in his bright, scarlet longjohns. The old man was so scared he hardly noticed Miranda's lack of clothing.

Over on the other side of the swaying motel court, Tregemmon and Christopher were piling out of their rooms. Then she saw Juliette and Emily come running out of a third room.

The old man standing beside Miranda turned and looked at her. He tried to smile, but he was too scared to carry it off. He shook his head and spoke in a high, quavering voice.

'Man, I sure do hate these damned things. I left California to get away from earthquakes.'

PART THREE

THE SOCORRO SEISMIC ANOMALY

'Hey, your boyfriend's taken my dog away from me.' The little man smiled at Juliette.

She turned to see Christopher smiling and patting a big grey dog that had flung itself down at his feet. 'Sorry,' he said. The dog was wagging its tail frantically as if greeting his long-lost master. 'I didn't mean to.'

The little man shrugged. 'That's OK, keep him,' he said affably. He winked at Juliette and returned to his seat behind the counter. Juliette realised that he had referred to Chris as her boyfriend, and she hadn't bothered to contradict him. What did that signify?

'A dog without loyalty is a worthless beast,' said the little man with mock despair. She tried not to stare at him. It wasn't easy because his face was extraordinarily wizened and gnarled, his features all mashed together in deep wrinkles like the bark on the curving bole of a tree.

He wore a cowboy hat, and a clean white shirt and jeans that must have been especially tailored to fit his squat, barrel-chested torso and his rather grotesque, stumpy, bandy legs.

His head was very large in contrast to those stubby limbs and torso. In fact he was what, in unkinder times, might have been called a dwarf.

'But if you folks don't mind,' said the little man, 'this bookshop is officially closed.'

The dwarf sat behind the counter in the middle of a big square room crowded with thousands of books, neatly lined up on shelves and tables.

Old armchairs were placed around the room for the comfort of browsers. A large Persian carpet stretched across the floor. It had obviously once been very beautiful but it was now threadbare and sun-faded.

The sun shone through the wide window behind Juliette, throwing backward shadows of lettering on the floor which read TAOS TONAL BOOK STORE: NEW AGE AND OCCULT OUR SPECIALTY.

The sunlight was warm and heavy. It gleamed on the polished wood of the store. The whole place smelt of books, a drowsy musty scent in the warm light.

Juliette shook off her drowsiness. She saw that Miranda had wandered over to a magazine rack. She went over and joined the girl, studying the titles on display. On the other side of the store, the men continued talking.

'Is your name Emmett Gorgon?' said Christopher.

The small man grinned. 'That's right. A blatant pseudonym, or *nom de guerre*, of course. Taken partly from the great hippie anarchist Emmett Grogan – we've got a couple of his books around here someplace, first editions at surprisingly reasonable prices – and partly, of course, from the Gorgon.'

He smiled, his battered, wrinkled face creasing further. 'That mythical creature who is so ugly it only takes one glimpse to turn you into stone.' He doffed his cowboy hat at Juliette in a gallant manner and smiled. Then he did the same to Miranda.

She felt she ought to return his smile because Miranda hadn't, and, besides, the little man was really quite sweet. Juliette couldn't help thinking how his body must have shaped his mind. He would have suffered considerable rejection and pain in his life.

Juliette became aware of Miranda beside her, flipping through the magazines. Poor Miranda.

She had been obviously troubled ever since the earthquake. Before that she had been concealing her grief over Danny's death.

Now she was flipping through a lurid-looking magazine. Juliette couldn't help peeking at it over the girl's shoulder. The photographs really were shocking.

Over by the counter Christopher was saying, 'I'm sorry

to drop in on you unannounced like this. But I got your name from some friends.'

'Don't apologise. Feel free to drop in unannounced any time, providing you bring beautiful young women with you. Beautiful young women... and fascinating small elfs.'

Juliette noticed that Emily had pushed a wheeled metal ladder to one of the bookcases and was scrambling up it like a climbing marsupial to reach a fat paperback on a high shelf. Typical. Juliette felt herself tensing up in case the little idiot tumbled off the ladder. But Emily was disgustingly well coordinated. As she lithely descended, clutching the book, the little man went over and joined her. 'Hello, elf.'

He took the book from Emily, who surrendered it reluctantly, and studied the cover.

'*History of Western Philosophy*, volume two. We have volume one and three as well, around here someplace.' He handed the book back to her and stared at the thousands of books neatly lining the shelves all around him.

'It's elves, not elfs,' said Emily diffidently. 'And don't worry about volume one and three. I've read them all already anyway.' She put the book back sniffily on a low shelf. 'Although I *am* fascinated by the way Bertrand Russell came so close to the truth and then faltered.'

She turned her back rudely on the little man and came over to join Miranda and Juliette at the magazine rack. 'I'm speaking of his mathematical work now, of course.'

The little man turned back to Christopher. 'So what exactly brings you to my humble establishment?'

'We're looking for somebody who expressed an interest in visiting Taos. And your bookshop seems to be the sort of place in Taos that he was likely to visit.'

'Well, I'm afraid you're asking the wrong midget. For one thing I haven't been in Taos for the last couple of weeks. In fact, I only stopped by today to collect the mail.'

He went to the counter and reached behind it and took out a large package. He held it up proudly. Then his face clouded. 'You see, my girlfriend's not too well.'

Emmett Gorgon paused and Juliette realised with surprise that his voice was choked with emotion. 'Rosie,' he said hoarsely, 'she's, well, let's just say that lately she hasn't been feeling too chipper. I've been staying with her out in the desert, taking care of her.'

He seemed to gather himself and, with an effort, got his emotions under control. He smiled again. 'So, like I say, I only came into town today because the post office was delivering something.' He patted the box and then, as if touching it had fired his excitement again, he began to unwrap it, tugging impatiently at the string on it.

Wrenching the string away, he began to tear the brown paper off the box. He paused for a moment and groped behind the counter until he found a gleaming silver letter opener. He used this to pop the box open, pulling out crumpled masses of newspaper, like the innards of a cardboard beast.

The newspaper had obviously been packed in the box as protection. Protection for something precious and delicate.

Juliette noticed that the newspaper had Chinese characters printed on it.

'Ever since I ordered this I've been worrying that it might be broken,' said the little man. 'I can hardly stand the suspense.' He quickly but carefully continued to open the parcel and paused tensely as he peered inside. Then a smile spread across his face.

'Nope, it's perfect. The US Mail somehow overlooked it.'

He grinned radiantly, plucking out handfuls of wrapping paper, as he unwrapped what looked like some kind of circular ceramic lid. He set the lid down on the counter and Juliette saw that it was made of brown and green porcelain. The little man continued to carefully fish other pieces of similarly coloured porcelain out of the box and assemble them.

What gradually emerged was a tall, graceful Chinese vase. Finely carved details on its brown surface were picked out in green. The vase had four fiercely curving dragons moulded on to it, spaced at regular intervals.

'It's beautiful,' said Juliette, moving away from the magazine rack. 'What is it?'

'A Chinese earthquake detector,' said Christopher Matthew. He walked over to the counter and inspected the vase. 'The ancient Chinese used these to determine the direction of the quake.' Now that she was closer Juliette could see that each dragon on the vase was holding a porcelain ball about the size of a marble in its jaws.

The balls were loosely held in the dragons' jaws and it seemed clear that the slightest vibration would dislodge them.

Below each dragon Emmett Gorgon placed a small porcelain frog with a cartoonishly gaping mouth, ready to catch the ceramic balls. It was really quite an elegant, ingenious device.

Emmett Gorgon pointed out the obvious. 'The slightest earth tremor would cause the ball to drop into the mouth of the appropriate frog, thus indicating the point of origin of the disturbance.'

'Circa third century BC,' said Christopher.

Emmett Gorgon whistled, impressed. 'That's pretty good, pardner. I can see you've been around a little.'

Suddenly his eyes narrowed with suspicion. He peered at Christopher. 'That reminds me, friend. I didn't quite catch your name.'

'Tregemmon calls him the Edge,' called Emily helpfully.

There might have been a flash of recognition in the small man's eyes. He developed a guarded tone in his voice. 'So what do you want from me?'

'As I mentioned, we're looking for someone,' said Christopher.

'Yeah, and as *I* mentioned I can't help you because I haven't been around since Rosie got sick.'

'The person we're after calls himself Mr Leiber.'

'Never heard of him,' said the midget. He began to carefully repack the Chinese vase in its box. 'Now maybe you folks will excuse me. As soon as I get this packed I'm going to shut up shop and hit the road.'

Just then Juliette turned to see her little sister at the

magazine rack, standing like a miniature replica of Miranda, holding exactly the same magazine and reading it with the same absorbed expression.

Juliette crossed the room in three swift strides. 'I'll take that,' she snarled, snatching at the magazine. Her intention was to wrench it away from Emily with the minimum of fuss, but Emily wasn't having any. She soon found that she was wrestling with her for possession of the magazine, in a highly undignified fashion, in the full and interested view of everyone. The shop had gone very quiet.

'What do you think you're doing?' shrieked Emily, piercing the silence with her high-pitched voice.

'This isn't suitable reading matter for someone your age,' said Juliette, trying to sound authoritative and reasonable.

The magazine suddenly came free – perhaps Emily had deliberately and devilishly released it – and Juliette went shooting back. She managed to recover her balance. Everyone was staring at her. She held up the magazine as though it was evidence. The magazine was devoted to 'strange phenomena'. The specific article that her sister had been reading concerned spontaneous human combustion and was illustrated with gruesome photos.

'I mean, look at this,' said Juliette.

Stark images of blackened skeletons and body parts. Charred hands and feet lying obscenely alone beside piles of black ash.

'How dare you try to censor what I read?' Emily suddenly resumed her offensive. She came and tried to snatch the magazine back.

Juliette held it up, out of her reach. 'You shouldn't be wallowing in lurid trash like this.' She glanced at the magazine. 'Yetis. Flying saucers.'

'But perhaps these arcane subjects have something to recommend them,' said Emily, rather pugnaciously. She had recovered her calm and Juliette kept a close eye on her. This was always when she was most dangerous. 'Take *déjà vu*, for instance. I had the oddest episode when you rescued me from the Halloween Hotel. It was just then that I first glimpsed Chris again. And then I got a surge of *déjà vu.* There was something extraordinary about the sensation. Like a distorted echo of memory. It was so eerie that one almost felt that in some absolute sense it had to signify something.' She looked at Juliette with a sanctimonious expression. 'This little epiphany opened my mind to wider possibilities in an almost mystical fashion. And one must always keep an open mind, don't you agree? So yes, even yetis and flying saucers.'

'Even spontaneous human combustion?'

'Even human combustion, most certainly. Besides, to return to our original point, what gives you the right to censor my reading matter?' A note of infantile grievance crept back into her voice. 'Give that magazine back at once. I was just about to read how Mrs Hetty Belstrom of Fort Lauderdale was transformed in the course of one memorable evening into a strange greasy residue clinging to the ceiling and light fixtures.'

'Look, I am a trained physician,' said Juliette. 'I've worked with bodies, both living and dead. I've sat my share of forensic exams. And, believe me, human flesh and bone simply don't burn in that fashion, spontaneously or otherwise.'

'I have a theory,' said Emily in her smuggest voice, 'which is best explained by an analogy with free radicals. Free radicals propagate in the body in a cascade of chemical events, a sort of metabolic chain reaction. And I believe that a similar chain reaction, on a much larger scale, could hijack basic metabolic processes and induce a meltdown of the organism, generating enormous, transient heat. *Sufficient* heat.'

Suddenly she jumped up and managed to snatch the magazine back from Juliette, who had dropped her guard in the soporific onslaught of Emily's monologue. 'So let me read it!' She gleefully danced away, clutching the magazine.

Juliette lost control. She heard herself snort furiously. 'Give it back.'

Emily dodged away. 'There are serious scientific issues at stake here.' Juliette pursued her across the bookshop.

As she fled, the little girl continued to speak as calmly as if delivering a lecture. 'I'm particularly intrigued by the nature of the metabolic event that starts the chain reaction.'

Juliette lunged at her. 'Give me that magazine!'

Emily skidded giggling across the smooth wooden floor of the shop, still holding the magazine. As she did so, she tripped on the old Persian carpet and fell sprawling against the magazine rack with a loud thud. Juliette felt the thud in her stomach.

The sound caused the big grey dog to twitch, startled, and rise up from his place on a sunlit patch of floor.

'Emily, are you all right?'

But Emily was grinning, apparently unscathed. The tall magazine rack, however, hadn't fared so well. It was still shuddering from the collision and magazines began to topple off its wooden shelves.

They fell in a shower of dust, flapping down like a flock of strange flat birds. Down they came, slapping on to the floor.

'Look at what you've done now,' said Juliette disgustedly. She bent over and grabbed the magazine that had been the original cause of their struggle, then set about picking up the other ones and restoring them to the shelves.

The men came over to help, Emmett Gorgon hopping down from the chair where he had been standing behind the counter.

'I'm terribly sorry about this,' said Juliette, her cheeks flushed with embarrassment. 'She's completely out of control.'

'That's OK,' said the little man. 'Nice to meet a youngster with a bit of spirit who actually *reads*. Just think, you could be saddled with an MTV zombie.'

'Mmm,' said Juliette, unconvinced that this was such a terrible thought.

While they tidied up the mess, Emily sat contentedly on the rug, not offering to help, busy reading another magazine which had spilt from a high shelf. Emmett Gorgon came over to her. 'While I'm not one to censor reading matter, I do think that's kind of a bad thing for a young elf to be looking at.'

The magazine was called *Unappreciated Tastes*, and it was subtitled, 'For connoisseurs of serial murder'.

Emily surrendered it to the little man with a disgusted sigh. 'I don't even know why we stock it,' he added, replacing the magazine on as high a shelf as he could reach. 'We've only ever had one customer sick enough to look at it. Sorry to take it away from you, elf, but I really do think it's for the best.'

Emily shrugged 'It's all right. But it's not the first time I've been exposed to what you would have as its mind-rotting propaganda. A girl called Nuala had a copy.'

The little man froze. He turned and looked at Emily. His gnarled face was pale.

'Nuala?'

FORTY-SIX

'Nuala was her name, I'm sure of it,' said Emmett Gorgon. 'She struck me as a nasty piece of work, even on such a short acquaintance.'

He grinned and shook his head. 'Mind you, some people say that's all a midget is,' he added facetiously. 'A short acquaintance.'

From his pocket he took a bunch of keys. To Emily the keys looked enormous, big and brass and jangling musically as he shook them, searching for the right one.

'She came into the store a couple of weeks ago. Just as I was getting ready to cash up the till and schlepp the day's takings over to the bank. But these two looked like potentially good customers. You know, they looked like they might have some money. There was just something about them. The way they stood. The way they moved. Like they were important people. So I went to the bank and I told Rosie to keep the store open and be sure and look after them. See if she could fleece them for some of the long green.'

He paused in his locking of the door and gleefully rubbed his fingers together. Then the light of greedy enthusiasm died in his doggy brown eyes. They filled with regret. 'I left her alone with those two weirdos.'

He shook his head. 'So it's my fault. Everything that happened afterward. If I hadn't left her, Rosie would still be OK now. Happy and full of life and laughing. Instead of . . . instead of like she is.'

There was silence for a moment. They stood awkwardly on the pavement, waiting for him to finish locking the door. But the little man seemed too upset to go on. Finally Christopher spoke. 'And there was a man with Nuala?'

312

'Yeah. I didn't get so good a look at him.' The little man shrugged sadly. 'He was nothing special. Just some middle-aged creep with a young broad. That was another reason I figured he must have money. Otherwise why would a young girl like that be hanging out with a middle-aged nothing?'

'How was he dressed?'

'Like a typical goofball tourist. Shorts, flip-flops, sunglasses. But there was a weird vibe about him.' He brutally twisted the final key in the bottom lock. 'I knew I shouldn't have trusted the son of a bitch.'

'Did you see his eyes?'

'No. Like I said, he was wearing sunglasses.'

Behind the store was a rusting fire escape with rubbish bins ranked underneath it. Beyond the bins a dusty red pickup truck was parked in a sunblasted empty lot.

Next to it Tregemmon had parked the minivan that they had rented in Vegas. The little man paused and looked at this large vehicle. Then he turned and looked at Tregemmon. 'I would have figured you more for the sports-car type.'

'Hell no,' said Tregemmon laconically. 'Give me a people carrier to drive and I'm a happy man.'

Emily elected to join Christopher in the pickup truck, with Emmett Gorgon driving, puffing on a cigar. She observed with fascination that he had rigged hand controls on the dashboard so that he didn't need to reach the brake pedal or accelerator.

Using his hand controls, Emmett Gorgon recklessly accelerated through the traffic, catching each light a split second before it turned red. Emily glanced back anxiously to see if the others were following. To her surprise, the minivan was right beside them, Tregemmon effortlessly keeping pace with the hurtling pickup truck.

'He drives that thing pretty good,' allowed Emmett Gorgon. 'The way he gooses it, it actually does move more like a sports car.'

'We call it the Lunar Excursion Module,' said Emily. She couldn't prevent a note of pride entering her voice.

'That reminds me. A clever little munchkin like yourself

313

should go see the Jasper Institute while you're in town.'

'I thought I was an elf.'

'Munchkin is better, trust me. The Jasper Institute is a whatyacallit, a planetarium. Plus a research lab. They got rooms full of computers buzzing away there, doing computer-type things. They've got equipment that can hear gnats fart on Saturn.' He winked at her. 'You'd love it.'

They had finally reached a red light that even the little man couldn't ignore and he brought the truck to a screeching halt with his hand controls. As they sat waiting at the lights Emily heard the burbling rumble of powerful engines. The sound pulled in beside them. There was something odd about it. It didn't sound like a car.

She saw Emmett Gorgon respond to it. His eyes narrowed with hatred and he leant over to glance surreptitiously into his mirror.

'The Las Cruces Saints. I wonder what those bastards are doing here.'

'A motorcycle gang?' said Christopher with interest. He looked at the friendship band he wore around his wrist.

'That's right,' said Emmett Gorgon. He glanced over at Christopher. 'Those boys are pretty far off their stomping ground. Las Cruces is way the hell south of here.'

Emmett Gorgon exhaled a big blue cloud of smoke and turned to Emily. 'Don't let those outlaw bikers put you off. Taos is a beautiful place. I hate to sound like the tourist board, but you really ought to check out the Pueblo Village. Fascinating insights into the culture of a lost people and all that shit. It's out east of El Prado – on the way to the Jasper Institute, as a matter of fact.'

'I'd love to go to this Jasper place,' said Emily. 'Their computer system sounds particularly interesting.'

'Great,' said Emmett Gorgon. 'I'll take you there.' Then his happy expression faded, replaced by a frown that creased his already much-wrinkled features. Now instead of a prune he looked like a *worried* prune.

'But it'll have to wait until we come back to Taos, OK? Right now our top priority is getting to Rosie.'

* * *

314

'I don't trust this midget,' said Juliette. 'He could be leading us to our deaths.'

'Isn't "midget" a rather derogatory term?' said Miranda.

Juliette frowned at her, trying to control her temper. The sight of the bikers at the traffic lights had unnerved her and now she was irrationally angry.

'The point is that we've hardly met this Emmett Gorgon and suddenly we're following him –'

'Which isn't easy, considering the way he drives,' said Tregemmon.

'Following him halfway across the state,' persisted Juliette. 'Has anyone looked at a map? Have you seen where we're going? Into the back of beyond. We are blindly following this midget and we don't even know who he is. Or even *what* he is.'

'He runs a bookshop.'

'Yes, of course,' said Juliette impatiently. 'But we don't know if he really saw Mr Leiber there, do we?'

Miranda shook her head, unconvinced. 'Why would he lie to us?'

'He didn't exactly strike me as a scrupulously honest businessman.'

'Short on morals, too?' chuckled Tregemmon.

'I don't think it's a laughing matter, Tregemmon. Say he actually does know Mr Leiber. What if he's working for him? Leading us all into a trap?'

Tregemmon shook his head. 'Nice thought, though. Thinking like that can help you stay alive. *Be suspicious.* But in this particular instance I don't think you've much to worry about.'

'And you heard what he said about the earthquakes,' added Miranda.

'Yes,' sighed Juliette. 'Who could possibly believe a story like that?'

The sudden silence in the vehicle was her only answer.

The red pickup the little man drove at such vibrating speed proved considerably less comfortable than what Tregemmon had dubbed the Lunar Excursion Module –

and frequently referred to by a range of less refined names.

But Juliette didn't mind. She happily accepted the discomfort; in fact she was full of excitement. This was her chance to quiz Emmett Gorgon and test her suspicions.

But she found that she couldn't think of anything to say. She was too distracted by the presence of Christopher Matthew beside her.

In the violent flood of events that had raced through her life recently, Juliette had quite forgotten how attracted she was to this man. Now she was intensely aware of his body pressing against hers, the occasional ticklish touch of his long hair on her cheek as he shook his head.

The smell of him, the sardonic flash of his smile in that rumpled face. The disturbing depths of his eyes.

Juliette began to wonder if she had ever really harboured any suspicions against Emmett Gorgon at all. Or was it all just an elaborate self-justification to seal herself in the hot cabin of this truck, pressed tight against Christopher?

Night had fallen across the desert now. Headlights flashed past them on the highway. Through the rear window of the truck, Juliette could see the black shape of Laughing Dog hunched against the deep blue sky, his long tongue lolling from his mouth, narrow handsome head pressed into the cool breeze.

'Doesn't your dog mind riding out there?'

'That ain't no dog, ma'am.' The little man grinned. 'That there's a hundred per cent coyote.'

FORTY-SEVEN

'Did you know that Laughing Dog is a coyote?'

'I think you mentioned it,' said Tregemmon. 'But only ten or eleven times.'

'Less of the hyperbole, please,' said Emily. 'I mentioned it once or twice at most. And did you know that coyotes are highly intelligent creatures? They have relatively large brains.'

Tregemmon yawned and shifted in his folding chair. Behind him, the motel's Pepsi machine began a renewed cycle of chugging and gurgling. 'If he's so smart, what's he doing hanging around with us?'

'Perhaps he likes us,' said the little girl primly. She reached over and patted Laughing Dog. The coyote lay beside her at the tiled rim of the motel's meagre swimming pool, his furry grey ribcage shuddering as he panted in the heat.

'The name coyote comes from *coyotl*,' said Emily. 'That's the ancient Aztec word for the species. They have a highly evolved body language and use postural signals to reinforce the rigidly hierarchical nature of their society. They are extremely sensitive to an individual's level of dominance in the group. I suspect that's why Laughing Dog threw himself at Christopher's feet when they first met.'

'In the case of me,' said a voice, 'it's usually women who throw themselves at my feet.'

They turned to see Emmett Gorgon waddling across the dusty motel court. The little man was dressed in a Pepsi baseball cap, sunglasses and a luridly coloured Hawaiian shirt, which hung down to his knees.

'Mind you,' he said, 'they haven't got a lot of room,

since I have such small feet. Some might even say petite.'

He took another lawn chair from the stack beside the pool and dragged it, scraping loudly, across the concrete.

'Join us, why don't you?' said Tregemmon lazily.

'Exactly my intention,' said Emmett Gorgon, unfolding the chair and slamming it down beside them. He took a cigar out of his shirt pocket.

'Are you going to smoke that thing?'

'That was my plan.'

'I suppose at least it'll keep the bugs away.'

'Do you want one? I've got a whole box in the truck.'

'I'll bet. No thanks. Tobacco's not my preferred smoke.'

'You should steer clear of that other junk. Do you know what marijuana is? It's hemp. They make hangman's ropes out of that stuff. Every time you smoke some, it's like putting a noose around your neck.'

Tregemmon nodded, quite unconcerned. He seemed content to sit placidly, his eyes shut in the sunlight.

Just then a door clattered open on the other side of the courtyard and Miranda emerged from one of the white stucco guest cabins.

'Come and join us,' yelled Emmett Gorgon, beckoning to her.

Miranda squinted at them, holding a hand up to shield her eyes from the sunlight. She gave a small shudder and called, 'No thanks. Ever since I met a man called Dr Buckminster I've had something of an aversion to swimming pools.'

'Aversion, shmersion,' persisted Emmett Gorgon good-naturedly. 'You just don't want to hang out with midgets.'

'That's not true!' said Miranda with irritation, coming over to join them. She sat down on the other side of Laughing Dog and ran her fingers through the thick fur on the nape of the coyote's neck.

Delighted at having a larger audience, Emily decided to press on with her lecture about coyotes. She had been doing some research and she found her newly acquired knowledge wondrous and fascinating. She was eager to share it.

318

'Do you know that coyotes seem to fall in love. Or at least they "bond with a partner", to use the jargon. This means that they form strong attachments with a partner of the opposite sex and mate for life unless –'

In a sudden flash of horror, Emily realised what she was saying. She stole a worried glance at Miranda. 'Unless one of them is killed,' she concluded in a tiny voice.

Then she stumbled on, not daring to look at Miranda. 'Normally, though, the male and female work together to raise a family of pups. They share equally in raising the young.'

Now she couldn't resist taking a sidelong glance at Miranda, to see how upset she was. After all, perhaps Miranda and Danny had planned to raise a family. Their own little litter of pups.

But Miranda had sunglasses on, rendering her pale-grey eyes unreadable. The Girl with Eyes like Rain, Danny had called her. 'Coyotes are very territorial,' continued Emily, moving quickly on to safer subject matter. 'When their territories overlap and the population ratios are at a certain critical point, they have even been known to interbreed with wolves.'

She paused at this point and stroked Laughing Dog's muzzle. 'For all we know, Laughing Dog might have some wolf blood in him.'

She broke off. Nobody was listening to her. Then Emily realised why. They were all staring at two figures hurrying towards the swimming pool. Juliette and Christopher.

'So what is downtown Albuquerque like?' drawled Tregemmon as they arrived.

He lazily shaded his eyes and squinted up at Christopher and Emily's sister. 'Have you got it sussed?'

'It's a metropolis beyond your imagining,' said Emmett Gorgon. The little man puffed happily on his cigar. 'Isn't that right?' He smiled expectantly at Christopher and Juliette.

They didn't smile back, however. Christopher's face was grim.

'What's the matter now?' said Tregemmon. He sat up in

his chair. He had a resigned and somewhat disgusted look on his face – a man whose holiday had been interrupted.

By way of reply, Christopher held up a newspaper. Across half the width of the front page a headline read RICHTER SEVEN SHOCK FOR PARKFIELD.

'I don't suppose there's time for us to stop at the Albuquerque Children's Museum,' said Emily. 'Or the Geology Museum.' She sat in the seat behind Tregemmon and Juliette, morosely flipping through a glossy tourist brochure which she had scooped up at the motel. 'Or the Explora Science Center. Explora? Loathsome misspelling, that.'

'I'm afraid not, honey,' said Tregemmon from the front seat of the minivan. 'We've got to get to Rosie before it's too late.' He peered out at the gleaming stream of traffic as he accelerated.

'Rosie,' snorted Juliette contemptuously. She stared out of the windscreen as they closed in on Emmett Gorgon's red pickup, where the others were riding. It was bouncing along a few car lengths ahead of them.

They were all headed out of town, southeast, towards Las Lunas and Route 25.

'I don't believe this nonsense about the earthquakes,' said Juliette.

'But you saw the newspaper.'

Juliette shrugged dismissively. 'Earthquakes are common in this part of the world, and they're even more common along the San Andreas fault. And that's precisely where Parkfield is situated. On a crucial flaw on the fault. It said so in the newspaper.'

'In point of fact,' said Emily, 'Parkfield is near the meeting of the Pacific and American crustal plates. They use lasers there, bounced off reflectors, to detect tiny movements in the Earth's crust.'

'But that was no tiny movement,' said Tregemmon. 'That was a hell of a big movement.'

Juliette silently agreed. She had seen the photographs in the newspaper, depicting the brutal devastation in the small California town. 'All of which supports my argument,' she said. 'There is nothing supernatural about this earthquake hitting Parkfield. According to the experts, they were overdue for one.'

'Visited by a seismic event of Richter six or greater every twenty-two years on average,' recited Emily in a singsong voice.

'Exactly,' said Juliette. 'So why are we racing after this midget with his crackpot story and his girlfriend waiting in the middle of the desert?'

Tregemmon didn't reply. He was concentrating on manoeuvring through the traffic as they sped out of Albuquerque.

In the back of the minivan, Emily was staring forlornly out at the shops as they flashed past. Tregemmon slowed for a traffic light, and for a moment they were obliged to pause outside a large department store.

In the store window was a gleaming display of matched leather luggage.

'She said I wouldn't need a suitcase,' murmured Emily.

'Beg your pardon, honey,' said Tregemmon, squinting at the traffic lights in the bright sunshine.

Emily nodded at the window display. 'Back at the Halloween Hotel, Nuala said I wouldn't need a suitcase because I wasn't going to live long enough to use one.'

A grim expression settled over Tregemmon's face. 'She did, did she?'

Instead of driving forward when the light changed, he turned left and pulled to a screeching halt outside the department store.

'What are you doing?' said Juliette.

'Proving that nasty little bitch Nuala was wrong.' He twisted the key and killed the ignition, then set about unbuckling his seat belt.

Juliette gaped. 'But we're supposed to be following the others.' Despite her avowed scepticism concerning Emmett Gorgon and his motives, Juliette didn't want to be separated from the red pickup truck with the others in it.

'This will only take a minute,' said Tregemmon. 'Wait

here.' He applied the handbrake and hopped out of the minivan. Three minutes later he emerged from the revolving glass door of the department store with a bright-red suitcase in his hand.

Emily squealed with delight when she saw it. Tregemmon grinned as he presented it to her. 'Just the first of many that you'll wear out in your travels around the world,' he said.

'My travels around the world,' repeated Emily. Her eyes were dreamy, as if she was seeing a vision of the future open up in front of her. For the first time.

She looked up at Tregemmon with eyes wide. 'Can I take it with me to all the different countries in the world?'

'That's the general idea.'

'Can I be a woman of mystery and chain-smoke cigarettes?'

'No you can't smoke –' said Juliette automatically, but Tregemmon cut her off. He looked at her for a moment, his eyes steely, then he turned and looked at her little sister again. 'Emma Lilly,' he said, 'you can do anything you want.'

'Emma Lilly?'

'That's right,' said Tregemmon. 'You've got a new suitcase and a new name. Now shut up and let me drive this dustbin.'

He pulled away from the kerb and set off in pursuit of Emmett Gorgon's pickup truck.

In the back, Emily sat clutching her gleaming new suitcase. 'Emma Lilly,' she chuckled.

FORTY-EIGHT

The air had grown cool as night settled over the desert. They were finally nearing their destination, but even the prospect of arrival couldn't keep Juliette awake.

She was riding in Emmett Gorgon's pickup truck with Christopher Matthew comfortably close beside her.

Laughing Dog was crouching patiently beyond the smeared window, in the back of the truck.

Juliette sat huddled in a sweater with the window open at her elbow, nodding off now and then to the sleepy buzz of tyres on the highway and the low roar of passing traffic. She absorbed the conversation between Emmett and Christopher in dreamy intervals.

'It came as a total surprise to me,' Emmett Gorgon was saying. 'I didn't think the big broad had any kind of real powers. I mean, shit, it was *me* who had to read up on the Indian lore and try and pound a few basic anthropological facts into her skull.'

Juliette chuckled sleepily.

'What are you laughing at?' said Emmett Gorgon.

'The way you call her the big broad.'

'Well, that's the way she was,' said Emmett Gorgon happily. 'My Rosie.' Then suddenly his voice changed, a note of pain creeping into it. 'The way she was,' he murmured.

Juliette winced, wishing she hadn't spoken. But after a moment Emmett Gorgon seemed to shake himself and recover some of his usual cheerfulness. 'We did pretty good, you know. Moneywise, I mean. We're a hell of a team when it comes to extracting the long green, Rosie and me. Before we got the bookstore we used to specialise in package tours.'

'Package tours?' said Christopher.

'You know, fleecing gullible New Age pilgrims who wanted to take a foray into the desert in search of spiritual enlightenment. Maybe a little mystical quest across the border to Sonora in pursuit of magic mushrooms and some spicy native sorcery. We did all that. Put on a show for the gringos.'

The little man took the cigar out of his mouth and examined the gnawed stub of it. 'The changing face of tourism, huh?' he grimaced. 'They used to be satisfied with a naked lady doing tricks with a burro. But, annoyingly enough, some of these pilgrims had done a little research. So, like I say, I had to pound a few basic anthropological facts into Rosie's head, so we could fool them. Or let them fool themselves. That's more like it. They wanted a good show, and we gave it to them. It was a nice little business. We published ads in college papers back east, plus word of mouth got us loads of new suckers – I mean clients. We were astonished by the response. Within two years we were able to pay off the mortgage on the bookstore. But I guess we shouldn't have been so surprised by our success.

'I mean, a female Yaqui sorcerer, a full-blooded coyote and a midget. How could we miss?'

Christopher's voice suddenly acquired a note of interest. 'Rosie is a Yaqui Indian?'

'Hell, no, that's just how we billed her ass, to fool the rubes. She could have been Chinese and they wouldn't have known the difference. But, as it happens, Rosie's from Mexico City. That's about all we know about her parentage. She's got a woman she calls her aunt but the old bat is actually no relation. Rosie is an orphan and this woman just kind of raised her.'

Juliette blinked her heavy-lidded eyes, trying to remain awake. 'How did you meet Rosie?'

'Bumped into her when she was a teenager, working in a topless bar in Abiquiu.'

'A topless bar?'

Emmett Gorgon turned and winked at Juliette. 'Hard to believe she'd go for me, eh? A big strapping lass like that, all covered with sweat and spangles?'

324

'That's not what I meant at all.'

Emmett Gorgon smiled at her slyly. 'You'd be surprised,' he said. 'Midgets get a lot of nookie.'

Juliette yawned. 'How humiliating. To work in one of those places.'

'It could be worse. They've got legalised brothels in Nevada just across the border. Rosie was lucky she didn't end up in one of them. Mind you, even if she had, you can bet she would have survived. She grew up in the toughest slums of Mexico City. Like I said, she didn't have any proper parents. She was orphaned in an earthquake.'

At the word 'earthquake' Juliette felt her heart sink. Here we go again, she thought.

The pickup rumbled along through the night. Finally Christopher Matthew spoke up. 'That was the earthquake where all the hotels collapsed.'

'Hotels, schools, hospitals, you name it. Rosie was just a tiny newborn baby. They dug her out of one of those collapsed hospitals. She was one of fifty-eight newborns they found alive. Some of them had been underground for as long as five days.'

Juliette frowned. 'How could they possibly be alive after all that time?'

'Apparently a survival mechanism snaps into action,' said Chris. 'The body responds as if it was still in the womb.' He sounded as if he knew what he was talking about. 'There's a slowing down of the metabolism. Like a state of hibernation.'

'Yeah, that's one theory, all right,' said Emmett Gorgon. 'Another is that goblins came up out of the depths of the Earth and suckled the babies and kept them alive.'

'And that's your theory?'

'Not at all. It's one dreamed up by Rosie's dreamboat of an aunt. She isn't really her aunt at all, of course. All Rosie's folks were killed in the quake. This so-called aunt is just an old witch who adopted her. And I do mean witch. I think they call it a *yerbera*. Old woman who deals in herbs and the like. I figure she took Rosie under her wing because she believed the kid had a kind of weird special power. Because she had been "born out of the womb of the Earth" . . .'

He fell silent again, for a long moment. When he spoke again his voice was low and serious.

'But what the fuck. Who knows? Maybe she was right.'

When Juliette woke again it was hours later. She sat up in her seat and rubbed the sleep out of her eyes.

On either side of the highway was empty desert, the rise and swell of it looking like a frozen ocean in the silver moonlight. She searched the sky for any sign of approaching dawn and found none. She checked her watch and saw that it was 3.27 a.m.

'Where are we?' she asked, her voice embarrassingly croaky.

'In the Socorro Seismic Anomaly,' said Christopher quietly.

'The what?'

'I was just explaining,' said Emmett Gorgon. He seemed pleased that she was awake. 'It's a term used by geophysicists. New Mexico has a fair amount of earthquake activity, and the quakes are pretty evenly scattered across the entire state . . .'

'Except for the Anomaly,' said Christopher.

'That's right.' Emmett Gorgon waved his hand at the windscreen and the desert landscape beyond. 'For some reason this area has a massive level of quake activity. It always has done, as far back as history goes. The seismic incidents just seem to cluster around here. The Anomaly is only two per cent of the total area of New Mexico, but it gets hammered with fifty per cent of the earthquakes. Nobody knows why. That's why they call it an anomaly.'

'You seem to know a lot about it,' said Juliette.

'I've been doing some reading.' He glanced at her. 'You know, some Indians have the theory that it's the navel of the world. But, listen, I'm no expert. A few weeks ago I'd never even heard of it.'

'So what brought you here?' said Chris.

'Nothing. Or at least I didn't know I was being brought

here.' The little man frowned. 'You see, ever since that day in the bookstore when she met that bastard Leiber, Rosie started acting strange.'

'Strange in what way?' said Juliette.

'Like she wasn't herself. I kept telling myself that everything was all right, that I was just imagining things. Or maybe she was moody. You know what women are like. I told myself it was just a phase, a bad patch, like all couples go through. But it broke my heart. There was something strange in her eyes, something wrong in the way she looked at me.' His voice faltered. 'I thought, I thought, you know, maybe she didn't love me any more. It was kind of a miracle that she ever did in the first place.' He cleared his throat.

'Then suddenly one morning, out of the blue, she decides to take off for Mexico to see her aunt.' He snapped his fingers. 'Just like that. She's all set to leave – without me. I have to beg her to wait five minutes while I get packed and lock up the store. I was so spooked I almost forgot about Laughing Dog.'

He glanced over his shoulder and looked at the coyote hunched on the rear of the truck, silhouetted against starlight. 'Luckily he jumped into the back of the truck just as we were leaving.'

The smile faded. 'But on that whole trip, and ever since, he's behaved differently toward Rosie. Like he's half scared of her or something. Anyhow, we drove down to Mexico and I kept kidding myself the whole way that maybe the trip would make everything right between us again. But it was like I wasn't even there. Or maybe like *she* wasn't there. She let me sleep with her. But that's all we did together. Sleep. Or at least she did. She turned her big bare back toward me and went off like somebody had thrown a switch. Rosie had always been a light sleeper, but not any more. She slept so deep it scared me. It was my turn to be the insomniac. I just lay there beside her wondering what the hell was going on. What I'd done wrong.'

'You didn't connect her behaviour to Mr Leiber's visit?' said Christopher.

'Not at that point, no. The thought crossed my mind, because I'd had a weird vibe from the fucker. But I thought, no, it couldn't be. I mean he'd been alone with her for . . . what? Half an hour? Forty minutes tops. What harm could he do in that time?' The little man's voice trembled.

After a moment he went on. 'Finally we got to Mexico City and found Rosie's aunt in the little dump where she lives near the Colonia Roma.'

'You said she was a wise woman?' said Christopher.

'Yeah, if that's what you want to call it.' The little man turned to Juliette. 'You know, like a kind of medicine woman.'

'Or sorcerer,' added Christopher, rather portentously and unnecessarily, she thought.

'That's right, although some of the locals said she was more of a *bruja*, a black magician. People in the neighbourhood were scared of her. But not Rosie. They were like mother and daughter. Here's a strange thing, though. After all that driving and Rosie's ants in the pants to get down there, you'd have thought at least we'd stay for a while. No way, José. One night and that was it – we were gone again.

'As soon as we arrived Rosie and the old crone were thick as thieves. They hurried off into a corner and started whispering together. Stayed up all night talking. I was sleeping in the truck with Laughing Dog. I never did find out what they were talking about. The next morning the old bat gives Rosie a box which is rattling like it's got glass in it or something. I sneak a look and see that it's full of jars. We stick the box in the truck and we take off again. Can you believe it? All that driving and we only stay there about ten hours.

'Then on the way back Rosie got real strange. She started sleeping longer and longer, even during the day. Everything she did got slower and kind of dreamy. It scared the hell out of me. She was like a clockwork toy winding down. We hadn't been talking much on the whole trip, but now she stopped altogether. Then one day we're

328

driving along, and I'm wondering what the hell I'm going to do, about to go crazy from the silent treatment. And suddenly she starts talking again. She says she wants me to stop the truck. She says she wants to go to bed. I said wait for the next motel. She says no, right here. She doesn't want to go home. She wants to stay right where we are. She says this is home now. I look around and we're, like, in the asshole of existence.

'But I found a place where we could stop.'

'And she's been there ever since?'

'*We've* been there. Together. Except when I had to go into Taos on urgent business. I fixed it up so that we could just about live there. Home sweet home. Right in the middle of nowhere. Except of course it wasn't the middle of nowhere.'

He frowned, his wrinkled features creasing in the tiny jewelled lights from the dashboard. 'It was smack in the middle of the Socorro Seismic Anomaly.'

After a long pause, Christopher spoke. 'What was in the jars her aunt gave her?'

'Chilli sauce,' said Emmett Gorgon. 'I'll say one thing for the old bitch: she always made a good chilli sauce.'

Juliette woke again as they bounced across ruts, their headlights probing ahead of them through the desert night to reveal a rough encampment. She saw an old-fashioned country mail box: a metal box on a stick. Beside it, a hand-lettered sign read SEISMIC CITY.

'I put that up,' said Emmett Gorgon proudly. 'I guess I can call it anything I like. The place is deserted now, except for me and Rosie.'

The place looked as though it had once been a caravan park. Mobile homes of various sizes and shapes stood perched on cinder blocks in the dusty grey expanse of what might once have been a carefully tended yard. Low fences of twisted wire marked areas where flower beds and shrubs had once flourished. Now all that remained were a few dry, dead stalks, sticking up like dead men's fingers in the harsh glare of the headlights.

The lights swung across the caravans. To Juliette they all looked empty, their windows shattered and doors sagging on hinges.

'We're here,' announced Emmett Gorgon. He turned off the engine and the glowing lights on the dashboard died. As the minivan pulled in beside them, Juliette saw a flicker of movement out of the corner of her eye. She turned to see a grey shape rippling lithely down to the ground from the back of the pickup.

There was the subdued thud of four paws landing on packed dirt, then Laughing Dog's eyes gleamed in the darkness as he loped off.

'I guess he's glad to be home again,' said Emmett Gorgon. 'I guess I am, too, if you can call this place home.'

Several of the abandoned caravans in Seismic City were still in good repair, and Juliette found herself and her sister billeted in one of these, sleeping on a surprisingly comfortable metal bunkbed. Its narrow rigid pallets reminded her cosily of childhood and holidays.

The next morning she woke to the sound of voices. Emily was already up and off, her bedding on the top bunk in unnecessarily massive disarray. Juliette got dressed and stepped out into the heat and dust and blinding daylight.

She squinted against the light, shading her eyes with her hand. As she crossed the yard she noticed that someone had drawn designs in the dirt with a stick.

Strange geometric patterns. Looping whorls and intricate spirals. They reminded Juliette of Australian Aboriginal art.

The others were all gathered around the entrance to a square tent, which had been attached to one of the larger caravans. In the shadowed doorway, enthroned in a bright-yellow inflatable child's armchair, was Emmett Gorgon. He had a can of beer in his hand, which had apparently come from a chiller chest which Tregemmon was sitting on.

Beside Tregemmon sat Emily, engrossed in a library book taken from a large pile on the floor.

But Juliette's eyes immediately went to Christopher, who was crouched, sitting on his heels rather convincingly in the manner of an Indian.

'Good morning,' said Emmett Gorgon, lifting his beer can. 'Would you like a brewski? The perfect breakfast.' He glanced at his wristwatch. 'Or lunch. We have a refrigerator full of them.'

'A refrigerator?'

'Sure.' Emmett Gorgon nodded at the back of his tent. 'Fridge. Freezer. TV. Video. All the comforts of home.'

'Where does the electricity come from?' said Juliette, more out of politeness than interest. She wanted to be alone with Christopher, having a civilised breakfast in a civilised place.

'I've got a small mobile generator out back,' said the little man proudly. 'Runs on gasoline.'

Juliette belatedly realised that she had been hearing the soft thudding of some kind of pump in the background ever since she woke up.

'Miranda can show you where the chemical toilet is,' said Emmett Gorgon. 'Like I said, all the comforts of home.' Then his voice grew more quiet and his smile faded. He glanced at his watch. 'After that I'll take you to meet Rosie.'

FORTY-NINE

They assembled outside the largest of the mobile homes, a silver and mint-green Winnebago.

Emmett Gorgon took a key out of his pocket and unlocked the door with what was almost a ceremonial air. He stepped inside, gesturing for the others to follow. But, before any of them could move, Laughing Dog came bounding up behind them, tail wagging, and writhed through the door.

Juliette followed the coyote into the dark caravan. The Winnebago was pleasantly cool inside but it had the indefinable, slightly sweet smell of a sickroom.

At the far end of the caravan was a shadowy room with a beaded curtain across the doorway, evidently a bedroom. Emmett Gorgon stood in this doorway, beckoning to them. They all approached, moving slowly and carefully, instinctively avoiding making any noise.

'Don't worry about trying to be quiet,' said the little man. He was speaking in a normal conversational voice, which sounded startlingly loud in the caravan, and somehow sacrilegious, like someone shouting in church.

'She isn't going to wake up,' he said.

They filed into the bedroom. The walls were covered with brightly coloured tapestries. It was a confined space, made even smaller by the large woman who lay in the bed.

Her smooth round face was untroubled and peaceful. One plump arm was tucked under her face like a contented child's. Her glossy black hair had been painstakingly plaited into braids which lay curled in gleaming black crescents on the white pillow beside her face.

To Juliette she looked like a placid peasant Madonna by

Diego Rivera. The sheets of the bed were clean and white, emphasising the rich golden brown of the woman's skin.

Her eyes were closed and the only sign of life was the slight rise and fall of the covers over her bulky body.

'My Rosie,' said the little man softly. 'Isn't she beautiful?' He turned and winked at them. 'And so quiet, too. She must be every man's dream come true.'

He was smiling, but there were tears in his eyes. Laughing Dog padded silently up to him and nudged the little man's hand with his nose. Emmett Gorgon absent-mindedly patted the coyote.

'And she never wakes up?' Christopher asked quietly.

'I got a doctor to look at her and he said it just looked like normal sleep. Normal! Huh!'

'I'm a doctor,' said Juliette suddenly. 'Let me examine her.' She bent down towards the big woman in the bed, but Emmett Gorgon took her arm.

'Not just now,' he said. 'Come on. Let's get out of here.' He walked back out of the bedroom and the others followed him into the narrow galley kitchen.

Emmett Gorgon went to the wall-mounted stove and climbed on to a stool. Standing on the stool, he ignited a burner under a large cooking pot. 'Pull up a seat,' he said to the others. He glanced at his watch. 'It shouldn't be long now.'

There were folding chairs and stools which tucked into ingenious alcoves, and soon the six of them were seated in the tiny kitchen, Emily deigning to perch on Miranda's lap.

She was still clutching one of the books she had found in Emmett Gorgon's tent. Apparently she had been devouring all the reading matter she could find, from the moment she woke up. 'We're in a region of the Rio Grande Rift that covers about two per cent of the area of New Mexico,' she announced. 'But it has an anomalous cluster of seismic incidents which account for around half of all the state's earthquake activity.'

'Yes,' said Miranda. 'Emmett told us about that.'

Emily continued, unperturbed. 'Around the cluster is

what they call a "halo" or ring of very low seismic activity. This aseismic halo persists even when the cutoff magnitude of the earthquakes under consideration is reduced.' She glanced up at them. 'Earthquakes appear in strange groupings with the strongest shocks, at least in recorded history, taking place in the so-called 1906–1907 swarm.'

Juliette broke in on her little sister's recital. She nodded towards the bedroom. 'Somehow I can't believe that a doctor came out here to examine Rosie and did nothing but simply tell you that she appeared to be sleeping.'

'You're right,' conceded Emmett Gorgon. 'That's not all he did. He also handed me a fucking big bill for the house call.'

'But I don't see how Rosie can simply be asleep all the time. Quite apart from everything else, she appears to be very well nourished.'

'You're about to see why,' said Emmett Gorgon. He glanced at his watch again and then turned to look at the bedroom. She followed his gaze and felt an abrupt shifting shock in the pit of her stomach.

Something was moving in the room, emerging from the shadows. The hairs stirred on the back of her neck. The beaded curtain in the doorway parted with a clattering sound and then spread open wide to reveal Rosie.

The sleeping woman had risen from her bed and was emerging from the bedroom, walking towards the kitchen. Her big brown body was completely nude, her stomach protruding, her smooth breasts the size of watermelons.

Her glossy black braids hung down on either side of her broad, placid face. They swayed in time with her large breasts as she walked towards them.

Her eyes remained squeezed shut and the expression on her face was somehow primally innocent, beatific. Her big feet slapped down on the linoleum floor, yet she seemed to glide forward effortlessly, floating, like a nude figure in a dream painting by Magritte.

Emmett Gorgon hopped on to his chair and turned quickly to the stove. He switched off the gas flame and lifted the lid off the pot. Clouds of steam rose from it, filling the room with the scent of onions and garlic as he placed a large wooden spoon in the pot.

'OK,' he said calmly. 'Everybody move to the back of the kitchen and make room for Rosie.'

'Is she sleepwalking?' asked Tregemmon.

'She appears to be,' whispered Juliette reluctantly.

'How did she get those bruises?' said Christopher. For indeed there were dark bruises dotted across the woman's smooth fleshy legs and arms.

The little man shrugged helplessly. 'It's a mystery. I keep a close watch on her day and night but I've never seen anything that might cause them.'

They watched as the big woman moved to the stove, lifted the wooden spoon and began to eat directly from the cooking pot.

'What's in there?' hissed Emily in a low voice. 'What's she eating?'

'You don't have to whisper,' said Emmett Gorgon. 'Just try and stay out of her way.'

The sleeping woman was eating with a relentless mechanical motion, shovelling the food into her mouth, swallowing without chewing and then shovelling more in. 'In answer to your question, Emily,' said Emmett Gorgon, 'she's eating chilli con carne.'

'Who cooks it?' said Christopher.

'I do, of course,' snapped the little man. He didn't take his eyes off Rosie as she finished eating, letting the wooden spoon fall from her fingers and clatter back into the pot of chilli. Then she wiped her mouth with a strangely dainty gesture and turned and walked back to the bedroom.

The beaded curtain clicked restlessly as she disappeared back into the shadows. Emmett Gorgon sighed with relief, wiping his brow.

He walked over to the refrigerator and took out a beer. He cracked the can open and took a sip before wandering back to the bedroom door.

The others drifted after him, peering over his shoulder at the heaped shape of the big woman in the bed, sleeping peacefully as if she had never stirred.

'Look at that face,' said Emmett Gorgon. 'Isn't that the face of an angel? Or maybe just a normal, healthy girl. Just a big beefy cheerleader bursting with health.' He sighed. 'Hard to believe I've been thinking about putting a pillow down on it and holding it there until she stops struggling.'

'What happens if the chilli isn't there on the stove for her?' said Christopher.

Emmett Gorgon led them back into the kitchen and opened a cupboard under the sink. 'In that case,' he said, 'she eats this stuff.' He held up an unlabelled jar with a yellow lid. It was full of some kind of dense red sauce. 'Straight from the jar.'

'What is it?' said Tregemmon.

'The chilli sauce that her aunt made for her.' He turned to Juliette. 'Remember I told you the old witch gave her a boxful back in Mexico City? The last thing Rosie said before she went to sleep was to make sure I kept the stuff nearby. It seemed really important to her. She made me promise. Not that she had to. She knew I'd do anything for her.'

'And that's all she eats?'

'That's all she seems to need. She'll open a jar and wolf it down neat. I can't stand to see her do that, though, so I use it in a recipe. My world-famous spicy beef chilli.' The little man attempted a smile, but it was feeble.

'What happens if the jars aren't there?' said Christopher.

'Funny you should say that.' The little man slumped into a chair. 'After a couple of days of this sleepwalking routine, I tried hiding them. I thought I might wean her on to better food and maybe even snap her out of this weirdo trance. So I made an omelette and left it on the stove for her. Meanwhile I took the jars and buried them outside.'

'What happened?'

'She ignored my omelette, walked out of the caravan and went right to the jars in a beeline. She dug them up like a dog digging up a bone.' He sighed again. 'I figured she must have smelled them somehow.'

'Smelled them when they were buried under the ground?' said Juliette.

'Do you have a better suggestion?' snapped the little man. 'After that, I tried getting rid of the stuff altogether. I drove into the nearest town and dropped the jars into a dumpster.' He grinned weakly. 'They made one hell of a satisfying crash.'

'So what did she do then?' said Tregemmon. 'Hitch-hike into town naked and jump into the dumpster?'

'She didn't have to,' said Emmett Gorgon bleakly. 'When I got back I found this waiting.' He returned to the cupboard under the sink and drew out a battered box wrapped in brown paper.

There was spidery handwriting in bright-blue ink on the paper, and a ragged row of Mexican postage stamps. 'Inside the package were six more jars of that red slop.'

'Her aunt sent them?'

'Yeah, that's right. But that's not the worst part. There was a postcard with them.' He reached into the wrapping paper and took out the postcard, which he handed to Christopher.

Juliette read it over his shoulder. On one side was a garishly coloured image of a crucified Christ. On the other, in the same spidery scrawl, were written the words, 'Having a wonderful time. Hope Rosalita enjoys her aunt's chilli.'

It was signed 'F Leiber, Esq'.

'Mr Leiber,' murmured Juliette. Much to her disgust she once again felt the small hairs stirring on the back of her neck.

'But how did he find Rosie's aunt?' she said.

Emmett Gorgon shrugged. 'Rosie must have told him when they met in the bookstore. Given him her address in the Colonia Roma. It seems they had quite a heart-to-heart chat in their half-hour together.' There was a note of jealousy in the small man's voice.

He returned the wrapping paper to the cupboard under the sink. 'Six more jars of the stuff. And they just happened to be waiting for me the morning I threw all the others away. What are the odds against that happening?'

'It was just a coincidence,' said Juliette.

337

Emmett Gorgon regarded her sardonically. 'Sure. Just a coincidence. But after that coincidence, sugar, I gave up. I figured I was up against forces beyond my control.' He picked up his can of beer and stared at it bleakly. 'That bastard Mr Leiber's got some powerful mojo. Powerful and mean.'

Christopher was still examining the postcard. 'How did they know where to send it?'

'We put the address on a letter Rosie wrote to her aunt. She had a last spasm of activity before she took to her bed. Like an animal before it hibernates for the winter.'

'I don't understand,' said Juliette, her impatience breaking through at last. 'What's all this got to do with earthquakes? And what is the supposed significance of the jars of chilli sauce?'

'There's nothing supposed about their significance,' responded Emmett Gorgon bad-temperedly. 'God, you shrinks really are a sceptical bunch.

'Do you know the joke about the two shrinks? Well, there's this shrink who's just moved into a new office. At the end of his first day he's locking up and he glances over to see another shrink locking up his office on the other side of the corridor. The second shrink says, "Good night." '

Juliette nodded wearily. 'And the first shrink watches him go and says, "I wonder what he meant by that." '

'Aw, you've heard it.'

'You were talking about chilli sauce.'

'Yeah, the stuff her aunt made. Well, if you don't believe me, try a spoonful yourself. Psychotropic dynamite. Rosie's aunt knows a thing or two about the native plants of Mexico, you bet. I think she's laced it with magic mushrooms. I had a teaspoonful. It put me out of action for hours. I woke up to find Laughing Dog sitting on my chest, whining. He probably thought I was out of action for good. When I opened my eyes he licked my face until I thought the skin was going to come off.'

'All right,' said Juliette, 'so you maintain the chilli sauce is some kind of drug. Perhaps a narcotic or hypnotic. That might explain why Rosie is constantly asleep. But what about the supposed connection with earthquakes?'

'Supposed, supposed,' muttered Emmett Gorgon. 'Follow me.'

Juliette was relieved to be out of the caravan. The sunlight outside was dazzling. Laughing Dog trotted off and vanished among the other mobile homes as Emmett Gorgon led the others to a bare patch of ground near his tent.

Here, scored in the dirt, were the strange drawings that Juliette had noticed earlier.

There were four of them in the sandy soil, each as large as a bedsheet. Their intricate geometric patterns consisted of loops, swirls and spirals.

There was something hypnotic about these, as though you might fall into them if you stared long enough, and be swept down to the centre of the Earth.

'Very impressive,' said Juliette. 'But what do they mean?'

Emmett Gorgon shrugged. 'I don't know. Rosie comes out at night sometimes, sleepwalking, and draws them in the sand.'

'They look like Aboriginal art,' said Miranda.

'Yes.' Christopher nodded thoughtfully. 'Artefacts associated with the Dreamtime.'

The little man shrugged. 'Whatever. I didn't know whether it was safer to leave them or rub them out, so I just left them. But I'll tell you what. The first one she drew was the night before they had that quake in Arizona that hit five on the Richter scale.'

'That was the one we felt!' said Miranda excitedly. 'In the motel outside Flagstaff. I'll never forget it.'

'Neither will that elderly gentleman from the next cabin,' said Tregemmon. 'That was probably the first time he's seen a naked woman since the Great War.'

'Flagstaff, eh? That would be the one.' Emmett Gorgon nodded. 'It hit just a few hours after Rosie came out sleepwalking and drew that picture in the dirt.'

'Pure coincidence,' said Juliette.

'Coincidence, eh? Come and look at these.' He led

them into the back of his tent. The floor was strewn with books and magazines and empty beer cans. The small refrigerator stood in one corner.

Juliette saw that scraps of paper were attached to the refrigerator with small magnets, in a strange echo of domesticity. Then she got a better look at the pieces of paper and saw that some were photographs.

Snapshots of Emmett Gorgon and Rosie in happier times: standing proudly in the bookshop in Taos; posing beside the battered red pickup truck; in hiking gear, walking beside Laughing Dog on a shady green forest trail.

Along with the photographs were newspaper clippings and drawings on scraps of paper. Juliette saw that the drawings were of the patterns in the sand outside, with dates and times written on them.

Emmett Gorgon began removing magnets, gathering a handful of the newspaper clippings. He removed three of them. The newsprint was already brittle, rapidly yellowing in the desert air. He shoved them at her.

'Coincidence, you said? Take a gander at these.' He held up the clippings one by one. 'Bogotá, Managua, Arizona.' He turned to his diagrams on the refrigerator. 'Each one hit the morning after Rosie did one of her sleepwalking drawings in the sand.'

He paused and took a folded piece of newsprint from his shirt pocket and spread it out on the refrigerator door, carefully fixing it in place with four magnets.

Miranda recognised it from the newspaper that Christopher had bought in Albuquerque. 'And Parkfield makes four. There's a new drawing out there in the sand. Rosie must have done that while we were away. I figure it was the night before the California quake.'

'I still don't see the connection,' said Juliette stubbornly.

'If you don't now, lady, you never will.'

'I don't see how the sleepwalking activity of a young woman can possibly be connected with seismic activity thousands of miles away.'

'Maybe not,' said Emmett Gorgon, 'but I bet your boyfriend can.'

340

Everyone turned to look at Christopher, who was staring thoughtfully at the newspaper clippings and the drawings of the patterns in the sand. He set them aside and glanced up at the others.

'Dream magic,' he said.

FIFTY

'Many cultures believe that magic can be enacted in dreams.' Christopher looked out of the door of the tent, towards the patch of ground with the strange patterns scratched on it.

'As Miranda observed, those drawings in the sand resemble Aboriginal Dreamtime artefacts.'

Juliette interrupted him. 'But this is completely irrational.' All at once she found that she was fighting to keep her temper. 'We are talking about dreams, subjective mental experience. How could they possibly affect reality?'

Christopher shook his head. 'You probably believe there's a sharp distinction between reality and dreams. After all, you come from a scientific background. That's what your medical training tells you. But in fact reality and dreams blend.'

'Amen,' said Emmett Gorgon.

'Mystical hogwash,' said Juliette.

'Better cut the Edge some slack,' observed Tregemmon. 'He's liable to be right in these matters.'

'I don't see how he possibly could be,' said Juliette.

Christopher was frowning, as if searching for the right words. 'It's all a question of consciousness. Consider the problem of human consciousness. How is it that our minds can perceive the world? Part of the answer is in the way our minds dream or, if you prefer, hallucinate. I believe that hallucinations are actually the raw material of our reality.'

Juliette frowned sceptically, but she found herself listening attentively.

'Our ability to dream, or hallucinate, is the basic powerhouse of our consciousness,' said Christopher. 'Dreams are the fundamental building blocks we use for assembling our perception of reality. Without them, we wouldn't be able to perceive anything at all.'

'Are you saying that life is just a dream?' said Juliette.

'Not all. At night, when we're asleep and dreaming, hallucinated thought holds sway in a pure form, without external interruption. It is the inner theatre of our imagination, sealed inside the bone arena of our skulls.'

Emily interrupted, 'And consider Rodolfo Llána of New York University, with his theory that the electro-psychological properties of the brain are the same awake and dreaming.'

'Oh, shut up, Emily, please,' said Juliette.

'In any case,' continued Christopher, 'we are shunting a steady stream of mental fantasy from our subcortex to our cortex. When we're awake, this stream of inner fantasy mixes with the flow of input from our senses. That is to say, it mixes with what we perceive of the reality "out there". And, like two streams of different-coloured water mixing, this blend becomes our waking consciousness.

'This explains why experience is so subjective. It's a blend of external reality and inner hallucination.'

'Inner hallucination,' said Juliette. She followed his argument but she wasn't sure she agreed with it.

'My point is that the same structures that give rise to dreams give rise to our perception of reality. Consciousness is a form of controlled hallucination. Dreams and reality form a continuum. A Möbius strip, with the twist occurring just behind our eyes. Somewhere in the prefrontal lobes.'

'Interesting notion,' said Emily, casually forming a Möbius strip with a piece of paper torn from a magazine. She showed it to Tregemmon.

'Yes, well it all sounds very scientific,' said Juliette, taking the strip from Emily and straightening it back into a normal ring of paper with two edges and two surfaces. 'But in fact there isn't any research or scholarship to support it.'

'On the contrary,' said Emily. 'Consider Merlin Donald's

mimetic models for representing reality and the external world. He argues that these inner representations may have been the dominant mode of cognition among nonverbal primates for millions of years. Julian Jaynes would argue that something similar has persisted in our species, right into recorded history.'

Juliette shook her head stubbornly and spoke with great finality. 'A dream is just electrical activity inside someone's skull.'

'Well, the electrical activity inside Rosie's skull seems to be having some pretty far-reaching effects,' murmured Emmett Gorgon. He picked up one of the newspaper clippings with a large photograph of earthquake-devastated Managua. 'Thanks to Mr Leiber.'

Juliette couldn't sleep.

It was late at night and she lay in the rapidly cooling interior of the bulbous old 1940s motorhome that had been assigned to her and her sister.

The caravan had ill-fitting doors that let the fine dust of the desert blow in. The metal structure creaked with every vagary of the night breeze.

Juliette thought of herself as a scientist, a rationalist. But even so she was tempted to find something vaguely menacing in those night noises.

She was lying on the bottom of two bunk beds fitted in a cramped alcove. On the bunk above her, her little sister was asleep.

There was always something both deeply alluring and deeply annoying about the perfect childlike peace on Emily's face when she slept. And the infuriating steadiness of her soft breathing made it impossible for Juliette to relax on the bunk below.

The sound struck her as positively smug. Finally she could stand it no longer. She got up and stared at her sister in the moonlight. As expected, Emily looked like an angel, lying there clutching her battered teddy bear.

Altogether she looked like a particularly cynical and cunning advertisement for childhood, one successfully intended to convey a lost Edenic time of peace and contentment.

The wind howled outside the caravan. Juliette felt cold and exhausted. She looked at the little girl clutching her teddy bear. Safe and secure and blissfully asleep. And a thought stole across Juliette's mind.

Why not? She'd tried everything else. Ludicrously, Juliette found herself stealthily extracting Mr Rafferty from her sister's grasp. She did it with such care that Emily didn't falter in her angelic sleep.

Juliette stood there for a moment clutching the teddy bear. She had memories of her own childhood toys. Benny the Badger, for instance, who had comforted her for years.

She climbed into bed with Mr Rafferty, feeling a little silly but fully expecting to find once again the sweet uncomplicated sleep of childhood. But instead she merely found herself lying there remembering how Emily had gone grubbing through the wreckage of the motel after the earthquake, searching for this teddy bear.

She'd enlisted Miranda to help her. It had seemed touching at the time. But now what Juliette kept dwelling on was the earthquake itself, and how terrifying it had been when the ground came alive under her feet. Like spending your whole life on a firm solid iceberg and then suddenly feeling it melt beneath you.

Juliette found herself sweating, her heartbeat ragged and anxious. She rolled over in her narrow bunk bed. Mr Rafferty lay on her pillow. Juliette looked at his battered, button-eyed countenance and sighed with disgust. 'You're not much help, are you?' she murmured.

Giving up all attempts at sleep, she quietly got up, dressed and went outside.

Under a moon as bright as a searchlight, the landscape was extraordinary. Juliette stared around. She was surrounded by a mundane collection of battered vehicles, yet in the moonlight they looked like a monument to a failed world, a civilisation lost in pursuit of the false gods of speed, travel and change that had ultimately been swallowed by the desert.

Beyond the caravan park was the open desert itself, bone-white in the moonlight. Shadows pooled like black ink among the distant hills.

Juliette stared at them for a long moment, moved by nameless emotions, until she was distracted by a noise from Emmett Gorgon's tent. She went over.

Despite the hour, the little man was busy at his table, unpacking something from a box. Juliette recognised it from the shop in Taos: the Chinese earthquake vase.

On the curved surface of the vase, four dragons stretched, looking elegant and sinister, with ceramic balls in their jaws and four-wide mouthed frogs waiting patiently below to catch them.

Emmett Gorgon carefully assembled the vase on the table top. 'You see this?' he said. 'I pray to God that none of these balls drop out of the dragons' mouths. But if they do, it will mean that somebody, somewhere, has had one. And all because of the spell Mr Leiber put on Rosie.'

Juliette forced herself to speak casually. 'A spell? Do you really believe that?'

'How else could it have happened? Something must have triggered the dream magic in Rosie. On her own she might have had a little power. Her old bitch of an aunt might have had a pinch more. But between them nothing like this. Nothing that could make a sleeping girl dream real earthquakes.'

Juliette felt a sinking feeling and the beginnings of a profound depression. He really believed it. It would be difficult – perhaps even dangerous – to try to shake the little man of his delusions.

Only a long careful process of discussion might help guide him back to normality. There was certainly nothing she could achieve tonight.

Emmett Gorgon looked at her, suddenly brightening. 'Did the Edge tell you about our plan?'

'Plan?'

'Yeah, me and him dreamed it up. A plan to break the spell and save Rosie.'

He hopped down from his chair and went into the

346

caravan. He came back carrying a wooden chopping board. The scarred old board was covered with chillies of all shapes and sizes. There were yellow, green and even purple peppers, although reds predominated. Some were as fresh and juicy-looking as ripe fruit. Others were shrivelled and dried and ancient.

'What do you think of them?' said Emmett Gorgon, stirring the chillies with his knife. 'Aren't they beauties?'

'What are they?'

'Mostly *Capsicum annuum*, with some *Capsicum frutescens* thrown in. In other words, hot chilli peppers.'

'I can see that. But what are they for?'

'Like I said, the Edge and me came up with a plan to save Rosie.'

'With chilli peppers?'

'The way we see it, Rosie's addicted to this drugged chilli sauce that her old bitch of an aunt made. So we're going to fight fire with fire. You remember that Rosie's aunt was a medicine woman? A herbalist? She was always monkeying around with magic mushrooms, jimson weed, datura, stuff like that. Especially the mushrooms. And when I ate her sauce, that's what it felt like. A trip on magic mushrooms. So me and the Edge figured that's the main active ingredient in the old witch's recipe, with maybe a bit of peyote thrown in, contributing some mescaline. Oh there's some chilli peppers in there, too. But they wouldn't be contributing to the mind-altering effect.'

'Of course not,' said Juliette impatiently. 'How could they? Chilli peppers aren't hallucinogenic.'

'Well, not normally.' The little man proudly inspected the huge selection of brightly coloured peppers on the chopping board. 'But these babies are.'

'How can they be?' Juliette was rapidly losing patience with this conversation. She was straining to remember her pharmacology, marshal her arguments. 'They're the wrong chemical composition. How could they have such an effect?'

Emmett Gorgon gestured at the chopping board. 'Well, shrinkie, you may not know it but hot chillies have a specific psychological effect when eaten. Each hot pepper we consume triggers an endorphin rush in our brain. That's why eating spicy food is pleasurable.'

'For some people.'

'For anyone with any sense, baby. Anyhow, you can combine the different rushes of the endorphins. Like combining the notes on a guitar to play a chord.'

Juliette thought this was a fanciful simile but she repressed the urge to comment.

'And these combinations trigger certain effects,' said Emmett Gorgon. 'Effects in the brain chemistry.'

'I see. And how does all this help Rosie?'

'In Taos I'm famous for my hallucinogenic chilli suppers. But that's just recreational drug use. Now we're going to use my drug magic to fight Mr Leiber's dream magic.'

Juliette shook her head impatiently. 'But, if you can cure Rosie just by feeding her one of your chilli concoctions, why haven't you done so already?'

The little man set the chopping board aside, carefully so as not to disturb the chillies. 'Oh, we're not feeding it to Rosie. She's way too far gone. We're going to feed it to Miranda.'

They were back in the small tent outside Emmett Gorgon's caravan before Juliette felt she could ask the obvious question.

'Why Miranda?'

'The Edge says she's telepathic, which is a stroke of luck. We can get her high on the chilli, so that she's in the same dream state as Rosie. Then send her in.'

'In?'

'Yeah, into Rosie's head.'

'Into Rosie's head. I see.'

'That's right. Send her in there so she can interfere with whatever Rosie's doing to cause the earthquakes.'

'In Rosie's dream.'

'That's right.'

'Miranda is going to enter Rosie's dream and take part in it.'

348

'That's right. Here, have a beer.'

Juliette accepted the beer. She felt weak with anger and frustration. Christopher had involved her in some mystical nonsense in the past, but this really was too much. Even allowing for the possibility that Miranda might have some kind of rudimentary telepathic powers, the rest of their scheme was still sublimely ridiculous.

Juliette felt exasperated and exhausted. 'I think I'll go to bed now if you don't mind,' she said.

'Mind? Hell, no. Let me get a flashlight and I'll walk you back.' Despite Juliette's protests he dug a battery torch out of a drawer and led her back out of the tent into the desert moonlight.

Halfway to her caravan they came to the large diagrams that Rosie had drawn in the sand. Juliette paused and looked at them. Emmett Gorgon stood beside her.

He sighed. 'It was when I first saw these things that I began to put two and two together. I knew that Rosie was eating that sauce, and having some weird dreams. But when I saw one of these, and the next day there was that earthquake . . .'

'Why don't you rub them out?'

'Rub them out? Are you crazy? I don't dare touch them. If just drawing them in the sand can cause an earthquake, who knows what rubbing them out might do? Why, just think about it.'

The little man kept talking, but Juliette wasn't listening. Something he'd said earlier had triggered an insight. Emmett Gorgon didn't know it, but he had explained something of vital importance.

He had said he'd seen the drawing in the sand, and *then the earthquakes had followed*. It was all just coincidence of course. But the association had been decisively forged in his mind. To him, the drawings and the earthquakes were connected.

In a sense, these drawings were the root of his delusion. Juliette stared down at them in the moonlight, and suddenly they seemed to symbolise all the superstition and block-headed, wrongheaded, delusional thinking in the world.

She felt an enormous surge of anger, and the anger gave rise to an instant decision, just as Emmett Gorgon asked her a question.

'I'm sorry. I missed that.'

'I said, are you going to go to bed, or are you just going to stand here all night looking at Rosie's art?'

'Actually, I think I will stay out here just a little longer.' Juliette fought to keep her voice normal, to conceal any trace of the decision she had just made. She turned casually away from the drawings. Emmett Gorgon mustn't suspect anything.

'It's very pleasant out here in the fresh air. If you just leave me the torch I'll find my way back to the caravan on my own.'

'OK, sure,' said the little man, holding the torch up to her. 'Say goodnight to the munchkin for me.'

'Of course I will.'

Juliette waited while Emmett Gorgon strolled back to his tent. Only when she was sure that she was absolutely alone and unobserved did she go back to her caravan and fetch the broom.

It was an old straw broom which she had noticed the evening before. It occupied a narrow, purpose-built alcove in the kitchen unit. Without waking Emily she took it from the caravan and went back outside, closing the door quietly behind her.

Back out in the moonlight she stood studying the patterns in the sand. They were so intricate that it almost seemed a shame.

But they were also the product of a disease process, a pathological combination of hysteria, drugs and somnambulism. A fascinating case, but it was having a debilitating effect on their entire group.

Juliette sighed. She was doing this for the greater good. She lifted the broom and began to sweep briskly.

As she did so, there was an odd coincidence. An unearthly sound rose over the desert. Liquid and yearning, it caused her whole body to go cold.

After a moment of perplexed terror, however, Juliette

realised that it was just Laughing Dog, or one of his brethren, singing to the desert night.

She forced a chuckle and continued her sweeping. Soon, all trace of the drawings had been removed.

She went back to bed in her cramped narrow bunk and slept like a baby.

FIFTY-ONE

When she finally woke up the next morning, Juliette found that her sister was already gone from the upper bunk. That was normal enough; Emily was restless, a habitual early riser.

So the first clue that something was seriously wrong came when Juliette realised the others were also missing from their various caravans.

She found them all gathered in Emmett Gorgon's tent. Christopher Matthew was sitting there watching the television. Tregemmon and Miranda and Emily were standing behind him, their eyes fixed on the screen.

Miranda was wearing nothing except a short dressing gown. The others looked as if they had dressed with equal haste.

As far as Juliette could determine, they were watching some kind of news programme. On the screen she saw some men crouching by a pile of rubble and then the image was gone, replaced by a serious-faced man talking rapidly into the camera in Spanish.

Before she could glean any more information she heard a sound behind her. Emmett Gorgon came out of the caravan. She turned to him. 'What's happening?'

The little man looked at her grimly. 'I'll tell you,' he said. 'Better than that, I'll show you.' He nodded at the Chinese earthquake vase on the table, exactly where they had left it last night. Emmett Gorgon looked at it, then at Juliette expectantly. 'What?' she said. 'I don't understand.'

'Take a closer look.'

Juliette stepped forward and inspected the vase. Then she saw. All four of the small ceramic balls had dropped from the dragon jaws into the wide waiting mouths of the frogs.

She stepped back hastily, finding something inexplicably repugnant about the sight. Her first impulsive thought was that this must be a trick that Emmett Gorgon was playing on her, that he had moved the balls himself.

'I don't understand,' she said. 'What does it mean?'

'It means earthquakes. Four of them. Last night.'

Christopher had turned away from the television. He opened a large atlas and began leafing through it as the others watched him.

'To the west we have Ensenada in Baja California,' he said, his fingers tracing the page. 'And the next one, the southernmost event. See? Approximately here, between Nuevos Ideal and Topia. Does anybody notice anything strange yet? No?' He looked up at Juliette. She shook her head. The map meant nothing to her.

'All right,' said Christopher. He turned to Emmett Gorgon. 'Do you mind if I draw on this?' The little man shook his head. 'Right,' said Christopher. 'Anyone got a pen?' Emily bounded forward with one.

'Thank you,' said Christopher. He began to draw small dots on the map. 'OK. Here's the Ensenada quake. And here's Nuevos Ideal. Now let me mark the third seismic event. It was east of us, in Texas. Here near Shreveport. Anyone see anything yet?'

'Oh my God,' said Miranda, staring down at the map.

'Here we go again,' murmured Tregemmon bleakly. He moved closer, scrutinising the atlas.

'What is it?' Juliette came forward so that she could see the map. 'What are you talking about?'

'Isn't it obvious?' said Emily. The little girl was rolling her eyes in disgust at her big sister's obtuseness. 'The pattern, of course.'

Juliette glared at her. 'What pattern?'

'It should become completely clear when I mark the fourth earthquake on the map,' said Chris. 'The one north of here. It took place in Casper, Wyoming.' He moved his pen and made a final mark on the map.

'I still don't see it.' Juliette felt an irrational surge of anger.

'How about now?' Christopher drew two lines across the map, one horizontal and one vertical. Each line connected two of the earthquake loci. As he drew them, Juliette felt a certain premonitory chill.

He lifted the pen away. On the page, the lines formed a perfect cross.

He was watching her with keen attention. 'And look at the point of intersection,' he said. Christopher tapped the point on the map. Juliette forced herself to look at it.

'It's in New Mexico,' she conceded reluctantly.

'It's more than that. It's in the Socorro Seismic Anomaly. Right smack on the spot where we are sitting right now.'

'X marks the spot,' agreed Tregemmon laconically.

Just then there was a cry from outside the tent. They all hurried out into the blinding daylight, dust rising under their feet, to find Emmett Gorgon standing outside Rosie's caravan.

He was staring at the ground, cursing. Laughing Dog cowered at his feet as he cursed and shouted.

'What's wrong?' said Tregemmon.

Emmett Gorgon spun around and stared at him. 'It doesn't make any sense! At least before it made some kind of sense.' He looked at the ground. 'For every drawing Rosie made there would be an earthquake.'

He shook his head again. 'But last night there were *four* new quakes, and this morning there isn't a single new drawing.'

Emily came and stood beside him, stooping to pat Laughing Dog as she studied the marks in the sandy soil: abstract swirls, nests of angular lines. 'You're right, Mr Gorgon. It's exactly the same as it was last night. Just the same four drawings. Completely unchanged.'

To Juliette their voices had faded to a meaningless buzzing. All she could hear was the roaring of blood in her own ears. She approached slowly, with great trepidation.

All too soon she was in a position, standing just behind the midget and his coyote, to see the markings on the ground.

She stared at them, and for a moment her vision became a blurred confusion of turbulent red, as if she was about to faint. Then her eyes cleared and she was forced to look at the drawings again. To look at the truth.

It was unimaginable, but there it was.

The drawings were back.

They were restored, exactly as they'd been before she raised her broom and obliterated them. Identical in every detail. As if she'd never touched them.

Had she really swept them away? Had she imagined it? Juliette felt reality begin to tip under her, like the deck of a ship in heavy seas.

'Yeah, they're just like we left them last night,' murmured Emmett Gorgon.

'No they're not,' she said in a small, frightened voice.

The others all looked at her. 'What do you mean?' demanded Christopher.

'I wiped them away last night.'

'What?'

'I took a broom and I wiped them all away.'

'You did *what*?' Emmett Gorgon was staring at her, his eyes bulging.

'I wiped them out. I removed every trace of them.'

'After what I told you?' Spittle was flying from the little man's mouth. 'After I told you how dangerous it could be?'

'With a broom?' said Emily dryly. 'The classical symbol of the witch?'

Her little sister was grinning at her. Juliette spun around to see that Christopher was also grinning. She wanted to smash his smug, complacent, grinning face in. Suddenly all her fear and confusion focused into a hard point of anger.

'How dare you be amused?' she demanded. 'Dozens of people died in those earthquakes. Perhaps hundreds.' She could hear her voice shaking, out of control with rage. 'And it's all my –'

Then she paused, like someone standing on the very edge of a precipice. Juliette fell silent, unwilling to complete her chain of thought. But Christopher completed it for her.

'And it's all your fault?'

Juliette felt her anger drain away in an instant. That was exactly what she'd been about to say. The implications of this statement began to penetrate her mind. She felt the beginning of an emotional disturbance, as profound as any seismic shift in the earth. Her paradigms and beliefs were suddenly a melting iceberg.

'I don't know,' she insisted, shaking her head. 'It seems impossible. But then, so does this.' She looked down at the four diagrams in the sand. 'As far as I can tell, they're identical to the ones I wiped out last night. Rosie must have redrawn them, accurate in every detail. And as she drew each one, there was a corresponding earthquake . . .'

'So you're beginning to believe in the power of dreams. Believe that magic is possible.'

'I don't know.' Juliette shook her head. It was too much to take in.

'Maybe it's a good thing.' Christopher smiled. 'Maybe it's a good thing that you did it.'

Juliette heard her voice go shrill with hysteria. 'A good thing that I caused four earthquakes?'

He remained calm. 'Maybe. Maybe your belief is the final piece of the puzzle that we need.'

'Need for what, for God's sake?'

'To defeat Mr Leiber.'

Juliette turned and ran. She ran from the ramshackle collection of caravans called Seismic City and the drawings in the sand and the truth that seemed to be hammering away at her mind. She fled into the desert.

It was perhaps ten minutes before Christopher came after her and found her. 'Why did you run away?' he said. She turned and stared at him.

'You'd be better off asking why I stopped running. And I did that because I realised I couldn't escape. What's happening is happening inside my head. I am starting to believe in this nonsense.' She looked at Christopher. 'Dreams. Sorcery. Earthquakes. I'm starting to believe. That's what scares me.'

356

He put his arms around her and she let him, reluctantly at first and then gradually melting. 'Why do we have to do this?' she said in a small voice. 'Why do we have to try to stop Mr Leiber?'

'Because it's my responsibility.'

'Your responsibility? How?'

Christopher's voice was steady and sad and matter-of-fact. 'Because I'm the one who unleashed Mr Leiber on the world.'

When they got back they found that Emmett Gorgon was wearing a chef's hat and a plasticised apron. On the apron was printed a grinning cartoon devil with a clutch of chilli peppers impaled on his pitchfork. HOT STUFF was written in large flaming letters above the devil.

'OK, folks,' he said. 'Tell your taste buds to fasten their seat belt, because they're about to experience the famous Emmett Gorgon chilli-con-carne experience.'

He was carrying a gleaming stainless-steel pot, which radiated heat off its curved shining lid that could be felt even in the boiling afternoon air of the tent. The little man sweated profusely as he lugged it towards the table, but he wouldn't allow anyone to help him.

The others were all seated around that table. Arranged in front of them were knives, forks, glasses and large bowls of rice covered with clean damp cloths. A big squat bottle of red wine sat in the centre of the table.

The little man set the pot down and wiped his sweating forehead. 'Get ready for a taste experience deluxe, my friends.' He wrapped his hands in one of the chequered cloths and lifted the lid off the pot.

An aromatic waft of steam rose from the pot and flowed across Juliette's face. She could smell the fragrance of garlic and other, subtler, spicier scents. It smelt delicious. Her mouth filled with saliva.

'Smells good, doesn't it?'

'It certainly does. What's in it?'

'Well, besides the obligatory beef and beans we have tomatoes, garlic, onions, mushrooms, celery, black olives, a large cinnamon stick, a dash of ketchup, a pinch of dried ginger, some tomato paste and . . .'

He reached for the large wine bottle, uncorked it and poured a gurgling measure into the pot. More steam came boiling out, spreading the smell of the fragrant mixture. 'And a generous splash of wine.'

'How wonderful,' said Emily sarcastically. Trust her to spoil the party, thought Juliette. Her little sister was staring at the plate on which sat a pair of large hamburgers. They were delicious-looking hamburgers in toasted sesame buns, fatly stuffed with green fronds of salad and golden tongues of cheese hanging out. Emily was toying with them critically, peering under the buns, then turning back to look at the pot of chilli.

'Why can't I have the chilli?' she grumbled, slamming her heels against the rungs of her chair.

'You know exactly why,' snapped Juliette.

'Hey, no arguing now.' Emmett Gorgon smiled at Emily. 'Did I not prepare two Grade-A prime munchkinburgers especially to compensate you?'

'Yes, I suppose you did,' allowed Emily sulkily.

'And do they not look mouthwateringly good?'

'Yes, I suppose they do.'

'Good.' The little man hopped up on to his chair. 'Then allow me to propose a toast. I'll keep it short, as you might expect from a man of my stature. Pass your glasses.'

He filled each glass with a generous dollop of red wine. Then he popped open a can of root beer and passed it to Emily.

The little man lifted his glass and turned to look at Miranda. 'Here's to our psychonaut. Miranda, baby, you're a brave girl.'

Miranda nodded modestly and then they all settled down to eat.

Despite the tantalising smell, Juliette found herself picking at her meal reluctantly. 'If it's just Miranda who's going to have this so-called "power dream" why do all of us have to eat the chilli?'

Emmett Gorgon called out good-naturedly. 'Hey, shrink baby, don't be such a tightass.'

'Yes, Juliette, don't be such a tightass,' chimed in Emily.

Juliette swung around, ready to shout at her little sister, but Christopher stopped her, and improved her mood considerably, simply by putting a hand on her shoulder. He said, 'I discussed this with Emmett.'

'That's right,' said the little man, busy at his pot. 'We discussed it.'

'I think sharing the meal with Miranda is a good idea.' Chris looked at Juliette. 'You of all people know how important set and setting are. If you want to think of it in anthropological terms, we are enacting a tribal ceremony. The entire group participates in the sacrament of a shared meal.'

'And here comes second helpings.' Emmett Gorgon set about serving splashy spoonfuls of chilli from the large pot.

'Sacrament,' said Juliette, careful not to sound sarcastic.

'Shared meal,' snorted Emily with none of her sister's reluctance for sarcasm. 'How shared can it be when I'm not even getting a spoonful?'

Juliette swivelled around and glared at her. 'That's because the chilli contains drugs that might permanently warp your growing mind.'

Emmett Gorgon rapped loudly on the pot with his wooden spoon. 'Hey, for the last time, will you two cut it out? Like the Edge says, we're supposed to be a happy, harmonious little group. We're supposed to help speed the dreamer on her way. Not bum her out.'

Everyone turned to look at Miranda, who was busy eating her second helping.

FIFTY-TWO

Miranda squinted up into the sun. Her head was buzzing with the drug. She didn't mind; it distracted her from thinking about Danny.

Laughing Dog trotted out of a patch of shadow and joined her at the head of the 'procession'.

For a moment Miranda experienced a strange sort of double vision. She was herself, here and now, in this trailer camp, walking along with her diminutive new friend Emmett Gorgon. But at the same time she was a Stone Age tribeswoman following a respectful distance behind the grotesque dwarf shaman as he led her across an ancient desert, under the eternal sledgehammer of the sun.

At the front of their small procession was a sacred beast, the shaman's familiar, and at the rear was the master shaman himself with his long white hair.

The sunlight shone down on her with a strange intensity, as if it was a fraction brighter than usual. In this enhanced light the objects around Miranda seemed charged with a special significance. The pitted chrome of the abandoned caravans. A broken beer bottle glinting in the sandy soil. The formal simplicity of a patch of weeds.

Then she was standing by a small green tent pitched in the dirt. The little man patted it proudly. 'The dream lodge,' he said, and spread the flap open.

Miranda crawled in. There were a sleeping bag and a pillow in the tent. It was cool inside, and the sunshine penetrated the fabric as a cool green glow that filled the small space. She heard a sound and turned to see Christopher looking in at her.

'Now,' he said. 'Hopefully the drug combined with the

ceremony we've enacted will allow you to actively enter as an agent in your dreams. Indeed, we hope that the hallucinatory effect of the sauce will put you on the same psychic wavelength as Rosie. Then, in a technique known as lucid or guided dreaming, we want you to enter into Rosie's dreams.'

'I know what to expect,' said Miranda. She felt drowsy and a little impatient. 'I just don't know what to *do*.'

'OK, once you're in her dream, you must somehow interfere with it. You must disrupt the magic she is enacting.'

'In plain English, stop her creating earthquakes,' added Emmett Gorgon.

'But how, exactly?'

'We can't tell you exactly,' said Christopher impatiently. 'Because we don't know what to expect. But the dream landscape is likely to be symbolic. Trust your instincts. There may be something that needs fixing or mending.'

'Or healing,' added Emmett Gorgon.

Miranda stared at them in disbelief. 'Is that all you can tell me?'

'Oh yes,' Christopher smiled. 'And look for a spirit guide.'

Look for a spirit guide? thought Miranda. What kind of advice was that?

She lay down, pondering the words. She pondered them for perhaps three seconds before she felt herself slide down into a deep velvet pit, and was fast asleep.

In fact Miranda experienced the best sleep she'd had since Danny had died. It was deep, restful and healing.

And, much to her chagrin, profoundly dreamless.

It had been blazing afternoon when she first lay down in the little green tent. Miranda woke to darkness and a cool desert evening. She crawled out of the sleeping bag, feeling a little zingy and pleasantly stoned.

She unzipped the flap and eased out of the tent – her inaccurately named 'dream lodge'.

As she emerged, she was startled to see Emmett Gorgon sitting there in a canvas folding chair. The little man was stationed a few feet from the tent, sipping a beer.

'Have you been here all this time?'

He belched and tossed the empty beer can aside. 'I had to keep an eye on you, didn't I? And somebody had to stay here and shoo Laughing Dog away.'

'Laughing Dog?'

'Yeah, damn stupid coyote. He took it into his head that he had to keep you company in that tent. Kept nosing around, trying to bother you. I kept dragging him away until he finally got the message. Poor old Laughing Dog. But we couldn't let him in. Disturbing you was the last thing we wanted to do.'

He peered at her anxiously. 'So how did it go?'

Miranda felt herself colouring with embarrassment. She was ashamed to admit the truth. 'I don't think I dreamt at all,' she said finally. 'I suppose it just didn't work.'

Emmett Gorgon shrugged philosophically. 'So it goes.'

'I'm sorry I couldn't help you,' said Miranda forlornly, and it couldn't have been more true.

Some of the little man's customary good humour returned. He smiled at her. 'Don't worry. It was worth it to see your friends get stoned. Come on. Let me show you.'

Miranda followed him back to the tent where they found Juliette sitting at the table. She was the only one there. The dishes from lunch were still spread across it, although one end had been cleared to make room for the Chinese earthquake vase.

Juliette was examining the vase with what was, quite obviously to Miranda, deeply stoned fascination.

She glanced up at them as they entered the tent. 'This is a quite beautiful piece of ceramic. Really quite beautiful. A fascinating culture, the Chinese.'

'Damned right,' said Emmett Gorgon. 'The ancient Chinese knew how to avoid earthquakes.'

'Really,' said Juliette, staring at them beadily. 'How fascinating.'

At that moment, Emily came racing into the tent. The little girl's eyes were ablaze with excitement. 'You really ought to see what's going on out there. Tregemmon is shooting at beer cans, using a torch in one hand and the gun in the other. He really is an incredible shot. Come and watch.'

Juliette stared at her sister, obviously trying to pretend she wasn't stoned. 'No, I'm going to go and make some notes,' she said, frowning seriously.

'Notes?'

'I'm having the most amazing insights. Formulating the most extraordinary theories.' She got up suddenly and lurched off, clutching a pad of notepaper.

Her sister watched her go. 'Suit yourself,' she murmured. Then she scooped up some empty beer cans and hurried out in the opposite direction.

'See what I mean?' said Emmett Gorgon. 'Your friends are a scream. I think I'll go and watch them shoot at beer cans. Want to join me?'

Miranda followed the little man out of the tent. 'I'm sorry the dream magic didn't work.'

'Who says it didn't?' Emmett Gorgon smiled at her. 'The night isn't over yet.'

FIFTY-THREE

Juliette woke up with a thick head and a dry tongue. Why was that?

Then she remembered, and she experienced an immediate pang of guilt. For years she had been a responsible professional, someone who wouldn't dream of touching drugs.

Of course, she had smoked a little dope years ago, as a callow medical student, but never anything stronger. And nothing since.

Juliette winced as she remembered last night. At first it seemed as if the chilli had had no effect. But she had found herself compelled to grab a pen and begin scribbling notes as madcap 'theories' sprang, one after another, across her mind.

At one point she'd become convinced that she'd formulated a revolutionary new therapy for mental illness. Convinced it would win her a Nobel prize, she had clutched her notepad and scribbled away for hours.

Now, lying in her narrow bunk, Juliette hardly dared look at these notes. Yet they had seemed so important at the time. She decided she might as well face the music. She reached over the side of the bunk and picked up the notepad.

Just as she did so, her sister wandered in, noisily brushing her teeth.

'If you're looking in there for the secret of life,' said Emily, mouth frothing with dentifrice, 'forget it. I read the first few pages and it was banal gibberish.'

Juliette dropped the notebook as if it had suddenly become hot. 'That's what I suspected,' she said quickly.

'If that's what it's like being "stoned", as you call it, then

I'm glad you didn't let me have any of your boring chilli.'

Juliette began to get dressed. 'You're quite right. The whole episode was a complete waste of time.'

'On the contrary, big sister.' Emily wiped her mouth and set her toothbrush aside. She broke into a dazzling grin.

'Come over to Emmett Gorgon's tent, where we are even now holding what Tregemmon is calling our "victory breakfast".'

Juliette saw that Miranda was seated at the table by Emmett Gorgon, looking bright and beautiful for someone who had supposedly enacted a sacred dream ritual. She was sipping a cup of coffee as Tregemmon appeared behind her, carrying a skillet full of sizzling rashers and two bright-yellow eggs.

He scraped them on to a plate in front of Chris and smiled at Juliette and Emily. 'I'm no cook but someone had to fix breakfast for our hero.' He nodded at Christopher.

'Christopher? I don't understand. I thought Miranda was supposed to be the one.'

'I was,' said Miranda with a chagrined expression. 'But as hard as I tried I couldn't seem to have any dreams. Or, at least, not the right ones. That was left to Chris.'

Christopher was now busy pouring champagne and orange juice into a large jug. 'I had a feeling we might need some champagne,' said Emmett Gorgon, winking.

Juliette gradually pieced the story together. Christopher told everyone about it as they sat down to breakfast.

And Juliette had the unwanted but immediate and powerful conviction that he was lying. Just like a real shaman or witch doctor, she thought, making the best of it when the tribe's so-called 'magic' failed.

As they ate Tregemmon's overcooked bacon and undercooked eggs and swallowed glasses of surprisingly good Buck's Fizz, Christopher told them the whole story.

'It was the strangest dream. Very vivid. I was right here. In the desert here, except there were no caravans and no highway. No sign of man at all. And the landscape was different. As though it was the way this place might have looked a million years ago. I was lying on the ground when Laughing Dog woke me up –'

'Laughing Dog?' Emmett Gorgon cursed and punched the table. 'Damn, now why didn't I think of that? I even said to look for a spirit guide. But it never occurred to me it would be this guy.'

He reached down to affectionately pet the coyote, who, Juliette noticed, was lying under the table, lolling at his feet.

'He was a hero,' said Chris. 'I couldn't have done it without him. We set off towards a mesa in the distance. As we neared the base of the mesa the terrain became very rocky. There didn't appear to be any way up, but in fact there was a path. I could never have found it, but Laughing Dog led the way.'

'Good boy,' said Emmett, patting the grey shape under the table.

'We climbed the mesa. It was a long climb and the footing was difficult. I didn't feel out of breath or tired, but I did get discouraged. It seemed to go on for ever. But, whenever I stopped, Laughing Dog would dance around me, whining until I started again.

'So we kept climbing. Climbing across these sharp, shifting rocks. But then, as we finally approached the top of the mesa, there was a crest, a kind of hillock, and the footing suddenly became soft, spongy, almost. And incredibly smooth. It felt strangely *pleasant* underfoot. There was a sort of rubbery texture to it.

'When we reached the top of the hillock I looked down on the desert. In the silver moonlight it was a spectacular view. There was a lake on the desert floor, on the far side of the mesa. The surface of the lake was smooth and black and still, with the moon reflected in the water. It was beautiful. I was staring at it when Laughing Dog began whining at my feet.

'I looked down at him and for the first time I got a good look at the hillock we were standing on. It was a big dome-shaped mound and, as I said, it was soft and smooth and rubbery. Now I saw that the mound sloped away, down towards two slightly smaller mounds. There was something strangely familiar about these. They both had dark patches at the centre. But by then I had seen what lay between the two mounds, and beyond them.

'It was a face. The enormous face of a woman. A sleeping woman. And that was when the dream took a very strange turn because I realised I was standing on the giant body of a naked woman. That's why the ground felt smooth and rubbery. It was *flesh*. The mound I was standing on was her stomach. The other two mounds were her breasts, and beyond that was her face. Then I looked at the face again and realised that it was Rosie.

'I became so frightened that I turned and ran. Laughing Dog loped after me as I tripped and fell, catching one of my feet in a small crater. As I freed myself I realised this must be Rosie's belly button.

'I felt the "earth" stir under me as though she was about to wake up. Maybe I tickled her awake, catching my foot in her navel like that. Anyway, she stirred. And as the "ground" moved under me it reminded me of being in an earthquake. I started running again. I found myself stumbling through a thick tangle of undergrowth . . .'

Christopher grinned ruefully. 'Of course, it wasn't undergrowth, it was her pubic hair. I was blundering around on her mons veneris. So at least I knew where I was. I got my bearings and, with Laughing Dog following, I fled across her thigh and slithered down off it on to the top of the mesa. The top of the mesa was flat as a bed. And a giant bed. And Rosie was lying on it. It was littered with clusters of boulders.

'As I climbed down off Rosie I felt her move. She was beginning to wake up. I didn't want her to see me, so I ran to take shelter behind some of those boulders. There was one large, pale, egg-shaped one which I was particularly drawn to, and I was going to hide behind it, but Laughing Dog wouldn't let me. He began growling so fiercely that I let him lead me away and we went and hid behind some other boulders instead. And it was just as well we did.

'By now Rosie was rising to her feet. She was enormous.

367

Her shoulders blotted out the stars. She reached down and picked up a big tree branch which was lying on the mesa. Then she bent over and began to scratch on the ground with it and I realised she was drawing a pattern. Like the patterns she draws outside the caravan when she's sleep-walking. Except vastly larger of course. I looked out from behind my boulder and I saw her scratching in the dirt using the big branch. It was like a pencil in her huge hand. Then, when she finished, she set the branch aside. And suddenly I realised I had witnessed the ritual she used for creating the earthquakes.'

'Exactly,' said Emily excitedly. 'The drawing of the pattern obviously equates with some kind of mental process, a sort of electrochemical template. Which somehow triggers the release of energy which in turn causes the –'

'But I was wrong.' Juliette felt a certain warm gratification as Chris cut her sister off. 'I had only witnessed half the ritual,' he said. 'Because, after she set the branch aside, she reached down with both hands and picked up one of the boulders from the mesa top. I saw that it was the milky white one. And it was a crystal. A giant raw crystal, uncut and unpolished. It glinted in the moonlight as she lifted it and then . . .'

Chris winced. 'And then she brought it smashing down on her own body with all her strength. Down on the flesh of one giant thigh. It made an enormous snapping sound, as though she had broken one of her own bones. And that was when it began.

'The whole desert seemed to shake. Off in the distance I heard a huge cracking sound, echoing Rosie's bone snapping, but much louder. And miles away, on the horizon, I saw a column of dust rising into the night.'

'An earthquake?' said Emily.

'Certainly,' said Christopher. 'To speak in shamanistic terms, the bones in Rosie's body were like the bones in the body of the Earth, and when she broke them she broke the bones of the Earth. A powerful metaphor for an earthquake. It makes sense.'

Juliette shrugged. 'But to you everything makes sense.

If it's true then why haven't we heard reports of another earthquake?'

Christopher turned to her, his dark eyes suddenly sardonic and angry. Juliette felt instantly less sure of herself.

'As it happens, at approximately the same time I was having this dream, the good people of Los Angeles experienced a very strange phenomenon. You see, all over that sprawling metropolis the frightened residents have installed earthquake detectors.'

'Earthquake detectors,' said Juliette sceptically.

Chris nodded. 'These devices were pioneered in Mexico after the big quake in 1985. They're designed to detect the initial shockwave of a large seismic event and set off an alarm. It's not much of an early-warning system; in the case of LA, they only provide thirty seconds to a minute's warning before the main quake hits. Still, it's enough time to get out of your house into the street, if you're lucky.' He reached across for the champagne bottle and poured himself another glass.

'Well, last night, all over LA, these alarms went off. It was all over the TV news. Tens of thousands of them. Baffled householders ran out into the street. Some people remained standing there for hours, they were so scared. Finally they all went back to bed, scratching their heads. Because no quake followed that initial shockwave.'

'What do you mean?' said Juliette.

'They got the warning of the event, but no event.'

'How could that be?'

Christopher shook his head. 'I don't know. But, from the cheapest, crudest earthquake alarm to the most sophisticated equipment in the university labs, they all told the same tale. A monster quake. Richter ten or greater. The warning shock hits, but the quake itself never materialises. It just vanishes. They're all baffled.'

Juliette felt a sudden flash of irritation towards Christopher. He was rather smug. He always had to have all the answers. 'But you have an explanation, don't you?' she said.

He shrugged. 'Certainly. I saw Rosie set off a quake in

369

her sleep. But dreamtime and real-world time are two very different things. Somehow, there in Rosie's dream, I managed to intervene and stop it before it spilt over into the real world.'

'Stop it? How could you stop it?'

Chris ignored her question and continued his story. 'After the dust settled, I looked out from behind my boulder and saw that Rosie was lying down on the ground again. She moaned softly as she went back to sleep. Obviously her leg was hurting where she'd hit it with the giant crystal. I felt sorry for her. In the moonlight I could see a bruise forming on her. Then, as I looked, I noticed that there were dark patches all over her body.'

'Bruises like the ones that we saw when she went sleep-walking,' said Emily. She glanced around for confirmation from Emmett Gorgon, but the little man had left the tent.

'Exactly,' agreed Chris.

'So that explains where she got them.'

Juliette resisted the impulse to say that all this proved nothing. Chris had simply seen the bruises and sub-sequently incorporated them into his dream. Assuming he had had a dream at all.

Chris continued. 'After a while the moaning stopped and I came out from behind the boulder to check on Rosie. She appeared to be fast asleep. I knew this was my chance. I went over to the giant crystal. Somehow I knew it was the key to the whole thing.'

'Somehow,' murmured Juliette disgustedly.

Chris seemed not to hear. 'Without the crystal she wouldn't be able to hurt herself and make the earthquake magic. I had to get rid of it. But how? It was far too big and heavy to lift. I stood there in the moonlight staring at it. If only I could destroy it. But how?

'Then I remembered that the crystal was only part of the magic. Rosie also did her drawings on the ground, using the branch.

'I had to deal with the branch too. That was easy enough. I could just take it to the edge of the mesa and throw it off. And that's when I got the idea. The branch could be useful. I went over to where it was lying beside Rosie and dragged it back to the crystal.

'The crystal was sitting in a depression in the ground, like an egg in a cup. I found I could work the narrow end of the branch under it. I shoved it in good and hard, so it was jutting out at an angle.

'Luckily the crystal was quite near the edge of the mesa. My weight on the lever was just enough to start it rolling.

'And, once it started, it didn't stop. It rolled down the steep incline towards the edge of the mesa, and soon it was going so quickly that I had to run to keep up. It went straight over the edge.

'I saw it fall at least a hundred feet before it hit an outcropping of rock on the side of the mesa. Then it started to bounce. It looked like a big egg in the moonlight. But not for long. After about the third bounce it shattered. A million pieces – tiny pieces of crystal. They flew up in a gleaming shower, filling the sky, spinning slowly.

'Then I dragged the tree branch to the edge of the mesa, and threw that over the side too. I went over to inspect Rosie. She was still asleep, but the expression on her giant face had changed. Somehow she looked happy and peaceful.'

How convenient, thought Juliette. How pat.

Christopher drained his glass. 'And then I woke up.'

'What a marvellous dream,' said Emily. 'Jung would have been proud of you. And you've obviously broken the spell.'

'Obviously,' said Juliette dryly. It was all ridiculous of course. And not just ridiculous but also potentially dangerous. Dangerous from a psychological standpoint. Particularly for Emmett Gorgon.

Thinking about the little man made Juliette realise that he hadn't returned to the tent.

'Where exactly is Emmett?' she said.

'Gone to sit beside Rosie,' said Tregemmon. 'He's going to hold her hand until she wakes up.'

'Until she wakes up?'

371

Christopher nodded. 'She's bound to wake up now. By my use of dream magic, I've broken the spell on her.'

Juliette wasn't able to keep her thoughts to herself any longer. 'What do you mean?' she hissed furiously. 'It's terrible to give that little man false hope.'

'False hope? But I –'

'You've done nothing more than experience a particularly vivid dream.' If that, she added silently. 'It is ridiculous for you to set any store by it whatsoever.'

'A particularly lucid, vivid, coherent dream.'

'Nothing that can't be attributed to the power of suggestion,' insisted Juliette. 'Or consuming a variety of powerful drugs. In fact, it was a classic wish-fulfilment dream. I'm sorry, but we are no nearer a solution than we were yesterday.'

There was a moment's bleak silence, and then Tregemmon spoke bleakly. 'You sure know how to break up a party.'

He poured the last of the champagne into his glass.

'I'm sorry,' said Juliette, calmly but firmly, 'but it's better you should all face reality. Rosie is still in an inexplicable coma.' Juliette had examined the woman herself; the coma was certainly beyond *her* powers of explanation.

'But she *is* going to wake up!' insisted Emily stubbornly.

'I don't think so,' said Juliette. She heard a sound behind her and turned towards the entrance of the tent. Emmett Gorgon was approaching. As he came nearer it became obvious that he was crying.

He stared at them, tears flowing freely down his face.

'What is it?' said Miranda, her voice full of concern.

'It's Rosie,' he said.

Juliette shook her head sternly. 'I knew it. I knew something would go wrong.'

'Wrong?' The little man wiped the tears from his face. 'She's wide awake.'

'Awake?' Juliette wasn't sure she'd heard properly.

'I'm sorry about all this crying,' said Emmett Gorgon. 'But, by God, I'm not ashamed of a few manly tears. I've got my baby back.' A shadow flickered in the sunlight behind him. 'Here she is now.'

He stood away from the entrance of the tent and Rosie came in. The big Mexican woman looked very different now that she was awake and fully dressed. She entered the tent hesitantly and smiled a tight, shy smile.

Emmett Gorgon took her hand. 'Rosie wants to apologise. She's completely ashamed that she's been sleepwalking in front of you folks naked. She feels so embarrassed that someone ought to fry an egg on her big blushing face.'

The big woman stood beside him, eyes lowered demurely towards the floor. Emmett Gorgon reached up and patted her on her big backside.

'But don't take that too seriously, folks. She did use to work in a strip club, after all.'

FIFTY-FOUR

Despite herself, Juliette was swept up in the spirit of the occasion. The party that ensued went on late into the night. Emmett Gorgon dug out some more bottles of champagne and, when these eventually ran out, the drinkers moved on to beer.

Music and smoke filled the tent and a rather woozy Juliette watched Miranda and Tregemmon dancing around a ghetto blaster.

She even had a dance herself. Finally, though, she decided it was getting late. Despite much sulking and protesting, she managed to drag Emily back to their caravan and make her brush her teeth and put her to bed.

Juliette could hear the others outside Emmett Gorgon's caravan, happy voices in the night. She could hear Christopher's voice. For a moment she was tempted to go back and join the party. To join him. But then exhaustion claimed her and she toppled into her bunk.

Maddeningly, she woke up two hours later and couldn't get back to sleep. Emily of course was happily lost in dreams on the top bunk. That didn't help. Juliette remained endlessly, echoingly awake. The sounds of the party had long since faded. She felt utterly alone. The only wakeful person in a peaceful, sleeping world. In the end she rolled over and picked up her torch and shone a beam of light across the dusty floor of the caravan. She was looking for something to read. Anything would do. Anything to distract her.

All she could see was the notepad she had used to such embarrassing effect the previous evening, recording her psychedelic musings.

Juliette sighed. She didn't look forward to reading it, but she decided she ought to. Just in case some genuine insight or memorable observation had slipped through the net of stoned banality.

But she was soon wincing. The first few pages were crowded with her sprawling handwriting and contained embarrassingly 'poetic' observations about psychiatry and the human mind.

These observations were in note form, occasionally bracketed by elaborately doodled flowers. The flowers were bad enough, but the notes read like an unholy hybrid of Rod McKuen and Abraham Maslow.

Juliette grew so embarrassed that she began to flip hastily through, skipping page after page packed with the same silly, stoned aphorisms in the same silly, stoned handwriting.

Then something rather odd caught her attention. On one of the pages the handwriting changed.

It changed abruptly and totally. From her looping scrawl it altered, in the middle of a line, to a jagged, spidery script that was completely alien.

For a moment Juliette wondered if someone had taken the pad from her and written on it. But she knew this was impossible. Not in the middle of a line of handwriting like that. And, besides, she knew that she had kept hold of the pad all evening.

She stared in puzzlement at the strange handwriting.

'I am,' it said, as though it was announcing the simple ontological fact of the writer's existence. But then on the next line the same words occurred again. And this time other words followed them.

In its entirety, the handwriting occupied only a few lines:

I am about to enact a terrible vengeance. You have interfered with a pet project of mine and I can hardly permit you to get away with that. I realise that you will not respond to this note because, as you can see –

And here the handwriting changed again, resuming the soft contours of Juliette's distinctive looping scrawl.

. . . as you can see it is now in your own hand. Obviously this entire message is nothing more than the result of some ridiculous undergraduate stoned behaviour by your own – that is to say, *my* own – unconscious mind.

Yes, you can believe that.

Or, on the other hand, you can pass along a message. Tell Christopher Matthew that I realise that I have been a little elusive lately, and I apologise. I guarantee that I shall meet him soon, for what I modestly call the Final Conflagration.

I think we shall stage it in sunny Taos, New Mexico.

Tell him it begins when he arrives.

And tell him one other thing. I am very angry about his interference with the earthquake magic. I went to rather a lot of trouble to arrange it and I don't appreciate anyone interfering.

I must take measures to indicate the true extent of my displeasure. I could hardly do anything else.

Yours fondly,

Franklin Leiber.

PS. I know you won't act on this message, since to do so would be to yield to irrational behaviour.

Juliette stared at the note for a long moment, her mind whirring with possible reactions. One was to leave the caravan and go running over to Christopher right away.

It was an incredible temptation to do just that. But the PS on the note was right. If she did, she would be yielding to superstition. Indeed, if she gave in to the note, she would be calling into question her own sanity.

So she let the notebook drop, fluttering to the floor of the caravan.

Then she rolled over in the narrow bunk bed, and fell asleep with strange suddenness.

Two hundred feet away, Miranda also was asleep.

She had got quite drunk at the victory party and stumbled back to her caravan to collapse on her spinning bed.

As she writhed down among her pillows she had discovered an unfamiliar shape. Mr Rafferty the teddy bear.
How had he got there? Never mind. He was a welcome
visitor.

Miranda fell asleep clutching the small battered shape
of the toy bear.

Soon she was dreaming. She found herself in the black
and silver desert, standing in the wilderness, under the
pure circle of the moon.

The ground felt soft and powdery under her bare feet. It
was more like soft, fine ashes than sand. There was a stand
of dead desert trees in front of her and in her dream
Miranda felt drawn towards it.

The high branches were a tangle of shadows in the silver
moonlight. Miranda peered into the shadows among the
trees, half expecting Laughing Dog to appear.

After all, he had appeared in Christopher's dream,
hadn't he? Miranda was delighted at the prospect of
seeing the coyote. And sure enough, after a moment or
two, there was a stirring of motion among the angular
trees. Their branches creaked in the moonlight and a
shape emerged from the shadows.

But it wasn't Laughing Dog. It was a man. He was
naked like herself, but he had such a mediocre average
body, potbellied and middle-aged, that she hardly noticed
it. The man's face, however, was something else. He
looked at her through dead eyes.

'Yes, I'm afraid it's me again,' said Mr Leiber.

FIFTY-FIVE

Absurdly, although he wasn't wearing a stitch of clothing, Mr Leiber was smoking a cigar. Clouds of smoke rose from his mouth as he exhaled expansively, floating upward, ghostly white in the moonlight.

He walked towards Miranda. The red tip of his cigar was the only colour in the monochrome landscape of the desert night. The cigar tip glowed cherry red as he puffed.

'I hope you don't mind me intruding like this,' he said. 'I mean, meeting in your dreams. It's getting to be a bit of a habit, isn't it? And habits can be so boring.'

He scrutinised the blunt burning stub of his cigar. 'But I'm afraid that I'm obliged, or "obligated" as our American friends would say, to pay you a visit. Because, you see, I'm afraid that I am rather unhappy with the way Christopher scotched my little earthquake enterprise.'

He puffed on the cigar again and smoke floated up past his eyes. Those eyes regarded her with infinite depths of intelligence, an intelligence now tinted with inhumanly powerful rage. 'I really should be paying a visit on Christopher himself. But for tiresome reasons I won't go into I'm unable to approach him on the same footing I can approach you.' He smiled a hideously empty smile at Miranda.

'You, yes I'm afraid it's you, Miranda.' He puffed on his cigar and the tip glowed cherry red. 'Now listen carefully. This won't take long. You may recall something that Emily said in the bookshop in Taos – she really is quite a clever little girl, isn't she? She had found this ghoulish magazine about paranormal phenomena. Then she offered a commentary, carrying on in rather technical terms about a strange metabolic phenomenon, a kind of cascade effect within the body. And some mumbo jumbo about free radicals. Yes? Do you remember? You can nod, my dear.'

Miranda was about to reply with a volley of icy abuse. But with a strange lapse, characteristic of dream logic, she found herself unable to speak. So, instead of scalding Mr Leiber with a stream of verbal obscenity, she found herself, maddeningly, nodding exactly as requested.

'Very well. And then Emily went on to mention some kind of metabolic event that started the chain reaction. Do you remember that?'

Miranda nodded again.

'Do you remember what that chain reaction was?'

Miranda shook her head.

'Well, allow me to remind you. Emily was discussing the subject of spontaneous combustion.'

Miranda felt a little chill of fear. She didn't want to listen to Mr Leiber. But she was unable to move.

Mr Leiber smiled. 'Spontaneous human combustion is a fascinating thing . . .' He lifted his cigar and stuck it back between his grinning teeth. He sucked on the cigar and the tip of it glowed a hot bright red.

The hot red seemed to spread until it filled Miranda's vision.

Red.

Hot.

Everything else was blotted out by this one sensation. Miranda stirred sleepily. She was terribly hot.

She became more fully awake and found that she had somehow got herself tangled in her sleeping bag. The bag had become a stifling shroud, trapping her sweating body.

She struggled to get free and discovered that her arm was stuck under her. Its circulation had been cut off, reducing it temporarily to a numbed paralysis.

Feeling a little ridiculous, she picked her arm up with her right hand and lifted it off, for all the world like a numb lump of meat. Removing the pressure helped a little, but in a moment the pain flared up again.

And now it was matched by another pain. An itching irritation in her numb and clumsy arm. Miranda laboriously rolled her arm over. To her astonishment she saw a burn forming on the smooth flesh.

She rose to her feet in alarm, kicking her sleeping bag aside. What was going on? Then a sudden wave of cramps hit her and it was so painful she forgot everything else.

She put her hand to her stomach, then snatched it away. What was happening? She could feel the heat radiating off her abdomen, as if from the surface of a skillet.

It was hard to tell in the grimy moonlight that penetrated the caravan windows, but the entire front of her body, from crotch to breastbone, seemed discoloured, a hot flushed shade of red. The colour of skin in a high fever.

Miranda scooped up the plastic bottle of water from the floor beside her bed and drank from it. Her throat pulsed as she greedily swallowed and felt the water travelling deep into her. Towards the source of that awful heat.

Almost immediately, the heat and the pain diminished. Miranda took a deep breath and sighed with relief. But, as she exhaled, her breath emerged in a billowing cloud of steam.

The steam shone in the moonlight. Miranda took one look at it and ran, stumbling out of the caravan and down the crude concrete blocks that served as steps.

In the moonlight she could see that there was a definite darkening of her skin, a huge oval that covered most of her body. As she looked at it the spot grew darker still, turning black. The centre of it began to char and crumble.

Miranda ran. She ran away from the caravans and out into the desert. The wind whipped at her. She ran across the uneven ground, feet flashing in the moonlight. Then she realised it wasn't moonlight.

The source of light was travelling with her, moving when she moved. A pale-blue glow that wavered in a wide arc.

Miranda instinctively searched for the source of the light, and when she found it she was too shocked to understand. The light was coming *from* her.

It was cast by a thin tongue of blue flame like the gas jet on a cooker. Except the flame was coming from her navel. It emerged from the black flaking skin, flowing out of her body. As she watched, the fissure split wider. Charred fragments floated away, opening a hole as big as a baby's mouth.

Blue flame poured out, illuminating the scene around her in bold strokes of light. The experience was eerie beyond imagining, but no longer painful. Some kind of terminal rush of natural anaesthetic had kicked in and Miranda felt strangely detached.

Finally, she was too tired to run and, besides, she could no longer see where she was going. The blast of flame coming out of her was rising so high it obscured her vision.

All she could see was a blue halo of flame floating up in front of her. Miranda stopped. Her legs trembled after the long run through the desert. She felt her body wobble. Then her legs gave way and she toppled to the ground.

She caught a glimpse of her own legs, standing some distance away from her. How could that be? Her feet were still firmly planted on the desert ground.

But the broken tops of her shins were standing there, burning like greasy black candles, blue flames licking up from them.

Miranda was beyond horror. This sight, in the desert night, seemed merely novel. Somewhere at the velvet edge of fading consciousness she suddenly felt the familiar tug of Danny's mind. Danny and the warmth of his love.

Was it a dying hallucination or genuine contact, reaching beyond the grave? It didn't matter. She let herself slip off in that direction.

But, before she lost consciousness, Miranda saw silver.

Drops of liquid silver, spilling on to the sand in front of her, as if the moon was crying tears.

The silver had a terrible beauty in the moonlight. She watched the molten splash of it on to the sand. With the last activity of her brain, she realised it was her fillings. The molten metal from her teeth spilling, like beautiful silver rain, on to the desert soil.

FIFTY-SIX

Juliette woke up to hear Emily shouting. There was nothing unusual in that. Emily had always been a strident child. But what *was* unusual was the sudden note of fear in the little girl's voice.

It brought Juliette to full consciousness. The bright clear moonlight of a desert night was beaming through the grimy windows of the caravan. The shouting was getting louder. And then suddenly Emily was beside her, flinging herself down on the bunk bed next to Juliette. She was clutching Juliette's notepad.

She looked pale and shaken. 'Look at this,' she wailed.

Juliette scratched her head sleepily, irritated at being dragged from sleep for something so trivial. 'What are you talking about?'

'The note from Mr Leiber.'

Juliette began to relax. 'Oh, that. It's nothing. Just some mental aberration.' She reached for the notepad. 'Look at it. Except for a few words, it's all obviously in my own handwriting.'

Emily refused to surrender the pad. 'Of course it is. He reached into your mind and wrote it with your hands.'

'Emily, that's ridiculous . . .' The small girl snorted furiously and hopped to her feet. 'What are you doing?'

Emily didn't answer. She pulled a sweater on over her pyjamas and grabbed a torch that was lying on the floor. She clicked it on, nodded with satisfaction and set off towards the door.

'Where are you going?'

'We have to react to that note. We have to see if everything's all right.'

'Wait until morning, Emily.'

'No.'

Juliette scrambled out of the bunk bed. 'Then at least wait for me.' But Emily didn't do that either and Juliette had to pursue her into the night in a most undignified fashion.

Emily hurried and her sister didn't catch up with her until they were in the darkness of the desert beyond the caravans. Emily stood there motionless, with the torch pointing at her small feet.

The torch was heavy in her hand. She stood stock still, staring ahead at Tregemmon and Christopher, who were already there, two shadowy figures in the night.

They were carrying torches of their own, shining them at the ground.

'Stay back, Emma Lilly,' ordered Tregemmon, glancing over his shoulder. He used their pet name, but there was something terribly cold about his voice.

Emily obeyed. She had no desire to see what had made Tregemmon's voice go so cold. A moment later her big sister came running up behind her. For an instant Emily considered trying to stop Juliette, but then she decided there was no point. Juliette was a grown-up and grown-ups insisted on doing things their own way.

She watched as Juliette slowed down and joined the hunched figures of Tregemmon and Christopher, the beams of the torches weaving all around them. Then the beams gradually steadied and came to fix on one particular spot on the ground.

They all bent down to examine this spot. Emily could hear their voices clearly on the cold night air.

'It's some kind of hoax,' said Juliette after a moment, her voice shaking. 'Look. It's just like in that ridiculous magazine. A pile of ashes in the shape of –' Then she stopped talking altogether for a moment. Neither of the men said anything.

Emily heard a soft rustling sound in the darkness and then a ghostly grey shape brushed past her knees. It was Laughing Dog. The coyote paused beside her, as if sensing

384

that there was something very wrong with the tableau ahead.

Or perhaps just wanting to comfort her.

Juliette began speaking again, babbling almost. Her voice was high-pitched and frantic. 'It can't be ...' she said. 'Someone's just taken some ashes and shaped them to look like her.'

'Don't touch it,' said Christopher. 'It's still hot.'

There was a forlorn cry which Emily was shocked to recognise as coming from Juliette.

'I told you not to touch it,' said Christopher wearily. 'Did you burn yourself?'

'No.' Then Juliette turned away from whatever the spectacle was on the ground and ran back towards Emily, sobbing. She buckled and fell to her knees. Emily had no idea what to do. Juliette threw her arms around her.

Laughing Dog watched solemnly.

'Oh God,' sobbed Juliette. 'The ashes fell apart when I touched them.'

She looked at Emily with her eyes full of tears. 'It was Miranda, and she just crumbled.'

The following day passed in a pall of gloom.

Laughing Dog seemed to sense the sadness of the occasion. Just after dawn he wandered out into the desert and investigated the pile of ashes that had once been a human being. And then he lifted his nose to the sky and began to howl.

Even Juliette found herself thinking that there was a note of almost human mourning in that cry.

As night fell she hurried to Emmett Gorgon's tent and was relieved to find Christopher sitting there, alone. 'I'm sorry about the note,' she said.

Christopher looked up blankly, coming back from whatever inner vistas preoccupied him. 'The note?'

Juliette found her voice was trembling. 'That's why everyone's angry with me, isn't it?'

'No one's angry with you. What are you talking about?'

'That note I wrote to myself. The one with the – the

message from Mr Leiber.' Juliette could hardly bring herself to say this. She felt as if she was opening her mind to superstition and madness. But it seemed that she didn't have a choice any more.

With her own eyes she had seen that pile of ashes, dwindling as it was scattered by the desert winds.

'It was a warning. I should have given you the note. You might have been able to do something. It's all my fault.' Juliette's voice trembled. 'I've killed Miranda, haven't I? Everyone blames me, don't they? And they're right.'

'Don't be ridiculous,' said Christopher softly. He had been distracted when Juliette first came into the tent but now he was giving her his full attention. There was a reassuring light of compassion in those extraordinary eyes. Juliette wanted to get as close as she could to his forgiving eyes. She moved forward.

And suddenly found herself in Christopher's arms. He was hugging her. His breath was warm on her face. They were pressed together at breast, belly and crotch. Juliette felt the warm pressure of his body against hers, and her emotions were taking a swift treacherous turn. A powerful wave of lust washed over her.

It was appalling to feel this way, with Miranda dead out there a few hundred yards away, dispersing into ash and memory.

But there it was. Juliette couldn't deny it. Lust was what she felt. She dug her face into Christopher's shoulder, then looked up at him. She gazed into his eyes for a moment, then her mouth was moving hungrily towards his.

Her skin tingled as their faces made contact. Their mouths drifted together and she felt an almost electrical shock.

Then there was a scuffling noise at the entrance to the tent and Emily came bursting in. Juliette and Christopher moved hastily apart, but the little girl didn't seem to have noticed anything.

'Tregemmon's back!' she said excitedly. Then she ran out again.

* * *

Juliette joined her little sister just as Tregemmon pulled up in the minivan. He rolled to a halt beside Emmett Gorgon's pickup. As the dust settled he climbed out and saw them standing waiting for him.

'Where have you been?' scolded Emily. 'We've all been terribly worried.'

'I'm sorry, but I had to go into town to buy something.' Tregemmon was holding an object wrapped in a towel.

'You already have a gun,' said Emily disdainfully. 'Why on Earth do you need another one?'

'This is a Sig Sauer P228. Nine millimetres.' Tregemmon unwrapped the gun. 'Holds more ammunition than the Ruger. Thirteen rounds. It weighs a shade over twenty-nine ounces. Barrel length three point eight six inches.'

'Yes, yes, that's enough details, thank you. But why do you *need* it?' She turned and looked at Juliette. 'Is it like you buying shoes? It doesn't matter how many pairs you have, you always need another one.'

Tregemmon grinned at them. 'Perhaps it's a little like that. Although I'd tend to make an argument about the need for superior fire power, that kind of thing.'

Abruptly, Emily looked away. 'Chris, what are you doing?' she said. Juliette looked around. Christopher was hurrying past them. He was coming from the direction of Miranda's caravan. He was clutching something. There was something faintly furtive in the way he moved.

'Chris!' called Emily again. 'What are you doing with Mr Rafferty?'

Chris turned reluctantly towards them as Emily came hurrying over, followed by Juliette and Tregemmon. 'This?' he said, looking at the teddy bear. 'I found it among Miranda's bedclothes. She was sleeping with it last night.' He hesitated. 'Just before it happened,' he said.

'Well, what of it?' said Emily. 'You're not suggesting that Mr Rafferty is in any way responsible for –'

She stopped and looked at him. 'Christopher, please. Mr Rafferty is harmless. He's sort of a floating comfort object, shared among the female members of our party. That's why Miranda had him. Why, even Juliette has had recourse to him on occasion.'

Juliette stared at her little sister. She hadn't realised that Emily knew about that.

Chris was nodding, as if this confirmed a suspicion he had. 'The night Mr Leiber wrote the note in her handwriting.'

'I suppose so,' said Emily. 'Why?'

'I think the connection is pretty clear,' said Christopher. He turned and walked away from them, still gripping the teddy bear.

'Christopher, please,' called Emily. 'What are you going to do with him?' she cried plaintively. But Christopher ignored her. He kept on walking, out into the desert. Emily turned to Tregemmon and Juliette. 'Please make him stop,' she begged.

'Stay here, Emily,' Juliette ordered, turning to follow Christopher. 'So what is the theory?' she said casually as she caught up with him. 'That the teddy bear somehow represents a connection with Mr Leiber?'

'It was Mr Leiber's girlfriend who gave it to Emily. And by all accounts Nuala isn't the type who's prone to kind gestures.'

'What are you saying?' said Tregemmon. 'That they planted the teddy bear on us?'

'Yes,' said Christopher. He kept on walking out into the desert. Night was falling now and Seismic City was becoming lost behind them in the shadows. Juliette felt a small irrational flicker of insecurity at leaving shelter so far behind.

'A teddy bear?' persisted Tregemmon. 'They planted a toy on us?'

'That's right,' said Christopher.

'Where are we going?' Juliette felt compelled to ask. They seemed to have come an awfully long way out into the desert and night was falling fast.

'We're looking for something I brought out here earlier. Ah, here it is.' Chris stopped beside a knee-high rectangular object standing on the ground behind a clump of weeds. Juliette recognised it as one of the spare petrol canisters from the minivan.

'What's that doing out here?' said Tregemmon.

'As I said, I brought it out here earlier. I was only waiting until nightfall. I didn't want Emily to see what I was doing. I didn't want her getting upset.'

'What's the petrol for?' said Juliette. Then she realised. 'Oh, I see.'

'They planted a teddy bear on us,' said Tregemmon in disgust. 'And now you're going to *burn* it.'

'I think that's the safest way to get rid of it.' He put Mr Rafferty on the ground and picked up the petrol can.

'What are you trying to say, Chris?' Juliette could hardly make out his face in the gathering gloom. None of them had thought to bring a torch. 'Are you saying that this teddy is some kind of sinister fetish? A voodoo doll?'

Christopher had been unscrewing the lid of the petrol can. Now he sighed wearily and put it down. 'Tregemmon, have you got a knife?'

'Why, is burning the bear suddenly not good enough? Are you going to stab it, too?' Now it was Tregemmon's turn to sigh as he handed Chris a pocket knife. 'You've really sunk low this time,' he said disgustedly. 'That little girl loves that bear, you know.'

By way of reply, Christopher unfolded the pocket knife, picked up the bear and slit its belly open. 'Here, look,' he said.

In the twilight Juliette saw him delve into the white cotton stuffing of the bear's innards and draw something out. 'Look at this.' He held it up. Juliette came close. It was a small sachet made of some porous material, like a tea bag.

'What is it?' said Tregemmon.

Chris cut it open and drew out a dark coil of strands. 'Hair?' said Juliette. Chris nodded. 'Human hair.'

'And you were expecting to find that?' said Tregemmon.

'I saw the bear had been opened up and then resealed. I noticed because of the stitching: the thread was different. So I was expecting to find *something*.' He examined the coil of hair. 'And I'm not too surprised to find this.'

Tregemmon frowned at the hair as though it was something unhygienic. 'Who does it belong to?'

'Mr Leiber?' suggested Juliette. She could see the way this was going. Christopher nodded.

'And its presence here is some sort of witchcraft gambit?' Despite her surface calmness, Juliette found that she was quite frightened by the discovery. The notion that someone else believed in such things was almost as disturbing as believing in them yourself.

'No,' said Christopher. 'I'd say it was more of a biochemical gambit.' He held up the strands of hair. 'I suspect Leiber's intention was to preserve some kind of pheromonal waft of himself and to pass it on to whoever came in contact with the teddy bear. To bring him to mind, as it were.'

'You're saying we're able to *smell* him?'

Chris returned the dark strands to the sachet. 'Well, it is body hair. It should be comparatively rich in chemical triggers, evolved when we were still smell-driven creatures. But which we can still detect, in minuscule quantities, on a subliminal level.'

Juliette immediately saw a flaw in this argument. 'Then that would be Emily who's been most exposed to it. She sleeps with the teddy bear almost every night. And apparently nothing sinister has happened to her.'

'Maybe she's immune,' said Christopher. 'After all, she's met Mr Leiber in person.'

'That's another problem,' said Juliette. 'Miranda and I never met him in person. In that case how could the smell of him possibly trigger memories of him?'

'Maybe you don't need to meet him. Maybe Leiber can have an effect on you just through his signature smell.'

'Maybe this, maybe that,' said Tregemmon impatiently. He took the sachet from Christopher. 'Let's burn this thing.'

'Burn it?' said Juliette.

Tregemmon glanced at Chris. 'I assume that's why he brought the petrol out here.'

'That's right.'

Tregemmon upended the petrol can. Juliette breathed the raw smell of the fuel and on top of that another smell, rank and unidentifiable and oddly unsettling.

Juliette saw the bright flash of a match and then

Tregemmon released it from his fingers and yellow flame splashed on to the sachet of hair. As it burnt the odd smell grew stronger for a moment and then dispersed.

'I hate the smell of burning hair,' said Tregemmon. 'Well, that's that,' he added, looking into the flames.

As Juliette watched, the small fire flared up, growing unnaturally high and bright. She moved a little further away.

And immediately the fire blazed up, the eerie sound of a coyote howling rose in the desert night.

'I wonder if that's Laughing Dog,' said Christopher.

Just then the fire died back down to normal and the sound of the coyote faded. Juliette watched the last small tongues of flame waver and die out.

Then suddenly it was dark.

'I'd heard that night falls quickly in the desert,' said Christopher. 'But this is ridiculous.'

'I can't see a thing,' said Tregemmon.

'It's some kind of temporary freak effect,' said Juliette. 'We were all staring into the fire.'

'You think it dazzled us or something?'

'Or something,' said Juliette confidently. But three minutes later they were all still standing in total darkness.

'Temporary freak effect?' said Tregemmon sardonically, and Christopher chuckled. Juliette felt irritated.

Christopher seemed to sense this. He took her hand. 'Well, that really was a very good theory,' he said. 'But it would appear that it's simply night and, yes, it really is this dark out in the desert.'

'I can't see the moon or stars,' said Tregemmon.

'It's an overcast night. Which way is Seismic City, do you reckon?'

'What am I, the faithful guide?' said Tregemmon bad-temperedly. 'Your guess is as good as mine.'

'All right,' said Christopher equably. 'I guess this direction.' He led Juliette by the hand, moving forward into the darkness.

'All right, all right, hang about,' said Tregemmon, hastening after them.

They wandered on in total blackness. Juliette didn't

mind. The night was mild and Christopher was beside her, holding her hand. Saving Tregemmon's irascible and sardonic presence, it would have been an intensely romantic occasion. A ride in the tunnel of love.

Juliette was lost in these thoughts when suddenly Christopher said, 'Did anybody pick up Mr Rafferty?'

'Shit, no,' said Tregemmon.

'Does it matter?' ventured Juliette.

'Of course it matters. Emily would have liked that bear back.'

'Wait a minute, did you hear something?' said Christopher.

'Don't start,' said Tregemmon. 'We're out here in the middle of the desert in total darkness. Don't start hearing things.'

But then they all heard it. A heavy lumbering sound, as of some great creature moving in the darkness close by. Juliette could hear the slurring of its big feet on the ground and the powerful hot sound of its breathing. It was very big and very close by.

'What is it?' she hissed.

'Do they get grizzlies this far south?' said Tregemmon softly.

A grizzly? A bear? Juliette listened to the big thing lumbering around them. It appeared to be circling them. Yes, it did sound like some kind of bear. Was that heavy breathing becoming quicker, more excited?

Being lost in the darkness had seemed like an adventure. Now it began to turn into a nightmare. Juliette found herself remembering what had happened to Miranda, last night, in the desert nearby. The horror of the memory hit her full force and fuelled her fear now.

The three of them stood very still, clustered together in the darkness as the big thing paced around them. Juliette felt rationality begin to slip away.

'What are we going to do?' breathed Tregemmon. 'Just stand here?'

'I'm not sure that I want to move with that thing out there.'

392

'If I could see it maybe I could shoot it.'

'Maybe you could shoot it,' said Christopher doubtfully. 'If it is a bear.'

Juliette didn't like this line of enquiry. 'Of course it's a bear,' she said quickly.

'That's my opinion,' agreed Tregemmon. 'But we'd better hear the Edge's opinion.'

'I think it's something we summoned up when we burnt the hair.'

'Nonsense, it's just a bear,' persisted Juliette. Just, she thought.

'The way that Mr Rafferty was just a bear?'

'Quiet,' said Tregemmon urgently.

The thing, whatever it was out there in the darkness, was now pawing the earth, an impatient sound full of the promise of impending violence.

Then another sound began in time with the pawing, a liquid rippling snarl that raised the hairs on the back of Juliette's neck.

'Stand behind me,' said Tregemmon, his voice constricted and unsteady. 'Both of you. I think it's going to charge.'

Just then Christopher said, 'Look. Over there.' Juliette turned to see a light. It was a tiny white glow, but it was the only light in this vast blackness and it was slowly coming closer.

The pawing stopped and the snarl dropped to an almost inaudible rumble, a menacing purr. The light bobbed as it approached them. Juliette could see now that it was the beam of a torch that someone was carrying. The thing in the darkness didn't seem to like the light. Juliette heard it give out a strange little high-pitched sound.

Then she realised that it wasn't the thing making the sound. It was the torch bearer calling out. And she recognised the voice.

'Chris, Tregemmon, Juliette. Where are you?'

It was Emily, her voice echoing in the night. 'Over here,' shouted Chris.

'Don't,' hissed Tregemmon. 'We don't want her over here. Not with that thing.'

But Juliette could hear the thing withdrawing into the darkness, a big beast moving with stealthy grace. The heavy paws came down with diminishing noise as it followed the terrain, pursuing the desert contours into the night.

Emily was close at hand now, the beam of the torch dancing along the ground in front of her. She lifted it and shone it on Juliette and the men; the three of them looked almost furtive caught in its brilliant beam. Juliette stared off into the darkness. There was no sign of the beast, whatever it had been.

'What are you doing out here?' said Emily.

'We might well ask you the same question,' replied Christopher.

Emily held up a small tattered object. Juliette recognised the teddy bear. 'I came to retrieve Mr Rafferty. I assume you're quite finished with him.'

Christopher too was scanning the darkness beyond the perimeter of the torch beam. Nothing moved in the desert night. 'Yes, I think we are.'

Emily was pointedly examining the slit in the belly of the teddy bear. 'There might have been something bad about him but I trust you've got rid of it.'

'I think we have, with your help.' Christopher took Juliette's hand and Tregemmon fell in beside them and they all followed Emily back to Seismic City.

'Someone's going to have to sew him up for me,' she said.

The following day they held a brief ceremony for Miranda. It couldn't be called a burial because there was nothing left to bury; the desert winds had carried the last of the ashes away.

Juliette still could not accept what had happened, despite the evidence of her own eyes. It didn't seem possible that a human life could end so arbitrarily and so completely in a wasteland like this. She was impressed with Christopher's behaviour, though. He had piled a cairn of rocks on the spot where they had found Miranda's scorched remains, and the few words he said were genuinely moving.

The ceremony cast a pall over their departure. They set off in the blazing heat of noon. Emily was the last to climb on board the minivan, naturally, dragging the beloved red suitcase Tregemmon had bought for her.

She sat down beside Juliette. It felt strange in the rear of the minivan without Miranda. It felt too big.

Juliette tried not to look through the window at the cairn of stones they were leaving behind.

Christopher wound down the window as Emmett Gorgon and Rosie came out of their tent to say goodbye. They looked forlorn. 'Are you sure you have to leave?' said the little man.

Christopher shrugged. 'You read Leiber's note. We have an appointment in Taos.'

'Listen – Rosie and me will come with you. We'll grab a few things and jump in the pickup. Just give us a couple of minutes.'

'No,' said Christopher firmly. 'Your part in this is over.'

The little man and his Mexican girlfriend waved until they were out of sight.

FIFTY-SEVEN

'How long does a thing like this normally last?' said Emily.

The wicker chair squealed as Tregemmon squirmed in embarrassment. 'Well, it's unpredictable.'

They were sitting in the afternoon sunlight outside the Cactus Garden Motel, ensconced in the bulbous pink wicker armchairs set out on the blond concrete patio. This was the eponymous cactus garden.

Just beyond the scraggly stands of cacti in ceramic pots was the pink stucco motel unit containing the other two members of their party.

'Honestly,' said Emily. 'What are they up to in there, those two?'

Tregemmon twitched as if he'd been struck. 'They're just talking,' he said hastily.

'Thanks for trying to dissemble in deference to my tenderness of years, Tregemmon. But let's not try to disguise the ugly truth. Those two are worse than animals.'

Tregemmon sighed, but he didn't say anything.

'The most sickening thing,' continued Emily, 'is that the motel staff have taken to referring to them as "the honeymooners".'

Tregemmon remained silent. They both stared at the pink stucco unit where Christopher and Juliette had been sealed for the last forty-eight hours, emerging, sheepishly, only to order large meals and dart back inside.

'But it's been two days now. Surely that's *plenty* of time.'

Tregemmon resumed squirming. 'Well, not necessarily.'

Emily sighed in disgust. 'Well, it can't go on much longer.'

396

But it did, and finally on the third day Tregemmon began to grow impatient, too. He disappeared into town and returned with a mobile phone. He wrote down the phone number and slipped the piece of paper under the door of Juliette and Christopher's motel unit.

Then he turned to the minivan, where Emily was waiting, sitting excitedly buckled up in the front seat, her red suitcase on the floor where she could keep an eye on it.

Tregemmon climbed in beside her and started the vehicle. He turned and grinned. 'OK, Emma Lilly. The vacation has begun.'

And it was indeed a vacation. They wandered randomly across the state, stopping wherever Emily chose.

She dragged Tregemmon to the Bradbury Science Museum in Los Alamos, lecturing him as they wandered among the exhibits.

'Los Alamos was of course birthplace of the atom bomb. If you can use the word "birth" to describe the origins of such a ghoulish implement. Did you know that when Oppenheimer detonated the first A-bomb he wasn't certain whether it would start a chain reaction which might destroy the Earth? He was *fairly* confident. Aren't we pleased about that?'

The Bradbury Science Museum was followed in quick succession by the Bandelier National Monument and the Los Alamos Historical Museum. Tregemmon suffered his boredom with grace and forbearance.

After Los Alamos they jigged back south to Santa Fe, where he also suffered nobly through the Institute of Native American Arts. Then, in quick succession, the Laboratory of Anthropology, the Capitol Arts Foundation and finally the Georgia O'Keefe Museum, where Emily bored Tregemmon into a glazed-eyed state by discussing the evolution of O'Keefe's imagery, using the photography of her mentor Stieglitz as a starting point.

She couldn't help it. She was having a whale of a time.

Every day they 'phoned home' and Emily suffered through the empty ritual of talking to her sister. It was a waste of time. Juliette wasn't really listening to what she was saying. Her mind was clearly elsewhere.

Juliette suddenly awoke in Christopher's arms.

She eased herself out of his embrace and rolled across the bed, detaching her sweat-sticky skin from his with a moist smacking sound like a kiss.

She lay back on the pillows and stared at the motel ceiling.

There was the churning noise of a car starting up in the courtyard outside and then headlights swept across the ceiling.

To Juliette the cracked ceiling revealed by those headlights was as beautiful as any landscape ever painted by human hand, and the sound of the car's engine might as well have been music.

She sighed and felt a languorous, refractive pleasure that seemed to fill every cell of her body. She had just woken from a catnap after a convulsive bout of lovemaking with Christopher that had lasted two or three hours.

She ran her hands down his lean body to the shrunken tangle of his genitalia. She cupped him for a moment before releasing him, chuckling at his lack of response.

The poor bloke was exhausted. She had worn him out. Images of their lovemaking played in her head, like brief highlights from a long and intensely personal X-rated film. She looked at Chris and was instantly seized with love and lust. The love was so intense it blotted out everything else in her mind. She floated on the warm tide of emotion for a long thoughtless moment. Finally it subsided sufficiently for Juliette to be able to think.

She saw that her clothes were still lying on the floor where she had discarded them days before. How many days? She had no idea. She had long ago lost track of whether it was day or night outside.

Juliette wasn't a psychiatrist working with her patient any more. I'm not a psychiatrist at all, she thought. I'm a hot whore in a Jacobean play.

The small motel room had grown heavy with the musky

smell of their lovemaking. At first Juliette had been ashamed. Now she was proud of it. It was a prehistoric, low-tide smell, as if the invisible ocean of life was brimming all around them.

Juliette leant over and kissed Christopher for the thousandth time. She still wanted him. She was his slut. His slave. She existed only to give him pleasure.

Then Chris woke up. His eyes opened immediately but he looked a little disorientated. Groggy.

'I had a dream,' he said.

He moved away from her embrace. Kicking the sheets off, he swung his legs over the side of the bed. Juliette realised something was wrong.

'Mr Leiber was in it,' he said.

She put a hand on his sweating shoulder. She could feel his heart hammering in his chest, vibrating through his ribs.

'Just like the dream Miranda told us about,' he said.

'I see.' Juliette nodded. 'And did Mr Leiber speak to you, as he did to Miranda?'

'Yes.'

'What did he say?'

'He said he was checking on us. Making sure that the compulsive sexuality was keeping us preoccupied.'

' "Compulsive sexuality"?'

'That's what he said. That's what he called it.'

'I like the sound of that.' Juliette rubbed her naked thighs against him. It was hot in the motel room. It was wet between her legs.

'You mean . . .' She tried to keep her mind on the conversation, but it wasn't easy. 'You mean he was suggesting that . . . somehow our own libidos are being – being used against us?'

'Yes. You could say he's put a spell on us.'

Her sweating body slipped against his. 'But that's ridiculous,' she said.

'Of course it is.'

FIFTY-EIGHT

After they'd made love, and slept again, and she'd once more lost track of time, Juliette's thoughts returned to something that had been bothering her.

'Besides, if it *was* a spell, why should Mr Leiber tell us? I mean, why would he reveal his plans like that?'

Christopher turned towards her. She could see he was having as much trouble concentrating on the conversation as she was.

'Because . . .' He put his arms around her.

'Yes?' Her legs drifted open.

'Because he thinks . . .' Christopher pushed his face into her hair, then slid it down to her neck. With his lips against her skin, his voice was muffled. 'He thinks we're not strong enough to resist his spell.'

But Juliette wasn't listening. All she could hear, legs akimbo, was the slow excited sound of her own breathing as Christopher entered her and they began making love again.

Finally, when they'd wrung the last drop of pleasure out of each other, Juliette closed her eyes and was swallowed up by sleep. She woke to find that Christopher had climbed out of bed.

She opened her eyes and there he was, standing in the moonlight. His burly, powerful body was naked except for the braided band on his wrist, a dark shape in the moonlight. Juliette remembered how it had saved his life, at Dr Buckminster's house.

She also remembered how he had got it, the bikers who had given it to him, and Shorty. Then they had closed over Shorty like an angry sea, to claim his life.

In the morning Juliette awoke, ravenous, to find Christopher sitting in an armchair by the window, dressed. She realised it was the first time in days that he'd donned his clothing. He looked at her bleakly as she sat up and yawned.

'We've wasted a great deal of time.'

Juliette shook her head and smiled a lopsided, drowsy grin. 'I wouldn't exactly call it wasted.'

Christopher came and sat on the edge of the bed. 'We've been under a spell.'

'So you said last night. Or was it the night before? But so what? If it was a spell, it got you what you wanted – didn't it?' She slid her long bare legs out from under the tangled sheets and playfully wrapped them around Christopher's waist.

She began to draw him across the bed towards her. He was between her naked legs and moving down towards her on the bed. Even though he was fully clothed she could feel his interest. Like a powerful force radiating from him. She knew, with satisfaction, that he wanted her.

Juliette closed her eyes and opened her mouth and hitched up her legs and got ready for a kiss.

But Christopher didn't kiss her. Instead, he pulled away, freeing himself from the grip of her legs.

'Juliette, stop it.' He went over to the beaten old wood-veneer cabinet that stood against the far wall of the motel bedroom. He picked up something from the top of it.

Juliette recognised her notepad, the one that contained the 'message' from Mr Leiber. She still didn't believe that the man had invaded her mind. There were plenty of other explanations for the note, even with its eerie change of handwriting.

She'd wanted to throw it away but Christopher had annoyingly insisted on keeping it.

Now he said, 'Mr Leiber has tricked us.' And he let the note drop to the floor.

'What do you mean?'

'He's kept us here in this motel for days.'

'Well, *something* certainly has.' Juliette let the sheet slide down, semiaccidentally, to reveal one of her bare breasts.

'Button it,' said Christopher. 'And stop playing the vamp. You're not going to seduce me.' He sounded firm about this, but Juliette noticed that he was careful not to come too near the bed where she was lying supine and naked.

'So. Mr Leiber's been delaying us here. He's been delaying *me*. Why?' He paced the room restlessly. 'It must be because he needs time. But for what? He must be preparing something. Something very big.'

Christopher paused and suddenly bent down to pick up the note from the floor. He stared at it. 'Very big. What could that be?' Then he froze.

He read from the note, speaking in a strangely soft, absent-minded voice. ' "The final conflagration . . ." ' He looked at Juliette.

'Oh Chris, please.'

'It means that Leiber is planning the end of the world.'

'I see,' said Juliette carefully. 'The end of the world.' She turned the concept over carefully in her mind. Somehow she ended up thinking about Miranda.

She thought of ashes blowing on the night wind, being carried over barren miles of desert, to disperse and vanish for ever. Cold ashes that were all that remained of a beautiful warm girl.

She looked at Christopher. 'I agree that Mr Leiber has some sort of dangerous power.'

'Good. That's a start.'

'And I certainly can't explain what happened to Miranda.'

'Of course not. It's beyond explanation.'

'But, Chris, you're talking about . . . enacting the apocalypse. That's rather different from burning one defenceless girl.'

'Maybe. But it's not a long way from creating earthquakes.'

402

Juliette frowned. 'But we have no firm evidence of a link between those earthquakes and any of your dream magic.'

Christopher gave a snort of disgust. 'No firm evidence,' he repeated.

He opened the door. 'I think Leiber will kill us all,' he said. 'Or worse. And you're giving me pissy sarcasm.'

'Chris, listen to me –'

Cool morning air was flowing through the open door past Christopher, on to Juliette, cooling the sweat on her skin.

'At the moment it's just emerging from a chaotic fog of possibilities,' he said. 'We can still avert it.' He pounded his fist into the palm of his hand. 'I might still have a fighting chance.' He turned and looked at her. 'But only if you help. Only if you're willing to believe.'

He suddenly came to the bed and stared down at her, peering deep into her eyes. 'But you don't believe, do you?'

He turned and walked out.

It took Juliette a few minutes to find her clothes, scattered as they were across the floor of the motel room, where they had remained for several days gathering dust.

As soon as she got dressed she followed Christopher outside. She stepped carefully in her bare feet. It was a bright, cold morning, the early hour when people with a long drive ahead of them were checking out and setting off.

There was a constant cough and roar of engines in the motor court just behind the cactus garden, where Juliette found Christopher sitting in one of the wicker armchairs.

She had paused to buy a cup of coffee from the machine behind the motel unit. The coffee smelt surprisingly good. She went to the wicker armchair beside Christopher. It creaked as she sat down.

'Did I hear you get up and go out in the middle of the night?'

'Yes, I went out and phoned Tregemmon.' Christopher frowned. 'He and Emily are just fine.'

He sighed, frowning in the desert morning. 'Juliette, don't you see? Leiber is the concrete dreamer. He can organise reality any way he pleases. He can do anything he wants. If he decides it's the end of the world, then it is.'

'Then why even bother to fight him? If what you say is true there's no way we can stop him. So we might as well just go back in that motel room and merrily fuck our brains out.'

Christopher flashed her an impatient look. 'Perhaps. I don't know if I can stop him.' His eyes had gone very cold. 'But I intend to try.'

'Chris, you say that this man has the power to control reality. How can you do battle with him? All on your own?'

Christopher stared across the parking area, smiling. 'It would appear that suddenly I'm not on my own.'

Juliette followed his gaze and saw with a pleasant shock that Tregemmon was ambling towards them in the morning light.

He was wearing sunglasses, strolling from the direction of the motor court with Emily following him. The minivan was parked behind them. Juliette realised that it must have arrived while they were talking.

'Good morning!' cried Emily. She came hurrying into the cactus garden, gravel skittering around her eager feet. She seemed full of energy but Tregemmon looked rather tired.

'Welcome back,' said Christopher as Juliette kissed her sister. 'Did you have some interesting adventures?'

'We learnt a lot about atom bombs.'

'And Georgia O'Keefe.' Tregemmon took off his sunglasses. 'You said something on the phone about needing us back here urgently. What's it all about?'

'Surely it's obvious, isn't it?' said Emily. 'Mr Leiber is planning to unweave the very fabric of existence. In short to bring about the end of the world.'

* * *

Juliette found a table for them in the clean busy coffee shop of the motel. Tregemmon and Emily hadn't had time to eat on the road that morning and she and Chris were understandably hungry all the time. So they all sat down in a booth together and ordered a large breakfast.

With the warm morning sun shining in on them across the highway, Juliette felt absurdly as if she was enjoying a family occasion.

Emily was busy demolishing a large plate of scrambled eggs and waffles. Between mouthfuls she glanced up at Christopher. 'Mr Leiber really is a most challenging opponent. But I have every confidence in you, Christopher. I'm looking forward to seeing how you deal with him.'

She wiped her small mouth daintily with a napkin and shoved her plate aside. 'Indeed, I've been having some thoughts on the matter myself.'

'That's very kind,' said Christopher. 'But I'm afraid you're not going to be here to see it.'

Emily stopped dead. 'I beg your pardon?'

'I spoke to your mother on the phone. I called her last night.'

'What exactly are you striving to tell me in this round-about fashion?'

'I've booked a ticket for you on the next flight back to England.'

Emily spun around and stared at Juliette accusingly. 'Did you know about this?'

Juliette found it ridiculously difficult to meet her gaze. 'Yes. I'm coming to the airport to see you off.'

'I'm afraid I have to stay here at the motel,' said Christopher. 'I have a few errands. So we'd better say goodbye now.'

'All right, goodbye,' snapped Emily. Then she fell into a sullen silence. When Tregemmon came into the coffee shop carrying her red suitcase, she refused to meet his eye.

She remained silent throughout the long drive to the airport. Juliette tried to keep up a stream of small talk, and Tregemmon was helpful enough, when he wasn't absorbed in his driving, but the atmosphere in the minivan had grown very strained by the time they finally arrived.

Tregemmon dropped them off while he found a parking space. Juliette took her little sister into the airport and collected her ticket at the check-in desk.

Tregemmon caught up with them just as they were approaching the departure gate. By now Juliette was having a terrible time; Emily had been dragging her feet and doing everything in her power to make it an unpleasant experience and delay the inevitable.

Her little face lit up for a moment when she saw Tregemmon, then the light faded and her sullen expression settled firmly back into place.

'Come on, Emma Lilly, cheer up.'

'I am not your Emma Lilly. You have forfeited any right to address me by such pathetic childish nicknames.'

'Oh, come on,' said Tregemmon in a jollying tone. 'What's the point in parting on bad terms?'

'What's the point in parting at all?' replied Emily harshly. 'For all you know, I might be a crucial weapon in your arsenal against Mr Leiber. And here you are cavalierly discarding me.'

'Baby, there's nothing you can do to help.'

'Of course there is,' said Emily fiercely. 'I'm a first-rate mind.' She stared at Juliette pointedly. 'And you certainly need one around here.' Despite herself, Juliette could feel anger rising. Emily certainly knew how to push those sibling buttons.

But then the little girl's expression softened and her lower lip trembled. 'Please don't send me home. You need me.'

'What if she's right?' said a voice.

'You stay out of this, Mum,' snarled Juliette. She had uttered these same words so many times throughout her life, during so many blazing arguments, that they'd become virtually automatic. She uttered them now quite without thinking. Only a fraction of a second later did her mind catch up with the significance.

Her mother wasn't here. She was thousands of miles

away, safely at home in England.

Juliette turned around slowly, not knowing what to fear more, the idea that she had started to hear voices, or the idea that –

'Hello, dear!' her mother beamed at her. She was standing behind them in the departure area, a big, battered, blue suitcase in each hand. She was wearing jeans and a hand-knitted sweater in garish, zigzag, ethnic colours which bulged with pompoms and other adornments. On her feet were equally ridiculous, purple, knitted boots with pale-blue leather soles.

It was as if she was dressed for an English – or indeed Tierra del Fuegan – winter. Incongruously, a white cowboy hat was perched on her head. She was smiling from ear to ear, her red face glowing.

Juliette made a deliberate effort to close her mouth. Her jaw had literally dropped at this ludicrous sight – presumably because her mouth was ready to say something even though her brain wasn't. Finally she managed to say something. 'Mum, you're in England.'

But her mother wasn't listening. She had dropped to her knees and flung her big arms around Emily, sobbing with joy. And, for once, Juliette's little sister didn't try to squirm away from a display of affection.

'You're safe,' sobbed her mother. 'Those horrible people took you away from me, but now you're safe! I was so worried, my love, my darling.' Tears streamed down her face as she buried it in Emily's hair.

'It's all right, Mum,' said Emily matter of factly. 'Tregemmon saved me, with the help of Christopher and –' Emily stopped and her face grew solemn. 'And Danny. And Miranda.'

Her mother rubbed Emily on the back to comfort her. 'Christopher told me all about it on the phone, dear. It's terrible, what happened to them.' She began to sob again. 'But at least you're safe. At least I have my baby.'

Juliette found she was both touched and embarrassed by the spectacle of her mother weeping over her little sister. She glanced around self-consciously, but found people in an airport departure lounge are inured to such emotional scenes.

Finally, her mother dried her eyes and released Emily from her bearlike embrace. But she insisted on taking one of the little girl's hands in her own and wouldn't release it. Emily didn't seem to mind.

Finally Juliette thought of something more to say. 'Mum?' Her mother wheeled around to look at her, smiling brightly. 'How in God's name did you get here?'

'Well, dear, it was easy enough. I flew. Christopher gave me the name of the airport and the time of the flight you were putting Emily on. So I did a little research – surfed the Internet – and found that I could fly here and intercept you before Emily left. It was a bit of a squeeze, but I made it.' Her eyes sparkled. 'Obviously fate intended for me to be here.'

Juliette decided that she must be firm. 'Well, I trust that fate also intends for you to turn smartly around and head straight back to England. With Emily.'

'Oh, I don't think so, dear. Now that I'm here I'll have to stay and have a little look around. I couldn't possibly fly all this way for nothing.'

'Well, who *is* going to accompany Emily? We can't just stick her on a plane on her own.'

'Of course not. Emily will have to stay here with us.'

'But Mum! We are in the middle of an extremely dangerous situation.'

All at once her mother's face grew serious. 'I know, dear. And that is the real reason that I have come to join you.' A distant, dreamy expression crept over her eyes. Juliette suppressed a groan. 'We are at the cusp of a great event. We are about to witness the final battle between two mighty sorcerers. The fate of the world hangs in the balance. It's like a huge hurricane about to sweep the world! And instead of hiding in England I'd rather be at the heart of the storm, with the ones I love.'

'Oh, I give up,' said Juliette. After listening to this speech she felt exhausted. 'I've had enough of this. I am going straight to the reservations desk and buying you a ticket. Emily's already got hers. If we hurry, we've just got time.'

'No.'

'What?'

'No, I am not going back to England, dear. You can dismiss that thought from your mind. Emily and I are here until this situation is over. Whatever happens, we shall face it together. As a family.'

Juliette felt a sinking feeling. She had heard this steely note in her mother's voice only on very rare occasions, but she knew what it meant. She reflected with despair how impossible it was to give orders to the person who had given birth to you.

She sighed and decided to abandon any direct attempt at arguing with her, for the time being at least.

But she couldn't quite manage to control her temper. 'Where did you get that ridiculous hat?' she said.

Her mother smiled, blithely ignoring any insult. 'Well, I know how much you hate my Oxfam sheep-herder's helmet. So I bought this at the airport shop here. It's a genuine stetson.' She smiled proudly, tilting it back at a rakish angle. 'I thought it would be more in keeping with the wilds of New Mexico.'

Juliette was too tired and defeated to give this the exasperated sigh it deserved. Tregemmon stepped forward. He was smiling and said, 'Don't pay any attention to her, Mrs R. You are very welcome here. And your stetson looks great on you.'

Juliette's mother beamed. 'Thank you, Tregemmon.'

'I don't suppose you'd like to do a little cooking while you're here?'

On the drive back to the motel, Juliette reflected how she had gone to the airport to rid herself of one encumbrance, only to return with two. God knew what Christopher would say.

Thinking of Chris made her uncomfortably aware of another problem. She was sharing a room with him at the motel. The very motel that was now visible in the distance.

And, if she didn't somehow manage to conceal all evidence of this in the first few seconds of arrival, her mother would realise that she and Chris had got together.

And her mother would then proceed to make her life hell by fatuously beaming with approval and generally buzzing around like a big fat Cupid who had successfully aimed one of love's arrows.

Juliette's thoughts were interrupted by a cry of delight from her mother in the front of the vehicle. She had caught sight of the motel with its giant sign, a hot-pink neon boomerang enclosing a glowing abstract cactus shaped like a jagged green flame.

Below this superstructure, in fiery cursive turquoise neon, were the words CACTUS GARDEN MOTEL.

This sign had her mother gasping with excitement and generally carrying on as if it were Versailles.

'Is this where we'll be staying? What a wonderful place.'

Juliette couldn't stop herself snapping, 'For heaven's sake, Mum, it's just a second-rate motel.'

Her mother swivelled around in the front seat and aimed her excited red face at Juliette. 'Oh, it is much more than that, dear. It is the site of power, our fortress for the battle to come. It is our Camelot. It is Christopher Matthew's crystal cave from which we shall launch a magical crusade against the evil of Mr Leiber.'

Her mother was still wearing the stetson. There was a gleaming fringe of sweat under the rim of the cowboy hat, crawling down her mother's forehead as she spoke. This had the general effect of making her look like an overweight madwoman.

'And Tregemmon is conveying us into the presence of the white wizard. Humanity's champion. Christopher Matthew.'

'And in such a classy vehicle,' murmured Tregemmon, applying the brakes as they glided into the car park.

Juliette was the first out of the minivan, hurrying into the motel unit she shared with Christopher. Her intention was to make a swift desperate attempt to tidy the bed and generally make the place look like something other than a den for shagging. She also intended to beg Christopher to conceal their affair from her mother.

But a few shocked seconds later she was wandering out to confront the others. They fell silent when they saw the note she was clutching in her hand.

'He's gone,' she said.

PART FOUR

THE JASPER INSTITUTE

'Since we're going to Taos anyway,' said Emily, examining first a brochure and then a folding road map, 'we may as well drop in on that place Emmett Gorgon told us about.' She passed the brochure to Juliette, who passed it along without interest to her mother.

'It's called the Jasper Institute,' said Emily. Juliette stared out of the window of the speeding minivan and wondered when she'd see Christopher again.

'I thought you'd already visited every cultural institution in New Mexico,' she said.

'Yes, and it was me that drove her round them,' added Tregemmon with a note of bitterness from the front seat.

'Well, you were a very model of patience, Tregemmon. I can't thank you enough,' said Emily in a distracted automatic tone. 'But this place is even more interesting than those others. It's a combined museum and research centre. They do statistical analysis there. The computers are linked to the "Big Ear", the Kraus-type radio telescope in Delaware, Ohio, and the VLA – the Very Large Array – in Socorro.'

'Not Socorro again,' murmured Tregemmon.

'Please. It's a fascinating place. Please can we go?'

'No, Emily.' Juliette decided she had to be firm. Somebody had to. Her mother obviously wasn't going to say anything. 'We're in Taos on urgent business. We have to find Christopher.'

'I think we ought to let her see it,' said Tregemmon suddenly.

'For heaven's sake, why?'

Tregemmon shrugged good-naturedly. 'Because it's as

good a place as any to kill time while we wait for the Edge to get in contact with us.'

Juliette glanced at him sharply. Did Tregemmon know something she didn't? 'And what makes you think he'll do that?'

Tregemmon tapped the cellular phone sitting on the dashboard. 'He has my number. He'll call us when he's ready.'

'And if he doesn't?'

Tregemmon shrugged again. 'Do you have any better suggestions?'

Juliette took the point.

'All right then,' said Tregemmon. 'We're going to drive right past the place, anyway.'

Indeed, ten minutes later alongside the highway the Jasper Institute loomed into view.

Juliette saw that it was housed in two separate buildings. The first was long and low, with an undulating white roof. Some American architect's clumsy attempt to be futuristic, the roof resembled the rippling shell of an oyster. Supporting it were perpendicular walls of glass – tall windows trellised with red steel girders.

But this structure was a tasteful piece of architectural restraint in comparison with its neighbour. This building chiefly consisted of a giant sphere, which unmistakably housed a planetarium. But the sphere had been painted to look like an enormous human eyeball, staring up at the sky.

The effect was achieved with alarming, almost photographic, clarity. Juliette repressed a shudder. The giant eye of the planetarium seemed to be staring up blindly into the grim turmoil of yellow and grey.

The sight of it angled up at the stormy sky like that was altogether eerie. It made her feel for a moment as if she had been transported into a Salvador Dali landscape.

'Eerie thing,' said her mother, annoyingly as if she had just read Juliette's mind.

'Ugly thing,' corrected Juliette.

'It's *supposed* to be watching the sky,' explained Emily

wearily. 'It's symbolic. The Jasper Institute is part of SETI, the Search for Extraterrestrial Intelligence.'

In front of the eye-shaped building was a broad sweep of carefully cultivated green lawn. The lush grass was watered by numerous sprinklers, all busy hurling rainbows. The green slab of lawn sloped down to the main entrance.

This was marked by a surprisingly small sign that read JASPER INSTITUTE, RESEARCH CENTER, MUSEUM, AND PLANETARIUM, and gave entrance times and prices.

As soon as he parked the van Tregemmon checked the prices and dug into his wallet. 'Here, this is on me. Now if you ladies will excuse me, I'm going to go off and do my own thing. Enjoy your visit, Emma Lilly.'

'And what exactly does your "own thing" consist of?' enquired Emily, rather snottily, thought Juliette.

'Well, I expect I'll find a quiet bar and shoot some pool, maybe have myself a beer. And wait for the phone to ring. It'll either be you girls calling me because you've finished looking around here, or it'll be the Edge.' Tregemmon's face grew serious. 'If it's the Edge I'll come and collect you.'

'All right,' said Emily reluctantly. 'I suppose that's a viable plan.'

Juliette walked with Emily and their mother across the car park towards the sweeping concrete profile of the oyster-shaped building. They passed the staff car park where a bumper sticker read ASTRONOMY IS LOOKING UP.

'Is that the museum?' she asked Emily as they approached the building. More as an attempt to be civil than because she cared about the answer.

'It also houses the computers and the research facility,' lectured Emily; she was in an almost exalted state, highly excited at the long-delayed treat finally in store. 'Which unfortunately is not open to the public. I'd love to have a poke around in their computers. Perhaps they'll let me in after we've done the museum and the planetarium.'

'Oh dear,' said their mother suddenly. 'I've forgotten my stetson. I'll just rush back and get it.'

417

'You don't need a hat, Mum,' said Juliette, trying to conceal the exasperation in her voice.

'We're going to be indoors the whole time,' added Emily.

But their mother ignored both of them. 'I'll only be a moment, dears,' she said, and trotted off.

Juliette and Emily exchanged identical expressions of weary disgust as their mother hurried back towards the minivan and Tregemmon.

Tregemmon was surprised to see Mrs Race back so soon. He had just been preparing to start the minivan and pull away.

'Forget something?'

'Not really, Tregemmon.' She picked up her cowboy hat from the back seat. 'I told the girls I was coming back for this, but in fact it was just an excuse. I came back because I wanted to wish you luck.'

'What do you mean?'

'I know you're setting off on a dangerous mission. All that talk of playing pool and drinking beer is just a smokescreen.'

Tregemmon was silent for a moment. Mrs Race might look a fool but she was actually very sharp. 'It's a fair cop,' he said.

'Don't worry, I won't tell the girls. But where are you really going, if I may ask?'

'To meet a midget who owns a bookstore.'

'Oh, Emmett Gorgon. Emily told me all about him.'

'Well, he gave the Edge the keys to the store. So I reckon he might have gone there. It's a good place to start the search, anyhow.'

'All right.' Mrs Race quickly squeezed his hand. 'Good luck.' Then she hurried off clutching her cowboy hat.

Tregemmon started the engine. In the rear-view mirror he saw the grim expression on his own face as he took the Sig Sauer out from under the seat and checked it. The gun was all right. It was ready. He put the minivan into gear.

He hadn't told Mrs Race that, if Christopher wasn't at the bookstore, there was a good chance Mr Leiber was.

The streets seemed strangely empty and Tregemmon made very good time crossing town. In fact there wasn't a traffic cop in sight and soon he was hurtling along.

After being stuck in traffic he found the clear streets intoxicating. His speed crept up inexorably until he was exceeding the legal limit by a considerable margin.

He was only ten blocks from the bookstore, and congratulating himself on having glanced at the city map only once, when the girl stepped out in front of him.

She simply stepped off the pavement and into the road as if he wasn't there, as if the minivan hurtling towards her didn't exist. She stuck her thumb out in a hitch-hiking pose and stood dully staring towards him, doughily unconcerned that he was going to smash her into a lifeless lump of meat.

Tregemmon stamped on the brakes. A flickering moment later – one of the longest moments of his life – the brakes began to take effect, soaking up the speed and momentum of the minivan. The vehicle came to a convulsive, juddering halt, its nose skewed violently towards the left lane.

His reflexes had reacted more swiftly than conscious thought in applying the brakes. Sweat dripped down Tregemmon's ribcage in a chill flow as he peered through the windscreen.

The minivan had lurched to a halt only a few inches from the girl. She stood there in the road peering up at him without undue interest.

She was wearing a fringed doeskin jacket thickly embossed with Native American beadwork. Her black punky hair was stiff with grease and she had gnawed, black-lacquered fingernails.

Insanely, one of her hands was still extended in a thumb-jutted hitch-hiking pose.

Tregemmon wound the window down with shaking hands. 'What the fuck do you think you're doing?' he yelled. In some distant corner of his mind he registered the fact that the girl was the first person he'd seen in these quiet streets.

'Thank you for stopping,' said the girl in an empty singsong voice. Before Tregemmon could stop her, she pulled the door open and climbed into the minivan beside him. 'Thank you for stopping to pick me up.'

'I didn't stop to pick you up, you stupid cow,' he snarled. He was still trying to adjust to the furious blast of adrenaline the near-accident had unleashed in his system.

'Yes you did,' said the girl in her sad empty voice. 'Not that it matters. Not that anything matters.' Tregemmon noticed that she was trembling. Her pupils were dilated, wide and black.

She was clearly scared out of her wits. She promptly buckled herself into her seatbelt and began nervously peering out at the empty streets.

'I'm sorry I shouted at you,' said Tregemmon, getting his temper back under control. 'But you shouldn't just step out into the street like that. People are driving too fast to stop.'

'No.' The girl shook her head quite emphatically.

'No what?'

'No people. No traffic.'

Tregemmon looked around. She was right. He hadn't really noticed, but the streets had gone from being strangely quiet to absolutely empty.

He felt an irrational cold thrill of fear.

'He's going to do it,' whispered the girl.

'What?'

'Everybody knows. Deep down inside, perhaps without even realising it, everybody knows.'

Tregemmon felt his skin crawl. 'I don't understand what you're talking about,' he said. 'Now, how about getting out of my vehicle?'

The girl spoke in her strange empty voice. 'Of course you understand. You feel it too.' Then she peered at him, as if seeing him for the first time. She was silent for a shocked moment and then she began to laugh. 'It's you.'

'What do you mean?'

'You're the Triggerman, aren't you?'

He stared at the girl. 'All right. Who are you?'

'We had to leave the Halloween Hotel before you slaughtered Comstock and Brilly.' A note of emotion was creeping into her voice. A hot little breath of excitement. 'But apparently you did an amazing job.'

Tregemmon stared at her with distaste. He knew who the girl was now. 'You're Mr Leiber's girlfriend.'

'My name is Nuala.'

'Why aren't you with him, Nuala?'

'I managed to slip away from them.'

'*Them?* Mr Leiber and who else?'

'I don't know how many exactly. Bikers.'

'Bikers?'

'A whole army of them. He's enlisted their assistance.'

'Oh, marvellous.'

Tregemmon started the engine again. He straightened the minivan and pulled forward.

'Where are you going?'

'To look up a friend.' The minivan sped through the empty streets. All the traffic lights seemed to be green.

'I saw the bikes parked outside,' said Tregemmon. 'I thought you'd been taken prisoner.'

'Well, luckily for me these are my friends.' Emmett Gorgon nodded at a beefy blonde woman wearing leather trousers and a sleeveless denim top. The denim top hardly contained the pale flesh of her torso. They were all standing in a small untidy kitchen with bright-yellow walls and a red linoleum floor. A man came into the kitchen. 'And this is Cricket.'

Cricket was a skinny, deeply tanned man with drooping white whiskers. Like Big Irma he was dressed in leather and frayed denim. He carried a baseball bat with a nail jutting from it.

'We were sent here by the Edge to look after the little dude,' said Cricket. Big Irma went to the sink and started making coffee while the men returned downstairs.

Tregemmon walked beside Emmett Gorgon, two steps ahead of him.

'Nuala told me that Mr Leiber had enlisted some bikers.'

'That's right,' said the little man. 'There's two gangs mixed up in this. The Las Cruces Saints are on our side. And a gang called Satan's Choice, surprisingly enough, are with Mr Leiber. By the way, where is Nuala?'

'I've got her handcuffed out in the minivan.'

'Lucky you,' said Emmett Gorgon.

Tregemmon glanced at Cricket, who had flopped into one of the armchairs in the bookstore, the spiked club resting across his knees. 'How did the Edge get these guys on his side?'

'Apparently one look at that thing on his wrist was all it took,' said Emmett Gorgon.

Tregemmon nodded. He should have guessed. 'That band the bikers gave him in England?'

The man called Cricket spoke up. 'He was wearing the band of power. That commands a lot of respect in the Outlaw Nation. When he asked us to come here, we said sure. Look after the little guy and his coyote.'

'Where is Laughing Dog?' said Tregemmon.

'Up on the roof,' shrugged the little man. 'Where else?'

It proved to be a redundant question on Tregemmon's part because a few minutes later Laughing Dog opened his jaws and began to howl. The sound carried eerily down from the roof as he escorted Nuala into the bookshop.

'See, the coyote knows.'

'All right, Nuala, that will do.'

'He knows what shall befall us. I never dreamt Mr Leiber would grow this powerful. I never imagined he would be able to do this.'

'OK, tootsie, can it,' said Emmett Gorgon firmly. He let them into the bookshop, where they stood, silent except for the unholy baying of Laughing Dog on the roof.

The mournful sound seemed to echo across the entire city.

422

'Listen to the message the coyote brings,' said Nuala.

'I'm beginning to wish you'd left her trussed up in the van,' said the little man.

'So am I,' said Tregemmon with feeling.

The biker called Cricket came up and tapped Emmett Gorgon on the shoulder. He nodded at Tregemmon. 'Since your friend has showed up maybe we don't need to stick around here any more.'

'My coyote got you spooked?'

'Your coyote and other things,' said Cricket placidly. Emmett Gorgon shrugged.

'OK, we'll take off then,' said Big Irma.

'We want to be at home with the kids,' added Cricket rather surprisingly. They walked out of the bookstore hand in hand and climbed on to their matching Harley Davidsons and gunned them to life.

The little man watched through the bookshop window as they roared away. 'I know how they feel. I just wish Rosie was here so I could huddle together with her and Laughing Dog.'

'What exactly is going on?' said Tregemmon.

'OK. Mr Leiber came here. And so did the Edge. Though not at the same time. They kind of used me as a message drop. Can you imagine what that was like? Acting as go-between for two such powerful, dangerous entities?'

'What was the message?' said Tregemmon impatiently.

'Oh, it was just about the place they're going to use for their meeting.'

'Meeting?'

'I think Leiber called it the Final Confrontation.'

'Marvellous,' said Tregemmon. 'Where is it happening?' But he practically had to shout to make himself heard. The howling from the roof was so loud now that it seemed to fill the entire building, reverberating through the empty rooms.

'I wish your coyote would shut up.'

'That's not Laughing Dog,' said Emmett Gorgon. He had a puzzled expression on his face. He opened a window

423

and leant out to listen. Tregemmon joined him and, after a moment, the truth began to dawn. They looked at each other.

'All his brethren have joined in,' said Nuala.

It was true. Laughing Dog was still howling from the rooftop, but now, from all over the city, dogs of every breed had joined in. They were baying in unison with the coyote's mournful song.

The unearthly sound rose and fell, echoing down the long stone canyons of the empty streets of Taos.

The little man closed the window and the sound abated but Tregemmon could still feel the hair on his neck standing on end.

Nuala began to giggle. 'They know. They know the end is coming.'

'Thanks, Nuala. That'll be all.'

'She may be a kook,' said Emmett Gorgon, 'but maybe she's got something. I can't help feeling a trifle anxious listening to that. Kind of makes a fellow want to be tucked up safely with his loved ones. By the way, where's the shrink and the munchkin?'

'They're safe all right. With their mother in fact.'

'Is that right?'

'Right now they're probably being bored silly at the planetarium.'

'Planetarium?' The little man was staring at him.

'I dropped them off at the Jasper Institute on the way over here. Why? What's wrong?'

SIXTY

A crudely lettered notice had been draped above the main entrance to the Jasper Institute.

Fashioned from what looked like a bed sheet, it read CLOSED TO THE PUBLIC. The sprinklers on the long, sloping, green lawns had ceased. The place looked silent and deserted.

Tregemmon felt a flutter of disquiet. Was he too late? Emmett Gorgon's words kept repeating in his head. 'The Jasper Institute. That's where Mr Leiber is meeting the Edge! That's where the final battle is going to be. And you left Emily there?'

Not just Emily, thought Tregemmon savagely, but her mum and her sister as well.

The entrance road to the Jasper Institute ran past the two main buildings and divided into a Y shape at the back. It ran in a cleft between the high sections of raised lawn, like a small canyon.

It hadn't seemed at all menacing when he had driven through it this afternoon but now, with its narrow high walls converging on an unseen destination, it looked like a death trap.

Tregemmon drove past the Jasper Institute and continued on for about half a mile.

Finally he locked the minivan in the courtyard of an unattended gas station and worked his way back on foot. It took him perhaps ten minutes of careful progress to reach the long sloping lawns of the institute.

He was carrying the Ruger as well as the Sig Sauer now, having agonised over the decision. The extra gun meant carrying more weight. But it also meant he had the option of the extra fire power, and that might prove crucial.

Night was falling. The giant eyeball of the planetarium looked even more ungodly, staring up at the lurid sunset sky. Moving along the sloping lawns, Tregemmon grew steadily less cautious about silence.

He could already hear a considerable clamour coming from the car park at the back of the buildings: shouting and engines and the occasional sharp distinct sound which might have been a backfire or a gunshot.

Working his way across the lawn towards the planetarium, he realised that at some point he would have to descend into the empty canyon of the approach road.

It was a prospect he didn't relish. He waited concealed in some bushes as a roar of engines announced the approach of unseen vehicles.

Half a dozen motorcycles swept into sight. As they flashed past, Tregemmon saw that the bikers all wore jackets or T-shirts with SATAN'S CHOICE emblazoned on them.

The motorcycles disappeared towards the car park. Tregemmon studied the situation carefully. At the rear of the planetarium the well-groomed lawn served to conceal the thin slot of a service alley, sunk below the level of the turf like an empty concrete moat.

The service alley curved around the back of the building. If he got in there he could see what was happening in the car park without being seen.

It was cool here, between the high concrete walls of the service alley. To his left was the outer wall of the planetarium, basement windows spaced generously along it at ground level.

Some of these windows were half concealed by the dumpsters. The dumpsters were tall and black and stood hulking in a long line. They looked like a military rank of squat black giants, patiently waiting for orders.

The wall opposite the dumpsters was featureless except for a metal ladder set into it. This gave access up on to the lawn. From the top of it Tregemmon would be able to see the car park. He hurried towards it.

The noise from the car park had diminished, but it had become oddly more disturbing. Tregemmon recognised the growl of motorcycle engines but there were other sounds, mixed in with them, low bestial cries that his mind was reluctant to identify.

He'd find out soon enough. Tregemmon moved towards the nearest ladder. To get to it he had to skirt a large spreading pool of motor oil covering the floor of the alley. As he stepped around it, alarm bells began to ring in the back of his mind. He paused, looking back at the dark puddle.

There was something odd about it. It wasn't reflecting light the way oil normally would. Tregemmon stared at the liquid for a long moment. Against the dark surface of the tarmac, in the shadows of the narrow alley, it was impossible to identify the colour of it. But Tregemmon already had an unhappy certainty about it.

He reluctantly traced the source of the liquid. It was draining from the dumpsters, coming from whatever load was bundled inside them. Tregemmon braced himself. He scrambled up the side of the nearest dumpster. Its curved lid was open, making it an easy matter to peer inside.

Under their curving hoodlike covers each dumpster consisted of a large hollow belly, a plastic walled space, big enough for a homeless person or two.

There was no one *living* in these dumpsters, however.

Tregemmon began methodically searching them all. None was less than half full. Despite the shock of what he found, his initial feeling of horror gradually slackened into relief.

It wasn't what he feared most. Tregemmon was relieved because none of the bodies belonged to anyone he knew.

The women and Christopher were still alive. He overcame his squeamishness and reached into one of the dumpsters and rolled some of the corpses over. They all appeared to be bikers. The nearest one was a grizzled middle-aged man, and on the back of his denim jacket the word SAINTS was lovingly embroidered.

Tregemmon remembered Emmett Gorgon's sardonic

expression when he had said, 'The Las Cruces Saints are fighting for us.'

Tregemmon let go of the dead man. He dropped away from his perch on the dumpster and landed on the ground. A commanding sense of unreality began to hold sway in his head.

He looked from the row of dumpsters up at the giant staring eye of the planetarium. The eye was peering into a sky that was darkening from indigo to purple.

Suddenly, silently, the floodlights ringing the building came on. The giant eye stared brightly up into the darkening night. Tregemmon felt a cold tremor run through his body. Maybe it really was the end of the world. Maybe the black magic and sorcery had begun in earnest.

Just then there was a roaring, wrenching sound behind him. It came from the direction of the car park and it sounded dramatic and final. Tregemmon scrambled up the ladder to see what was happening.

As his face cleared the top of the wall he saw the strangest thing. A biker was floating in the air, some twenty feet above the car park. The man wore a leather jacket and greasy jeans. Under his jacket he was wearing a tie-dyed T-shirt with the word SAINTS and a cartoon halo crudely printed on it.

He was just floating there, silhouetted against the purple evening sky, defying gravity. In fact he was rising gently, like a cunningly wrought and incredibly lifelike helium balloon. His eyes were shut and he had a dreamy expression on his face.

For a split second Tregemmon knew he was witnessing an act of outright magic. Then logic came crashing back and the world suddenly made sense again.

He saw the motorcycle the floating man had just vacated as it followed its terminal trajectory across the car park. The concrete post it had just smashed into was tilted at a queasy angle, shards of tan stone crumbling from it to expose a dark core of metal bars. The front of the motorcycle was crushed into a blunt mess as a result of that impact – the same impact that had thrown its rider into the air like a toy.

Tregemmon was simply witnessing his reaching the peak of his arc.

Now the floating man began to descend swiftly towards the ground where knots of bikers stood waiting for him, diverse weapons glinting in their hands. By that time, however, Tregemmon was already slipping from the ladder, dropping back into the alley.

There were voices approaching, echoing off the narrow walls. He couldn't tell how many were coming but there were a lot of them.

Tregemmon knew he had to hide, and there was no choice about his hiding place. He pulled himself up and into one of the dumpsters full of corpses.

'I understand your men have just dispatched the last of the Saints,' said a man's voice, growing steadily closer.

'It sounds like it,' said a second man.

'Place him in the dumpster, then.'

'We're on the case, Mr Leiber.'

By now the two men were emerging from the curve of the service alley into the area with the dumpsters. One of them was tall and heavily muscled, with a shaven head. He wore combat boots and camouflage trousers. His arms and torso were bare. On his chest were tattooed the words SATAN'S CHOICE, and much else besides.

His entire body, including his shaven scalp, appeared to be completely covered with the garish writhing colours of tattoos.

His companion was quite a different proposition. This was Tregemmon's first glimpse of the man called Mr Leiber. At first there didn't seem to be much to him. A soft, balding, middle-aged nonentity, about the same build and height as Christopher Matthew.

But this man was a total contrast. After a moment his very ordinariness became disturbing. There was something false about it, like a false skin that might at any moment split open to hatch something quite different.

As soon as Tregemmon thought this, Mr Leiber gave a twitch and began to stare around the alley, as if he sensed something.

Tregemmon instantly closed his eyes and let his body go limp. He had managed to worm his way into one of the half-open dumpsters, writhing down among the dead bodies. His reluctance to hide in here had vanished when he realised it was a matter of survival. With a little luck he would be safe in this grisly hiding place.

His eyes were shut now but he could still hear the activity below. A group of bikers were joining Mr Leiber and the tattooed man.

'Get the last of them into the dumpster quickly,' said Mr Leiber, a note of command in his voice. Tregemmon remained silent and limp as the dumpster shook and the meaty weight of several new corpses was piled on top of him.

On the dead Tregemmon could smell leather and blood and petrol and the rank terminal ripeness of human fear.

'Your followers have done well, Needle Man,' said Mr Leiber.

'It has been their privilege to help the Bringer of Light in the Last Days.'

'Yes, yes. Now can we get down to the main order of business?'

'OK. Just give my people ten minutes to get their act together. Then we'll go into the planetarium and get them for you.'

'If you encounter a black man with dreadlocks along the way, kill him immediately. He is extremely dangerous. The others, however, I want perfectly intact. I can't emphasise that too strongly. You can do what you want with the women later, but initially I don't want them or Christopher Matthew damaged in any way.' There was something deeply disturbing about the droning voice, like a machine operating at the wrong frequency.

In the dumpster Tregemmon's heart leapt. The others were alive.

'Won't be easy,' said the Needle Man, 'but I'll see that it gets done.'

'Good. Now if you'll excuse me I believe Herr Hammersfeeld is rather alarmed by our activities on the hallowed grounds of his beloved institute.'

'Mr Leiber! Mr Leiber!' called a petulant voice in a foreign accent. Under the mound of corpses, Tregemmon risked opening his eyes to narrow slits. Piled as he was near the top, and with the dumpster lid wedged open by the abundance of bodies, he was able to see tolerably well.

A small untidy man in a rumpled white lab coat was hurrying along the curving alley. He had a bland pink face whose babylike appearance was somehow unaltered by the smooth bald spot in the centre of his head or his moustacheless silver beard. Tregemmon had once heard that you should never trust a man with a beard but no moustache.

'Here he comes now,' said Mr Leiber to the tattooed thug. 'I advise you to close the lid of that dumpster so as not to alarm the poor man.'

'No problem,' said Needle Man. He signalled to his men.

Tregemmon closed his eyes again as the bikers scrambled back on to the dumpster. There was a rustling sound and the hood came slamming firmly down on the pile of corpses. The impact drove Tregemmon down. Darkness closed over him. The voices outside took on a strange muffled quality.

Mr Leiber ordered the Needle Man and the other bikers to go away. Then the little man in the lab coat was gasping breathlessly. 'Mr Leiber! Mr Leiber, are you sure that the danger's over?'

'The danger, Herr Hammersfeeld?'

'That nasty business in the parking lot,' said the scientist impatiently. 'Are you sure that the last of our assailants have been dealt with?'

'Ah, yes,' said Mr Leiber. 'I should think so, yes.'

'But why on Earth did these people come here to the institute and attack us?'

'Because you have some very grave news to impart to humanity, Herr Professor.'

'But they can't kill the truth by killing me.'

'My dear sir, who knows what was going on in the minds of these barbarians?'

'Pardon me. But I must say that our attackers are hard to distinguish from . . . from some of your colleagues.'

Mr Leiber lowered his voice. 'Needle Man and his rowdies are not the allies I would have preferred, true. But needs must when the devil drives, as the saying goes. You see, I had no choice, with the local forces of law and order apparently seized by some strange paralysis.'

'But why is this?' said the scientist querulously. 'Why are the police paralysed?'

'Civil unrest, I should think.'

'Civil unrest?'

'Resulting from your discovery,' said Mr Leiber with just a note of respectful awe in his voice. 'Word of it must have leaked out, Herr Hammersfeeld.'

'But how?' muttered the scientist. 'I am still gathering data.'

The voices began to grow fainter, as Mr Leiber and his companion moved away.

'As you can imagine, news travels very fast with something like this.'

'I suppose so.'

As soon as the voices had faded safely away, Tregemmon scrambled out of his hiding place in the mound of corpses and set about trying to push open the lid of the dumpster. This didn't prove particularly easy, not least because the pile of bodies kept shifting under his weight whenever he braced himself to begin pushing at it.

As if in compensation, the first window he came to after sliding down from the dumpster proved to be open on the inside. On the outside it was nothing more than a sheet of screen mesh in a metal frame, designed to allow cool breezes in and keep insects out. Tregemmon kicked it in.

The mesh burst and the frame distorted. The only sound was a soggy metallic ripping. Tregemmon slid through the opening, into the basement of the planetarium. He was inside what appeared to be a small washroom. He stepped down, first on to the closed lid of a toilet, then on to the orange and black tiles of the floor.

He froze. The washroom door was swinging inward as

someone came in. Tregemmon already had the Sig Sauer out, because the automatic's high ammunition count made it the weapon of choice for unknown situations.

He pulled the door open and discovered two startled young eyes staring up at him.

'Tregemmon!'

'Emma Lilly!'

Tregemmon hugged the little girl, sweeping her briefly off her feet and setting her back down. He didn't let go of his gun while doing any of this, however, and he was soon busy assessing the room they were now standing in.

It was a small office with a metal desk and cheap filing cabinets lined up along the wall. There was only one door, opposite them, windowless and apparently locked.

'Tregemmon, there's blood on you.'

'Don't worry, honey, it's not mine. I had to hide in a dumpster. Now listen, are the others safe? Your mum and Juliette and the Edge?'

'Yes. They all conspired to leave me in this boring janitorial office. For some reason they thought I'd be safer here than upstairs.'

'You are, unless somebody comes in the way I did ... What's the matter?'

With alarming suddenness Emily had burst into tears. As she sobbed she managed to squeeze out a few strained words. 'Tregemmon, I'm so glad you're alive.'

'Hey, hey now, baby. Don't fall apart on me. I need your brains. What happened after I left you here?'

'Well ...' Emily wiped her tears. 'Chris turned up with his friends and then Mr Leiber turned up with his. They began fighting. We were trapped in here in the planetarium. Like being attacked in a fort. It was terrifying. It was just like one of those frontier sieges we saw so realistically evoked in dioramas at the various museums on what I've come to think of as our cultural tour.'

'Sure, our cultural tour. And you said the others are all upstairs?'

'Except for Christopher. He's just gone outside.'

'He's done what?'

'Well, apparently he has an idea about how to defeat the enemy. Some kind of behavioural thing. It involves tribal magic.'

'Yeah,' said Tregemmon darkly. 'Tribal magic. That makes sense.'

'Unfortunately it requires him to capture their leader.'

'Their what?' said Tregemmon sharply. 'Their leader?'

'I'm afraid so.'

'Oh, great. That'll be easy.'

'Christopher has a gun,' added Emily.

'Worse yet. He'll probably blow his own foot off with it,' said Tregemmon unhappily.

Juliette was standing beside a meteor.

It was the central feature of the planetarium's carpeted lobby, an awesome chunk of space rock mounted on a smooth marble pedestal. To Juliette it seemed altogether sinister.

On one side of the huge pitted stone were a giftshop and restaurant; to the other was the curving corridor that housed a museum. The dark corridor glowed with the mysterious shapes of illuminated science exhibits. On another occasion Juliette might have been intrigued with the place.

Now she was more concerned with escape routes.

A central staircase rose from the meteor towards the planetarium's domed auditorium. A curved observation gallery looked down from its perimeter. This was where she had stationed her mother, hopefully out of harm's way, assuming she would bloody well stay put.

Juliette stood beside the big stone shape of the meteor, breathing the conditioned air in shallow anxious gasps as she waited for Christopher to return from his suicidal errand.

She could hardly believe it when she finally saw him, still in one piece, walking up the stairs to the glass doors. And he wasn't alone. Walking close at his side was a tall man.

In contrast to Christopher's long white hair, this man

was completely bald. And, as he got closer, she saw that what she had taken to be dirt all over the man was actually tattoos.

He approached the planetarium close at Christopher's side. Christopher was holding a gun almost negligently in his left hand.

Juliette stepped out from behind the meteor and ran to the door. She unbolted it and the men stepped inside. She couldn't stop his name bursting from her lips. 'Chris!'

He nodded at her calmly. 'This is the Needle Man, so named because of his plethora of tattoos. He is completely covered with them and apparently they tell the story of his life. He was moved to do this ridiculous thing to himself by a Ray Bradbury story.' There was something strange about Christopher's voice.

The Needle Man nodded affably at Chris, a gleam of approval in his eyes. 'Hey, man, how did you know that?'

Juliette approached the pair with caution. They were still standing very close together. 'I can't believe you captured him,' she said.

'I didn't,' said Christopher.

'He means he didn't use any recognised conventional mortal methods of capture.'

Juliette wheeled around to see that, against her express instructions, her mother had left her hiding place and come downstairs to join the conversation.

She beamed at Juliette. 'He means he captured him with *sorcery*, dear.'

'No,' replied Christopher wearily. 'I mean I didn't capture him at all.' He let the pistol slide out of his hand and fall to the carpet with a thump.

'Chris, your gun!'

'It's unloaded anyway. They unloaded it when they captured me.'

'I don't understand,' said Juliette. She could hear a note of hysteria beginning to creep into her voice. 'What do you mean, they captured you?'

'Needle Man captured me and took my gun away and made me walk back in here. He's holding a gun on me right now.' Christopher stepped away to reveal that Needle Man was indeed pressing a gun to his ribs. Juliette could see that the tattooed man had a good working knowledge of anatomy. If he fired, Christopher's heart would certainly be blasted into a tangle of intricate ruined tissue.

The Needle Man smiled. 'I only went to all this trouble because Mr Leiber wants you ladies intact.'

Juliette's heart lurched as he walked towards her mother and patted her on the face. 'But he said later on we could do what we wanted with you.' He pinched her plump cheek between thumb and forefinger and squeezed until colour flushed the skin.

Juliette's mother was trying hard to be brave but she had tears in her eyes. 'Fat old women bleed real good,' said the Needle Man in the friendly informative tone of a public-service bulletin.

'Not around me they don't. And keep the gun pointed at the floor the way it is right now. If you so much as twitch I'm going to spoil those tattoos.'

'Tregemmon!' Juliette and her mother spoke in unison. They must have sounded ridiculous, like a well-rehearsed chorus or something, because Tregemmon chuckled.

Then, with a few short strides he was beside the Needle Man and brought his gun down on the tattooed skull with a savage chopping motion.

Juliette winced at the brutal sound of metal connecting with bone, but it appeared to have the desired effect. The Needle Man went down in folding sections, first on to his knees, then face down on to the carpeted floor, where he lay motionless.

'Tregemmon, you're covered with blood!'

'It's a long story, but it's not mine so don't worry, Mrs R.'

'Excellent timing, Tregemmon,' said Christopher. 'I was worried for a minute there that you wouldn't turn up.'

Tregemmon barked a laugh. 'Can you believe him? He has the balls to go out there and lure the biker leader inside, and then he's so soft in the head that he counts on me turning up to finish the job for him.'

'I knew something would happen,' said Christopher. He walked to the glass doors and bolted them again. Then he pressed a button on the wall and metal shutters began to descend over the entrance, blotting out the daylight. 'Something always does,' he added.

He paused and looked down at his wrist. 'Now, isn't that interesting?'

'What?'

Christopher held up his arm so they could see the woven wristband that was tied there. Except it was no longer tied. As Juliette watched, the wristband appeared to writhe like a caterpillar and loosen itself and then slither from Christopher's wrist, fluttering down to the carpet.

'It untied itself,' he said, looking down at the band. 'I suppose that means the debt has been paid.'

'Like I needed to see that,' said Tregemmon.

'More than paid,' added Christopher firmly. 'From what I saw outside, the last of the Saints is dead. They sacrificed themselves for us. They were brave men. We wouldn't have got this far without them.'

Juliette found herself wondering if Christopher had surreptitiously untied the wristband just before he brought it to their attention.

'All right, all right,' said Tregemmon. 'I'm sure that's all very true, but what do we do now? What is Mr Leiber up to? I saw him out there with a little guy called Hammersfeld.'

'Herr Hammersfeeld,' said a high childish voice. 'He's the research director here.'

Juliette lurched around to see Emily emerging from the shadowed tunnel of the museum.

'I thought I told you to stay in the basement,' she snapped.

'I thought it was inadvisable,' said her little sister with heavy sarcasm, 'given that armed bikers are pouring in through the windows.'

'Shit,' said Tregemmon.

'They must have worked out that something was wrong,' said Christopher. 'He's been gone too long.'

He nodded at the Needle Man, who was now woozily coming around on the carpet. Christopher glanced at Tregemmon. 'I only need a few minutes with him. Can you hold them off?'

'Yes, of course,' said Tregemmon grimly. 'I'll hold them off while you do your hoodoo shit.'

'I'll snap the hierarchy into action.'

'Yes, that sounds like a particularly good idea,' said Tregemmon. He sounded bitter. He started down the dark museum tunnel, heading towards the basement. As he disappeared into the shadow he glanced over his shoulder. 'Just make sure you get it right.'

Tregemmon hurried through the dark curving museum, past glowing exhibits. A dinosaur skeleton loomed eerily above him.

In a glowing perspex cube a small industrial robot endlessly riveted the same piece of metal with idiotic patience.

Tregemmon registered these things with a tiny fraction of his attention. He felt keyed up but strangely relaxed. He knew what must be done and had a pretty good idea of how to do it.

There were two routes up from the basement: the elevator and, opposite it, the staircase. He'd had a chance to study both briefly when he made his own way upstairs.

The elevator was no bother. It would be easy enough to disable. The staircase was more problematical.

It was a shining modern construction of steel and glass. A huge glass cylinder slanted down into a transparent section of the floor. This cylinder was effectively the stairwell, the open mouth of it giving access to the skeletal steel frame of the staircase.

At the foot of the stairs were the public toilets and, beyond these, a sealed area of janitorial offices where he'd found Emily. The open glass tube that formed the stairwell was bad news from a security point of view.

It meant Tregemmon couldn't seal the door to the stairs, because there was no door. But fortunately the stairwell also served as part of an exhibit, dedicated to the optical-illusion art of Escher.

Hanging from the ceiling above it was a second steel staircase, this one with mirrored glass on the steps so that people walking down to the basement could look up and see themselves apparently ascending to the ceiling.

This second staircase was a heavy slab of steel and glass, cunningly suspended from the roof by six cables. If those cables were to break it would come crashing down into the open mouth of the stairwell and block it very effectively indeed.

The stairwell.

Why did that word disturb him? Tregemmon shrugged off the thought. He had no time to worry about it now. He was in sight of the suspended staircase. He walked a few swift steps closer and chose his position. The mass of steel and glass gleamed against the dark ceiling. He took careful aim at the furthest of the six cables. The Sig Sauer bobbed nervously in his hand.

That was strange. Normally Tregemmon could rely on himself to be rock-steady when sighting a target. But now his hand was trembling like a leaf. Tregemmon fought to control it.

He had to shoot the cable. He had to seal the stairwell. He had to do it now.

But his hand wouldn't stop shaking. Tregemmon made himself fire anyway, praying that his reflexes would take over. He squeezed the trigger twice as the muzzle of the gun wavered crazily around. The bullets went caroming upward to be lost somewhere in the darkness above.

What was wrong with him? He had to pull himself together. He had to block the stairwell.

The stairwell . . . Suddenly he understood why that word disturbed him.

It had been in a *stairwell* in the Halloween Hotel that he had shot and killed the wrong man. An innocent man.

The memory came welling back from the darkness of

439

his mind. Tregemmon fought it off. Why was this happening now? He had never suffered this kind of lacerating self-doubt before.

Mr Leiber. The thought suddenly came into his mind. Mr Leiber was the mindfuck maestro. He must be doing it. Just as Tregemmon realised this, he glimpsed a blur of movement out of the corner of his eye.

A biker. At the foot of the stairs, running up towards him. Behind him, Tregemmon could see an angry mob boiling down the corridor.

Instantly Tregemmon's hand steadied. He looked up at the ceiling, took aim at the cable and fired. The bullet clipped the bracket that secured the cable and winged off into the darkness.

Tregemmon fired again, minutely correcting his aim. The cable split apart with a loud musical noise and melted away into the darkness. The suspended staircase tipped fractionally before the remaining cables took up the load.

The lead biker was reaching the top of the stairs now. He was carrying some kind of machine pistol and he tried to fire it at Tregemmon while he was running. The bullets sprayed around Tregemmon, missing him by a considerable distance.

Tregemmon turned around and shot him without ceremony. The man fell back down the stairs, rolling past two more bikers, the frontrunners in the pack that was now rising out of the basement like a flood of dark water.

The two lead bikers were only halfway up the stairs, so Tregemmon turned his attention to the next cable. He got this one on the first shot, neatly slicing it and causing it to whiplash with an angry singing note louder than the last one. The suspended staircase juddered violently for a moment and then steadied. He had to shoot one more cable.

But there was no time now. The two bikers had reached the top of the stairs. They were both armed and, unlike their comrade, they paused to take careful aim.

Tregemmon shot them both. The first man fell back immediately, crashing into the pathway of the mob, slowing them down for a precious few seconds.

440

But the second man took the bullet, grabbed the stair rail for a moment, then began to lift his gun again.

So Tregemmon shot him again, reluctantly using up another precious bullet. The man crashed down into the crowd of bikers following, and his arrival gave them second thoughts. They paused halfway up the stairs.

Good. Tregemmon took the opportunity to reload the Sig Sauer.

He returned his attention to the gleaming mass of the suspended staircase. The middle wire on the near side seemed the logical one to take out next. Tregemmon aimed and fired.

He hit it first time.

Just as well, since the bikers had recovered their nerve and were coming up the stairs again. Unfortunately, the suspended staircase was still attached to the ceiling. Despite being tilted at a drunken angle, it wasn't quite ready to go.

The first wave of bikers were reaching the top of the stairs. They were driven by the momentum of the men behind them so they were unable to stop and take aim. Tregemmon had the advantage. He turned and fired five bullets into the mass, taking careful aim and getting good effect with each one.

Once again, the sudden arrival of casualties caused the mass of men on the stairs to halt. After a hesitant second they retreated down the staircase to reconsider tactics. Tregemmon smiled. In a moment there would be no tactics to consider.

Tregemmon returned his attention to the crazily leaning staircase hanging above them. The next cable would definitely cause it to let go. Tregemmon took aim carefully.

Just then he heard a whispering sound. The elevator. He had forgotten about the elevator. He twisted around to face it as its doors hushed open.

There were five men inside. They had guns.

Tregemmon switched to the Ruger and killed them all.

He dropped the now useless revolver on to the carpet. There was no time to reload. He could hear the sound of the bikers rushing up the stairs, taking advantage of his momentary distraction.

Tregemmon didn't waste time looking at the approaching mob on the staircase. Instead he turned to its mirror image on the ceiling. The suspended staircase was now hanging at a steep awkward angle, the remaining cables drawn taut.

Tregemmon chose one of them, aimed and fired. The cable dissolved with a tormented bass twang and the staircase tipped clumsily, snapping the remaining supports. It came away from the ceiling with apparent slowness, rotating slightly as it dropped.

Tregemmon watched as the heavy staircase plunged downward like a crashing spaceship. It dropped into the open stairwell, crushing the front wave of bikers.

There were moans and cries and the screeching scrape of metal against reinforced glass. The mass of steel settled into the glass throat of the stairwell and lodged there.

The rods of the staircase were like prison bars keeping the surviving bikers trapped.

Tregemmon turned away and picked up the Ruger from the floor. He began to reload it with shaking hands. The elevator was blocked with bodies, its doors endlessly reopening and trying to close, like a ghastly mouth. But it meant no one could come up that way.

They were secure for the time being.

As Tregemmon started back along the dark curving corridor of the museum he heard an unsettling sound, a tormented screech followed by a heavy echoing clang. The bikers were apparently trying to shift the steel mass of the staircase; by the sound of it they had lifted it for a moment before its weight overcame them and forced them to drop it back into place.

They'd failed. This time. Tregemmon wondered how long it would continue to hold them.

SIXTY-ONE

Tregemmon came trotting up to Juliette. 'Where's Emily?' he said. 'Where's your mum?'

'They're safe,' she said. 'They're upstairs.' She nodded to the circular balcony that ringed the domed auditorium above them.

They were standing beside the meteor in the foyer of the planetarium. Tregemmon looked strange – half frightened, half joyous. Juliette had read about the exalted states sometimes achieved by men in combat.

'Are you all right?' she said. 'My God. It sounded like you were fighting a small war back there.'

Tregemmon nodded at her, seeming grateful for her concern. Then he glanced back at the dark tunnel of the museum. 'I haven't heard the barricade being moved since that first attempt. Which could be construed as either reassuring or ominous.'

'What do you mean?' said Juliette.

'I suspect our chums the bikers are even now working with tools to clear the stairwell. But don't worry.'

'Don't worry?' Juliette didn't know if this was some kind of macabre gallows humour.

'Now what about the Edge and our tattooed pal?'

'He took him in there.' Juliette nodded at the giftshop on the other side of the foyer. She was straining her ears to listen for the bikers, who in her mind were like fiends clawing their way up from the underworld. Tregemmon had said they might break through at any moment.

Tregemmon was staring through the glass walls of the giftshop. Inside Christopher could be seen talking and gesturing with his hands. The Needle Man gave every appearance of listening intently.

Tregemmon turned back to her. 'What the hell is going on?'

'I wish I knew,' said Juliette with feeling. Just then an enormous metallic crash came echoing down the dark museum corridor. She almost jumped out of her skin.

The fiends from the underworld had clearly broken through.

Tregemmon wiped a thin film of sweat from his upper lip. 'I don't know how long it's going to hold them,' he said in a worried voice.

Juliette sagged with relief. So it was still holding. Thank God.

'Don't worry,' said a voice. They both looked up to see that Christopher had emerged from the giftshop. The Needle Man stood behind him. He had a strange sleepy expression on his tattooed face.

The metallic sound came again. It didn't seem to bother Christopher. He was calm and relaxed. 'Join me upstairs,' he said.

He gestured for them to follow him and began to ascend the carpeted steps towards the auditorium. Juliette exchanged a glance with Tregemmon and followed.

The Needle Man remained standing by the meteor.

Juliette glanced back at him. 'What's wrong with him?' she said. 'He didn't seem to notice us.'

'That's right,' said Tregemmon. 'Like he was in a trance or something.' He called up to Christopher. 'Did you hypnotise him?'

'Something like that,' said Chris.

They reached the top of the stairs and Juliette's mother and Emily came rushing towards them out of the shadows.

'Are you all right, Tregemmon?'

'I'm fine, Emma Lilly.'

'Thank heavens for that,' said Juliette's mother.

'What do we do now?'

'Stay up here and watch the show,' said Christopher dryly.

At the foot of the steps the Needle Man was standing motionless beside the meteor, looking like a man lost in thought. Once again there came the reverberating sound of metal shifting, ringing along the museum corridor.

'It sounds like they're breaking through.' Juliette tried to keep the note of fear out of her voice.

'Don't worry. We'll be safe up here,' said Christopher.

'I wish I shared your confidence.' But Juliette's words were lost in an enormous metallic crash from the museum corridor. It was followed by a bellowing roar of triumph from massed voices. 'They're coming,' said Tregemmon laconically.

By the meteor, the Needle Man suddenly shook himself like a dog waking up. He seemed to throw off his trance state just as the first bikers burst from the shadows of the museum corridor. They were followed swiftly by a dozen more. The men congregated around the Needle Man, evidently delighted to be reunited with their leader.

The bikers surged ebulliently around the meteor as still more of their number poured out of the museum. A tall, heavily muscled man with a grizzled grey beard stepped forth from the crowd and embraced the Needle Man.

'That will be his second in command,' murmured Christopher.

'What exactly is going on?' Juliette had tried to stay silent. But she felt if she didn't talk she would start screaming. The sight of the heavily armed mob milling below had turned her bowels cold.

'Just watch,' said Christopher.

Juliette was watching and she was horrified. At least fifty bikers had now emerged from the museum shadows. They were all clustered in a huge crowd around the Needle Man, flashing hostile glances up towards the balcony.

Juliette shrank back from the hatred in those eyes. Even someone without her knowledge of human behaviour could easily see this was a mob that promised violence.

Juliette studied them with a sick feeling in her stomach. Hard-faced angry men with flushed excited countenances. She was startled to see that there were also three or four women in the mob. Their faces were even more blunted

445

with hatred than those of the men.

'How are we going to stop these people?' Juliette found herself saying. Her voice sounded nakedly fearful. 'They're going to come up here and they're going to –'

'I am on the case,' said Christopher sharply. 'As you've seen, biker society is quasi-tribal in nature. More importantly it is quite rigidly hierarchical. Perfect for our purposes. I have already primed their leader.'

'Primed? Chris, what in God's name are you talking about?'

'Those people down there are in a highly suggestible state.'

'So?'

'So they are vulnerable to manipulation.'

'Couldn't we try to convert them to a gospel of love and understanding?' said Juliette's mother, her own voice quavering.

'Unfortunately they're not programmed for that,' replied Christopher. 'They're programmed for violence.'

Down below the biker leader had held up his hands for silence. In a few seconds the planetarium grew uncomfortably quiet. 'The time has come,' yelled the Needle Man. His voice echoed around the building with the hectoring tones of a television evangelist. He pointed to the balcony. Juliette felt herself shrinking back again. 'There they are. Look at them. They are all that stands between the dark lord and the consummation of his great project.'

'That's a fucking funny way for a biker to talk,' said Tregemmon.

'Indeed,' said Christopher.

'I suppose Mr Leiber fried his brain.'

'Now let's get them for him!' cried the Needle Man. 'We won't even break a sweat doing it. Only one of them is any good with a gun. Once we've got rid of him, the rest are pussies. Can you believe they had me prisoner and they just let me go?'

The bikers bellowed with laughter at their leader's wit. His second in command slapped him on the shoulder. The

Needle Man turned to a gaunt boy holding a double-barrelled shotgun that was almost as tall as he was. Needle Man took the gun from him and brandished the heavy weapon overhead as if it were weightless. 'That freak with the white hair up there. The one they call the Edge. He thinks he's worked some kind of voodoo on me!'

The bikers all roared with laughter. The Needle Man joined in heartily, and then he turned and lifted his shotgun and fired it squarely into the face of his second in command.

Juliette's mother gave a small cry of horror and covered Emily's eyes. Tregemmon turned to Christopher. There was an expression on his face somewhere between fear and admiration. 'Is this your handiwork?'

'It's starting,' said Christopher.

'Mum, will you take your hand off my face?' said Emily in a muffled voice. 'I can't breathe.'

'I'm sorry, dear. I just didn't want you seeing that terrible thing.'

'There's worse to come,' said Emily bluntly.

'Dear!'

'It's true. If I have interpreted Christopher correctly then we are about to witness something extraordinary.'

Below them, the crowd had frozen. There was another gunshot from somewhere in the mass of bikers, and then silence. Juliette peered over the balcony. They were all standing there, perfectly motionless, in their postures of a moment earlier. Frozen.

This sudden paralysis of the mob was somehow more frightening than its murderous rage had been. Juliette shivered. She found herself reluctantly turning to her little sister for an explanation. 'What's happening?'

'You might say that Christopher has cast a spell on them,' said Emily in an annoyingly didactic tone. 'Or, if you wanted to talk in more scientific terms, he is manipulating group dynamics.'

'And that's one hell of a group,' said Christopher, nodding at the motorcycle gang below. 'Now they're reverting to primal conditions. Tribal behaviour will apply.'

'But why did the Needle Man kill his second in command?' said Juliette's mother in a worried voice. 'And what was that other shot we heard?'

'Well, every group has a leader,' said Christopher. 'Someone at the top of the social pecking order. In this case it was the Needle Man. But there's also someone at the bottom, whom you might call the scapegoat. You know, the kid at school everyone else picks on, even the most bullied of the other children.' Christopher smiled. 'So the leader and the scapegoat are at the two ends of a clearly defined pecking order.' His smile faded. 'And this pecking order is ultimately founded on fear and resentment and maintained by the threat of pure aggression. It is a situation charged with enormous latent violence.'

He looked down on the crowd below. There was a note of regret in his voice. 'And I have just unleashed that violence.'

Juliette frowned. It made a kind of sense. 'You mean they're working their way through the chain of command?'

'Yes, simultaneously from the top and the bottom. In as strict a sequence as their sense of hierarchy allows.'

'But they're not doing anything now,' she said. She nodded at the crowd below. It was as still as a forest of statues.

'Yes, they are,' said Christopher. 'They're busy displaying their hierarchy. Look at them.'

Juliette leant over the balcony and saw that a strange silent ritual was taking place below. The crowd of bikers, frozen a moment ago, were losing their paralysis. A flickering of movement spread through the crowd.

The movement consisted of small subtle alterations of posture in relation to each other. It was repetitive and there was some curious pattern to it, like an intricate, rigid folk dance, one that required the minimum of physical movement. Or perhaps a ritualised performance like Noh theatre.

'Those are threat and dominance postures propagating through the group,' explained Christopher. 'They are establishing very clearly the pecking order. In rehearsal for what is about to happen.'

'This is the fascinating part,' said Emily, edging nearer the railing to get a better look. Juliette promptly grabbed her and dragged her back. 'Mum, cover her eyes again.'

'Thank you for letting me indulge my scientific curiosity,' snarled Emily, struggling in her grasp. After a moment she gave up and began to sulk. 'But you can't blame me for being fascinated. The hierarchy of a human group is normally an invisible structure. Here we will see its shape starkly revealed as resentment rises upwards and contempt flows downwards along clearly defined contours.'

'And with lethal force,' said Christopher. 'You were right, Juliette. Don't let her watch.'

'I don't have to watch,' said Emily snottily. 'I know what's going to happen. The anatomy of the human hierarchy is about to be revealed to us in the most brutal terms.'

She said something else as well, but Juliette didn't hear it. Her voice was drowned out by a thunder of gunfire from below.

It was over surprisingly quickly. Finally just a few sporadic gunshots echoed through the planetarium. Then a disturbing silence.

'They didn't waste any time wiping each other out,' said Tregemmon, looking at the bodies strewn across the carpets. Juliette was shocked to see that *he* looked shocked.

'Assuming that they *have* wiped each other out,' replied Christopher.

'Now, that's what I'm worried about too. I haven't seen the body of the leader anywhere.' Tregemmon glanced back at the dark curving tunnel of the museum. Here and there among the glowing exhibits were the dark shapes of bodies scattered on the carpet. 'That tattooed fucker would have been difficult to miss.'

'We're also missing the scapegoat. I haven't seen his body anywhere.' Christopher suddenly moved forward, drifting like a ghost in the darkness with his white hair. He was moving on to the next glowing exhibit, a diorama of some cavemen. 'Wait, damn it,' said Tregemmon. 'I'm supposed to be covering your back.' He hurried after Christopher. Juliette came next, followed by her mother and Emily.

'Three here,' said Christopher. He was standing beside the diorama. There were indeed three more bodies in the shadowy space behind it. Juliette saw that they were locked in the last embrace of an orgy of murder.

But the biker leader wasn't among them. 'No sign of Needle Man?'

'And no sign of the scapegoat. Did anyone see what he looked like?'

'Weaselly little fellow,' said Tregemmon.

'Yes,' said Emily. 'It was obvious that he was one of life's perpetual underdogs. But today he had been transformed.'

'I thought Mum was covering your eyes,' said Juliette.

'Call it a fleeting impression,' replied Emily. 'Suddenly all his buried hatred and resentment burst forth. After a lifetime of humiliation, old scores were settled.'

Juliette repressed a shudder. She had seen far too much herself. She had seen the scapegoat setting about his work. There had been a kind of unholy aura around the little man as he set about his systematic slaughter, first with a handgun and then swinging a socket wrench.

Juliette shut out the memory. She forced herself to think of something else. 'It's curious that the scapegoat and the leader were the two survivors.'

'No it isn't. It's perfectly obvious,' said Emily. 'Looking at it from a structural point of view, it was the most likely outcome for this horrid ballet of behavioural violence.'

'Exactly,' said Christopher. 'Having slaughtered their way along the hierarchy they met in the middle, so to speak.'

'Then perhaps they've also . . . put paid to each other,' said Juliette's mother. She was treading gingerly along the museum corridor as if it were a minefield. There were bodies everywhere.

450

Tregemmon shook his head sadly. 'I wish you ladies had stayed upstairs.'

'But she's right.' Juliette felt she had to defend her mother when she was right; it happened so seldom. 'I don't think anyone could have survived that bloodbath.'

Tregemmon said, 'I'm tempted to start thinking that way myself.' He grinned. 'But don't forget the Edge here is carrying a gun. I gave him a pistol, so it isn't safe in about a ten-mile vicinity.'

'I'm not great with weapons, it's true,' said Christopher. 'I'm certainly not in your league, Tregemmon. But I'm sure I can manage to shoot the right person, when he turns up.'

'That's what I like to hear. Let's nail the fucker and go home.'

'The right person?' said Juliette. 'What do you mean?'

Tregemmon looked at her. 'I'll give you one guess.'

'You mean you intend to shoot Mr Leiber?'

'On sight.'

'But you can't just murder him.'

'On the contrary,' said Tregemmon. 'After what he did to Miranda I've got no problem with that at all.'

Juliette turned and looked at Christopher. 'But Chris, you can't.'

Chris was busy peering behind a glowing exhibit consisting of coloured balls on silver rings set against a backdrop of stars and galaxies. The sign on the exhibit read OUR SOLAR SYSTEM.

'I certainly can,' he said. 'You know what Leiber's going to do if we don't stop him.'

'You don't honestly believe that, do you?' Juliette's voice was getting frayed with anger. 'It's all hokum. He doesn't have the power to do any such thing.' Even to herself she didn't sound entirely convinced.

Tregemmon swallowed and asked, 'Do what, exactly?'

'I can't begin to tell you,' said Juliette curtly. She didn't want to think about it. 'It's too ridiculous.'

Chris shrugged, looking at Tregemmon. 'It's something we learnt while you were gone. Here at the Jasper Institute they have very sophisticated computers. They would be the first to see it. The first to know it.'

'See what? Know what?'

'If it's coming,' said Juliette wearily.

'Coming?'

'A cosmic catastrophe,' she said, making a hideous attempt to pass it off lightly. 'An astronomical event.'

'Oh shit,' said Tregemmon. He turned slowly and looked at the model of the solar system. Mounted on one of the silver rings, the Earth was the size of a pool ball. Juliette imagined another pool ball skimming towards it across the smooth velvet of space.

She imagined the sharp hard snap of contact . . .

'Oh shit,' murmured Tregemmon, and she knew he'd worked it out. 'Don't tell me that –'

'It's not going to happen,' said Juliette hastily.

'How can you say that?' Emily was glaring at her. 'You heard what Herr Hammersfeeld said.'

'All right,' conceded Juliette. 'All right, it's true that Herr Hammersfeeld is the director of this place. And it's true he was terribly distressed about what he calls his data.' She took a deep breath. 'All that may be true. But just because Mr Leiber has managed to deceive Hammersfeeld doesn't mean we have to believe it.'

'I suspect he has sufficient belief for his purposes without us,' said Christopher. 'And now he's shaping his preferred reality.'

Juliette looked at the model of the solar system, thinking again of the sharp impact of pool balls.

'Don't they say that's what killed the dinosaurs?' said Tregemmon.

'Don't worry, Tregemmon,' said Juliette. 'We're talking about one man here. He couldn't possibly cause such a thing to happen. He couldn't influence the movement of a massive chunk of rock from space.'

She turned to Christopher, feeling a desperate need to break through. 'Chris, please see reason. It's totally impossible.'

'No it's not. Consider Carl Sagan.' Christopher nodded at a large illuminated map of Mars. 'I heard him give a lecture at the Royal Academy, about the so-called canals of Mars. He scattered some polystyrene fragments against a black cloth and he asked if any of us could see the shape of canals among that random mass. And, of course, we could. That is one of the attributes of the human mind. We make a pattern out of chaos according to our preconceptions.'

Christopher's eyes gleamed under his mane of white hair. 'In exactly the same way we build our everyday reality, extracting it from the chaos of sensory input. And Mr Leiber has the power to influence those vital preconceptions.'

'He is what Christopher calls a local-reality controller,' said Emily. 'Although I prefer Pickett's term, "the paradigm driver".'

Tregemmon checked his gun. 'Just get me in range and I'll drive his paradigm for him.'

'Christopher,' said Juliette desperately. 'You may believe this, but that doesn't make it true.'

'Listen to him, dear,' said Juliette's mother. 'He is one of the Wise. They have the magical powers of the good, and work in harmony with the natural forces of the Earth.'

Juliette ignored her mother's ravings. 'Christopher,' she said desperately. 'When we met, you were in a mental institution and you were in there for a good reason. I believe you have a fixation and somehow it is at the root of all this.'

Christopher looked at her suspiciously. 'What do you mean?'

'You're afraid that Mr Leiber is controlling you.'

'No,' said a voice from the shadows. 'What really scares him is the exact opposite.'

Tregemmon's gun came up automatically as a man emerged from the dark tunnel of the museum. He stepped into the glow of light from the solar-system display and Tregemmon saw that this was Mr Leiber.

It was the first time Tregemmon had ever seen him clearly, but there was something eerily familiar about him.

453

Everyone stared at Leiber. He seemed perfectly relaxed. A rather tall, undistinguished, middle-aged businessman losing the war against his own potbelly. A balding nonentity.

Tregemmon recovered before any of the others. 'This is very convenient,' he said. He moved towards Mr Leiber and aimed the Sig Sauer at his head.

Mr Leiber smiled. 'Are you going to shoot me? Go ahead. But how do you know that you won't also kill your friend here?' He nodded at Christopher Matthew.

Tregemmon hesitated. 'What's he talking about?'

'Ignore him.' Christopher's voice was impatient. 'Just shoot him.'

'By all means do so,' said Leiber. 'But the bullet may also kill the man you call Christopher Matthew. Because, after all, we are the same man.'

'He's just fucking with your mind, Tregemmon. Ignore him. Do it.'

'No, he won't do it. Look at him hesitate. You see, he knows I'm telling the truth.' Mr Leiber smiled his empty smile. 'Now that we're standing side by side it must be obvious.'

Tregemmon was still pointing his gun at Mr Leiber but somehow it was clear that he was no longer ready to use it.

Juliette could see why. There was an eerie resemblance between the two men. Leiber had thinning hair and Christopher's was white and much longer, but this was a superficial distinction.

The real difference lay in their demeanour. Both men inhabited similar bodies, but what their very different personalities had done with those bodies was extraordinary. Posture, bearing, mannerisms, everything about the way they held themselves was different. Like two different creatures inhabiting identical shells.

But above all what distinguished them was the almost autistic stiffness and vacancy of Leiber's behaviour.

There was still no denying their physical similarity. They might have been brothers. Twins.

'I believe the lovely psychiatrist is baffled about the

duality of our nature,' said Leiber. 'Well, it's very simple really. You see, there is no Franklin Leiber. There is no Christopher Matthew.'

Juliette looked at Christopher to see what he made of this, but he was just listening quietly, with what might have been a look of resignation on his face.

'But there once was a man, a very troubled man, called Matthew Franklin. A man with unusual powers but one who was quite insane. Hilariously he stumbled into a government project, a behavioural-weapons research project, and accidentally became enmeshed in it. The experience sharply increased his already considerable powers. And it even restored his sanity. Or rather, I should say the man restored his own sanity. Tell the lady what I mean, Christopher.'

Christopher remained silent.

Juliette's mind was a jumble of conflicting thoughts. She remembered seeing the name Matthew Franklin on a folder on Chad's desk. Back at the Abbey a thousand years ago. Could Leiber be telling the truth?

'All right,' he continued in his hollow monotonic voice. 'If you won't tell them, I will. One day Matthew Franklin healed himself. He did this by splitting himself into two separate entities. Christopher Matthew and Franklin Leiber. The trauma of the separation caused his hair to turn white and mine to start falling out. But otherwise we were physically identical but so utterly different in mannerism that many people would never notice that we're the same man. You might say that I lack the sugar coating of personality which Christopher rather selfishly kept for himself. Indeed, there's a lot of good stuff I didn't get. In fact, I mostly got what you might call the bad stuff. That was the point of it. Christopher wanted to shed his insanity, to shear it off like a calving iceberg.'

Juliette listened in fascination. Could it be true? It was absurd, but she was beginning to believe him.

Mr Leiber smiled. His face had all the character of a paper bag, but his eyes were dark and strange. 'And that's me. The insanity. It worked. He got rid of me. But it didn't really work.' He turned and stared at Christopher.

'Because along with his madness he also gave away his power.' Under his dead eyes his mouth smiled. 'A truly astonishing portion of power.'

Christopher turned to Tregemmon. 'Kill him,' he said.

'But is it true?' said Tregemmon. 'If I kill him will I also kill you?'

'No. He's just bullshitting. Do it.'

Mr Leiber waggled his finger. 'He says that. But he can't be sure. And you wouldn't want it to happen, would you, Tregemmon? You wouldn't want to kill the wrong man again, would you?'

It was the final mindfuck. Tregemmon's hand was slick with sweat, spreading like oil across the grip of the pistol. But still he managed the business of putting the barrel of the gun right up against the shining skin of Mr Leiber's head.

He avoided those eyes. All he had in his field of vision was the gun barrel pressing into the sparse white hair, flecks of dandruff all around it.

'This is for Miranda and Danny,' he said. He began to squeeze the trigger and immediately a gunshot rang through the museum.

For an idiot instant Tregemmon thought that he'd fired, but then he realised impatiently that that wasn't it at all.

He'd been shot. He felt his body falling towards a floor that floated dreamily up to meet him.

Tregemmon fought to remain conscious. He didn't know where he'd been shot, but his entire torso had gone numb. He lay on the floor and tried to move. He couldn't.

Mr Leiber walked past him. Then out of the corner of his eye Tregemmon saw another figure step out from behind the solar-system exhibit. It was the biker Christopher called the scapegoat. The weaselly little man was carrying a gun. It looked like a police Python.

With a flicker of disgust Tregemmon realised that he'd been shot by the runt of the pack.

There was a terrible piercing noise echoing through the planetarium and it took a moment for Tregemmon to identify it as Emily screaming. Screaming his name.

The little girl was struggling, trying to run towards him. But her mother was holding her back. The scapegoat was pointing his gun at them. Emily's screams gradually faded into sobs and Tregemmon heard the distant sound of other voices.

Mr Leiber was talking to Christopher. 'Incidentally, bravo,' he said. 'That hierarchical chain reaction you initiated in the bikers was really very clever of you. It severely depleted the ranks of my assistants. They would have gone on obligingly killing each other to the last man if I hadn't intervened.'

The scapegoat crept forward and took Christopher's gun away. Then he went and stood respectfully beside Mr Leiber. He kept his gun on them.

Mr Leiber glanced at his watch and then he reached down into the solar-system display and tapped the pool ball that represented the Earth. 'Poor Herr Hammersfeeld,' he said. 'He's very upset with his findings, you know. Keeps going back to the computers hoping there's some mistake. It's all too much like some vulgar Hollywood opus for his middle European sensibilities.'

'You can't do it,' said Juliette. She sounded as if she had begun to believe he could.

'Why not? It's a bit of an old chestnut, I know. But I couldn't resist. Anyway it was either that or having the aliens land. And this seemed marginally more plausible.'

Mr Leiber smiled. 'And, after all, belief is my currency.'

As Tregemmon lay motionless on the floor he discovered that there was still a tiny spark of sensation in the numb mass of his body, like a flame embedded in ice. He began to wonder if perhaps he could move.

Leiber turned to Christopher. 'Well, Christopher, what do you have to say? Don't just stand there like some knock-kneed puritan who's farted in a crowded elevator. Let's duke it out. The final battle. God and the devil fighting for the fate of the world. A confrontation to decide once and for all who is the more powerful. Like some stirringly primitive revivalist painting.'

457

Christopher said nothing. Juliette broke in. 'But you'll die too.'

Mr Leiber looked at her. 'What? Oh, the comet. The comet is just a convenient device, my dear. My real interest is in harvesting the global tidal wave of belief that will occur when the poor innocent souls who inhabit this benighted world see a comet in the sky. Once it appears I might change it into something else at the very last moment, a great flaming eagle, say, or a feather pillow. And then think of the power *that* will give me. Imagine the Herr Hammersfeelds of the world trying to account for that.'

Lying on the carpet, Tregemmon suddenly knew that Mr Leiber was going to win after all. The knowledge gave him a final racing flow of strength. His Sig Sauer was on the carpet where he'd dropped it. Within reach.

He would have only one chance. He rehearsed carefully the move in his mind. He would have to roll over and pick up the gun. It would then be two shots. First the scapegoat. The little man was still pointing his gun at Christopher and at Emily.

He would have to be rendered harmless. And then Mr Leiber. One bullet each. He didn't have the strength for any more. He couldn't afford to miss.

Looking at Emily through slitted eyes, Tregemmon knew he couldn't afford to miss.

He felt the flow within him grow and spread and reach its maximum size. Before it could begin to die back again, he made his move. He rolled over, his body moving like a numb lump of meat – but no matter, because his hand was obediently reaching for the Sig, picking it up. He kept rolling.

The scapegoat had seen him but it didn't matter because it was too late now. Tregemmon aimed and fired and the weaselly little man went down. He kept rolling, kept the gun held high, Mr Leiber coming into his sights –

And then there was a movement out of the darkness and a heavy gleaming shape stamped down on to his hand. A boot. A motorcycle boot.

His fingers spread open involuntarily, the gun spilling from them. He looked up and saw the biker called the Needle Man. He must have been waiting in the shadows of the museum corridor, in case he was needed. Now his tattooed face stared down at Tregemmon's.

There was no hatred or anger in that stare, no discernible emotion at all, as he pointed the gun at Tregemmon's head and fired.

There was a flash of light and a moment of wonder in Tregemmon's mind. Then all his thoughts and feelings were obliterated in one final brutal smear.

Juliette stared in shock. Emily made a choking sound and broke free from her mother. She threw herself on to Tregemmon's body, sobbing hysterically. The tattooed biker stepped back in embarrassment and disgust.

Mr Leiber glanced at his watch. 'Not long now.' He looked at the tattooed biker. 'Needle Man, I no longer have need of your services.'

'I understand, my lord.'

'Oh, and by the way, congratulations on emerging as the winner from your group hierarchy.' Mr Leiber gestured at the corpses of the bikers lying strewn all around.

'Thank you, my lord. Goodbye.'

'Yes, you'd better go now,' said Mr Leiber.

The Needle Man put his gun in his mouth and pulled the trigger. Juliette turned hastily away before she saw his tattooed skull dissolve. She blundered blindly into Christopher's arms. He held her and with her eyes firmly closed she heard her mother utter a little cry of horror. Slowly she opened her eyes again.

The Needle Man was lying dead on the floor now. Nearby Emily was still sobbing on Tregemmon's corpse. Her mother in turn was trying to comfort her, hugging her like a big clumsy bear.

The sound of the little girl's sobbing was as steady and constant as the beating of a heart. Then abruptly it stopped.

Emily snuffled for a moment and then she looked up

from Tregemmon's body. Her gaze fixed on Mr Leiber, her eyes wide and wet, shining with grief and hatred.

'Do you know something, Mr Leiber?' she said.

Mr Leiber seemed taken aback by having the little girl address him, suddenly so calmly. 'I beg your pardon?'

'The belief of a child is a very powerful thing,' said Emily, her voice as cold as ice.

At the sound of her voice, Christopher seemed to take heart. He let go of Juliette and stepped forward.

'Especially,' continued Emily, 'when that child is a prodigy with a phenomenally powerful mind.'

'Yes,' said Christopher. There was a fierce new light in his eyes. 'And especially when all her mental resources have been focused by a terrible tragedy.'

Emily nodded. Juliette shuddered to see that she had a spot of Tregemmon's blood on her face. It gave the little girl an unearthly appearance, like a caste mark or shamanistic tattoo.

'Imagine the emotional mental power created by an event like a sacrifice. A sacrifice as potent as . . .' Emily's voice faltered. 'As this . . .' She looked down at the dead man.

Her voice quivered on the verge of tears and then recovered. 'But my loss confers enormous power on me.'

Mr Leiber stirred uneasily under her gaze.

'She's right.' Christopher grinned savagely.

'Now I see the truth,' said Emily. There was no hint of tears in her voice any more. 'You are nothing, Mr Leiber. Or, to be more accurate, you are merely what you appear to be. A mediocre, ordinary mortal. You have no power. You are no threat.'

'Don't be ludicrous,' said Mr Leiber. But he said it perhaps a fraction too hastily.

'It's not ludicrous. It's what I believe. And there is no belief as strong as that of a child.'

'Quite ludicrous.' Mr Leiber seemed to regain his confidence. He gestured at the corpses on the floor. 'Look around you, look at my believers. They stretch as far as the eye can see. My army. An army at my beck and call.'

'They're all dead,' said Christopher. 'Who's to say they ever were your believers?'

'That's right,' cried Juliette's mother gleefully. 'You've isolated yourself from your source of psychic energy.'

'You're cut off from the necessary pool of belief, Leiber.' Christopher was grinning. 'You've cut yourself off.' He nodded at the tattooed corpse on the floor. 'You even got rid of Needle Man. That was a mistake. He was the last of your believers.'

Juliette's mother nodded, beaming triumphantly. 'That's right. Your followers are all dead. The only living souls around you are united in a chorus against you. Take my hands, girls. Let's all hold hands and link our energies.'

She held out her plump pink hands. Juliette impatiently ignored her, and so did Emily.

But their mother remained confident. She turned to Mr Leiber, speaking with considerable force. 'We don't believe in you, Mr Leiber!'

She turned back and seized Juliette's hand. 'Join in, dear! He's cut off from his source of power. We can make him wither away – like Count Dracula when the sunlight hits him.'

Juliette shrugged her mother off, both frightened and angered by this torrent of nonsense. As she freed herself she heard Mr Leiber talking.

'Ridiculous,' he said. 'My followers are legion.' Juliette noticed that a note of mild alarm had crept into his voice. 'All we need to do is step outside this planetarium and find one of them.'

Christopher grinned defiantly. 'Shall we do just that?'

Mr Leiber looked at him, hesitating. Then there was a sound, a scuffling in the shadows. Someone was approaching along the museum corridor.

Mr Leiber smiled, all his confidence returning. 'I don't think we'll even have to do that. One appears to be coming to us.'

A moment later a small figure in a white coat emerged from the shadows. He was staring at the corpses and shaking his head in utter despair. 'My God, this place, this place,' he said.

'Ah, Herr Hammersfeeld,' called Mr Leiber. 'You have come at a very opportune moment. Perhaps you could repeat your findings to these good people.' Mr Leiber leant over the solar system and tapped the pool-ball model of the Earth.

The little man didn't seem to hear him. He looked at the bodies, at Emily hugging Tregemmon, then at Juliette. His eyes were vague but then they cleared, like a man emerging from a reverie. 'My findings . . . my findings, ah yes.' His face brightened a little. 'Yes, one must retain the big picture.' He made a feeble attempt to smile at Juliette. 'We may be surrounded by slaughter. But somehow, God forgive me, all this death seems worth it.'

'Sorry?' said Mr Leiber politely.

'I am a scientist. I am not normally given to quasi-poetic utterances. But I feel we have all narrowly escaped the shadow of the dark angel.'

'I beg your pardon?'

Herr Hammersfeeld shrugged. 'Of course, we didn't really. There never really was any danger. It was all a computer error, thank God. Now excuse me.'

Mr Leiber stared at him. 'Wait.'

'No.' Herr Hammersfeeld hurried away. 'I must prevent word of the nonexistent "threat" reaching anyone else, before my institute becomes a laughing stock.' He trotted along the curving museum corridor, vanishing from sight.

Mr Leiber stared after him, an appalled expression on his face. He turned and looked at Christopher.

'I win,' said Christopher.

And then, with no conscious thought at all, Juliette found herself bending down and picking up Tregemmon's gun from the floor. She raised it and pointed it at Mr Leiber and then she found herself squeezing the trigger and shooting and shooting until it was empty.

Mr Leiber's expression as she blasted him out of existence was one of almost comical surprise, as if he never could have imagined things turning out like this for him.

He lurched backwards and fell heavily and mortally to the floor.

Juliette dropped the empty gun on to the carpet beside him. 'Well done, dear,' said her mother. She clumsily patted Juliette on the shoulder.

SIXTY-TWO

Juliette stared down at Mr Leiber's body. Whatever disturbing presence had once animated that shell was now quite gone. In death he looked pathetic instead of formidable.

Gradually other impressions began to filter into Juliette's mind, along with a vague but growing sense of alarm.

She realised she had just shot and killed a man. She was a doctor dedicated to saving lives and she had just taken one.

Juliette felt a hand on her shoulder and turned to see Christopher there.

He was smiling at her. There was something very different about his eyes. 'So you weren't just along for the ride. Well done.' He gently took the gun away from her.

Juliette told herself that she had been in the grip of some force completely beyond her rational control. 'I don't know why I shot him,' she said aloud. Her voice began to waver. 'You have to believe me. It was a compulsion.'

But Christopher wasn't listening to her. He had turned away and now knelt beside Emily. She was sobbing over Tregemmon's body. Christopher touched her gently on the shoulder.

'In a way Mr Leiber succeeded,' he said.

'What do you mean?' said Emily tearfully.

'The world did end today. It always ends when somebody dies.' Emily turned and sobbed on Christopher's chest.

And as he knelt there, comforting her little sister in this museum full of corpses, Christopher proceeded to give what amounted to a valediction to Tregemmon.

Juliette's mother took her hand as they listened. He said

that Tregemmon was unique and could never be replaced. They now lived in a quite different world, one poorer for the loss of him.

Juliette soon found warm salt tears flowing down her cheeks. She wiped her face and watched Christopher as he spoke. She realised what was different about his eyes. Looking into them, it was as though the agitated water in a pool had suddenly become still. She recognised that some terrible emotional turmoil had ended for this man.

She was looking into the eyes of someone who had become somehow purged, purified, shriven.

When he stopped speaking, her mother hurried to Emily and scooped her up in a bear hug. 'Come on, dear,' she said.

Emily allowed herself to be separated from Tregemmon. Christopher, however, remained kneeling on the floor. He leant forward and put his hands on Tregemmon's chest.

For a second Juliette found herself wondering crazily if he was going to perform some kind of magic and bring the dead man back to life. But all he did was pluck out some car keys from the pocket of Tregemmon's bloodstained jacket.

Christopher led them out of the planetarium, unlocking the steel shutters and taking them through the glass doors at the front of the building. As they walked down the concrete steps, the night air smelt sweet. Juliette turned and looked back at the planetarium, a giant eye staring up into the heavens.

She decisively turned away from the grotesque building and hurried after the others. A warm feeling was growing inside her as she watched Christopher.

She felt he was leading them out of the place of death. She noticed that he hadn't bothered to take a gun with him. Presumably because there would be no more need for guns.

Juliette braced herself to see more bodies but out here in the car park there were none. Rather there were dozens

465

of motorbikes parked in haphazard fashion. She had the disturbing thought that no one was going to be riding these bikes home.

Beyond the motorcycles were several cars. Their footsteps were loud in the empty car park. Juliette realised that, but for their footsteps, the world was utterly silent. There wasn't even a sigh of wind.

She looked up at the sky. It was slashed to the west with sunset. The lurid streaks of colour reminded her of a melting ice lolly. For some reason she remembered the taste of those childhood confections, sweet and frozen.

Frozen.

She looked at the sky again. Something very odd was going on. It had been sunset hours ago, when Tregemmon arrived at the planetarium and joined them. It was still sunset now. That was impossible. It was as if time had frozen.

Juliette shook her head. Perhaps she was confused. Perhaps it hadn't been sunset earlier. It couldn't have been.

Now Christopher had arrived beside a pale-blue Mustang convertible and he was unlocking it. Juliette wanted to ask him where he'd got the car but she felt too numb to talk.

Christopher started the car and drove them, like an ordinary family at the end of an ordinary day, out of the car park and on to the highway.

A few minutes up the road Christopher stopped at a gas station. Juliette saw that the minivan was parked in the forecourt. Christopher pulled up beside it in the Mustang and took out the keys he'd removed from Tregemmon's jacket. He held them out towards Juliette. She was startled.

'Don't you want to drive?'

'I'm not coming with you,' said Christopher.

She didn't believe what she was hearing.

Christopher nodded at her mother and Emily. 'Go with them. With your family. Fly back to England.'

'Chris. What are you saying?'

'Drive to the airport and don't stop or open the windows until you get there. And for God's sake don't get out anywhere.'

The gas station was brightly lit but deserted. The minivan was the only vehicle parked there under the brilliant lights. It was illuminated like a stage set. Once again Christopher held the keys out to Juliette, the shadow of his arm clear on the concrete. 'You'd better go now.'

'Christopher, what are you saying? I want to be with you. I love you.'

'There was some component of that,' allowed Christopher. 'And Mr Leiber used it against us.'

'What?'

'Juliette, you don't believe in me. You never have.'

'I love you. I want you.'

Christopher shrugged. Juliette realised it wasn't just his eyes. His whole manner had changed. He looked somehow peaceful, healed; happy. Her heart pinched as she began to realise that this was a happiness she would not be sharing.

'A long period of hostile doubt,' he continued, 'followed by a brief spasm of sexual obsession. Do you call that love?'

Juliette found herself at a loss for words. She felt as if she had been punched in the stomach. 'But –'

'But you don't believe in me even now,' said Christopher. 'And perhaps that's for the best.' Down the road the bulging unreal eye of the planetarium stared up into the garish sky.

'I suggest for your own peace of mind you simply believe that I was some kind of charismatic madman with amazingly persuasive fantasies. That I tricked you into sharing those fantasies.'

Once again he offered her the keys and this time Juliette numbly accepted them. She turned to the minivan, where her mother and Emily were waiting. 'Tregemmon used to call this the people carrier,' said Emily. 'He had a lot of names for it, some of them very rude.' Her voice trembled a little, but she very bravely kept herself from crying.

But then Juliette slid the door of the van open and there in the back Emily saw something: the red suitcase that Tregemmon had bought for her. She dissolved into tears.

Christopher must have heard, because he came back from his car and patted her on the back. 'Be brave, Emma Lilly,' he said. He looked at the others.

'All of you listen to me,' he said. 'Juliette, I don't care if you believe me or not. Just for once, do as I say.' He glanced up at the sky. Juliette numbly registered that it was still arrested in the same moment of sunset.

'At this instant,' said Christopher, 'reality is like a painting that is still wet. Conditions are very unsettled. So I want you to drive straight to the airport and don't stop until you get there. As I said, don't open the windows or the doors. And stay in the vehicle. Got that? Good.' He kissed Juliette, hugged Emily and her mother, and left.

As Juliette watched the Mustang pull away she realised with a hollow feeling that this was the last time she'd ever see him.

She tried to decide whether to wave or not, and then suddenly it was too late. The little car had dwindled in the distance.

Juliette looked up at the sky over the highway and saw that the sunset was no longer frozen. In fact night was falling with great rapidity. Something else was changing, too. She realised that the peculiar silence was over.

From every direction, manmade noise was rising, gently but steadily. The noise level of the urban night was coming up all around her, like someone gradually turning the sound up on a video. From all over the city came the cry of sirens, but also music, radios, distant laughter and shouts.

The sound of arguments, the grumbling of distant traffic and, somehow most profoundly, the lonely roaring of a jet high in the sky above.

She felt a touch on her arm and turned to see her mother standing there. 'Don't be too hurt, dear,' she said. 'He was being cruel to be kind. He had to sever the bond between you, because he knows it's for the best. The path of a sorcerer is a lonely one. None may travel it beside him without coming to harm. He knows that, and he loves you and he's merely seeking to protect you.'

'Oh, Mum, fuck off,' said Juliette wearily. 'I never want to hear another word about wizards or magic or this sorcery nonsense.'

'He was right.' Her mother shook her head in wonder. 'You don't believe, even now, do you?' There was no malice in her voice, just pity.

'I suppose if you let yourself believe, your whole world would crumble.'

'That's exactly what Christopher said,' added Emily, who had crept out of the van to join them. Juliette had had enough of talk. She wanted to be gone from this place. She shooed her mother and sister back into the minivan.

Once she was inside the vehicle she realised that night had arrived quite completely. Peering into the darkness, Juliette fumbled for headlights, then started the engine. Reminding herself that she had to drive on the right, she edged out of the gas station and into the street, joining the thickening traffic.

The streets and sidewalks of Taos were coming to life around them as they drove along the highway. With her mother nervously map reading, they set off towards the airport.

After driving for about ten minutes, Juliette saw a police car stopped under a street light at the side of the road. Pulled in behind it was a mud-spattered Volkswagen Beetle containing a pale, stick-thin, middle-aged couple who were receiving some kind of traffic citation with ill grace.

Juliette eased her brakes on and pulled over to stop just in front of the police car.

'Juliette,' said her sister sharply.

'What are you doing, dear?' said her mother.

'Christopher told you not to stop!'

'Be quiet, Emily. We have to tell someone in authority what happened back there. I'll say I heard some shots as we drove past the Jasper Institute.'

469

'Christopher said not to get out of the car! He said not to open the window!'

'That's right! Don't do it, dear –'

Juliette ignored her mother and her sister, and pressed the button for the window on the driver's side. The window began to buzz obediently down. Juliette turned to look outside.

One of the policemen was still busy writing a ticket for the couple in the Volkswagen. The other one was climbing out of the patrol car, coming over to see what Juliette wanted.

Juliette felt a sudden lurch of fear. Something was wrong. The window beside her was humming slowly open but, instead of revealing the policeman walking towards her, all it revealed was a strange oily mist. Juliette rubbed her eyes, but in the back of the car her mother and Emily were obviously seeing the same thing, because they began to scream.

All around them, every other window revealed a normal urban street scene. Passing traffic and a police car parked under a street light. But the window Juliette was opening revealed nothing but a roiling grey mist.

The mist glowed as though there was a light concealed somewhere within it. It shifted and gleamed with an odd kind of intermittent sparkling as if it were wet.

'Close the window! Close it!'

Without thinking, Juliette hit the button and the window lurched to a halt in its descent and began to shiver clumsily upward again. As it closed, the scene outside did not return to normal.

Instead she saw the same glowing mist. Only now it was pierced with flashes of colour, polychromatic swirls like the shimmering rainbow on an oil slick.

No one said anything. They all sat there, staring at the window. It took a long sickening moment for the oil-slick shimmer to subside and then, after another endless moment, the swirls of colour began to fall back into familiar contours, solidifying once again into street, Volkswagen, alert and suspicious face of the policeman.

470

He stood watching them with a doubtful expression as Juliette hastily slipped the handbrake and put her foot down on the accelerator. The minivan slipped back into the traffic and roared away. The policeman watched them go.

The view outside Juliette's window had stabilised now and seemed to remain normal. No one in the van said anything. No one said anything all the way to the airport.

When they reached the airport they sat in the minivan for a full hour before they dared open the door and get out, stepping into the humid air of a hot evening and the sights and sounds of a world that was solid and real and smelt of aircraft fuel.

As they walked towards the departure gate, Juliette realised something ironic. Christopher had been right. She hadn't believed. Not even after Miranda, not even after Leiber.

But, after buzzing down her window and seeing a wet opalescent void where the world should be, she believed all right.

The departure gate was to her left. Her mother and Emily were lagging behind her. Juliette walked around the corner and slammed straight into a man coming the other way.

He stepped back. It was Chris. 'What a coincidence,' he said. He stepped forward again as he took her in his arms and pressed his mouth against hers.

Juliette sank into a kiss so total that it swallowed her consciousness. She almost didn't notice the weary sigh of disgust from her little sister, or the delighted buzzing of her mother as she circled them like a fat contented bee.

THE VERDICT OF THE REVIEWERS

As *The Wise* was going to press the first reviews were appearing of the three books that launched the Virgin Worlds imprint. Here is a selection of the press comments.

MIRRORMAN by Trevor Hoyle

'An intriguing blend of Horror and Fantasy.'
Starburst #248, April 1999

'[Trevor Hoyle] is worth 50 of your Ludlums and Archers.'
Glasgow Herald

HAVENSTAR by Glenda Noramly

'*Havenstar* is an original, engrossing page-turner of a Fantasy. You want strange and powerful magic, world-changing heroism, and courage in unlikely places – it's here.'

'Terrific stuff – this author is one to watch.'

'Rating: 10/10.'
Starburst #248, April 1999

MNEMOSYNE'S KISS by Peter J Evans

'A great debut from a promising new talent.'
Starburst #248, April 1999

'Classic cyberpunk . . . slickly written, swiftly paced, and tosses in enough exotic locations, corrupt corporations and assorted lowlifes to keep the narrative racing along.'

'It's hard to believe that *Mnemosyne's Kiss* is Evans' debut novel, given the confidence of his writing and the tightness of the plotting. His two female characters are utterly believable and as dysfunctional and nasty as any Chandleresque male.'
SFX #50, April 1999